THE GOOD DEATH OF KATE MONTCLAIR

The
Good Death
of Kate
Montclair

Daniel McInerny

CHRISM
PRESS

Chrism Press, a division of WhiteFire Publishing
13607 Bedford Rd NE
Cumberland, MD 21502

ISBNs:
978-1-946531-46-9 (paperback)
978-1-946531-47-6 (eBook)

THIS BOOK IS FOR
MISS AMY
MY STURDY SHELTER

EDITOR'S PREFACE

Let the record reflect that I refused this job when first offered—that cold November morning, puffs of mist rising in the mountains like rifle smoke from a Blue-Gray skirmish, as I sat beside Kate on her bed holding her hand.

"You're going to refuse my dying wish?" she said. "That's cold, dude."

"I can't do it, Kate. Ask Adele to do it."

"I want *you* to do it."

"I can't."

"Why? Is it because you don't agree with my decision?"

"It's not that."

"Then why?"

"Because I'm in love with you, and that doesn't make me the best candidate for a cold-eyed editor."

I felt the pressure relax on my hand. "You can't fall in love with all the dying girls, Benedict."

"No? Watch me." I let go of her hand and placed mine gently over hers. "I don't expect you to say anything, Kate. I just need you to know it."

"Thank you."

I looked down at my grubby boots.

"I guess it must be love," she continued, "because I haven't showered in four days and I smell like rotten eggs."

"You're beautiful."

"You're delusional. Anyway. I'll have Miranda put the manuscript and a zip drive with the file in the bottom drawer of my desk downstairs. If you change your mind…"

A few moments later, she added, "I know this is cold comfort, Benedict, but in other circumstances, I would have liked to have given us a try. I've enjoyed seeing you again. Playing detective. I appreciate the fact that you didn't pity me. But the thing is, I have to catch a bus. I'm afraid I'm on a pretty tight schedule."

Pretty tight indeed. Kate Montclair's bus departed the next morning, November 2, All Souls Day. Regrettably, I was not present when her death occurred. The reasons for this are complicated and not ones I'm particularly proud of. The thing is, I did disagree with her decision. Not for all the best reasons but simply because I wasn't ready to let her go. I really was in love with her. Even so, I failed to act as I should have done. I left the house, and for my punishment, I live with the fact that I wasn't there for her when she needed me most.

No, that's not right. Kate didn't need me in the end; she passed out of this world just fine without me, on the terms she had accepted, with dignity and grace. I just wish I had been there beside her, to feed on her impressive fortitude and to let her know that I was with her. When I left Five Hearths, Kate's house in Fauquier County, I did not take her manuscript or zip drive with me, and I never expected to see her memoir again.

I did, however, go back to Five Hearths briefly on the afternoon of November 3. I needed to retrieve a bag with my passport in it that I had left in the guest room. As I drove up to the house, I was jarred by the sight of yellow barricade tape across the front door as well as the side door into the mud room and kitchen. I parked my rental car and, with the extra set of keys Kate had given me, opened the side door and slipped underneath the tape into the house. Entering the familiar kitchen, seeing her ROMA apron hanging on the doorknob of the pantry, the thought struck me as it had not yet done with such force:

She is not here. She is no longer part of this universe, and I will never see her again.

I went upstairs to get my bag, but both curiosity and grief would not allow me to pass her bedroom without going in. Yet the door was not only closed but locked; I supposed by the police. I found my bag in the guest room and slung it onto the bed. I started rummaging for my passport when I noticed something underneath a pair of jeans. It was the manuscript of Kate's memoir, with the zip drive taped to the front page. Cheeky monkey. I could just see her giving Miranda directions to leave it, not in her office desk downstairs, but here in my bag. I don't know how I might have reacted to this if the events of the day before had not occurred, but now, more than ever, I was determined to have nothing to do with this memoir. When I had found my passport and repacked my bag, I hurried downstairs, tossed the memoir and zip drive onto the desk in Kate's office, and left the house, I thought forever.

My flight from Dulles to Heathrow didn't leave until the next evening, so I spent a sleepless night in a hotel room in Gainesville. I lay in bed through the early morning hours like a shipwrecked sailor, exhausted by the awful business of death. I had been in the States since early in the summer. I had come to be with my mother during her final illness, and after her burial, while I was still in DC packing up her apartment, I happily reconnected with Kate, only to discover that she too was approaching her last end. It had been a grim six months, full of catastrophe as Kate would say, and I'd had enough. I wanted no part of whatever "final transition celebration" Kate had planned with Adele—such a thing had nothing to do with me. I just wanted to get on a plane.

The next morning, as I was checking out of the hotel, the woman behind the desk informed me that someone had left me a package. She handed me a manila envelope, inside of which was Kate's memoir and zip drive. I glanced around the lobby of the hotel, wondering from what hiding place Miranda was watching me.

"I don't suppose she left a phone number or address?" I asked the woman behind the desk.

"A man left that for you."

"Oh." I smiled wearily. "Of course."

Not having any interest in the memoir but uneasy about throwing it away, I put it with the zip drive on a closet shelf in my London apartment and did my best to forget about it. I never read the thing—never even glanced at it. Kate was going to be part of me for the rest of my life, and I would treasure until my own dying breath those precious days we spent together during her final week, but I refused to spend even one more second with the decision she recounted in her memoir and her desire to publicize it to the world.

I resumed my sere and fugitive existence. I had one or two requests for service to consider, and after the new contracts were signed, I was off again. I spent some weeks in Paris, followed by several months in Spain. By the next September, I was in Scotland, in a market town called Dumfries. I had been brought there by the tottering sanctuary of the thirteenth-century church of St. Teneu, otherwise one of the most intact Romanesque churches in Scotland, which I and my team had been commissioned to restore. I had been staying in Dumfries for nearly two months, in yet another Airbnb—a simple but pleasant cottage attached to a larger house owned by a voluble widow named Deborah. Deborah was lonely, and often when I got home in the evening, she poked her head out the door and invited me in for a "wee dram." She never asked me to wear a mask or whether I was vaxxed. I spent many summer evenings in an easy chair in Deborah's sitting room enjoying the golden flame of her scotch spreading through me while she talked of her husband, long dead, and her children far way in Aberdeen, Edinburgh, and London. I was happy to listen to her—or rather, I was happy to smile and half-listen, for like Deborah, my one comfort was memory. While she spun her stories, I let my memory drift back to those days in Rome, when Kate, Adele, the Codys, and I were young, and to the tragedy that brought us, or offered us at least, a little wisdom. I reflected on how the aftermath of that tragedy had dogged us through the years and into middle age. I thought about how it had brought me to that bedroom in Chappaqua, New York, where once I sat with Veronica Cody and told her that I loved her, and how it had brought me to that other bedroom at Five Hearths, where once I sat with Kate Montclair and, improbably, told her the same.

One September evening, I had just said goodnight to Deborah and returned to the cottage with the nightcap she insisted I take with me when my mobile rang. The caller ID indicated "Unknown Number." For the past ten months, whenever a call came in from a number I didn't recognize, my chest seized at the thought that it might be Miranda. I had not heard from her or any report of her since I left the States. The police had alerted homeless shelters and indigent mental health facilities across the Atlantic seaboard and beyond, but no one had reported seeing her. She had gone underground, and this time, though I did not quite admit it to myself, I reckoned I had lost her forever.

But when I picked up the call, I was greeted by her uncharacteristically bright and cheery voice.

"Heidy-ho, neighbor! What's going on, Benedict?"

"Miranda? Thank God! Where are you?"

"How's the editing of Kate's memoir coming along? It's got a great plot twist, but you'll need to write that up. You've been working on it, haven't you? Kate needs that book out, like now."

"Miranda, where are you?"

"I'd give you three guesses, but it'd be a waste. I'm here again. I'm at Five Hearths."

Thus began my slow realization that Kate's story was not yet over. She still had something important she wanted to say, and she needed me, not only to edit her memoir, but to complete it.

What I present before the reader is the full account of Kate's final illness. Out of necessity, I have had to put the ending in my own words, but by then it was my story, too, mine and Miranda's and the Codys' and, of course, Adele's. In a way, it has been one story all along, the story that has been unfolding since our youthful days in Rome—the story that came to such a foul and joyous resolution in the good death of Kate Montclair.

Benedict Aquila
Hampstead, London
January 1, 2022

THE GOOD DEATH OF KATE MONTCLAIR

Being the Memoir of Her Final Illness

For love of a task excellently done
For the love of beauty
I have put in the work
I have suffered and toiled.
With honesty I declare I have consulted the rubric
And reviewed my list of habitual errors.
With integrity I declare
this is not a first draft
And that what I submit is wholly my own.
Thus acknowledging that I remain an apprentice
With still much to do on my way toward mastery
I commend this work to your discernment
Humbly requesting it be deemed acceptable
Pending the appropriate alterations.

Kate Montclair

PART I

Midway through the Journey of Our Life

CHAPTER ONE

We awaited news of my fate in Dr. Brawny Ladd's hobbit-sized examining room. Dr. Brawny Ladd is my neuro-oncologist at MedStar Georgetown University Hospital. Or he was until recently, when I retired him. His real name is Dr. Gregory Ladd, but Lisa and I call him Dr. Brawny Ladd because he's cute and seems to be no stranger to the gym. Lisa is my good friend from school. She teaches in Brook Farm's art department. She was with me for moral support, though only via Zoom due to the hospital's COVID restrictions.

When he arrived in the examining room, all masked up like me, Dr. Brawny Ladd took the chair from behind the tiny desk and sat down right in front of me—so close, in fact, that the sexual energy, at least on my end, crackled to life. Amazing, that even in my parlous state, my biochemistry yearned for pleasure and connection, and above all the hope of security within this virtual stranger's brawny embrace. But how unsuited are our needs to this world. A world where there exists bone cancer in children. Which is heated by a sun scheduled to die in a few billion years. A world with tsunamis, hurricanes, and droughts, not to mention our newest friend, COVID-19. A world in time, with a past that cannot be undone. All our mistakes set forever in metaphysical concrete.

As his voice slid down his throat and he looked with grave interest at the poster on the back of his door for the previous year's Glioblastoma Awareness Day, Dr. Brawny Ladd lowered the boom about my biopsy. And before I was even sure I had heard him correctly, he downshifted into full masculine technician mode. *"Let's Attack the Problem!"* Not with surgery, for he agreed with his even more esteemed colleague Dr. Chakrabarti that the insidiousness with which the tumor had wrapped itself around the tissues of my brain ruled that out, but with chemo and radiation that, he hoped, would shrink the tumor and allow for "a longer period of acceptable to perhaps even excellent functioning."

But I was not really listening. As soon as I was sure I had heard him say "Glioblastoma Multiforme Stage IV" (those spiky Roman numerals are like nails in the lid of the coffin) I was gone, wondering if I would lose my hair (the hair first, always), about what I would do with Five Hearths, about the timing of my resignation from school, about how I would finance a burial plot, about whether cremation would be cheaper, about whether anyone besides Lisa and Evie and Everett and a handful of former students would miss me. I was thinking, too, of a good headline for my obituary:

> Kate Montclair, Who Was Never Able to Come to Terms with Life in a Cosmos Ill-Suited to Her Aspirations, Loves, and Heartfelt Demands for Meaning, Is Cut Down by the Hand of Said Cosmos, Cruelly Below the Median Age of Death for a Person of Her Gender and Demographic Status, at 55

Or maybe 56, if I made it past my next birthday.

Eventually, dear, dreamy, ever-so-proactive Dr. Brawny Ladd picked up on the fact that, even though Lisa was fully engaged from my laptop, I had checked out. He stopped and defaulted to the first, perhaps only, talking point he remembered from Bedside Manner 101. He asked if I had any questions.

Just two. Why would a good God, supposing for the moment one exists, allow such a rotten thing to happen to such a sweet gal in the prime of life? And second, Dr. Brawny Ladd, given that I don't see a ring on your finger, how would you like to take a dying woman to dinner? You won't have to worry about a long commitment!

The question I voiced was far more prosaic, not to say dull-witted.

"So, I'm really dying?"

Poor Dr. Brawny Ladd. I had forced him to lay down his technician's arms and address me like a human being. With those big brown eyes, he gave me a sad "You got me" look and nodded. He was so forlorn. I wanted to hug him and tell him everything was going to be all right.

"I have fifteen months, more or less," I said. "That's what I've read."

"Every case is different," he replied. "We're not done fighting yet. We haven't even started."

"That's right," Lisa echoed.

"What can I expect?" I said. "I mean, what's my life going to be like?"

"Pain will increase, but we'll be able to neutralize it pretty well with medication. But you may experience more headaches, weakness, memory loss. Oftentimes patients experience problems with speech. But we're going to put together a game plan."

A game plan. Rah rah sis boom bah. Like it's halftime of the big game and we're 21 points down. I smiled back at him, appreciative of the sentiment but in no mood for fantasy. He pressed on.

"There's also something called fractionated radiosurgery. Sometimes called a cyberknife. For patients with inoperable GBM's, we've had some success with a three times daily RT." (The Brawny Ladd loved his acronyms.) "The idea is to slow the tumor's rate of growth so as to extend the patient prognosis as long as possible. We'd give you the three doses of radiation about four hours apart."

I replied, somewhat non-technically, "You'd zap me *three times a day*? How often would I have to do this?"

"Five days a week. Our RT lounge is very comfortable."

"*Five days a week?* Does your RT lounge offer hot rocks massages? Free liquor? How many weeks am I supposed to do this?"

"The protocol typically runs between six and seven weeks."

I tell you, if Dr. Brawny Ladd weren't so gosh-darned cute when he's in full black-ops mode, I would have laughed him out of that examining room. Six to seven weeks of thrice-daily zappings! He was like a little boy with a new water pistol; he just needed to shoot his radiation gun at *something*. I almost said yes because I knew it would make him so happy.

"How much more time would the cyberthingy give me?"

"For a small percentage of patients, the procedure has given them years."

"But for most?"

"Several more months, perhaps. Some months."

When school ends in June, and I know I have "some months" of freedom ahead of me, I am giddy with anticipation. A few summer months is a new world, rich and varied in alluring possibility. But "some months" tacked on to the end of a miserable slog through a fatal illness is a black hole of nothingness. A senseless prolongation of the awful inevitable.

"I'm not sure…"

Dr. Brawny Ladd had one more arrow in his quiver. "Some new protocols have shown some promise. There's a clinical trial for Stage IV Glio patients going on now at the Cleveland Clinic. But it's a Phase 1 trial—meaning that they're still trying to figure out the right dosage of the new drug and its impact on the body."

"How could I participate in a clinical trial in Cleveland?"

"You'd have to relocate for a time."

"It's bad enough having brain cancer—but in Cleveland?"

The more I listened to Dr. Brawny Ladd, the more I needed to get out of that examination room. I felt like I had been buried alive in it, with the Brawny Ladd nestled beside me ready to whisper encouraging pro-tips on how to conserve oxygen. I let him ramble for a while, but when I began to hyperventilate, I rose from my chair.

"Well, doctor, you've given me a lot to think about."

"I understand," he said. "Keep in mind that your best bet is to act quickly."

"I just have to think—the semester just started."

At this, Lisa nearly reached out from Zoomland to shake me. "Kate, I want you to forget about your classes. Your job right now is to focus on yourself. There's a long-term sub policy in place for this kind of emergency."

I knew Lisa meant this to be helpful, but I hardly found it so. Like most people, a fair amount of my identity was wrapped up in what I did for twelve to sixteen hours every day, so it was more than a little unsettling to have it ripped away so suddenly. I was a teacher. I had just started my thirty-second school year. I had lived with this rhythm almost all my life: the promise of new birth each August, the purchasing of school supplies, writing for the first time in the virgin planner, the ardent list of professional resolutions, the sheer giddiness induced by books and ideas, the newly arrived batch of fresh-scrubbed faces, some of whom I would one day count among my friends. How I loved it all, despite its many, many frustrations. Could it be possible that I had taught my final class?

"I'd just like some time to think," I said. "This is all happening kind of—"

"Kate," Lisa interrupted again. "Sweetie. You need to move on this."

I brushed her off by not looking at the screen. With my eyes fixed on Dr. Brawny Ladd, I said, "Can I call you?"

No doubt he was gobsmacked by my reaction, but he didn't break character.

"Absolutely." He got up. "Talk to your family and we'll make a plan."

"Thank you, Dr. Ladd. I don't have a family. But thank you."

Before I even got to the elevator, I had gone through all five of Kübler-Ross's Five Stages of Grief. Denial, anger, depression, bargaining, acceptance. She seems to have forgotten total existential bewilderment. It's not at all the same as anger. It's not, "I'm mad because fate is taking my life from me." It's more like how you feel when you watch a foreign film and you don't get the abrupt and enigmatic ending.

Wait. That's it? It's over? Could someone please tell me what that was supposed to be about?

"Are you tracking me, Kate?" Lisa asked. By this point, I had made it to her car in the hospital parking lot. She was behind the wheel, and I was in the passenger seat.

"Yes," I said.

"I don't think you're tracking me. That's OK. I'm tracking for you."

"Yes."

"What about a second opinion? I'm calling my sister-in-law in Baltimore tonight, the nurse up at Hopkins. We're going to get you into their cancer center."

"I dunno, Lisa."

"We're not done fighting, Kate, you got that? You *got* that? It's your choice how you want to proceed, but you heard the Brawny Ladd. Whatever you choose, you have to move on it."

"Can't I just—am I allowed to think?"

"I'm not trying to pressure you!"

"No?"

After this shot to the mouth, we went to our corners. In the stormy silence, I formulated a new plan.

"You know," I said, "I think I'm going to take a walk."

"A walk? OK, let's go for a walk. Where do you want to walk to? Want to go get a drink? Want to get drunk? C'mon, let's do it. We'll have a late lunch and get drunk."

"Don't take this personally, Lisa, but I think I'd like to be alone. Do you mind?"

"I don't want to leave you alone, sweetie."

"I know you don't. But I'm OK."

"I don't think you're OK."

"Well, *of course* I'm not OK. But I need to be alone. We introverts process differently. You'd want to talk it all out. I want to perpend."

"Perpend?"

"Contemplate. Cogitate. Chew over."

"Where are you going to go?"

"I have no idea. It's a lovely day. I think I saw a notice for a shuttle to Dupont Circle. Maybe I'll hop on the shuttle."

"Fine. You want to be alone."

"Thank you."

"But I'm going to call you in two hours," Lisa said. "You're staying in the city tonight? At the apartment?"

"Yeah. I guess. Yeah."

"Good. I'll call you in two hours."

"In two hours."

"Yes."

"When you get home, take a big soak in the bath. Pour yourself a glass of wine. Put on *Pride and Prejudice,* the episode where Colin Firth strips down to his undershirt and dives into the lake. But I'm going to call you before that. In two hours."

"Two hours."

"I'm right here with you, sweetie. We're going to fight this. You got that? And we're going to *win.*"

As we parted, Lisa gave me a long hug and whispered, "Good thoughts, sweetie. You've got all my good thoughts."

Actually, as I rode the MedStar shuttle to Dupont Circle, all I had were bouncing thoughts. Bounce, bounce, bounce. Bouncing around my mind like tennis balls.

So I will die having never accomplished with my writing what I had hoped to accomplish. Unless…unless tomorrow, while my energy is still good, I get up early and get back to that essay…

So we beat on, boats against the current. I wonder how many essays on *The Great Gatsby* I've read in my life. Hundreds, certainly. Thousands? Practically all forgettable. Both Gatsby and I, in the end, get punished for our romantic readiness. Last spring, however, at the end of our *Gatsby* unit, I finally read one that surprised me. By Alice Nwaoloko, not even one of my best students. She set the rubric emphatically aside and wrote it in the form of a diary entry by "Mrs. Daisy Gatsby," now divorced from Tom Buchanan and the unhappy wife of Mr. Jay Gatsby. They have been living in Gatsby's mansion in West Egg for six months, more than long enough for them to come to hate one another. While Gatsby spends his days meeting with his Presidential Exploratory Committee and visiting his new mistress, Daisy is planning a solo vacation in Tuscany in the hope of finding herself—*and* a hunky new love interest, just like Julia Roberts does in *Eat, Pray, Love.*

Is that what would have happened to us, Mr. Cody? Would you eventually have gotten sick of me, and would I have ended up as I am anyway, a catastrophist, one who repeats self-loving affirmations three times a day after meals and has had a fling or two with a hunky stranger, but who still doesn't have a clue who she is or what anything is about?

> Catastrophist (noun)
> definition of catastrophist
>> : an exotic breed, almost entirely extinct; not a pessimist, as a pessimist anticipates bad things happening in the future; a catastrophist realizes that something horribly catastrophic has happened in the past but that most people have had the event wiped from their memories; the catastrophist's memory was also wiped, but imperfectly, as the catastrophist remains aware that something terrible happened and that its effects remain very much with us.

As I rumbled along on the shuttle, I indulged myself in an imaginary conversation with Chloe, my therapist. "OK," Imaginary Chloe was saying, "you're dying. Let's look it squarely in the eye. What feelings come to mind?"

"That it's all been a waste."

"What has been a waste?"

"My life."

"Why?"

"Because nothing has come to anything. Nothing has come to a climax and resolution. I can't even detect a narrative. It's just a series of disconnected, for the most part unhappy, episodes. Hey! That's Aristotle's definition of a bad tragedy: a string of disconnected episodes. I can't even say my life has been a good tragedy."

"There have been disappointments," Imaginary Chloe said. "Agreed. But surely you've found some satisfaction in teaching?"

"To a point, sure. There are worse things than spending your life trying to turn kids on to literature and good writing. At Christmas, kids bake me my share of cookies and mini banana bread loaves and leave me heartwarming notes along with Starbucks gift cards, so something must be working.

"But before you get all Mr. Chips on me, consider the case of Rachel Lord.

"Rachel Lord was the brightest, most gifted student I have ever taught. Period, end of discussion. You have to understand, in my classroom, written compositions can only be submitted under the following 'affidavit' signed by the author, a statement ending with the words:

So, acknowledging that I remain an apprentice
With still much to do on my way toward mastery
I commend this work to your discernment
Humbly requesting it be deemed acceptable
Pending the appropriate alterations.

After I grade the draft and students 'confess' their writing 'sins' to me, students are given the 'penance' of correcting their mistakes in a fresh draft. It is *exceedingly* rare for essays to go through less than three drafts. Indeed, the phrase I write on penultimate, almost-but-not-quite-ready essay drafts, 'Acceptable, with alterations,' has become a shibboleth among my students and always serves as the caption to my photograph in the school yearbook.

"But on two legendary occasions, a student has handed in to me, as a *first draft*, a perfect essay in terms of literary analysis, critical thinking, grammar, and composition—an essay requiring absolutely *no alterations*—and Rachel Lord was that student on both occasions. No word a lie, this kid was writing publishable poetry as a sophomore in high school. She graduated from Brook Farm and went on to get a BA in English from Harvard, then did graduate work at Cal-Berkeley. Then last week, Lisa told me that she saw an alumna's Facebook post that said Rachel Lord had committed suicide. Overdosed on pills in a seedy hotel room in Palo Alto.

"Why, Rachel? What happened to what we used to feel when we read 'I heard a Fly buzz—when I died' or *The Bell Jar*? What happened to the feeling that we would never be the same again, that our lives were going to burn in every moment from then on?"

Why wasn't the poetry enough to keep the catastrophe at bay?

When I got off the air-conditioned shuttle at Dupont and was assaulted by a blast of late-August DC humidity, I realized that I was still wearing a mask. (I keep a collection of booklovers COVID masks in my purse, and all day I had been wearing the one featuring cartoons of Jane Austen's major couples.) I ripped the mask off my face and stuffed it in my purse. If COVID wanted to kill me, it was going to have to get in line.

As I walked, it occurred to me that, when you got right down to it, death was kind of a mysterious thing.

I remembered two years ago, asleep in my childhood bedroom at Five Hearths, being awakened in the middle of the night and hearing my mother in her death delirium calling out through the darkness for *her* mother, long dead and deeply despised.

I remembered my friend Bianca Enderby dying of leukemia right at the start of senior year in high school. I think it's fair to call her my friend. We weren't super close, but we had, on two different occasions—once at a party and once in the corner of the stands at a football game—long and intense conversations about "life." We girls all followed her final illness with fanatical melodrama, and when the news of her death was finally announced at school, we collapsed, inconsolable, into one another's arms. Even some of the boys cried. We girls piled teddy bears around her locker. We made a pile of teddy bears that came up to our waists. Why? Why did we suddenly adopt a metaphysics that saw Bianca Enderby being ferried across the Styx comforted by 137 teddy bears? And what about Lisa's metaphysics? What did she think "good thoughts" were going to accomplish? By sending out her "good thoughts," did she think she was beaming into my brain tissue some special New Age healing energy?

I was thinking of people I should call. I'm an only child whose parents are deceased and who has no children of her own. Frankly, there aren't a lot of people to call. Does one call the man one was never really married to? I can imagine that conversation.

Me: *"Hi, Tim, I'm dying."*

Tim: *"No problem, Kate. Because the thing is, you were already dead to me."*

No, what Tim would actually say is that he would pray for me, which would bother me even more than a snarky comment. When Mom died, he sent a condolence note saying that a Mass would be said for "the repose of her soul" at his church in Houston. I wrote back and thanked him, though I refrained from saying that when the priest came to see her in the hospital, Mom told him to get lost.

I don't think I'll call Tim. I don't owe him anything anymore, not even a goodbye.

So where do you go after you learn that you have a malignant tumor growing like an asparagus bed in your brain?

My go-to place is Cool Beans near Dupont Circle, the best coffee shop in the District. During the school year, it's where I lurk in the late afternoons to numb the pain of adolescent fumbling at composition with a dark chocolate mocha and a pastry. Something about the clean lines of the shop's decor, the white-tiled walls, the built-in bookshelves, the gleaming silver of the espresso machines, and even the barista sporting the ski cap and the sleeve of colored tats, I find particularly comforting. I should write them an online review:

> *Need a place to decompress after your doc has told you that your*
> *days are numbered? Head straight to Cool Beans! The coffee and*

*pastries are top-notch, and you can sit quietly and anonymously
for hours while you ponder the meaninglessness of the indescrib-
able physical and emotional suffering you are about to endure.
Five stars!*

As I walked in the door, two idle baristas, both wearing conventional hospital masks, greeted me like so many skulls with broad, blue-toothed grins.
An Asian woman reading a thriller at a nearby table wore a mask, a plastic
visor, and a colorful shawl swaddled around her neck.

Seating was limited to half capacity, but I still found the perfect little
two-seater in the corner. I sat down with my 530-calorie dark chocolate mocha and 800-calorie pastry. Some people would want to sit and cry; all I
wanted was carbs and sugar.

I had just sat down when I got a text from Lisa, a smartphone stock image
of Wonder Woman flexing her bicep with a caption in all caps:

WE'RE COMING FOR YOU, CANCER!
YOU JUST MESSED WITH THE WRONG GIRL!!!!!!!!

Good ol' Lisa. I was awful to her at the hospital. She's just the kind of
friend you want with you in a foxhole such as this. Still, it struck me that
there was something a little pathetic about her kind of Never Say Die swagger.
Because the truth is, I was very likely dying. And pretty soon too. The cancer
cells weren't "attacking" me in any intentional sense. They were just doing
what they were supposed to do, playing their role in the general catastrophe.
I didn't begrudge Lisa the desire to fight. I really didn't. But I would also have
found it refreshing if someone went around with a T-shirt that said:

I HAVE BRAIN CANCER,
AND I'LL BE CHECKING OUT BEFORE LONG

And on the back:

DID I MENTION THAT YOU'RE MORTAL TOO?

I replied to Lisa's text by inviting her to spend the weekend with me at
Five Hearths. I wanted to make it up to her, but it wasn't just that. Usually when I lit out for my bolt-hole in Fauquier County, I was answering

the call of the anchorite. I wanted nothing other than to curl up for one of my eremite weekends of reading, movie watching, cooking, bath taking, wine drinking, and compulsive journaling. This coming weekend, however, I didn't think I could endure without some company. And Lisa knew the rule of being a good guest:

THE RULE OF ST. KATE
Article XXIV
Guests Are Allowed at Five Hearths Only If They Know How to Be Alone and Thus Don't Require Constant Attention,
with the Exception, Of Course, of Dinner and the Evening Movie

As I ate my pastry, I marveled at how, just a week earlier, I was in my sweltering classroom at Brook Farm, death the furthest thing from my mind. I was just beginning English I Honors Period 3. Sixteen hyperachieving first-years, all in their COVID masks sitting six feet apart, like a collection of prodigiously gifted med students. I had just begun a vivid narrative of the summer when the teenage Mary Godwin, not yet married to Percy Bysshe Shelley, traveled with the poet to the Villa Diodati on Lake Geneva, where they rented a house along with Mary's half-sister Clare, the irrepressible Lord Byron, and Byron's personal physician, John Polidori. Students tended to perk up when I detailed the various entanglements of free love in which this group of extraordinary young people involved themselves, and how they passed the cold, wet summer composing ghost stories, the future Mary Shelley's *Frankenstein* and Polidori's *The Vampyre* being the only two that were ever completed. But as I was telling this story, I suddenly could not remember the date of that fateful summer. It wasn't just that I couldn't pinpoint the year; I couldn't remember what *century* I was supposed to be in. For several tormenting moments, I had nothing—as though my memory of all things Mary Shelley had been removed, like a video from YouTube, leaving only a grey screen with an unhappy face looking back at me.

Highly trained professional that I am, I began to fake my way through the lesson. For what happened next, I must rely on the eye-witness account of the ineffable Ms. Bridey Schlupp and her Rampaging Run-Ons, in which all my failures as a teacher of grammar and composition lie before me…

Bridey Schlupp
Ms. Montclair
English I Honors Period 3
August 23, 2020

For love of a task excellently done
For the love of beauty
I have put in the work
I have suffered and toiled.
With honesty I declare I have consulted the rubric
And reviewed my list of habitual errors.
With integrity I declare
this is not a first draft
And that what I submit is wholly my own.
Thus acknowledging that I remain an apprentice
With still much to do on my way toward mastery
I commend this work to your discernment
Humbly requesting it be deemed acceptable
Pending the appropriate alterations.
Bridey Schlupp

Close Observation Writing Assignment #1
Ms. Montclair's "FrankenSeizure"

Rubric:
- Word count: no fewer than 800 words
- Must make observations using each of the five senses at least once
- Must employ at least one good simile and one good metaphor
- Must employ at least five strong verb sentence dress-ups
- Must correctly employ at least five distinct vocabulary words from *Vocabulary Adventure* Units 1-3

So, at first we all thought Ms. Montclair was pranking us because she had just pranked us at the beginning of class.

Five minutes after the bell we were all wondering where she was when she *hurled* [strong verb] herself out of the storage closet with *cherry-colored stage blood* [sense: sight] all over her face *alleging* [*Vocabulary Adventure* Unit 1] she had been attacked by Victor Frankenstein's "creature"—still alive after all these years because he/it is "virtually immortal." Why??? Because her father's real name was really "Frankenstein" and the creature is out *to annihilate* [strong verb] all members of the House of Frankenstein including Ms. Montclair (real name: "Victoria Frankenstein") unless she makes the creature a mate (gross!) using the physics lab here at school and the recipe her great-great grandfather *bequeathed* [*Vocabulary Adventure* Unit 1] to her. Lol!

So given Ms. Montclair's *propensity* (*Vocabulary Adventure*, Unit 3) for classroom hijinks I don't think us students should be very much blamed for not realizing that she was having a real seizure especially since she was just talking to us about Mary Shelley and how when writing "Frankenstein" she (Shelley) had been reading about Luigi Galvani and his nephew Giovanni Aldini and there [sic] experiments trying to bring the dead back to life using electricity otherwise known as Galvanization. Truly it was just like Ms. Montclair to roll around on the floor like she had just been galvanized. (By the way, I believe her having a seizure right after lecturing on galvanization is situational as opposed to dramatic irony because in this case, the opposite of *Oedipus the King*, the audience—us students—were not aware of what was happening beforehand. *Do I get a bonus point???*)

The first sign for me though that this wasn't some classroom gag was when I saw little globules of foam *exude* [strong verb] from Ms. Montclair's mouth like the little blobs that squirt out of the canister of Redi-Whip when it has been pretty well cleaned out [simile]. When she started foaming at the mouth, Liz Matthews *screeched* [strong verb/sense: hearing] and then everybody started freaking out and I experienced in my mouth the acidic backwash from my lunch [sense: taste] which is often the *prelude* [*Vocabulary Adventure* Unit 1] to hurling. It did not help that I was sitting quite near to Several Boys Who Shall Remain Nameless who had just come from P.E. and so *reeked* [strong verb/sense: smell] of Axe. Miraculously however I managed not to wretch [sic]. Jilly Carson meanwhile maintained a cool head as she told T.J. Stromberg to run down and get Ms. Horst, our nurse. T.J. *bolted* [strong verb] out the door leaving the room in *pandemonium* (*Vocabulary Adventure*, Unit 2).

Liz Matthews, the aforesaid screecher, who also suffers from a peanut allergy, then had an idea that she thought would be majorly helpful. She took out her EpiPen and stabbed Ms. Montclair in the leg [sense: touch]. It was not a bad idea but we only learned later from Ms. Horst that a severe allergic reaction is not the same thing as a seizure and so—*plot twist!*—the EpiPen didn't work. Thankfully then Ms. Horst arrived and told us all to sit down and remain calm. She knelt down next to Ms. Montclair who was still shaking but not so wildly now. Ms. Horst didn't do anything like holding Ms. Montclair down or putting something in Ms. Montclairs [sic] mouth. Liz Matthews had heard that seizure patients can choke on their own tongues and die but Ms. Horst said that was an old wife's tale and that she should know because she is an old wife. Lol!

Soon Ms. Montclair was dead to the world [metaphor]. Then she began to snore, which totally cracked us up. Her snoring sounded like when a spoon gets caught in the garbage disposal [simile—sorry Ms. M!]. When the bell rang at the end of the period none of us wanted to leave due to acute FOMO. But when the paramedics arrived Ms. Horst told us to skedaddle to 4th period and let the paramedics do their stuff. (btw I swear one of them looked just like the dad in *The Quiet Place* [allusion].) We were all pretty freaked out but Ms. Horst told us not to worry because Ms. Montclair was going to be just fine. Which I hope she is. Feel better, Ms. Montclair!!!

The kids told me later that I passed out, dropped right to the floor, where my arms and my legs went rigid. They described how I arched my back as though I was desperate to expel something from my mouth.

I was like this for about a minute. Then I began to convulse and emit specks of foam from my mouth. No one was timing this phase, but the kids swear my whole body was shaking for close to two minutes before the spasms began to subside. After they stopped, I lay there unconscious for several minutes. And yes, Bridey, snoring. But it could have been far worse. Based upon what I later read about seizures, I can only be grateful that I experienced no lack of control of my bladder or bowels.

When I started to come back to consciousness, I could see figures moving around, but at first they only looked like trees walking, as the man said. These were my traumatized kids flitting anxiously around me.

"Welcome back, hon."

It was Karla Horst, our school nurse, kneeling beside me.

"Where am I?" I said. "What happened?"

"You've had a seizure, Kate. I called 911. The ambulance is on its way."

I had never had a seizure before. Knew nothing about them. Karla's voice was calm, but her hands shook as she gently rolled me onto my side and did her best to comfort me. It took a long time for the ambulance to arrive—twenty minutes, I later learned. While we waited, Karla asked me just to rest and not talk, and so I lay there assuming the worst, preparing myself for death. With unfolded laundry still on the guest room bed in my apartment. With the frying pan from my morning omelet still soaking in the sink. With the humorous essay I had been working on fitfully all summer at Five Hearths still unfinished and unfunny in the open notebook on my desk. Weird what comes to you in the final moments, or in what you take to be the final moments, of your life. I remembered, when I was twelve or so, my father returning home from a cross-country trip. He said half-jokingly to my mother about his flight home in a turbulent storm: "We were all saying the

Act of Contrition." I tried to recall it. But I ended up mumbling Grace Before Meals: "Bless us, O Lord, for these thy gifts, which we are about to receive…"

Not that it mattered. I didn't believe there was anyone at the other end of the line, and I hadn't since I was fourteen.

I remembered, too, looking up into a clear night sky at the morning star.

I was young and in Rome, and I was sitting on the ground holding Mr. Cody with his head in my lap and my legs weirdly splayed, like I had just attempted and miserably failed to execute one of my majestic seventh-grade splits. I had my arms around his neck and my face buried in his hair. And I said to him, "Well, Mr. Cody, look how I'm going out. On my classroom floor. I am fifty-five years old. You might not even recognize me if you saw me. Not completely gone to seed, but still, not your manic pixie dream girl anymore. Just a middle-aged lady who's spent the last thirty years trying to learn how to deal with the catastrophe." Little Miranda, meanwhile, was curled up beside her daddy with her head on his tummy, as though expecting him to wake any moment and roughhouse with her. I couldn't tell her that he was dead. I didn't know how. Where are you, little Miranda? How I've always wanted to find you. This, too, alas, I am going to have to leave unfinished…

As I sipped my mocha, I watched, at a right-angle to me a few tables away, two twentysomethings, their masks tucked under their chins: a tall, handsome Caucasian man with an All-American jawline, and a stunning African-American woman with high cheekbones and a megawatt smile. They were both in business attire: he in a seersucker jacket and navy-blue slacks, and she in a sleeveless pale green dress with a professional hemline right at the knee. Recent college grads, apparently, working their first big jobs in the city, indentured servants to some law firm or PR firm or think-tank. I wasn't sure at first whether it was a date. It was possibly just a pick-me-up dose of caffeine between colleagues before they went back to work. But then he said something that made her laugh, and she looked down at her coffee, unable to handle the pressure of his gaze but basking in it nonetheless, and then I knew perhaps better than they did that it was a date. Nature's wheel had begun to turn. The young had found their way into one another's arms, little thinking about where the ride would end. What did the poet say? Birth, copulation, and death. Again and again and again.

Sometimes I feel like we're all Londoners in 1941 who have to get up every morning and paw through the rubble of the Blitz. Except that in our case, we are all so shell-shocked that we've forgotten there's even a war on. We think we're living our best life now.

The young lovers got up to go. As they put on their masks, I had this desperate, catastrophist's need to go over and warn them. Tell them that something had gone horribly wrong and, though I'm not sure what it was, I was sure that our masks weren't going to help any of us.

They headed for the door. Should I run after them? At least to tell them that I was rooting for them, even though the game was rigged and they couldn't possibly win?

But they wouldn't understand, and how could I blame them? I couldn't make sense of it myself.

What do you think happened, Mr. Cody? Did we do something wrong? Is this diagnosis my punishment, the final proof that I've never deserved to be happy? You have to help me figure this out quickly, because pretty soon your long-ago Ms. Montclair is going to return to dust.

I'm afraid I may have given you the wrong impression. This is not a cancer memoir. I loathe cancer memoirs. You know what song I can't get out of my head whenever I think of cancer memoirs?

> *Johnny could only sing one note*
> *And the note he sings was this*
> *Ah!*

The Judy Garland version, natch.

Cancer memoirs all say the same thing. That is, after they drag us through all the dreary cancer memoir tropes: the sense that Something is Not Right, the Anxious Waiting for Medical Test Results, the Grave Diagnosis, the Denial, the Rage, the Loss of Normalcy, the Loss of Hair, and Yadda Yadda, until, One Fine Day, the Cancerous Author has…an Epiphany! "Jeepers! It was Right There in Front of Me the Whole Time! How Could I Not Have

Seen It? *You Have to Live Every Moment.* It's a Vale of Tears, Baby, But There's Beauty and Love and Grace If You Can Only Live Deep and Suck Out All the Marrow of Life. Every Moment: Making Scrambled Eggs for the Kids. Reading Silently with Your Partner Before Bedtime. The Smell of Coffee and All That's Too Much for Emily Webb in Act III of *Our Town*. Do You See It Now? Cancer or No Cancer, You Have to Live Every Moment Like It's Your Last!"

This, of course, is all bunk.

I mean, I'm not against a little consciousness-raising. I'm an English teacher: I can understand the value of paying attention. But the problem with living in the moment is that moments *pass*. In fact, logically speaking, I'm not sure it's even possible to live *in* the moment. I'm straining here, trying to remember the lectures on time from the philosophy elective I took junior year. Was it Bergson? Heidegger? Anyway, what is time but the experience of a *continuous flow*? It's a ride on an express, not a local. There are no stops, at least not until you get to the end of the line. And when you get to the end of the line, it's no longer *you* there. It's a corpse.

Ergo, there's no such thing as living in the moment. There's only a pressing of one's face to the window of the train as the landscape whizzes by.

This is not a cancer memoir. So what is it? A *Confessions*? That would imply there is someone to confess to.

On the most basic level, this is the book Adele asked me to write. "You're under the cosh, darling. I know it's not the book you've always dreamed of writing. But it's the book fate has offered you. It's the book you were *meant* to write."

This is an account of my experiences in the Death Symposium and of what I have decided to do. Names, places, and dates will have to be changed if it is ever published, but I will leave that job to others. I cannot write about this experience by hiding all the identifiers under black ink like in a classified document. I'm going to name names and reveal the locations. But I will also be careful. At Adele's request, I am keeping the laptop, when I'm not using it, in a strongbox in my bedroom closet, and no one has a key but me. And yes, I am actually going to type. I have always written by hand, have never used a computer for any piece of writing that meant anything to me. But I do not trust my strength in the coming days and weeks, and so I will type, type against the dying of the light.

What is the Death Symposium, you ask? Come with me back to the coffee shop.

The young lovers gone, the mocha and pastry dispatched, I started work on an eminently practical End-of-Life To-Do List. But my reflections were rudely intruded upon. A middle-aged woman with stalagmites of hot purple hair sat down at the table six feet from me. She was giving a lecture via cell phone, at theatrical levels of projection, to a sister or girlfriend *who simply had to learn to stop being so needy around a boyfriend who clearly had no respect for her.*

I did my best to ignore the lecture and go back to my list, but the woman's voice shattered my concentration, not to mention compromised the glass windows of the coffee shop. I should have exited stage left, with a withering look in her direction, but nonconfrontational jellyfish that I am, I instead concocted a plan to use the Ladies. Then, upon my return, if she were still on the phone, I would buy another coffee and retreat with it up to the mezzanine.

On my way into the Ladies, I was arrested by a notice pinned to the bulletin board on the wall. The advertisement was printed with black lettering on white paper bordered with blood-red skeletons lined up head to toe:

> **The Washington, DC Death Symposium** invites you to an exploration of the things that really matter. In a compassionate, confidential, and non-judgmental environment, we discuss topics that our death-denying culture has sadly made taboo.
>
> *What song would you like at your funeral?*
> *Describe what a "peaceful" death means for you.*
> *How do you prepare for death and dying?*
> *Who gets your collection of garden gnomes when you're gone?*
>
> And did we mention tea and cake?
>
> **Coming to you every first Thursday of the month at 7:30 p.m. Cool Beans Coffee, 732 P Street NW (off Dupont Circle).** Come for a frank, FUN discussion of death, dying,

and what it means to be fully alive. Bring a friend, and we'll see you there!

Meanwhile, check us out on Facebook and Instagram.

I'm not the kind of person who reads, let alone responds to, notices on bulletin boards in public spaces. Especially ones printed up like an invitation to a Halloween party. But the blood-red skeletons caught my eye, as did the name of the group: *The Death Symposium*, an intriguing mixture of the philosophical and macabre. The neatness of the advertisement too, the cost that must have gone into printing it—assuming these were hanging all over the District—hinted that perhaps this was not some motley collection of urban eccentrics but a group of some substance and commitment.

When I got back to my table, the stalagmite woman was quietly engrossed by her phone. I sat down, opened Facebook, and found the page I wanted: *The Washington, DC Death Symposium*. The stream was populated by memes with inspiring quotations, links to helpful articles about the grieving process, instructions on how to start one's own local chapter. But I also found a link to a website. I clicked and found a well-presented page with an About tab at the top.

When I clicked on About, I came to a page presented in the form of a letter encouraging interested seekers to visit the Death Symposium. My eye tumbled down the letter as I scrolled, and at the bottom, I found a digital signature. As I read the name, not only the day's momentous news but also the years fell away around me. It was a name that worked upon me like one of those cooking smells that transports you back to childhood.

Beneath the signature was a studio portrait of Adele herself. I had not seen her in thirteen years. She wore her sixty years with typical elegance. Her hair was now icy white, done in a pixie, and she posed with a green cape wrapped dramatically around her shoulder. She remained a strikingly beautiful woman.

"Hey! Do you know her?"

The stalagmite woman was now beside me, having invited herself right into my personal space.

"I do." I was about to add, "We used to be very good friends," but she blew right through me.

"Adele is *fabulous*. That *accent*! She is my *favorite* person in the world.

Have you been to the Death Symposium? There's a meeting next week, I think. On Thursday. Oh, you've *got* to come. I missed the last one, and I've been *really* feeling it. I know it sounds weird but just come! You'll *love* it. Who would have thought talking about death could be so fun?"

No, the overall effect of stumbling upon Adele in this way was not as piquant as a cooking smell from childhood. It was more a feeling of curiosity that my life might be capable of such poetic closure, as my end joined up with my beginning.

For I did used to know Adele Schraeder. We used to be very good friends.

CHAPTER TWO

The next morning, I called the second-in-command at school, Jeremy Whittleston, and asked for a week of emergency sick-leave. I said that I hadn't been feeling well and that I needed to get a "test" done, and to his socially awkward, emotionally out-of-touch credit, he asked for no further justification. As soon as I was off the phone with Jeremy, I started packing my bag, looking forward to hitting the road as soon as the morning rush hour died down.

When I saw my Morning Mountain a few hours later, and my dear old house awash in the August sun, I felt more myself than I had since the seizure. Lisa had told me not expect her until evening, so I had the day to myself. I unpacked, readied the guest room for Lisa, threw in a load of laundry, and then took to the front porch to eat a lunch of locally sourced veggies, fruit, and cheese for protein, complemented with a glass of Ox-Eye pinot noir, my favorite Virginia wine, redolent of a pioneer smokehouse. I sipped my wine and looked with satisfaction on my lands and messuages, and, as I did, the glaring, antiseptic corridors of MedStar Georgetown University Hospital swirled down the drain of my consciousness like a bad dream upon waking.

I couldn't stop looking at my Morning Mountain. That's what I've called it ever since I can remember: "Morning Mountain." It's the highest part of the ridge on the horizon. There's a pretty good view of it from the window of the bedroom I used as a child. Growing up, when I awoke in the mornings, I would always go first to the window and say, "Hello, Morning Mountain." In my green girlhood, usually alone and always with my notebook, I hiked its back countless times. It was the place where I worked everything out. Where I decided that I and my high school boyfriend, Tommy Seger, didn't have what it took to go the distance, and where I staked everything on the dream that there was someone else out there for me. Where I wrote some of my best sketches for my college comedy troupe, Funny Ha-Ha or Funny Strange, and imagined myself as a standup comedian who, like Woody Allen, parlayed a standup act into a serious writing and directing career. It was my place of hope and promise, when it still seemed possible to believe in such things.

My efforts quacking myself online had sharpened my sense of what to expect:

- More headaches (including migraines)
- Nausea and vomiting
- Cognitive/memory issues
- Speech issues
- Possible blindness
- More seizures
- At the end, difficulty swallowing

Soon enough, my familiar existence would be deeply compromised by medical treatments, the indignities of loss of independence, the increasing use of drugs to numb the pain. The thought of all this shriveled my bowels.

While online the night before, I had also visited an online cancer chat group.

> *When I got my Glio diagnosis, my doc gave me the standard 14 months tops, but I'm now more than two years into my recovery, and I feel great. So all of you out there dealing with Glio, don't believe what anybody says. Just stay positive and know that you're going to beat this!*

Foolishly, I ended up Googling this stouthearted soul and came upon his obituary. He passed about three months after writing this post.

In my bed at Five Hearths, on a beautiful spring morning if I could make it that far, looking out onto my Morning Mountain—that is where I wanted it to end.

But enough. I was breaking my newest rule:

THE RULE OF ST. KATE
Article CCCXIX
While On an Eremite Weekend at Five Hearths,
Thoughts of Death Are Not to Be Entertained

How strange it was that I had stumbled upon Adele Schraeder on this week of all weeks. How strange that here, in the eleventh hour, she had come back into my life.

I was sitting on my porch at Five Hearths gazing out at my Morning Mountain, but I was also a new teacher who'd just arrived in Rome. In fact, it was my first day on campus at Wildwood International Catholic School, which everyone—students, teachers, and staff alike—referred to as WIX. I was walking between my new roommates, Lauren and Consuela, who had started teaching at WIX the year before. They were showing me the way to the new faculty orientation.

We were halfway down the walk that led from the front gate to the main administration building when I saw a young woman come out the front doors. In her T-shirt, jeans, and sandals, she might have been mistaken for one of the senior girls, but—as I knew from a picture of the faculty that Lauren had shown me—Adele Schraeder was, in fact, one of my new colleagues and older than I by four years. She had on a jaunty, wide-brimmed straw hat, from under which her ginger hair splayed upon her shoulders, shimmering in the sun.

She tripped down the stairs, and at the bottom she was met, as if out of thin air, by three of the senior girls—I did not yet know them as such—who had arrived back to campus early for RA training. As they approached us, Adele told the girls in the magisterial tones of her British accent:

"We don't have to take this from the sisters, and we won't. We will rally, my lovelies. We will agitate."

As they passed me on the walk, the senior girls hushed their conspiratorial voices and regarded the three of us with barely polite suspicion. Adele herself, with those bright blue, sharp-witted eyes, nodded to me with—was it a *pert* smile? Indicating what? A certain condescension, perhaps? Because she knew who I was and that, as a new teacher, I was helpless to do anything in the classroom but grind young souls into dust, destroying any delight they might take in learning with my slavish acceptance of techniques and lesson plans designed for large-scale industrialized education?

"They gave you *her* class," Lauren said to me after Adele and her coterie had passed. "To punish her, I suppose. Senior English Honors. Adele's been teaching that class for three years."

"Punish her for what?"

"In the spring, Bijou Arden's mother found her with birth control. Mrs. Arden is über Catholic and a boffo benefactor to the school. Or used to be. Mrs. Arden told Sr. Helen Marie that she suspects Bijou got the stuff from Adele, and do you know what Sr. Helen Marie said back to her? I got this straight from Bijou herself. Sr. Helen Marie said, 'But Mrs. Arden, isn't Bijou using contraceptives better than her being unmarried and pregnant?' Mrs. Arden stormed out. She was going to pull Bijou from the school, but Bijou convinced her to let her finish her senior year."

"Adele denied everything, of course," said Consuela with an arch look. "So we can't officially say that giving you her class was a punishment. But Adele sure thinks it was. I heard her saying so just the other day."

Bijou Arden. She was one of the senior girls who had materialized at Adele's side, and in time I came to know her as the leading member of Adele's coterie. Her father, the former British High Commissioner of Malta, died of a heart attack when she was ten, and since then Bijou had run a little wild. She sat in the back of my fourth period senior English honors class, silent, aloof, her languid green eyes studying me under half-shuttered lids. The girls wore uniforms, the traditional Catholic school plaid skirt, white blouse, and sweater, and Bijou always made sure that her skirt was rolled a daring inch above the required mark, that her socks were bunched at the ankles rather than stretched up to the knee, just as every girl at the beginning of the year was instructed not to do.

"Why did Bijou's mother suspect Adele of giving Bijou the birth control?" I asked Lauren and Consuela.

The two smiled knowingly at one another.

"Parents have complained before about Adele being a little too chummy with students. Mrs. Arden knows her reputation."

"Late in the spring semester, we were informed of a new rule," Consuela said. "There's to be no more fraternizing with students off-campus. Without a doubt, that's aimed at Adele."

"Really?"

"She's always meeting with her girls o.c.," Lauren explained. "You see them everywhere: cafés, restaurants, museums. She'll keep meeting with them too. Don't you worry. If there's one thing about Adele, she always does just as she pleases."

I lay down after lunch for a short nap, which turned out to last nearly three hours. I slept in the master bedroom now, my mother's old bedroom, not least because it has the best view of my Morning Mountain. For a long time after my nap, I stood at the window, gazing at the mountain and reeling in the years. Then, after freshening up a bit, I put on a mask and walked over to say hello to Evie and Everett, my rich and attractive elderly neighbors out of Central Casting. I love 'em so much. They both have perpetually tanned skin that bespeaks wealth and a Virginia landowner's pedigree that antedates the Revolution. They're both thin as rails, too, and beautifully straw bale blonde. Everett is a retired big-time DC lawyer. His hair is receding in dignified fashion, but Evie's is full and always styled with that girlish flip in the back. She's pushing seventy-five, but a grey hair would not dare to infiltrate that gorgeous head.

"Hey, Miss Katie!" Evie sang when she opened the door and ushered me in. She always calls me Miss Katie, my name in Proper Southern Lady Talk. "Everett will be so glad to see you. He was just saying the other day that he hasn't seen you since the night we got back from Banff right before the lockdown."

I found them getting ready to go to a meeting of the executive committee of the Upperville Horse & Colt Show, which was happening the next weekend. We all had masks on, but even so, knowing how especially fearful they were about COVID, I kept my distance at more than six feet. They both looked so cute. Evie in her breeches and boots and Everett as Mr. Dapper Virginia Gentleman in his open-collared blue Oxford and perfectly creased tan slacks.

Everett's eyes popped as he remembered something. "Hey, Miss Katie! I've got something for you."

He bounded upstairs, and Evie walked me out onto the front porch. As per habit, she asked about what she calls my "love life."

"Have you seen Whatsisname again, the lawyer for the whatsis?" When it comes to girl talk, Evie doesn't sweat the details.

"You mean Eric?"

"The one who sent you the dozen roses."

"That was Eric." Eric was a friend of a friend of a friend of Lisa's whom Evie tried to persuade me to see again after a disastrous first date in which he took me to a Nationals game. I have never been a fan of baseball, and after three-and-a-half hours of watching grown men scratch themselves and spit, while Eric fed me endless stats and trivia relieved only by a cup of cheap warm beer and an undercooked hot dog, I was ready to get me to a nunnery.

"I haven't seen him," I said.

"But he sent you roses!"

"Evie, he's the most boring man in the federal government. And that's saying something. I'd rather spend an evening talking to his roses."

"Oh, well. I'm going to tell Walker to call you."

Mentioning Walker is also a habitual part of these conversations. Walker is Evie and Everett's only living child, a handsome middle-aged man who does something inscrutable involving commercial real estate out in San Diego. "Walker's a skirt chaser," Everett often said with a rakish wink, not at all unproud of his son's exploits. Evie would then swat Everett on the shoulder. It was an old routine.

"Have you lost weight?" Evie asked as we stepped onto the porch. I felt a *frisson* of panic, as though she'd noticed the cancer sucking the life out of me. "Because you look *fabulous*. I mean it! With that figure, I would think men would have to take a number to get a date with you."

I didn't even consider mentioning my diagnosis. I didn't think I could pull that off yet. Twenty-five years ago, Evie and Everett had lost their daughter, Cricket, then twenty-three, to non-Hodgkin lymphoma. Evie had mentioned this fact to me exactly once, early in our friendship, and Everett had never referred to it. There was no memento of Cricket in the house, except for one photograph on the bureau in a spare bedroom. I found it one day as I was snooping around the house. I had come over to feed the dogs, as Evie and Everett were out of town, and couldn't resist the temptation to explore. The photograph showed mother and daughter seated outside at what looked like an Italian trattoria, smiling broadly at the camera. They were both blonde beauties, Cricket, seventeen or eighteen at the time, the image of her mother.

Once, on one of Walker's visits home, he took me out to dinner in Leesburg. In the course of the evening, I asked him about Cricket, older than him by two years.

"She was something," Walker said. "She could sing like you wouldn't believe. I mean, a professional-level talent. She was at Juilliard when she got sick. Who knows what she would have gone on to do."

I confessed my snooping around the house and seeing the photograph upstairs.

"I took that picture," he said. "We were in Rome on Cricket's high school graduation trip, the summer before she went to Juilliard."

"Your folks never talk about her."

"No. What can be more devastating than watching your own child, all youth, beauty, and talent, slowly wither away? It nearly killed Mother. It's hard to imagine Evie depressed, but she didn't leave the house for nearly a year."

Ever since that conversation, I had understood why, when we met, Evie was so immediately taken with me. So, no, I did not mention the diagnosis.

Everett returned to the porch bearing a gift bag. "I've been doing a little online shopping," he said in his best ole-time radio manner. "Think of it as an early birthday present."

I opened the gift bag and found—ooh-la-la!—a cornucopia of swag from the GirlyGun Store: one hot pink Smith & Wesson pistol, one inside-the-waistband holster, one outside-the-waistband holster, one leather concealed-carry handbag, one pair of pink chrome earmuffs, and one package of bullets.

Everett liked to shoot, and he liked that I liked to shoot. One Saturday, he invited me with him to the range, and I surprised myself by how much I got into it. I was not a little intoxicated by the sense of power the gun gave me, but I also warmed to the idea that I, as a single woman living alone, much of the time in an urban setting, had a sure means of defending myself.

"I forgot the safety glasses," Everett said, "but we'll pick some up next time we go to the range."

"I'm speechless, Everett." I kissed him on the cheek. "And thank you, Evie, for letting him do this."

"I wanted to get you a spa day," Evie rolled her eyes, "but I was out-gunned."

We laughed and made shooting jokes for a while, but then it was time for them to go. I gave Evie a big hug on the pebbled drive as Everett pulled out of the garage in his late-in-life crisis, a silver Jag.

Evie got in, and as the top rolled behind her head, she said, "I hope you'll get a ride in."

"I'd like to, if it's all right."

"You know you don't have to ask. It's a gorgeous afternoon. I'll talk to Walker. If he doesn't call you this weekend, let me know."

"We'll cut him out of the will." Everett winked.

And they were off to their committee, while I was off to the barn.

Evie and Everett kept two horses, Lucy and Ethel, which they allowed me to ride any time I liked. I'd taken riding lessons in the summers as a child, but I was never really a horse kid. But when Evie and Everett and I got to be friends, they encouraged me to take up riding again. Everett refreshed me on the basics, including how to saddle and brush, and since then I rode every chance I got. Their acreage was large enough for a good canter, but there was a cut in the fence between our two properties so that I also had my own five acres at my disposal.

I saddled up Ethel, a sweetheart of a grey-maned Appaloosa, and took her out. It was indeed a gorgeous afternoon. The strength of Ethel supporting me was a comfort, and the combination of the clear, mellow air and the smell of the deep green clumps of Everett's newly mown grass raised my spirits.

After a good canter around the properties, I walked Ethel to my favorite nooks and crannies while I talked with Evie and Everett in my head.

How do you guys do it? You make it look so easy. You never betray any sign that anything has happened. Is this how you manage it? With your committees and fundraisers, your dinners out with other horse-minded friends and your long vacations in places like Banff and Stockholm from which you return full of funny stories and interesting cultural tidbits? I wonder at how you haven't closed yourselves in. You pride yourselves on your independent spirit, yet you never fail to come to the assistance of those who need you. You call your dogs your "granddogs" and give generously to organizations working to save the planet. You act as if the evils of the world are only unfortunate mistakes that can be remedied with a little common sense, a little cash, and a reminder that we are all in this together. I suppose it helps to be wealthy as Midas and with no physical sufferings beyond Evie's cataracts and Everett's need of a knee replacement. But I've seen that photograph put just out of sight on the bureau in the guest room. I know you know what it feels like outside the bubble, to stand out in the rain and take the full brunt of the storm. So how are you able to drive off smiling to your committee in your silver Jag? Would you please tell me how you do it?

I'd left the gift bag with the rest of the swag in the barn, but I'd brought the loaded pistol with me. When I got to the top of my favorite hill, well away from my house, I spied two squirrels scratching around the lone giant oak tree. I pointed the pistol at them and, rather uncharacteristically I hasten to add, unleashed GirlyGun Armageddon.

"Did you make the appointment?" Lisa asked as soon as I let her into the house.

"Appointment?"

"C'mon, Kate." Lisa set her suitcase down and faced me squarely. "You didn't call the Brawny Ladd and make an appointment?"

"This is the 'I'm Thinking About It' portion of the festivities."

"I thought that was yesterday."

"I'm having a good long think."

"What do you think your options are?"

"Why are we talking about this right now? Here in the kitchen? Before you've even put your jammies in your jammy drawer? Before we've even had a *drink*?"

Maybe it had been unrealistic to think that I could keep from getting into this topic with Lisa for two whole days. As I finished making our dinner—lemony chicken arugula quinoa salad with avocado and creamy basil dressing, right off the Foodierama website—I decided on a different strategy: surrender.

"I'll make the call first thing Monday morning," I told her as soon as we sat down to eat on the back deck.

"Good girl." After her first taste of the crisp pinot grigio, Lisa added, "You can't waste time, sweetie. Cancer never sleeps."

"You know who I bumped into yesterday after I left you?" I had already tired of the subject of my impending doom. "Virtually bumped into, that is. One of my oldest friends—you've never met her—Adele Schraeder. I taught with her in Rome when I was a mere slip of a girl."

"That's cool. You found her on Facebook or something?"

After an almost imperceptible hesitation, I answered yes. "She's actually in DC now."

"Really? And she hasn't called you?"

The question put me on the defensive. "Oh, that's not so surprising. We haven't been *that* close for many years."

"What is she doing in DC?"

"She has some kind of business. Calls herself a 'transition celebrant.'"

"I've heard of those," Lisa said, munching arugula. "My sister suggested I hire one when I divorced Bob. I probably should have. They're kind of a cross between a therapist and an event planner. That's really cool. You should call her."

Relieved that Lisa hadn't dismissed Adele's profession as kookery, I was encouraged to press on. "She also runs this discussion group called the Death Symposium."

"That sounds creepy. What is it?"

"Kind of like a book club, but instead of talking about a book, you talk about death. And you'll never guess where they meet! At Cool Beans."

"So, it's people sitting around *drinking coffee* and talking about *death*?"

"I guess. Yeah."

Lisa held in mid-air the quivering slice of lemony chicken skewered upon her fork. "You're not thinking of going."

"I thought I might, to see Adele, at least."

Lisa's fork clattered upon her plate. "You are *not* going to the Death Seminar. It's the unhealthiest thing you could possibly do! Tell me that you will not go."

"Why are you so opposed to it?"

"Because it's…it's *depressing*. It's *ghoulish*! Take your friend to dinner or something, but don't sit around with a bunch of neurotics at the coffee shop talking about death."

"OK, sheesh, I'll take her to dinner. Sorry I ever mentioned it."

But did I really want to give up seeing Adele in her element at the Death Symposium? Something in me was eager to see what this eccentric little subculture was all about. I *wanted* to talk out loud with others about what a "peaceful" death meant for me. And if Adele was in the middle of it, stirring the pot, there was no way that it wasn't going to be something special.

Late in the afternoon on Saturday, while in bed with a book, I reached for my phone and went again to the Death Symposium website. I looked intently into Adele's eyes as they stared back at me from her picture.

I said I would always be here for you, darling. Did you think I was going to leave you alone at the end? Just come! Of course we have our eccentrics, but believe me, you're not going to find straighter talk than at a Death Symposium. There's truth in our advertising. We don't dance around the big stuff. If there's a method in the madness, we'll help you find it. C'mon! When life has you by the throat, what else can you do but philosophize? And hey, if you hate it, at least we'll reconnect.

After reading blog posts on the site for a while, I went into the bathroom. When I returned, Lisa was lying sideways across the end of my bed, having come in to check on me. I had left my phone on the comforter, and the screen had not yet gone to "sleep." Lisa looked at me with a sad, disappointed expression, as if she had caught me surfing porn.

"Perhaps our problem with death," I said, standing there with one knee resting on the mattress and my arms folded across my chest, "is that we look at it too subjectively. We long to remain in existence as an *individual consciousness*. Which, after all, makes a certain amount of sense. Because that's how we've evolved to confront the world.

"But what if we reframe the whole problem? What if we seek not to remain in existence as an individual consciousness? What if we seek, instead, to appreciate that our material constituents, even when they are no longer able to support individual consciousness, will live forever mingled with the cosmos—maybe even one day contributing to a *new* individual consciousness somewhere else in the universe?"

Lisa waited a good while before answering with measured calm. "What if, instead of focusing on death, we made a gameplan for your recovery?"

"What's wrong with focusing on death? Don't you think it's unhealthy that we're always shunting it to the side, ignoring it, *suppressing* it? My mother's funeral took place over two days in a fake living room at a funeral home with wall-to-wall rugs, massive, noise-canceling curtains, and piped-in classical music, and never once did anyone get a glimpse of her corpse. *I* saw her corpse on the day she died, and it was the second corpse I had ever seen *in my life*. And I don't expect to ever see a corpse again."

"You don't find the desire to see corpses a little morbid?"

"Not when someone I love has died. Come with me to the Death Symposium."

"You want me to—"

"I'm not saying that just because one day my elemental particles will still be a part of the universe that I'm comforted. I'm only saying that I'm interested in the effort to comes to terms with the problem of mortality." I pointed at my phone. "The guy who wrote that blog was taking death seriously. As if it were *the most important thing*."

Lisa, the energy spilling out of her now, rose and repositioned herself on her haunches. "I agree on one thing with your blogger. You need to reframe the challenge. You need to start thinking about how you want to live the rest of your *life*."

The next day, Sunday, was sunny and pleasant. I felt well enough to saddle up Lucy for Lisa and Ethel for myself again, and we went for a saunter around Five Hearths. Afterwards we made brunch, and then, my energy shot, I repaired to my bedroom once more. An hour later, I awoke with the most overpowering Post-Sunday Nap Melancholia. Anybody know what I mean?

Whenever I wake up from a Sunday nap, especially if it's a beautiful day, I come to consciousness so unbearably melancholy. Where have I been? In the backyard here at Five Hearths with my dad, hitting rotten green apples with a nine-iron over the fence. Riding my bike down Covert Hill, hot wind in my face, coasting with my arms stretched wide at my sides. In Rome's Trastevere neighborhood on the first night I met Adele.

As the conscious mind dozes beneath an umbrella, the tide of the subconscious leaves its sad detritus along the shore.

What was the name of that trattoria in Trastevere? I don't remember. It was the first weekend of the school year, and my new friend, Rory, a Dubliner who taught in the history department, had invited me to join him and several of our other colleagues for dinner at a trattoria they liked. Dutch treat, of course. Adele arrived late, accompanied by an elegantly dressed, silver-haired Italian man who, in his late forties (I'm guessing), could still turn every female head in the room. Unbelievably, even though we taught in the same department, I had not yet met Adele. Our respective teaching schedules did not allow our paths to cross. But beyond that, she kept most assiduously to herself and to her "girls." You could never find her prepping alone in her classroom before first bell or after last bell. She never came into the faculty lounge. Even during this dinner at the trattoria, the dynamics of the various conversations did not facilitate an introduction. And the longer she sat as an unintroduced colleague at the opposite end of our long table, the more embarrassed I became, as if my social class did not permit an introduction. After the meal, our group huddled on the corner outside the trattoria to plan the rest of the evening. Adele and her silver fox stood right behind me talking to Rory, a conversation I listened to intently.

"Allow me to get this straight," Rory said to Adele. "You are proposing to screen a lascivious art film in the dead of night at a Catholic boys' school?"

That's exactly what Adele was proposing. It was her friend Massimo's film—"The Massimo," as we called him, an avant-garde student filmmaker—and Adele wanted her escort for the evening, a real-live Italian film producer named Roberto, to see it because Mr. Cody was in it, and she wanted Roberto to cast Mr. Cody in his new film. But the only way to screen The Massimo's film was to use the projector at WIX's sibling school across town, Mater Dei.

"Students from both WIX and Mater Dei appear as extras in the film," Adele said to Rory. "It is a coeducational enterprise."

So why did I get involved with shenanigans that could have cost me my job? Why didn't I make an excuse and run for the hills? Yes, I was young, far from home, and eager for friendship, but this does not explain everything. Believe me, my getting involved had nothing to do with an interest in The Massimo's film or getting Mr. Cody, whom I hadn't even met, an audition. It had more to do with Adele. As everyone started making plans to troop over to Mater Dei, a hand touched my shoulder.

"Could you hold this, darling?" Adele asked me. "Roberto needs to make another call." She handed me a half-finished bottle of wine, which I held while she dug Roberto's early model, brick-sized mobile phone out of her bag. Did she even know my name? Did she introduce herself or say anything else to me? I had no memory of either. All I remembered was getting into Rory's Fiat. A stupid thing to do, I suppose, but I have never regretted doing it.

"I like your poster," Adele said to me as Rory's Fiat jiggled down the narrow streets of Trastevere looking for a way out of the maze. "*Non te quaesiveris extra.*"

"Oh. Yes. A friend of mine in college made that for me."

I had a framed black-and-white photograph, blown up poster-size, on the wall of my classroom. It showed me on my Morning Mountain, sitting on a rock overlooking the Blue Ridge, accompanied by a quote from Emerson. *Non te quaesiveris extra.* "Do not seek for things outside yourself." I still have it on my bedroom wall at Five Hearths.

"I popped into your classroom to see you the other day," Adele said, "but you weren't there. So I admired your poster."

I didn't know how to continue. But she did.

"I hear you're doing a wonderful job with Senior Honors."

"Who told you that?" I asked, unable to suppress my curiosity.

"More than one of the girls. Even Bijou Arden, who's the hardest nut of all, thinks you're, 'like, a totally rad dudette.' She says this with great irony, of course, but with Bijou great irony is what passes for total sincerity."

I replied with something self-deprecating that Adele brushed aside.

"None of that, please. Clearly you have the gift. I am constitutionally unsuited to teach British literature. I always pass quickly over Jane Austen, praising her rather nasty personal letters—what fun they are to read aloud to the girls!—but dismissing the banality of her conventional happy endings. I luxuriate far too long with the Romantic poets. Then I spend the next three months with my beloved Jane Eyre, meanwhile forgetting all about Dickens, who couldn't write a woman to save his Victorian soul. You see, my problem with teaching is that I always end up teaching *me.*"

We snuck into the projection room at Mater Dei, which turned out to be only my first fireable offense of the evening. To my horror, Bijou Arden was already there waiting for us, snuggled on a moldy sofa with her French boyfriend, Patrice.

Right before the screening commenced, The Massimo himself asked to sit on the folding chair next to me. "Would you need some wine?" He smiled at me. "I get you the bottle, yes? Then we become intimate."

I tried not to stare at him bug-eyed as I prayed that his real meaning was lost in translation.

"I'm fine," I said. "I don't need any wine, thank you."

"You are a teacher at Wildwood?" he said.

"Yes."

"With Adele?"

"Yes."

The Massimo pressed his hands together prayerfully underneath his stubbly chin. With great concentration, he struggled to find the right, the most deserving words.

"Adele! She is *la bella donna britannica*! *Che affascinante. Che astuzia!*"

"What is *astuzia*?" I asked, having been able to put together the rest.

"Ah! *Astuzia*. Maybe…." But after great mental exertion, he shook his head. I had asked too much of his English vocabulary. In the end, he tapped a forefinger against the side of his skull and smiled.

The lights went down, the projector rattled to life, and we were plunged into the surrealistic world of The Massimo's bizarre imagination. The Massimo wrote and directed the thing while also playing his own protagonist. His scenes have settled in my memory like a disconnected montage from an ancient nightmare:

> The Massimo in bed, smoking, as a woman sleeps beside him. The camera pulls back, and we discover that the bed is in the middle of the crowd around the Spanish Steps.
>
> The Massimo lounging in his bath while a different woman berates him. The camera pulls back, and we discover that the bathtub is in the middle of the Colosseum.
>
> The Massimo eating cereal at a kitchen table, while the Grim Reaper, holding a scythe, stands ominously behind him.
>
> A dream sequence in which a crowd of women dressed in togas stab The Massimo countless times like he is some kind of Julius Caesar. When The Massimo falls, his own toga

drenched in blood, the women raise their bloody daggers triumphantly and cheer.

But what I remember best was seeing Mr. Cody for the first time. His character was involved in some kind of espionage subplot with a woman played by none other than Adele. I remember only fragments from a sequence of him and Adele in the Vatican Museums, shot in jiggly, hand-held *Cinéma vérité* (if only to avoid the security guards):

INT. VATICAN MUSEUMS – DAY

Shot looking down from the top of the museum's famous spiral staircase. As the ENGLISHWOMAN walks down the stairs, a MYSTERIOUS MAN follows from a spiral behind.

INT. VATICAN MUSEUMS – NOT EXACTLY CONTINUOUS

As they stand, backs to the camera, in the Sistine Chapel, contemplating Michelangelo's *The Last Judgment*, the Englishwoman surreptitiously transfers an envelope from her purse to the guidebook of the Mysterious Man.

EXT. OUTDOOR SEATING AT A CAFÉ – PROBS LATER SAME DAY

The Mysterious Man, sitting alone, is approached by a waiter bearing something on a small salver. The Mysterious Man picks up the something, only to discover…

INSERT

that it is a piece of honey-flavored candy.

EXT. OUTDOOR SEATING AT A CAFÉ – CONTINUOUS

Horrified, the Mysterious Man looks up and finds the Englishwoman smiling at him from across the piazza. The Mysterious Man gets up to run, but four men in ski masks suddenly appear out of nowhere and seize him…

Now, how this espionage subplot was connected to the film's main plot and The Massimo's various romantic liaisons was anybody's guess, and it didn't help that Mr. Cody's and Adele's dialogue (spare and, I would later learn, turgidly symbolic) was more than my meager Italian could handle. But I wasn't in the least concerned with any of that. I was mesmerized by Mr. Cody from the moment he appeared on screen. There he was, my Mr. Cody, in all his lithesomeness, suavity, babyface, tousled hair. Of course, he wasn't yet my Mr. Cody. But before the film was over, I wished he were.

Halfway through the film, The Massimo vacated his seat beside me, unable to bear the suspense of the audience's reaction to his work. Which was just as well. When the film ended, but before the lights came up, Roberto, in the row behind me, asked Adele, "Is your friend insane?"

"Which one, darling?"

"The one who concocted that madness we just watched. How did he get a bathtub inside the Colosseum?"

"Forget The Massimo," Adele said. "Tell me what you think of the chap who played my asset."

"What do you mean, 'asset?'"

"I was a treacherous spy, darling. The honeypot. Didn't you get that?"

"I didn't get anything but a headache."

"It doesn't matter. The point is, the chap I did scenes with is the one who is going to star in your next film."

"I thought you were the best part of the film," Roberto replied.

"Pish! I only did it for a lark. Michael Cody is the man you want. He's worked in the West End, you know."

I was riveted to this conversation, eager to hear more about Mr. Cody's career in the West End, and also whether Adele's charm would be enough to persuade Roberto to give him an audition. But before she was able to seal the deal, the evening reached its harrowing climax. A loud knock sounded at the sliding glass door.

"Don't turn on the lights!" Rory ordered us. "Stay quiet and do nothing."

"Open the door, Bijou!" called a boy's voice. "I know you're in there."

"Good Lord!" I heard Bijou laugh. "It's Head Boy Petrus!"

"Who's Head Boy Petrus?" someone asked.

"My excessively school-spirited brother Peter."

Bijou and Patrice snuggled closer on the moldy sofa, stifling hilarity.

"Cover for me, won't you, darling?" Adele squatted beside my chair.

"Sorry?"

"Don't let anybody know I was here. Especially don't say that I invited Bijou."

"What do you want me to say?"

"Let the Muse guide you." She smiled, took Roberto's arm, and disappeared through a door behind the screen.

The knocking on the door became violent. Finally, Rory walked over and opened the sliding door. A boy pushed past him into the room and turned on the lights. It must have seemed like the raid of an opium den. The Massimo's film had induced a general state of narcotic torpor, and the room of groggy, well-oiled *cinéastes* groaned at the interruption.

"What is it, Peter?" asked Rory.

"I am just looking for my sister, Bijou," the boy said as he scanned the room with a predatory eye. He looked every inch the part of the preppy head boy with his razor-parted hair, boat shoes, and collar of his school polo titled obnoxiously skywards. He glared at his teacher.

"Do you know, Mr. Dunne, there are two women in the swimming pool?"

"Really?" said Rory with sincere innocence. "How extraordinary. What do you need, Peter?"

"I need to get my sister back to Wildwood. Is Miss Schraeder here?"

Rory turned fearfully and noticed that Adele and Roberto had melted into the night. "No, she's not," he said, relieved. "Why do you want Ms. Schraeder?"

"I need to know whether Bijou came with Miss Schraeder."

"*Ms.* Schraeder isn't here. The screening of this film was a coeducational enterprise." Rory struggled to reestablish his authority, a difficult job against the backdrop of giggles from the women in the swimming pool.

"How did you get here, Bijou?" the brother demanded of his sister.

"None of your business, moron."

"Mother will be interested to know."

"Turn me in if you must, Petrus, but you're not going to scare me."

"How did you get here?" the brother shouted.

It was a sibling standoff.

Until a voice said, "She's not here."

These words, if you can believe it, were uttered by yours truly. Even more improbable were the words that followed:

"I'm Ms. Montclair. I teach at Wildwood. I can assure you that Ms. Schraeder is not here."

The room nodded in confirmation of my account. I did not dare look at Bijou.

As Peter considered the plausibility of my story, someone appeared behind him.

"Hello, Cody," said Rory.

"Evening, Rory," said Mr. Cody, leaning beautifully against the doorjamb in jeans and a T-shirt and no shoes. "Enjoying an evening of the cinematic arts?"

"We've been screening The Massimo's latest celluloid extravaganza. You were quite good in it, by the way, Cody. It only made sense to screen it here, some of our students being in it—swathed in all decency, of course. It's a coeducational enterprise."

"Of course," smiled Mr. Cody. "Are those some of WIX's finest faculty in the swimming pool?"

"Art and exuberance often travel together," Rory conceded. "I will ex-piscinate them forthwith."

Mr. Cody smiled to himself as Rory, happy to escape, strode past to clear the swimming pool.

"Mr. Cody," said Peter, panicked that the moment was getting away from him, "I need to know how my sister got here tonight. My mother ordered me to tell her if I ever saw my sister with Miss Schraeder."

"How did you get here tonight, Bijou?" Mr. Cody asked.

"Walked right through the door." Bijou smiled at him.

Mr. Cody looked calmly at Peter, then back at Bijou. "It's past visiting hours, Bijou."

"Is it?" Bijou put a hand to her chest in mock surprise.

"It is. Patrice, Peter, why don't you wait for me up in my room."

Then, in perfect Italian, Mr. Cody informed the Italians in the room that the evening's entertainment was over. Then he told the rest of us in English.

"Mr. Cody, may I speak with you privately," said Peter.

"I'll see you upstairs, Peter. Let me see our guests out first."

With the look of a thwarted Javert, the boy Peter exited in a huff. The rest of the expedition trooped out. As I passed him on the patio, Mr. Cody, with an impish grin, leaned forward and said to me, "And please tell Ms. Schraeder I said goodnight."

Somewhere in the middle of this reverie, I began to feel sick, and eventually I had to crash into my bathroom. After I finished being sick, I closed the bathroom door and washed my face and brushed my teeth. Not confident I could even make it back to my bed, I sat down on the edge of the bathtub. I pillowed my head on my folded arms and tried to settle my breathing and my thoughts. Maybe twenty minutes passed before I heard Lisa's voice from the bedroom, asking whether I was all right. I stood up, steadied myself, opened the bathroom door, smiled, and told her I was fine. I also told her how thankful I was, not only for her help this weekend but for her help the whole past week since my seizure. We hugged, and she went back downstairs, leaving me to think about what I didn't tell her: that, at an undefined moment during my interlude of intestinal distress, I had come to a decision. On Thursday night, I was going to the Death Symposium.

PART II

The Lands Beyond the Sun

CHAPTER ONE

So what do you wear to a Death Symposium, one where you will see an old friend whom you haven't seen in thirteen years?

I went with stylish causal. Faded, mid-rise jeans, cuffed above the ankle, brown boots, white blouse, black leather jacket, accessorized with my new Kors bag and a scarf for a COVID mask. As an unexpected bonus, my gal Brittany had a cancellation, and I was able to get my hair done the afternoon beforehand.

Why thirteen years? It is not easy to say.

After I left WIX, the summer after my second year, Adele and I established the habit of exchanging long letters, a practice we kept up for the better part of two decades. Three times we went on "holiday" together in Europe, and once I met her in New York to celebrate my fortieth birthday. But eventually, our communication became fitful. You might think the rise of email and the advent of social media would have made it easier for our correspondence to continue, but from the start, Adele was Amish toward all things digital. "The digital world is not only a distraction, it is an abstraction. When I want to speak to someone, I want to look into their eyes or at least encounter their bodily presence through their handwriting." Meanwhile, the internet had turned me into a dopamine addict, and the writing of letters became as foreign to me as handwritten recipe cards. Oddly, phone calls were never our thing. A couple of times, we attempted a transatlantic natter, but each time it proved an anticlimax. The telephone tamed her vivaciousness. For Adele, it was neither fish nor fowl, neither a live performance nor the prepared script of a personal letter. As the years went by, our communication dwindled to birthday greetings and Christmas cards, always expressing the wish for us to get together the next year. Eventually, even these were foregone, though when Tim and I divorced, I dropped Adele a note to that effect. Two weeks later, she returned a card with the single line: *If a temple is to be erected, a temple must be destroyed.*

The last time I vacationed with Adele, we toured Brontë country up in Yorkshire, and afterward I spent a week with her in London. Though her face was a little fuller and pencil-line circles had formed under her eyes, she was still beautiful, still mercurial, still very much Adele. Unfortunately, I was also still very much myself. Still teaching, still not happy with Tim, still stagnant in pursuit of my creative ambitions. But we had fun together on that trip. In London, we went out a lot with her friends—art people, writers, political agitators—and Adele introduced me to a nice divorcee, the owner of a Soho art gallery, with whom afterwards I emailed pointlessly for a couple of months (Gareth—I had forgotten about him!). But I have always suspected that on that trip I somehow proved a disappointment to her. She never said anything, but when I remember the look on her face when I hugged her at the tube station on my way to Heathrow, I think I see a trace of pity in her eyes mingled with the sadness of farewell. Or is this merely the filter formed by my insecurity?

The audience taking up real estate in my head is an eclectic group, one which wouldn't mix well in real life. My mother is there, of course, along with all the bright young things in the English honors crowd, both in my own high school class and in the classes I've taught through the years. Tim's new wife is there too (sad, I know, but that's why they call it therapy). And, finally, Adele. Not *finally*, because Adele, ever since that night in Rome over thirty years ago when I covered for her at Mater Dei, has been the closest, loudest, most persistent member of my audience. Others seem to watch me from a distance, lobbing comments from the sofa like relatives at the holidays. But Adele is always right there at my elbow, providing an incessant stream of dismayed commentary:

"Why don't you do something with this closet, darling? You've got everything all higgledy-piggledy…

"Is this how you want to spend your life, Kate? On your deathbed, you're not going to wish you had spent more hours watching telly…

"Why are you playing by the school's rules? You're the talent in the organization, not those mandarins in the administration…"

Even more than my mother, I think, Adele is the one I have always wanted to please.

The real Adele, of course, would detest my allowing her to play such a role in my imagination. She would be the first to remind me that only I can confer upon myself a sense of self-worth. Many times over the years, I have bid her psychic image goodbye, thanking her for her years of contributions but assuring her that her services are no longer required. And she would leave me for a while, but only for a while. One morning, I would be getting dressed for work, and I would see her standing right behind me in the mirror, staring down at the love handles I acquired over Christmas.

So, sure, yes, I was anxious about seeing her again. And I was feeling badly for feeling anxious about it. And I was afraid of her reaction when I told her that I was still teaching high school English and that my writing ambitions remained unfulfilled. I had nothing to be embarrassed about. I knew that. Mindfully, I stepped back and examined, with the curiosity of a naturalist, this desire to impress, to perform for her. What a waste of time, allowing myself to be measured by someone else. I resolved once more: *Non te quaesiveris extra.* I was still that girl looking out over the mountains. I answered to no one but me.

It was twenty minutes to eight when my Uber dropped me at the coffee shop. I hoped that the symposium (official start time, 7:30 p.m.) would be in full swing and that I could slip into a seat without fanfare. I was surprised not to find the group assembled on the busy, buzzing main floor. Then I saw a fortysomething woman come out of the Ladies with the unmistakable look of a gal who has just reapplied eye makeup to freshen a tired face that has been at work all day. She ascended the stairs to the mezzanine. By her skeleton-teeth COVID mask, I could only surmise that she was on her way to talk about death.

I followed the woman up the stairs with bated breath, but I might have breathed easily. Adele wasn't even there yet.

Who *was* there was a rather large group—larger than I imagined it would be—sitting around two long tables pushed together. I wondered how they were allowed to gather up here, disregarding social distancing guidelines. But then again, Adele was running the show.

I made a beeline to the empty seat at the end of the table farthest away from the stairs. Keeping my head down, I took my journal out of my purse and uncorked my pen. Only after I had spread my journal on my lap and found the next blank page did I raise my head and make a survey of the room.

First impression: even in their COVID masks (doggie masks, Egyptian key-of-life masks, flower-petal masks, and so on), they looked comfortingly normal. I had expected, especially given the downtown location, a bunch of lonely and unclubbable oddballs: whacked-out homeless people enticed by the offer of cake; amateur philosophers looking for a soapbox; mousey, grief-stricken widows with no one else to talk to. But this group looked like a faculty meeting at school. Not that my faculty was a paradigm of good social adjustment and mental health. But they're *folks*, you know? As these seemed to be. Along with the woman whom I saw come out of the Ladies, I recognized the woman with the stalagmites of hot purple hair whom I had encountered at the coffee shop the previous week. We nodded hello. She and most of the other women were dressed business casual, apparently having come straight from work, and perhaps having made a pit stop at a salad hut for dinner. I saw good shoes; I saw, on balance, good hair. Two or three had luxury notebooks like mine. These were women I recognized: mid-life, college-educated professionals trying to figure out what was going on with the universe.

Not that they were all middle-aged women. Two elderly ladies—one Caucasian, one African-American—in matching pastel cloth masks, had clearly, like me, just been to the salon. Next to them, in your basic paper mask, was a rumpled, portly, elderly gentleman with dyed, copper-colored hair. Across from them was, I suspected, the only married couple in the group. They were Caucasian, sixtyish. The woman was perched on the edge of her chair, posture erect, hands folded before her on the table, large eyes wide and apprehensive like today was the first day of school. The husband sat in a more relaxed—not to say slumped—position beside her, mumbling irreverent, sniggering criticism. Beside this married couple, in colorful sugar skull masks, was an obese college girl from George Washington University (according to her T-shirt), accompanied by an equally obese young man. I wondered whether a fellow student had committed suicide. With me at my table were three young people, two women and a man who all worked, I found out later, at the Toy Theatre a few blocks away. One was admin, another was in marketing, and the third did costumes. Directly across from me was a distinguished African-American man in a nice suit, the only male government worker in the room, I was guessing, and, I was also guessing, a recent widower.

Some twenty souls in all, counting myself, mainly women of a certain age with a sprinkling of men. The ethnic make-up was tolerably diverse: mostly Caucasian, with three African-Americans, one Latina, and one Asian. When I came in, they were discussing a legal question with passionate sincerity.

"Virginia law allows it."

"But DC law doesn't, which makes me furious."

"What's really ironic is that the pet cemetery only allows owners to be buried alongside their pets. *Alongside*, but not *with*."

"That's criminal! If we snuggle in bed together in life, then why can't we snuggle in bed together in death?"

"In Ancient Egypt, you could be buried along with your cat. They'd even mummify the little darling for you."

"That's because cats were considered divine."

"Well, my Mr. Roboto certainly thinks he's a god!"

Hearty laughter at this.

"Maybe we need to claim that they're our children. Not *like* our children. But our *children*."

"*Corgi Mom x2*. It's not just a bumper sticker anymore."

"But can you be buried with a *human* child?"

"I don't see why not."

"Who are these people preventing us from being buried any way we want?"

"Fascists!"

"Hear, hear!"

"This may be slightly off topic, but did you know you can memorialize a social media profile? So that the profile remains online—like *forever*—for people to post their love on, or for you simply to scroll back through. I did it for my Gizmo's profile page, and it's such a comfort to read through the old posts. Sometimes other pets in his former playgroup will post that they are still thinking about him."

"That is so sweet."

"So sweet."

I'm not a pet person. If we're talking dogs and cats, in particular, I have no desire to keep one. The very thought of some creature in my house getting hair all over my sofa is too much for me to handle. But I'm well aware that I'm in a minority. Pretty much everyone else on the planet, including this group of death symposiasts, can't seem to live—or die—without them. Lisa, for example, has this enormous dog (don't ask me—I don't know the names of the breeds) and every morning before sun-up, she blurps into her sweats and goes tramping through the neighborhood wearing her one Michael Jackson plastic glove and carrying a poop bag. I'm sorry—is that supposed to be fun? Many people find it to be. In my DC neighborhood, I constantly see people who otherwise would never look at one another as they pass by on the street—or, heaven forbid, stop and say hello—tarry together on the corner, bonding over their dogs. Isn't it a natural progression that they would want to be buried with them? But then again, why is it that we look to the animal world for that final consolation against the coldness of death? Is it because our pet is the only thing we've found in life that does not disappoint our yearning for love and loyalty? And if so, isn't that unutterably sad?

I was thinking of raising these questions. Why be a wallflower? Why not embrace this group as a brilliant attempt to speak what the rest of the world finds unspeakable? But I was afraid that my questions would come across as too harsh. They didn't know me yet. They would think I was making fun of them.

The conversation segued into the question of burial at home. I was interested in this, as I had been wondering whether it would be possible to be buried at Five Hearths. The woman I had seen come out of the Ladies had looked into it for her father and was daunted by the restrictions and the permits that needed to be obtained, at least in Maryland. I was making a note to myself to look up the Virginia and Fauquier County laws when the sound of someone coming up the stairs diverted my attention.

It was *her*.

Not yet noticing Adele's arrival, the first-day-of-school woman was in the middle of saying something like, "When our son passed—"

Adele heard this phrase and stopped the woman. "Human beings don't *pass*, darling. They are not gall stones. Human beings *die*. Life systems fail and we come to an end, full stop. That is our dignity. And this is our first rule at the Death Symposium: we refer to death by its proper name. No euphemisms. No fear."

All tongues were silenced. All eyes in the room gaped at her. Not least mine. *This was Adele. This was my old friend.*

"Now," Adele flashed a smile to the group as she plunked her bag down at the end of the far table where the facilitator's chair had been kept vacant for her. "Let us eat and drink and tell sad stories of the death of kings!"

She was not wearing a mask. She examined the table in the corner where refreshments had been laid out, and satisfaction lit in her eyes when she saw that someone had performed to point her instructions for setting out the crockery and cake.

In essentials, she was just as I remembered her: all smiles, all bright-eyed intelligence, all fabulously shod and outfitted. But new was this icy white pixie (her own shade or dyed?), and the designer reading glasses perched on top of her head, and the age lines on her forehead and the corners of her mouth (impossible to obscure entirely with makeup). She was carrying a little more weight than when I last saw her, but she remained tall and, for a woman pushing sixty, admirably slender. In fact, she looked quite jealous-making. She looked like a woman to whom Nature had issued a challenge and who had risen to it with a spit in Nature's face.

I kept my head down, strangely shy of direct eye contact with her, yet irrationally afraid of failing to be recognized.

Adele was still getting settled in the facilitator's chair, still chatting with the young man seated on her right, whom she seemed to know well, when I noticed a woman skulking up the stairs, exactly the kind of vagabond I had expected to find here. She was, like Adele, without a mask, dressed in black jeans and a tattered leather jacket over a black tee. On her feet, she sported a pair of old-school, high-top black Converse All-Stars, and on her head, she wore a black ski cap, from under which scraggly strands of hair, naturally dark but dyed with streaks of violet, escaped like the vines of an exotic creeping plant. Slung over one shoulder, she carried a pink, Disney Princess backpack, designed for a seven-year-old girl. She held something in her hand, too, but I couldn't tell what it was.

She hesitated upon the stair just long enough for Adele to sense her presence. When she saw her, Adele, for an instant, registered exasperation in the downturn of her mouth, just as she might have reacted to a child who had gotten out of bed during an important dinner party. But just as quickly, she turned her attention back to the group with a broad smile.

"So sorry I'm late, everyone, but I just nipped up to New York for the day and my train home was late. I see one or two new faces. Welcome. My name is Adele Schraeder. I'm the founder and facilitator of the Washington, DC Death Symposium. By day, I run my own shop as a transition celebrant. It's so good to be with you—"

The husband of the first-day-of-school woman and the old man with the copper-colored hair looked at her moonily like little boys smitten with the teacher. No one seemed disappointed that the discussion of home burial had been interrupted.

"Well done you for having a productive discussion without me. But would you mind terribly if I changed tack? I had planned a think-pair-share activity for this evening. I thought we'd do the think and pair portions before tea and cake. Afterwards, we can come back and share the results of our pairs conversations. Anyone interested in talking about sex?"

Amid rowdy cheers and laughter, Adele took the reading glasses from her head, positioned them on the end of her imperious nose, and framed us in her penetrating gaze.

"At the end of our last meeting, dearest chucks, we were talking about the value of remaining grounded in the body. I'd like to pick up right there. The desire to escape reality is omnipresent. Television, porn, the immortal longings of various religions. *Reality is earthly*. Outside our head. It's the graveyard littered with a thousand corpses.

"But while we are among the living, reality is this animate body, this forked carcass we carry around. So one way in which we can learn to face reality is to come to terms with our bodies. Attend to my metaphor: *come to terms*. One comes to terms with one's enemy in order to put an end to hostilities. My point is, we must make *peace* with our bodies. We may not love our body—perhaps few do. But we have to learn to regard our body as essentially *who we are*, not something we are trapped in. In fact, I declare that the body is the source of all wisdom. Thus speaketh Zarathustra: 'There is more reason in your body than in your best reason.' One manifestation of this wisdom is sex. Anybody here in favor of sex?"

Enthusiastic agreement all around. One or two ribald asides.

"Tonight, I want to invite you to think about those times when you have listened to the wisdom of your bodies when it comes to sex, when you have refused to deny your erotic nature. Whether in the naughty adolescent escapade or in the dangerous liaison—or simply in an incandescent carnal extravaganza enjoyed in your imagination—I want you to think about what you can learn about yourself when you embrace yourself as an embodied, sexual animal. Let's start with a private think, ten minutes or so, journaling if you like. Then I'll put you into pairs. But don't worry. Everything shared on this mezzanine stays on this mezzanine. We must learn to trust one another. Names can be changed to protect the insatiable. Off you go."

I wondered whether I might get a chance to speak to Adele now, but she went right over to confront the street woman on the stairs. I watched as she led the woman down to the main floor and presumably out of the coffee shop.

Most of the symposiasts were journaling, so I looked down at mine. Soon I was remembering the first time Adele took an active interest in my sex life, that Saturday morning in the Campo de' Fiori as we walked among the stalls of the farmer's market admiring the packages of fresh spices, the rows of eggplants as brilliant as Fabergé eggs, the endless varieties of olive oil and vinegar and *giardiniera*. It was there that the defining episode of my Roman years begins to take its lovely and tragic shape.

"What is your opinion of Michael Cody?" Adele asked me as we stopped at one of the vegetable stalls for green beans.

"I'm not sure I have an opinion," I said. "I've hardly said more than hello to him. He seems nice."

I hesitated to say anything further, as I didn't know what sort of conversation she was angling for. Did she want to reveal to me that they were dating? Or did she want to complain about his unwanted attentions? If I had learned anything about Mr. Cody from Lauren and Consuela, it was that he was crazy about Adele. Even my girls had picked up on that much.

To make a little mad money, I had parlayed my high school tennis team experience into a coach's position at WIX. One afternoon after practice, we were walking back to the locker room from the courts when Jenny Dyer asked, "Ms. Montclair, what if we just boycotted the whole thing?" Tension among the girls was running high due to the upcoming fall formal hosted by the boys at Mater Dei.

"I think you should take Ms. Schraeder's advice," I replied, "and go to the dance as a group. Think about it. You'll still get asked to dance, and you won't have to deal with all the nonsense of who's going with whom."

Tessa, a squat, buxom American, lifted her chin and did her best Ms. Schraeder impression. "An adolescent boy, my darlings, is a mere collection of appetites. Humor him, girls, but do not indulge him. Save romance for when you find a *man*, if you ever have the good fortune of doing so."

"I believe Ms. Schraeder has found *her* man," smiled Jenny archly.

"I beg your pardon, Miss Jenny?" I whirled around to reprimand this cheek.

Jenny giggled the more and looked to her comrades for support. "It's not exactly a secret, is it?"

"What isn't?" I said, trying to mask my keen interest.

Jenny turned up her hands and said, "Ms. Schraeder and Mr. Cody from Mater Dei? C'mon, Ms. Montclair. You can't tell us you haven't noticed that he's always over here hanging around her."

No, I could not truthfully say that I had not seen Mr. Cody in the late afternoons zipping onto campus on his black Vespa, walking with Adele around the perimeter of the school, and sometimes riding away with her on the back of the Vespa.

And one day before the semester started, I had noticed him surreptitiously sketching her during one of our dual faculty meetings. As WIX and Mater Dei allied themselves in all sorts of various ways, our faculties met together at the beginning of each school year to cement relationships and plan events. At the beginning of my first year at WIX, we hosted the Mater Dei faculty in our auditorium, and from my seat in one of the back rows, between the heads and torsos of my colleagues, I watched Mr. Cody sketch Adele—his eyes brushing up and down as he studied the contours of her face, the brisk motions of his hand, the frown of dissatisfaction with his work, the irked erasures. His thick brown bangs fell into his eyes as he drew, and each time he raised his head, he raked his hair back and rubbed his pencil across that week's version of the beard that he grew—and compulsively shaved and regrew—as if his own face were a sketch he was trying to perfect. The facial hair was part of his artistic persona. It was also, as I later teased him, an effort to maturate the sweet babyface that still defined him in his twenty-sixth year. He was indeed a good-looking young man, Mr. Cody, and all the women in the school, young and old, were smitten with him, including—very much including—me.

But was Adele smitten? Part of the mystery between them was uncovered that morning in the Campo de' Fiori.

"I want to know," Adele said to me, "what you *really* think of him. Do you fancy him?"

I endeavored to spare my blushes by saying, "He seems awfully fond of you."

"Pish. We're good friends. That's all."

"You're not going out with him?"

"Certainly not."

"Why 'certainly not?' He clearly likes you."

"Michael Cody doesn't know what he wants."

"Has he ever asked you out? Like, on a real date?"

"All the time, poor booby."

"What? You don't like him?"

"Of course I like him."

"Then why don't you go out with him?"

"Don't be silly."

"What's silly? He's cute."

"Aha! The libido quickens."

"I mean it. Why won't you go out with him?"

I half-expected Adele to drop the bombshell, "Because I'm a lesbian." But she didn't, because it wasn't true. What caused the confusion was that Adele, even in *her* twenty-sixth year, was not able to articulate for herself, much less for other people, that her attraction to men was governed by the image of her adored father. She preferred older men—her father had been fifteen years older than her mother—men who, like her father, were charismatic, amoral but not apolitical, and leery of conventional relationships. The figure of Roberto had shown up time and again throughout the years. When it came to men closer to her own age, she took on the role of the nurturing goddess, instructed by Zeus to move the hero's plot along. To her, Mr. Cody was not a subject of sexual interest but a talent to be furthered, a cause to be supported, a project.

"He's a hugely talented actor," she explained to me that morning in the Campo de' Fiori. "He shouldn't be wasting his life teaching school. Did you know that a few years back he was in a show in the West End? He needs to get back on those boards. *You* saw him in The Massimo's film. It's plain he's got the chops. He wants to start his own theatre company."

"Why doesn't he? What's stopping him from going back to London?"

Adele struggled with her reply. "He's lost his way."

"How?"

"By forgetting to be brave. He needs rescuing. And you need a sexual awakening."

"I beg your pardon?" I turned around to make sure no English-speaking marketers could overhear our conversation.

"That is, with a *real man*. I'm not talking about the boys from college. You need sex so that you can learn to go beyond sex. It is above all a work of compassion."

"Why compassion? Why *rescuing*?"

"Oh, perhaps I'm being dramatic. But Michael needs someone to help him believe in himself again."

"But I don't understand why *you* don't undertake this great work of charity."

"Michael Cody is not my mission," said Adele, "at least not in the way you imagine. My mission is more that of the midwife. I'm like Socrates in reverse. Instead of leading people to the great heaven of ideas, I lead them to the body."

But who was Adele Schraeder? Where did she come from?

She was a Londoner born to British parents. Her father was the editor of a socialist weekly, and her mother had been a schoolteacher who died young of leukemia. Adele always took great pride in the fact that her mother, before she started teaching, played bit parts in a couple of Ealing Studios comedies from the 1950s. "Her comic timing was always pristine," she liked to say, "not least when she conceived *me*." She'd known her father longer and better, of course, and unabashedly adored him and his quixotic politics. "Daddy's heyday was the Thatcher administration, when he and the paper became a prominent gadfly. Indeed, if Margaret Thatcher had never existed, my father would have had to invent her." From her mother, Adele inherited her beauty and sense of style, her quick wit and gift for mimicry. To her father, she owed her magpie mind and taste for crusades.

As an adolescent, Adele attended a comprehensive high school in London—a public school, in the American sense. At sixteen, she had a boyfriend six or seven years older than she. By the time she was eighteen, she worked regularly as a model, spending weekends on photoshoots all over England. She was not keen on university, but after graduation, she moved to New York and enrolled at the New School, where she entertained vague thoughts of becoming an artist or an actress. There she learned to dislike Americans, whom she believed, with rare exceptions, were genetically incapable of conceptual thought. After a year, she transferred to the London School of Economics, where she majored in philosophy.

After college, she still took the odd modeling or acting job—Roberto was not wrong about her talent—but by this point she had discovered her taste for Ideas, for movements and counter-movements, revolutions and manifestoes. This meant that she made herself unemployable. Eventually, she did what every liberal arts major does when she's desperate for work: she turned to teaching.

By the time I came to WIX, Adele had already taught there for two years and would remain for five years in total. She took a job at an international school in Rome because a job was offered and because Rome sounded like an adventure. But at WIX, despite her idiosyncratic and at times titillating lesson plans—*The Last Tango in Paris,* I assure you, was not an official part of the WIX English curriculum—Adele was not a popular teacher. Her mannerisms and enthusiasm made her a figure of fun for most of her students. She had little ability, much less patience, to connect with the bored adolescent female. She had no empathy for those who could not follow her zigzagging tangents. Her methods were lost on ninety percent of her students. But for that last ten percent, she was an idol.

On her return to the mezzanine, Adele found me. She enfolded me in a long, hard hug.

"Is this really my Kate? Is this really, really, *really* my old friend?"

We were both in tears. My eyeliner was ruined. I started to pull away from the hug, but she pulled me right back. (How reluctant we are, we tiny, love-starved humans, to share physical contact, but how we relish it when it comes!)

"Don't you look absolutely brilliant," she said as we parted. "Where are you now?"

I explained to her that I still lived here, split between DC and Five Hearths.

"I'm sorry. I thought you moved away after your divorce."

"I probably told you I was going to, but in the end I stayed."

"So, you've been here all along, and I haven't seen you?" She didn't say it as an admonishment, but as a way of saying how glad she was to see me.

"I didn't know you were here either," I said.

"Goodness me, I've missed you, Kate!" She held me by the shoulders, looked at me with the old, fierce intensity that, when she wanted to make use of it, made me feel like I was the only person in the world whom she would ever think about noticing. "How on earth did you find us?"

Not *me*, but *us*. Adele never thought of herself as a lone operator but always as the vanguard of a *movement*. I told her about seeing the advertisement on the bulletin board downstairs. In response she cried, "Fate! Karma! Kismet! Sheer dumb luck! Whatever! You're here!"

She gave me another hug for good measure, but when she pulled away, her eyes hardened as she looked at me. "Kate Montclair, you are dying!"

She just said I looked brilliant. How could she know about my tumor?

But when she saw my worried reaction, she hurried to explain. "Not *today*, necessarily! That's just how we greet one another in the Death Symposium. Our version of 'I'm Jane X, and I'm an alcoholic.'"

An intense urge to tell Adele my news lunged for the surface, like a drowning person desperate for air. I wanted to say, *You are right. I am! I am dying!* But I didn't, of course. How heavy would that be? To greet an old friend with the fact that one had a median fifteen months to live.

"Now," Adele went on, "we're going to catch up later, but first you're going to talk about your most recent experience of sexual euphoria with someone you've never met. Don't worry," she added *sotto voce*. "I won't stick you with Mr. Edmondson. Tales of his sexual exploits can be rather unsettling. I'm going to put you with—"

She scanned the room for a candidate, but before she could settle on one, she was interrupted by a young, athletic-looking British woman in a mask emblazoned with some sports team logo. I remembered seeing her sitting downstairs when I came into the coffee shop. She had not hitherto been part of the symposium, but she and Adele began to confer. Not wanting to be a bother, I touched Adele on the shoulder to indicate that I would take care of myself.

But there really wasn't anyone left to pair with, except the odd creature I had seen earlier skulking on the stairs. Despite Adele's best efforts, she had returned. She sat on the floor against the balcony that overlooked the main floor. I decided to pair up with her. I needed a partner, and with this one I was betting I could avoid the subject of sex entirely.

"May I?" I asked, indicating with my eyes the spot next to her on the floor.

She looked dully at me, then back at the crowd below on the main floor. She fiddled with some kind of device in her hand. I took her silence for consent and sat down.

I was forced to move her Disney Princess backpack so that I didn't sit down on it. She panicked when I touched it and ripped it from me. What was the significance of carrying such a thing? Was she crying out for the comfort and protection of Prince Charming, the substitute father? Or was it merely an ironic accessory, the Disney princess showcased as the enemy of the people?

"My name is Kate." I smiled at her.

No response.

"This is my first time here."

No response.

"Have you been here before?"

No response. This was going to be easier than I thought. All I needed to do was sit here and bide my time until tea and cake. I looked at the other pairs around the room as with embarrassed looks and giggles they divulged their sexual secrets. What would I talk about if I had a partner who wasn't mute?

Carl, my Miami Beach mistake from three winters ago? Steve, my Sanibel slipup from further back? Each regretted as soon as the moment of pleasure subsided. My body wasn't as wise as Adele thought.

I looked more closely at what the woman fiddled with in her hands. It looked like some kind of old-school recording device that used cassettes. When she noticed me staring at it, she stuffed the thing into a pocket of her leather jacket. Then she said, as a kind of incantation, "I am the handmaid in service to the prophet."

I noticed for the first time what she was wearing around her neck. The sight of the thing astonished me. How did she come across a green scapular? On the inside of her right arm, a tattooed name in large vertical, Gothic letters read NORMA.

"Is your name Norma?" I asked.

After a moment's pause, she tucked the scapular back inside her tee, turned to me, and said, "I am the handmaid in service to the prophet. What someone says in the final moments is not what's important. What's important is the decision made in the moment of courage. I have to work tomorrow. I work on Mondays, Wednesdays, Fridays, and Sundays. The trick about the pool is that you have to keep the chlorine and the pH levels within an acceptable balance. Manny taught me how to do it. He looks after me. Irene said she would look after me, but I said I didn't want any of her money."

It was like listening to AM radio in the middle of the night as you drive down the highway with two channels vying for dominance. Her body language indicated anxiety, but her face showed no affect whatsoever, and her voice was as flat and mechanical as that of one of my freshmen boys reciting poetry.

The woman looked at me, as if with her stream of cracked consciousness she had confused herself. She began to gnaw on the pad of her right index finger. On the inside of her left wrist were furrows of knife-thin brown scabs, marks I knew well from the wrists of so many of my girls at school.

"May I help you in any way?" I asked. "Do you have a safe place to live?"

She said in return, "I just didn't like to hear her cry."

"Because I can help you find a safe place. You don't need to be on the street. Do you mind telling me where you live?"

No answer.

I looked at the green strap of the scapular hanging around her neck. I had not seen a green scapular since my days in Rome, more than thirty years ago, when they were at the heart of a great mystery that absorbed my friends and me. How uncanny to see one here today. I searched the woman's face more thoroughly. She was lovely, however hard she had worked to deconstruct her beauty. Yet her poor skin was unnaturally brown and blotchy for her age, in a way that reminded me of one of my miniature rose bushes with blight. What *was* her age? She was definitely past her twenties. Mid-thirties, maybe? Miranda would be in her mid-thirties. But this woman's name, if the tat on her arm was any indication, was Norma. And at any rate, why would Miranda be living on the streets in Washington, DC?

I kept asking the woman her name, about where she lived, about her job. But I didn't learn anything before Adele called us to refreshments.

Refreshments, of course, were tea and cake—a cake not bought from the coffee shop itself but smuggled in from a caterer. It was a rather macabre confection, iced with the blackest of dark chocolates and decorated around its curve with dancing skeletons like figures on a zoetrope. With water boiled in a large electric water kettle, the super-fit woman who interrupted us earlier, Adele's former professional soccer player turned assistant, Carly, brewed loose-leaf Earl Grey in real teapots, which she poured into bone china teacups, each one imprinted with a grinning skull set against a dying rose.

During refreshments I began meeting people. Appearing through a thick cloud of perfume were the two elderly women in pastels. Octogenarians, they were not shy to tell me. They hailed from a chichi retirement home called Arcadia up near Rock Creek Park. The house van bore them to and fro every first Thursday.

"There used to be three of them from Arcadia, but one just died," a young man named Julian explained to me as soon as I excused myself from these ladies. "Watch out for the small one. She just buried husband number three, and she's already looking for her next victim. And I think we can guess who it is," he added, nodding across the room to Mr. Edmondson, the copper-haired duffer.

Julian was a hospice nurse and a great friend of Adele. He was the one who sat at her right hand. We immediately hit it off. As we ate our cake, the two of us started talking to the two obese GW undergrads. I both wanted to chastise and to feel sorry for the young woman, who had not let her weight dissuade her from following skinny girl fashion and squeezing every roll of fat into a pair of tights. The geeky boy standing next to her in black T-shirt and black jeans had zero muscle tone, and his skin was as white as the underbelly of a largemouth bass, as if the only light he'd seen in years was the blue light from his laptop screen. He looked on blankly as the girl, all undergraduate bubbliness, told Julian and me about the "Beyoncé Mass" they had attended the previous weekend.

Throughout the refreshments I kept a lookout for my troubled friend. She did not mix and mingle. She remained seated on the floor looking dully into space until most everyone had gotten their tea and cake. Then she stole up to the refreshment table, wrapped two pieces of cake in several large napkins, stuffed her booty into the Disney Princess backpack, and returned to her spot on the floor.

"Who is that woman?" I asked Adele before the session resumed.

"Which?"

"That woman over there on the floor."

"Couldn't tell you. Some street urchin with serious mental health issues."

"I asked if I could help her but—"

"Don't. I tried to help her when she first came here. But she doesn't take the help. She only fixates upon you and never leaves you alone."

An agitation, a moral disquiet, would not allow me to let the subject rest. I wanted to ask Adele if she had seen the woman's green scapular, but I didn't. I thought it would make me look pathetically obsessive if, just minutes after reuniting with Adele, I brought up the Codys.

My concern for the street woman turned out to be pointless. When next I looked around, she was gone.

A few minutes later, Adele signaled the end of refreshments and the start of the group share. Once I was seated, I noticed a new member had joined us. Daringly maskless, he had taken a seat near Adele at the front. He sat diagonally from me, so I saw his face clearly. At first I wasn't sure it was him, but then he removed all doubt by turning and giving me a nod and a smile. My oh my, even Benedict Aquila had succumbed to time. His face was a crag now, red, with age lines everywhere: frown lines, tear troughs, deep nasolabial folds, eye wrinkles, crow's feet. A "Before" picture for a men's anti-aging cream. Still, there was method in all this chaos theory of his skin. It drew attention to his eyes: two tiny full moons of brightly illumined gray that took in the world with an odd mixture of weariness and curiosity. Once he had been the consummate slacker—the guy who used to bum nights on people's couches, who smoked pot with the grounds crew at Mater Dei, who almost never wore anything on his feet, and who somehow always got someone else to pay for his meal. But here, in his sport coat, slacks, and nice shoes, he looked respectable. And his face, in a way it had never struck me when we were kids, was not unattractive. Men age so much better than women. When Benedict was young, his large nose, short chin, and mop of brown hair gave him a sort of shifty, rat-like appearance. He looked like the mobster's kid brother who ends up betraying the family. But he'd grown into his face. The age lines, the added weight, and the pencil moustache combined to give him a weathered dignity. Even his nose, which used to dominate his face like a meteor that had crash-landed onto a cornfield, now displayed its incongruity more like that of a cathedral dominating a small medieval town.

Why he was there I had no idea. I didn't even know he was living in the States—which wasn't surprising given that I hadn't really kept up with Benedict during the past thirty years. He used to write me after I returned from Italy. Long, deeply personal letters out of all proportion to the degree that we had been friends. I might have replied once or twice in the most perfunctory way. But then I stopped replying, and though his long letters continued for a while, he eventually grabbed a social cue and stopped writing.

I guess I shouldn't have been surprised that Benedict was there. He was always showing up. Adele, for reasons that were mysterious, liked having him around. I asked her about it once, early on in our friendship.

"Does he have a crush on you?"

"Benny? That's a load of tosh."

"But he's always hanging around."

"Benny is always everywhere. He's like the ether."

I never got a more concrete reason for her allowing him to hover. I decided that it was his general posture as a rebel without a couch that attracted him to her as a kindred spirit. Mr. Cody's loyalty to him was more easily explained. They both loved doing improv comedy at bars and clubs around Rome. Benedict had been a member of the Footlights comedy troupe at Cambridge until he got kicked out for helping himself to the cash register, and Mr. Cody always credited Benedict with helping him develop his comic timing. I performed with them a few times. With Mater Dei's South African math teacher Dickie Grobbelaar, we formed a company we called Roman Holiday. But for all this light-hearted proximity, I never warmed to Benedict. For one thing, his feet stank. For another, my moral principles, though fairly elastic, become rigid as steel when it comes to embezzling from college comedy troupes. That always struck me as an act ranking in heinousness only just above stealing money from the Girl Scouts. I could take a pie in the face from him on stage, but I could never forgive him in my heart. Mr. Cody explained to me that Benedict had stolen the money because his father had cut him off, and that eventually he had returned everything he had stolen. But that didn't absolve him in my eyes. And on top of it all, he once tried to warn me off seeing Mr. Cody in the most disgusting way imaginable.

This was at one of the weekend parties Benedict's mother, still the countess though divorced from the count, used to allow us to have at her villa near Tivoli, outside Rome. It was a groggy Sunday afternoon after a long Saturday night of playing *Casablanca*, a drinking game in which one watches the eponymous movie and has to drink a shot each time one of the characters lights a cigarette. No small challenge. Mr. Cody and others were shaking out the cobwebs by playing soccer on the lawn. Benedict, unshaved and, as always, barefoot, found me enjoying a solitary coffee on the patio and reading *Ulysses*, which he saw as an opportunity to bring me up to speed on certain facts.

"Don't get me wrong, Kate. Cody is my friend. But I'm your friend too. I want you to know that I have everyone's best interests at heart."

"What are you trying to say, Benedict?"

"Please don't be angry."

"I'm not angry. I just don't understand what you're trying to say."

"I'm trying to say that I'm pretty confident—absolutely confident, actually—that Cody is seeing someone else."

"Is that so?"

"She's actually a friend of mine."

"A friend of yours."

"Yes."

"And who is this friend?"

"I can't say."

Of course it was Adele. Why didn't he just say it? Not that it mattered. Mr. Cody and I already understood one another regarding his friendship with Adele.

"You can't say. I see."

"But I know they're still together."

"So it seems we have a love triangle, Benedict. How deliciously dramatic."

"You're angry. I'm sorry if I talked out of turn."

"Are you, Benedict? Are you, really?"

I went back to my reading, or pretended to, but he stayed there watching me, weighing in his mind, I supposed, whether to tell me it was Adele.

"You know," he said, looking at my book, "Dante has an interesting take on Ulysses."

Benedict, who was fluently bilingual, taught the upper-level courses in Italian at Mater Dei, including an elective on *The Divine Comedy*. As Adele liked to quip, having to listen to Benedict blather on about Dante was its own ring of hell.

"Dante writes something of a sequel to the *Odyssey*. He imagines Ulysses back home in Ithaca, after all his adventures, but still restless. It's not just that he wants to get back to sea; he wants knowledge. *A divenir del mondo esperto:* 'to gain experience of the world.' Not even his love for his wife and son, Penelope and Telemachus, can hold him back. So he gets the band back together, his old comrades, and they set sail. They sail all the way to the Straits of Gibraltar, the boundary which the gods have set to human exploration. But Ulysses urges them on. *Non vogliate negar l'esperienza, di retro al sol:* 'Do not refuse experience of the lands beyond the sun.' They keep going until they get to the South Pole. And there they see on the horizon a mountain shore, a mountain higher than any of them has ever seen. They cheer their great discovery, but just as they do a whirlwind arises and batters their ship. It plunges them into the sea, and they drown."

At the time, this little speech didn't strike me as a warning; it struck me as pedantry, boorishness, obtuseness. One minute he was accusing the man I was dating of seeing someone else, and the next we were chatting about great literature? Give me a break. I wanted Benedict to plunge into the sea and drown. But in the end, I just gave him the dead-eye and said, "Is this going to be on the test?"

"I meant well, Kate."

"Busybodies always do."

He got up to go, but before leaving he said, "Please don't tell Cody I mentioned this to you."

Of course I mentioned it to Mr. Cody, and all he did was laugh.

"I reckon he might be talking about me and Janet Abbey," he said. "Yes, I admit, I confess, we went out a couple of times in the spring. But we never went *out*. In fact, *she* gave *me* the mitten. Not that I regret anything. It was a mitten I was glad to accept. We were totally unsuited for one another."

"Who's Janet Abbey?"

"Algebra teacher. Left for another job after last school year."

"Where?"

"Across town at St. Giles. The British International School."

I felt badly for pressing even this hard on the Janet Abbey question. Who Mr. Cody had dated in the past was no business of mine.

He laughed again. "Do you know what I think? I think Benny was making a play for *you*. I'm serious! It's the only thing that explains such an elaborate lie."

Back at the Death Symposium, Adele was calling us to order.

"Let's hear what you've been thinking and talking about in your pairs."

No one volunteered until she playfully chided the group. With glowing blushes, one of the women from the Toy Theatre started to unpack the secrets of her sexual life, but as is the way of these things, it didn't take long before the conversation lurched in a new direction. All of a sudden—don't ask me how—we were talking about assisted suicide.

Then the husband of the first-day-of-school woman, who had been rolling his eyes all night, sat up, folded his hands on the table, and mansplained how all this "right-to-die nonsense" leads to a "slippery slope." "Pretty soon," he added in his best cable-news manner, "people are going to be popping a suicide pill every time they have a bad day."

Look, I'm generally a non-confrontational person. I have trouble speaking my mind at faculty meetings when all we're talking about are proctoring duties. But this guy's smugness—the way in which he kept both righteous eyes closed the whole time he spewed his idiocy, like it was too much for him even to *look* at us—needed to be smacked back. I jumped into the fray, not waiting to be called on.

"I won't comment on the logic of your last remark," I said, "nor the patronizing way in which you've trivialized a deadly serious and personal issue. What I will say is this: Who are you to instruct anyone on how they should make decisions about the most important matters in their life? A decision to die in the midst of a grave illness is a private matter of conscience, and no government, no political party—*no one*—should attempt to coerce that decision."

Applause broke out around the table as soon as I finished speaking.

The man shook his head, as if I were not worthy of being responded to, and returned to his slumped position in his chair. Adele endeavored to restore order. But before she could do so, someone interjected a question aimed at me.

"Would you be able to tell us more about what you mean by 'conscience?'"

It was Benedict. He looked down the table at me with a puzzled expression. Not the mock puzzled expression used by the conceited debater as a rhetorical weapon. But real puzzlement. I wasn't quite sure how to answer.

"I mean what everybody means," I said. "Your sense of what's right. The place where you get in touch with what you value most."

Benedict turned to Adele and asked, "May I follow up?"

"Quickly, Socrates," Adele replied mordantly over the frame of her glasses.

"I'm just curious—" Benedict looked back to me— "whose values your conscience puts you in touch with?"

"Mine," I replied. "Whose else?"

"That's a good question. You see, what troubles me is that whenever I think about my conscience, I think of myself as being *judged*." He paused for a moment before going on. "I don't think of conscience as getting in touch with what I value most. I think of myself as under scrutiny. That I've done something I shouldn't have done and someone is angry with me."

"Did you go to Catholic school?" someone smirked.

"Freud has a theory about that, Benny," Adele said. "You have an overdeveloped superego. Speaking of Freud, we've gotten far away from the topic of sex—"

"I guess what I'm wondering," Benedict pressed on, looking at me, "is whether it makes sense for us to put ourselves under judgment."

My cheeks grew warm with the awareness that everyone was looking at me. "I'm sorry—I don't—"

"If conscience provides the standard of value—if conscience is the *judge*—then how can a person serve as both the judge and the accused?"

After a moment's thought I responded, "I don't think I agree with your courtroom metaphor. For me, conscience is more like reading one of my old journals on a rainy Sunday afternoon. As I read, I measure myself now against myself then—with, I hope, dollops of self-compassion. Given new experience in life, new insight, new information, don't we reflect on what we value and change our minds if needs be? Isn't conscience just another word for personal growth? I suppose in some sense we stand in 'judgment' over our former selves, but I think it's more productive if we think in terms of acceptance rather than judgment."

"Beautifully said." Adele smiled at me.

"You may be right." Benedict nodded almost sadly. "It's just—that's not how it feels to *me*."

"Kate has touched on something crucial," Adele said by way of bringing the rest of the room back into the discussion. "We are never bound by our thinking at any one moment of our lives. We can always stand back from our present self and ask whether we are living up to that *fullness of life* we most deeply desire. That's a tremendous power we have. But how often do we use it?"

Immediately after the Death Symposium broke up, around nine thirty, Adele was mobbed by needy symposiasts. As I stood and packed up my notebook, I checked to see, out of the corner of my eye, whether Benedict was making his way toward me. Most surprisingly, he was not. He had gone over to talk to the street woman, who was still sitting by the balcony. He leaned down and tried to engage her in conversation, just as I had tried to do. Then, from the pocket of his trousers, he took out a wad of bills and handed them to her. She took them eagerly, and as she did, Benedict, strangely, glanced at me. I turned away. When I looked up again the woman was scooting down the stairs with her money and Benedict was watching her go.

By the time he turned around again, I had recovered my manners. He hesitated to come forward, so I strode up to him with a big smile on my face.

Cheek kiss with a hug? Air kiss with a hug? Just a hug? Who knew what the ground rules were. In any event, Benedict went for the full-on cheek kiss while I went for the plain hug, no fries. He ended up kind of kissing me on the back of the head, while I sort of stumbled into his ear.

"My apologies for coming on a little strong back there," he said. "I have a keen interest in ethics, I suppose because I don't have any."

"I was just disappointed that you didn't bring in Dante."

He laughed and stepped back to drink me in, perhaps with a tad too much eagerness. "You look fantastic, Kate."

"I look like a woman who already gets the senior discount at the department store, Benedict."

"That's just capitalism working an angle. Really, Kate, you look marvelous."

"You're very kind." Was I supposed to return the compliment? I had no idea. I *think* I said—I *hope* I said—that he was looking well. Anyway, it was hard to believe that I was really looking at yet another figure from my mythic past. Adele, Benedict—it was as if the gods had returned.

"What are you doing in DC?" I asked. "It's strange how everyone from my youth is converging on this tiny diamond of overcrowded real estate."

"I've been living here off and on for the past several months, in fact, while my mother was in her final illness."

"Oh, no!"

"It's all right. She died a couple of months ago. I don't know if you remember my mother?"

"She was impossible to forget. *The countess.* I'm so sorry for your loss."

"Thank you. I appreciate that."

When I asked Benedict what he did for a living, he explained that he ran a consultancy in historic building restoration specializing in medieval churches and abbeys. After his stint at Mater Dei, he had earned a degree in architecture, then found his way into the restoration business.

I wondered if he had seen that the street woman had been wearing a green scapular. There was no question of asking him about it. That subject was closed between us, never to be opened again. Still, I wondered if he had seen it. Especially given that, as we talked, he seemed to keep checking the stairs. Was he hoping to see the street woman return?

"I have to run, Kate," he said. "But why don't we get together for a drink? I'm probably the last person you'd want to get a drink with, but I wouldn't keep you long. I'd love to catch up."

Spare me, Benedict, whatever this was. False humility. Obsequiousness. Playing the outcast. Quite right: you're the last person I'd want to get a drink with.

"Maybe so," I said. "This week is busy but—"

"Why don't we take each other's numbers?" He was already digging his phone out of his pocket. What did I care? I could ignore his texts for the rest of my short life. After we exchanged cell numbers, he added, "I'll be in touch."

Then he was off—I hoped for the last time.

Adele was still involved with her admirers, but I interjected myself into the throng to make plans to get together with her the following night.

"I'm so looking forward to a good natter," she said. "Let me take you to my friend Rav's new venture up in Cleveland Park. Your Mama's Tandoor. The latest addition to his haute Indian cuisine empire. He's just reopened after the lockdown."

I told her it sounded marvelous and asked if she wanted to exchange cell numbers.

"Don't believe in digital," she said. "I own no computer. No mobile. How about smoke signals? Do you do smoke signals? Oh well, Carly helms the electronic gidgety-gadgets at our house. She'll give you the number."

As we parted, I found myself resenting this flash of the *grande dame*. Who was she to deflect me to her assistant? But I tried to remind myself, this is Adele. She could never be bothered with anything other than the current bee in her bonnet. Besides, she had symposiasts to say goodnight to.

Carly was at the refreshments table packing up the crockery in a large plastic storage tub. She was loud, jovial, mannish, with a short haircut made for the playing field. So she and Adele lived together? I was all nosiness as I introduced myself and explained who I was.

"How long have you been Adele's assistant?" I asked.

"Since right before she came to the States. New York, then here in DC."

"Adele was in New York? I didn't know that."

"Yeah. For a year or so."

"Where do you work from? Home?"

"From Adele's house, yeah."

"Adele's house?"

"Yeah. I live in the basement and have an office on the ground floor."

Not wanting to look too surprised by this, I explained my desire to exchange cell numbers. We took out our phones and made the new contacts, but before I said goodnight, I did a little more research in preparation for my dinner with Adele.

"So, what is a transition celebrant exactly?"

"Someone who helps people through big changes in life. You know, marriage, divorce, anniversary, death."

"Death?"

"Oh yeah. The deathday celebration is becoming quite popular."

"Deathday celebration? What is that?"

Carly held the already bubble-wrapped teapot from the table. Through the thick plastic, the skull on the teapot's fat belly grinned at me with an effect like that of a funhouse mirror.

"The deathday is like the opposite of a birthday," she said. "A celebration of life at the end of life."

"How does anyone do that?" I asked. "How does anyone know the day they are going to die? Or do people just pick a day to celebrate?"

Carly laughed—flushed?—as she placed the bubble-wrapped teapot in the plastic tub.

"That's her gift," she said, looking for the next item from the table to bubble wrap. "Adele helps people find just the right day."

CHAPTER TWO

Five stars for Your Mama's Tandoor. Super yummy with a cozy decor. Adele's friend, Rav, treated us to small plates of eggplant and mixed tomatoes. I ordered my lamb curry before I realized Adele was now a vegetarian, but guilt subsided as soon as I tasted the succulent, spicy meat. Starting with dessert, we went through two entire pots of chai masala tea, losing ourselves within that fragrant cloud of cardamom and cinnamon.

What had Adele Schraeder been doing for the past decade? "Stirring pots," as she liked to say. She had continued to live in London, but (surprise to me) for most of that time lived with a man named Roger, who was older (of course), wealthy, and a notable patron of the arts. They were together some seven or eight years, until, three years ago, Roger died of heart failure.

"Daddy died only a month before Roger. I never saw Daddy's body. I was on holiday with a friend in Prague, and by the time I got home the body was already at the morgue. It never occurred to me to ask to see it. I made the decision to cremate him so that I could spread his ashes in the Thames. I thought he would have liked that. But even at the time I had a sense, a most inarticulate sense, that this was *wrong*. That this wasn't the proper way to say farewell. Like everyone else, I buried the feeling—pardon the pun—and went on my way, not realizing that my inability to countenance death was stifling my satisfaction with life."

I inserted that this had been my same experience with my mother. But although she touched my hand in condolence, Adele did not slow down for my memories. She was too full of her subject.

"But then I heard Dr. Ashton give a lecture on the philosophy of the Death Symposium. He's a brilliant man. A specialist in the psychology of grief. Immediately, I realized, '*This!* This is what the world is yearning for and doesn't know it.'"

As she said this, Adele tapped a claw of freshly manicured nails on the table for emphasis. Then she took a sip of tea, warming even more to her theme.

"We live in a culture that sanitizes death, keeps it out of view. The result is that we don't know *how* to speak about it, and we don't *like* to speak about it. Have you noticed that we can't even say the word anymore? Dr. Ashton founded the Death Symposium to address our mass repression. That's exactly what it is—*repression*—and it's killing us. We're neurotically afraid of coming to the end of our lives, and the result is that we fail to live."

All through this speech, the desire to tell my news once again lunged for the surface. Chief reason for: Why not? What was the point in hiding it? Chief reason against: an indistinct and possibly misplaced feeling that it would put unnecessary pressure on the renewal of our friendship.

Given Adele's current crusade, it seemed silly to hesitate. And yet, I was not ready to pull the trigger. I didn't want to appear weak in front of her, I guess. I didn't want to reveal that my disappointed existence would never have the opportunity to reach—what had she called it yesterday?—the *fullness*.

"So what did you do after you heard Dr. Ashton's lecture?" I asked.

"I began to read his work. I started going to the Death Symposium. There are two full versions running in London, widely popular, and many others popping up elsewhere." She mentioned a famous British actor who had publicly championed the cause. "But it took Roger's death to really galvanize me. Even as the men from the funeral home carried his body out of the house, I saw what I had to do. I began a course with Dr. Ashton and received certification from the Death Symposium Institute as a transition celebrant. And I was just getting ready to put out my shingle when one day Dr. Ashton said to me, 'What I really want is for the Death Symposium to conquer America.' That was the second thunderbolt. You see, though Roger bequeathed the bulk of his fortune to his grown children, and even left a legacy to his ex-wife—he was a good, decent man—he also left me a tidy little sum. I had the means and the opportunity to start a new chapter in my life. With Daddy and Roger gone, it was the perfect time to pull up roots. I told Dr. Ashton, 'Choose me! I'm ready to conquer America.' We decided that New York would be the natural place to start. A month later, I had opened the North American Theatre of the Death Symposium."

"Why didn't you stay in New York?"

"Why didn't St. Paul stay in Philippi? I had the Good News to spread. We took off in New York like a rocket. Before I had unpacked my toothbrush in Manhattan, I was running two versions of the Death Symposium and hustling to keep up with my growing business. Mercifully, I had Carly to do all the admin work. Still, it was hard to keep up with it all. I trained a bright young spark named Emma to take over my facilitator's chair at one of the weekly symposia. But things kept mushrooming. People have such a hunger for what we're doing. Meanwhile, Dr. Ashton wanted to see the Death Symposium in more US cities, so Emma studied for her certificate and opened up her own shop as a transition celebrant in Brooklyn, and I moved down here to DC."

"Why here?"

"It's the most powerful and influential city in the world. Why not?"

"And Carly came with you. You two live together?"

"Carly's my girl Friday. Couldn't live without her. She does everything for me: cooks, cleans, books appointments, and races about the metropolis hunting me down real tea."

"Where did you find her?"

"She was one of my students from way back. Ace footballer. Played professionally for the Chelsea Women until she blew out her knee. Oh, Kate!" Adele reached across the table and took my hand. "It's so good to see you. Catch me up on your last decade. I want to hear everything."

I offered her, instead of "everything," a brisk overview of my rather uneventful past thirteen years. Keeping my hand to the plough at Brook Farm Academy. My struggles to maintain Five Hearths. All in about a minute and a half.

"Any men in your life?" she asked. "Have a bit of a pash for anyone in particular?"

"Not at present."

"That's all right. *Non te quaesiveris extra*, what what?"

"Tell me more about you and Roger."

"Oh—as I said, he was a dear man. Interested in everything and passionate about art. We knew one another for a long time before one day I woke up and realized we were living together. Neither one of us had the slightest inclination to accommodate the other in any way whatsoever, so we lived our lives as the best of friends. I don't believe we ever had an argument. His children are lovely too. Never showed me the least resentment. Seemed glad, in fact, that their father had found someone who didn't plague his heart out."

When I asked how she and Roger met, she surprised me.

"Remember The Massimo?"

"The Massimo! I haven't heard that name in thirty years."

"He's still making films, you know. Perhaps a toucher more mainstream, if you can believe it. Sometime in the late noughties, he met Roger and persuaded him to back one of his films. When it was done, Roger helped get the film into Cannes, and The Massimo, whom I had stayed in contact with, invited me to come down for the parties. I met Roger over a red carpet mojito. We had a bop on the dance floor, and I thought, 'I may be able to tolerate a man who can dance like this.'"

The mention of The Massimo put me in mind of the old Rome crowd. "How weird to see Benedict Aquila last night. When did you two reconnect?"

"Oh, we've always stayed connected. He started coming to the Death Symposium with his mother before she died. Remember the countess?"

"Vividly. Why was she living in DC?"

"She grew up here, though from her twenties she lived in Italy. For her final years, however, she wanted to return to the States, but as soon as she landed here in DC, she became ill and took to her bed in a local 'retirement community.' The kind that keeps the poor dears busy all day with *tai chi* and watercolors because if they stop for a moment they might actually have a think about the meaning of their lives. I abhor what we do to the elderly in our culture. That's why I make sure to get Death Symposium adverts on every bulletin board in every one of those gulags. That's how the countess heard of us."

"The countess never struck me as someone who would want to sit around and talk about death, even over tea and cake."

"What did Dr. Johnson say? The prospect of death wonderfully concentrates the mind."

My attention was pulled back to my sparring session with Benedict at the symposium and to the street woman to whom he had given money. At the Death Symposium, I had decided against mentioning the street woman's green scapular to Adele, but now I couldn't resist.

"That street woman from last night. Did you see that she was wearing a green scapular?"

"No, I didn't."

"I hadn't seen one of those in forever."

Adele shrugged her shoulders, which was enough to dissuade me from asking if she knew where Miranda Cody lived now.

The green scapular first came to my attention one night at Sunday dinner, my first fall in Rome. I was host along with my friend Astrid, who taught German at WIX. While we were getting the dinner ready in Astrid's kitchen, Lucas Holloway, who taught science at WIX, and his girlfriend, Shia Lu, who taught math, revealed that they had found a green scapular underneath one of their pillows.

"Underneath your pillow!" I said as I refreshed the tumblers with our cheap, grocery store Chianti. "Why would anyone put a green thingy—"

"—scapular—" said Lucas.

"—scapular underneath your pillow?"

"I take it," replied Lucas, "that the culprit is directing his prayers against the arena of my and Shia Lu's iniquity."

"The arena of our *what*—?" squawked Shia Lu.

"What I want to know," Lucas continued, "is how the culprit got into our apartment. Clearly, it's someone who knows the intimate details of our personal lives, who knows when Shia Lu and I are home and when we are not. Who may be watching us right now."

"OK," said Shia Lu, "you're starting to creep me out. Should we call the police?"

"The *Roman* police?" Lucas scoffed.

"If nothing else, it's unlawful entry."

"May I ask a question?" I interrupted. "Simply as a point of information. What *is* a green scapular?"

Lucas reached into his jeans pocket and brought out a mysterious article, which he held up to the light over the dining table. Attached on either end of a green cord was a square of green cloth. On a smaller square of white cloth attached to the green square was a picture of the Virgin Mary holding her exposed heart. On the other side of each green square, again on a smaller square of white cloth, was an enlarged image of that same heart underneath a cross. The heart had a sword thrust through it and was bleeding. Encircling this image were the words *Immaculate Heart of Mary, Pray for Us Now and at the Hour of Our Death.*

"Ghoulish," said Shia Lu.

"I was kinda, sorta, not really raised Catholic, yet I've never heard of a green scapular," I said. "What are you supposed to *do* with it?"

Lucas smiled and nodded in the way he did when a student's question teed him up for one of his patented lecturettes.

"Scapulars are worn around the neck and underneath the clothing as tokens of devotion. According to my research yesterday in the school library, there are two kinds of scapulars, green and brown. The brown—that is, the scapular of Our Lady of Mount Carmel—is more popular. In 1251, the Blessed Virgin Mary appeared to St. Simon Stock, Superior General of the Carmelite Order, and presented him with the brown scapular as a 'garment of grace.' St. Alphonsus Liguori was buried wearing the brown scapular, and years later, when his grave was opened—"

"You're babbling, dearest," said Shia Lu. "What does this have to do with our little mystery?"

"I am merely drawing the appropriate preliminary distinction. Our culprit has chosen to give out the *green* scapular, which the Virgin Mary, in 1840, presented to Sr. Justine Bisqueyburo."

"*Por supuesto,*" Shia Lu said, reaching for the bread.

"The Virgin Mary told Sr. Justine that if someone is unable or unwilling to wear the green scapular, then it can be placed or even hidden among his or her possessions. One can then say the mandatory daily prayer, 'Immaculate Heart of Mary, pray for us now and at the hour of our death,' for the sake of the person not wearing the scapular, and he or she will receive special graces."

"So someone thinks we're *dying*?" Shia Lu wondered.

"Think of it as a talisman against harm," replied Lucas.

Adele contributed nothing to this part of the conversation. I watched her as she sat apart from the rest of us, cross-legged on the floor beside the bookcase where Astrid kept her record albums and cassettes. Adele studied the cover art and liner notes on the albums and sipped her wine. Her only reaction to the discussion was an eyeroll she shared privately with me.

It was something of an event that Adele was even with us. Though she was an integral member of our crew, she rarely appeared at Sunday dinner. She was nearly always elsewhere, an elsewhere that typically involved some form of missionary zeal: a meeting of the local Greenpeace chapter; a lecture at the American University of Rome by a renowned Communist politician; an anti-apartheid demonstration outside the South African embassy. Once or twice I joined her on these adventures, but I much preferred a glass of wine and "the crack," as Rory called it, at Sunday dinner.

"This is all a bore, kids," Adele said, putting aside Astrid's copy of Bob Dylan's *Slow Train Coming.*

"Aren't you at all interested?" Lucas asked her.

"Not even a little bit."

"Not the tiniest bit curious?"

"I find it a bore."

"So who do you think's doing it?"

"Haven't got a clue, mate. Given the weirdness of it, I suppose it's one of the sisters—"

This was met by Lucas with sharp derision.

"There isn't a sister at WIX under *sixty-five!* I don't see any of them sneaking into our apartment. Besides, I think they would be more interested in putting Sandinista propaganda underneath our pillows."

"Who else would care enough to do it?" asked Adele. "Obviously, it's someone with strong religious motivation. I suppose it could be one of the Holy Rollers."

The Holy Rollers were a group of serious and homely girls, mostly Spanish and Portuguese and one or two Americans, who wore little doilies on their heads at Mass and their skirts down to their ankles, and who had attempted to launch a sexual abstinence crusade that was roundly mocked by all beyond their tiny circle. I usually saw them kneeling in front of the statue of Mary in the garden behind the main administration building, saying the rosary. Not even the sisters seemed to like them. They certainly gave them no encouragement. Adele, I thought, was onto something. I could easily imagine the Holy Rollers talking in condemning whispers about the sexual manners of their teachers and sneaking into apartments to plant green scapulars, all in the firm confidence that they were saving endangered souls.

"But how would the Holy Rollers know that Shia Lu and I are living together?" Lucas countered.

"They look," Adele said. "They see. Anyway, you should be proud that you got singled out for attention. It's a sign you're doing something right. Let them hide their green scapulars. If I got one, I would wear it around my neck at school as a badge of honor."

Back at Your Mama's Tandoor, the pot of chai masala was gone and Adele had paid the bill for dinner, hearing none of my pleas to contribute. The balmy night was pleasant as we exited the chilly air conditioning of the restaurant. I had driven my car. Carly had brought Adele, and had sat in the car all through dinner, engrossed by her phone. She did not appear in the least impatient when Adele and I loitered in the parking lot to talk.

"I haven't asked you about your writing," Adele said.

I muttered something about the humorous essay I had started over the summer. The sound of my voice sickened me.

"I want you to write something about the Death Symposium," Adele said. "I think you're the perfect person to do it."

"What kind of thing?"

"An eyewitness account. A gospel. What do they call it these days? Narrative nonfiction?"

Adele flattered me while she made her pitch. But as she did, that desperate, drowning person inside me made one final, aching lunge for air.

"I'm afraid I won't have the time," I blurted out.

"Pish. You have all the time you'd care to commit to it."

I looked at her steadily and said, "All the time I'd care to commit is precisely what I don't have."

We sat in my car as, through tears, I told her my story. She held me by both my hands, following every word I said with furious interest. Once I had the basics out, she gave me a long, silent hug.

I found it awkward that she didn't bother to alert Carly. "Don't worry about Carly," Adele assured me. "She gets paid to wait for me. It's in her job description."

We sat in my car for nearly an hour. I answered as patiently as I could her string of well-meaning but tedious questions. Had I gotten a second opinion? Had I looked into clinical trials? Alternative treatments? When did my chemo and radiation begin?

"I haven't scheduled it yet."

"Why not?"

"It's hard to see what the point would be. I'm driving my beautiful neuro-oncologist bonkers, waiting so long. It's been over a week since my diagnosis, and I haven't even suited up for battle. He was ready to rock-and-roll that day. He called me himself this morning, hoping to get the chemo and radiation routine rolling. I explained to him that I was still thinking through my options. He asked if I had been experiencing 'low mood.' He said 'low mood' is a normal reaction to such a diagnosis and that he would be happy to write me a prescription for an antidepressant. 'Low mood!' Whatever happened to 'fear and trembling?' The first casualty of catastrophe is the language. I told him—politely, of course—that he could keep his pills.

"I'm dying, Adele," I concluded. "There's nothing to do but get ready."

Black rivulets of eyeliner trickled down her cheeks. She took me by the shoulders, just as she had at the Death Symposium, and locked me into her gaze. "You're not going to go through this alone, Kate Montclair."

I nodded and ripped another tissue from the box I'd put on the panel above the dash.

"I'm going to be here for you the whole way. No disrespect to your friend Lisa, but this is what I *do*. I help people in just this position every day."

"Thank you," I said before I blew my nose with a resounding honk.

Before we parted she said, "I want you to come to my house for dinner this Sunday night. Every month, I hold a meeting of the inner circle. Like the philosophers of old, I have my exoteric teaching and my esoteric teaching. Nights at the coffee shop are for the common stock, the *hoi polloi*. Those meetings have value in and of themselves, but they also serve as a net by which I catch the occasional exotic fish. You, Kate dear, belong among my exotics. No, you don't need to bring anything but yourself. Do you want me to have Carly come get you? Let me know if you change your mind. Meanwhile, you call me at any hour of the day or night. I mean it. Don't you dare worry about whether you're bothering me. I want you to lean on me. I want you to put yourself entirely into my hands."

CHAPTER THREE

I drove back to Five Hearths after my dinner with Adele, as I wanted to spend the weekend in the country. I felt saner there, close to my Morning Mountain. On Saturday, I woke up long before dawn and couldn't get back to sleep.

When you wake up to death, you can go in one of two directions.

The first is to shore your fragments against your ruin: settle your finances, organize your closets, give away unwanted clothes to charity, arrange to spend time with friends, do maintenance on your property in preparation for putting it on the market, finish that piece of writing.

The second response is to let go: do nothing, stare out the window, wander through the rooms of your house summoning its ghosts, waste time on the internet, sleep. Because, after all, what is the point?

Today was a day of the second response. Aided by rain.

With my coffee, I read—more like skimmed—stuff online, none of which brought me enlightenment or wisdom, consolation or courage. Who was it that said technology only allows us to do stupid things faster?

Afterward I crawled back into bed and wrote in my memoir for an hour. Then it occurred to me to open Kate's Cabinet of Curiosities (a fireproof box of treasures that I keep on a shelf in my closet). I sat on my bed for another hour and sifted through them. In my old WIX class planner I found, waiting like a pressed flower, my and Mr. Cody's green scapular.

Around one o'clock, I lay down to rest for five minutes. I woke up at four thirty.

By this time, it was getting harder to avoid certain obligations. The first was Lisa. She had been texting me at what seemed like ten-minute intervals.

Just wondering what the gameplan is. I'm right here with you, sweetheart!

Let me know your plan. I'm making up a batch of Jewish peni-
cillin (chicken soup) and can bring it over whenever.

Doing ok? ur not ghosting me, right? The silence is driving me
to drink (even more).

I hadn't returned any of these texts because I hadn't scheduled my chemo and radiation, and I didn't want to be scolded for it. What was I doing not scheduling chemo and radiation? Conducting research, I told myself.

The other night, after I got home from the Death Symposium, I visited some websites and cancer chat groups online, trying to get a better sense of what life would be like on chemo and radiation. The level of pain some of these poor souls had to endure frightened me. And the *time* they had to spend in hospitals. I spent six months with my mother in and out of cancer wards, leading her through her doomed regimen of chemo and radiation like General Custer's chief military strategist at Little Big Horn. I swore to myself then that I wasn't going to die like that. It was just so *degrading*, not to mention brutal on both body and psyche. And toward what end? A few extra months of enfeebled life, tops.

Homeopathic remedies? Sure, I looked them up too. I liked the idea of simply bulking up on coconut oil and flaxseed and foregoing chemo and radiation. At least until the pain got really bad, why not?

But here's the rub. At some point the pain was going to get really bad.

But isn't that where hospice came in, and I began to exit stage left, doped up on morphine?

My favorite guy from these cancer chat groups was the guy who, when diagnosed with inoperable Stage IV Glioblastoma Multiforme, did exactly nothing. I mean nothing. No chemo. No radiation. Not even a sprinkle of flaxseed on his morning yogurt. He just said to the tumor, "Do your worst," and now he's into his third year post-diagnosis. That guy was my hero. I wanted to be like him. I wanted to say to the tumor, "Do your worst," and go back to my regularly scheduled programming. If the evil machine of the universe wanted to gobble me up, then let it come get me. Meantime, I would be chillaxing with a glass of wine on the porch.

I picked up my phone and texted Lisa.

*Sorry, not ghosting you! At Five Hearths dealing with mainte-
nance men on about five different home repair projects. Getting
this money pit ready for the market. Will call 2morrow if not
2nite.*

When you've got cancer, such a text is not lying; it's called self-care. But it
wasn't a total lie, anyway. I had begun at least to *think* about getting the house
ready to be put on the market.

The second obligation had to do with school. Since the diagnosis, I had
been on leave "for personal reasons." Tabitha Davie, my head of school, had
texted me the day before, asking how I was. I had a big decision to make
about teaching. Did I soldier on to the bitter end, or did I turn in my badge
and walk away now? The more I thought about it, the more it seemed unac-
ceptable to keep on teaching. Not only would my energy have diminishing
returns, but I would only further traumatize the students. It was also best for
the school that I resign while the school year was still young and a replacement would be able to start more or less from the beginning. I texted Tabitha,
saying nothing yet about my condition but asking for an in-person meeting
on Monday.

Then there was Benedict. When it came to setting up drinks, he didn't let
the moss grow under his texting thumbs. I heard from him on Friday afternoon, just as I was getting ready to meet Adele.

*So great seeing you last night. How about drinks this weekend?
Any night works for me.*

I didn't respond to him right away. The trick of it was to sound enthusiastic while putting him off indefinitely. I finally replied.

*So great seeing YOU! In the country this weekend as I inherited
my mother's 5-acre money pit. Lots to do getting it ready for the
market. Can we touch base again next week?*

He texted back right away.

Best of luck with the house. Yes, let's aim for next week.

After these exertions, I made myself a dinner of Costco meatloaf and mashed potatoes, which I enjoyed while watching *Sense and Sensibility*. Comfort food, comfort movie. Afterward I deleted the Weight Watchers app on my phone. If they weren't going to give me extra points for being gravely ill, then we were finished. I ate the remaining portion of mashed potatoes right out of the plastic tray while doing the dishes.

Sunday was a hard day. I walked over in the rain to Evie and Everett's and told them my news. Evie burst into tears and escaped to her room for about ten minutes. I was a mess too, but I made use of the time alone with Everett to ask if he would manage the sale of Five Hearths if I couldn't get it done before my bus arrived. He said he would be glad to. A weight off my mind.

When Evie returned, we stood in the living room and hugged and cried some more.

"I hate that cancer!" she kept saying. "I hate it. I hate it. I hate it!"

"You and me both, Evie," I said as I kissed her forehead. "But, hey, if this is what it takes to get Walker to step up the pace of his wooing, it's the price I gotta pay."

Gallows humor. The only way through such moments.

That first night at the Death Symposium, Carly had given me an introductory packet of materials. Inside was a brochure detailing the history of the Death Symposium movement, an advertising flyer for Adele's transition celebrant consultancy along with her business card, a black COVID mask with a skeletal smile, and a booklet entitled *The Art of Death*, full of advice about how to begin thinking about one's death as well as tips about how to talk about death productively with friends and family. Inside the booklet were some questions intended to be guides for meditation. *What is your greatest experience of suffering?*

That one's easy. It began in our little theatre at WIX, that first fall in Rome. Mr. Cody was slouched in a third row seat, a clipboard resting on his knee, a pensive index finger at ninety degrees on his cheek. And there I was sitting next to him, hyper-aware of the proximity, and every time he leaned his head toward mine to confer or to make a light joke, I went taut like one of those push-button puppets that when you release its plunger goes ramrod straight.

It was callbacks for the fall show, Thornton Wilder's *Our Town*, that old

high school chestnut. Since the late sixties when the Sexual Revolution ushered in the idea of co-ed productions, the drama club had been a combined
effort of both WIX and Mater Dei. The schools took turns hosting the show,
and this year WIX enjoyed the honor. I was there at the auditions because he'd
asked me to "consult," based upon what he saw me do at the improv night the
previous weekend. Adele and I and a few others had gone to see him, Dickie,
and Benedict do comedy improv at Childe Harold's, one of the English bars
in Rome. For one of the sketches, they needed a fourth and Adele pushed me
up on stage. The sketch was a noirish detective story that required a femme
fatale. My "Dollface" was something of a hit, and the sketch won first prize
for the night: a bottle of champagne, which the boys gifted to me. Big fun.

But it was also a strange night. During the prizes giveaway, some crazy
woman locked herself in the storeroom behind the bar and lit a case of alcohol on fire. The bar owner broke down the door with an axe and firemen
rushed in. The fire didn't get beyond the storeroom, and thankfully the woman only suffered from smoke inhalation, but it was still pretty unsettling. And
a mystery too, what the poor thing was trying to do. I never got a good look
at her, but I vividly remember the white and orange buggy of the Roman
ambulance, its siren keening, rollicking away with her inside.

For an hour, Mr. Cody and I watched the students audition. Afterward,
he asked me if I would I be available after school the next day for one last
discussion about the cast list. We could grab an espresso at the Caffè Ogygia,
a coffee bar popular with us teachers, on the corner across from the front gate
of Wildwood.

Careful, girl, I told myself that evening as I rode the bus home. *Even if this
flurry of attention is more than about the play, this is a man who, until recently,
was in hot pursuit of your good friend. Do you really want to be the rebound girl
who gets dumped in two weeks when he realizes that you've been no more than an
emotional crutch? And why are you even thinking that he could be interested in
you in that way? Maybe he is just happy to talk to someone who shares his passion
for drama?*

I also wondered what he was doing teaching drama in a Catholic boys
school. Why had he left London and a promising professional career that
most young actors would saw off their right arm for? *Mr. Cody has lost his
way,* Adele said. What did that mean? A broken heart? A professional crisis?

It must have been hard making a living as a stage actor. Possibly one of his performances had gotten negative reviews and producers were reluctant to hire him. But why Rome? If he wanted so badly to get back into the theatre, why not stay in London?

The evening deepened. As the bus wheezed along the Corso, I looked out the window, absorbed by the brilliant windows of the glam clothing and bag shops. I remembered how during a break in the auditions he had made me laugh by imitating the *basso profundo* voice of the portly boy who auditioned for Mr. Gibbs. I thought of his little pursed smile, the one he made when he knew he'd said something cute. Maybe my need to be cautious was only my insecurity talking? Maybe Adele was right, and I was the one who could help him find his way again?

The bus clattered to a stop. With a hiss, the contraption sank, and then the doors rattled open. An old crone dressed in widow's black and laden with two grocery bags boarded the bus. She shouldered her way down the main aisle thick with standing passengers. "*Scusi,*" she mumbled. "*Permesso ... 'messo.*" Though it was not evident in her chalky, crumpled features, even she, I fantasized, had once felt herself carried away by longing for a man. They had married young, and she bore him children, and sooner or later he died, leaving her to remember him sadly each morning as she wrapped her black kerchief around her gray head. The man sitting next to me yielded his seat to her, and she plumped down beside me with all the burden of her bulky frame and heavy bags. How strange that she had nudged her way down the aisle of standing passengers to take a seat next to me. She struck me like a visitation, like Poe's raven alighting upon the bust of Pallas, come to tell me, "Nevermore."

I spent the evening worrying about what to wear. We were meeting right after school, so whatever I wore would also be work clothes. He had seen me in my best jeans that first farcical night at Mater Dei and my two favorite pairs of school slacks on the days of auditions. The proletariat-loving sisters didn't require the female faculty to wear skirts, and I rarely did. But I considered wearing my below-the-knee navy blue skirt until I decided that it was too cold to tramp down to the café in anything but pants. In the end, I settled for a classic English-teacher fall ensemble: brown corduroys, auburn sweater with jacket, and thick, pumpkin-colored scarf. A look that said, "I'm ready either for a romantic walk in the autumn woods or for grading sixty-five essays on self-knowledge in *Emma.*" It was a good pick, because he himself came looking like my twin in a brown corduroy jacket and loosened pumpkin knit tie.

"We look like we should have our own TV show," I said as we compared our outfits. "The mild-mannered schoolteachers who solve mysteries on the weekends."

He laughed and added, "But who along the way are always quarreling about the true identity of the Dark Lady of the sonnets."

There really wasn't anything more to discuss about the cast list, but he was having so much fun obsessing over every decision that I did my best to appear concerned about whether Gretchen Fowler's pantomime skills were up to scratch. When at last he declared the list carved in stone, he ordered us another round of espressos to celebrate. His treat both rounds: good sign.

Except then there was a bad sign.

The second round of espressos arrived, and as we were adding the *zucchero,* he said, "Well, I feel really good about the list."

"You should," I said. "I don't think any of the kids will have reason to complain. Casting two Emilys was a masterstroke."

"Don't credit me. It was Adele's idea."

"Really?" I replied, as all my pumped-up he's-treating-for-the-espressos excitement hurtled down my torso like an elevator whose cords had been cut. "When did you talk to her?"

"Oh, we've been talking all week. She knows these kids and all their teenage dynamics. Bijou's one of her favorite girls, and she's been advocating for her to be the second Emily. Last night I was still wavering, but Adele convinced me that Bijou could pull off doe-eyed innocence."

OK. I guess you had to hit me over the head. This wasn't a date. I sat back in my chair and did my best to transition from the charmed and charming possible female lead to the cool and collegial nice new friend. I then observed, simply by way of establishing the facts:

"You and Adele seem pretty tight."

"Yeah. She's a pal. You two are growing pretty tight as well, I understand."

"She's a pal."

After another moment I asked him how long he had known her.

"We met not long after I came to Rome. She took me in hand, as she likes to put it."

"She does that," I said. "She's quite manic, isn't she? Something grabs her, and off she goes."

"Funny you say that," he replied, "because that's a word I use for her myself."

"What word?"

"Manic. Mania. For the ancient Greeks, *mania* meant you were in the grip of the gods. That's what I call her: 'maenad.'"

"What's a maenad?"

"Maenads were female followers of Dionysus, the god the Romans called Bacchus. He used wine to whip the maenads into a frenzy, and they followed him into the woods as raving 'maniacs,' where they would tear wild animals apart and indulge in sexual orgies."

"Lovely," I said with a sardonic smile before downing the last of my espresso.

"I just mean that she's a great—an *enthusiast*," he said. "Don't get me wrong. I love Adele. Everybody loves Adele."

Sick to death of Adele, I asked him, "So what brought you to Rome?" My tone was all Joe Friday; I just wanted to get the facts on this guy to satiate my curiosity before I went home. He took out a cigarette, then put it away when he noticed the *NON FUMARE* sign.

"Does one need a reason to come to Rome?"

"I think when one is working professionally as an actor in London, yes, one does."

He cocked his head back and scrutinized me. Then he relaxed and smiled. "I have no doubt Adele exaggerated whatever meager success I enjoyed in London."

"But why give it up?"

"I haven't."

"You needed a break?"

"I was tired, yeah. I needed a change of scene."

The next sequence was more perfunctory as he answered basic questions about his upbringing and education, most of which information I had already learned from Adele. He grew up in New York City, where his father was the headmaster of the British international school in Manhattan. In high school, he fell in love with acting, and by his senior year, he was determined to make a career of it. He earned a place at RADA—the Royal Academy for Dramatic Arts—as one of the two American citizens accepted that year. By the end of his third year in the three-year program, he had already played some minor television roles and secured an agent. Six months later, he played Edmund in a West End revival of *Long Day's Journey into Night*.

But he grew increasingly uncomfortable as he answered my questions. He was not eager to discuss his acting career. He displayed neither honest pride nor winsome self-deprecation as he recounted the details of his *curriculum vitae*. I had to pull out of him the names of the television shows and plays he had appeared in. Until, abruptly, he had to leave. No explanation. Only that he was "late for something."

The waiter saw us leaving and rushed over with *il conto*. Without even looking at the bill, Mr. Cody handed the waiter a 10,000 *lire* note and kept walking. I felt like I had been dismissed.

His Vespa was parked diagonally along the curb outside the café. He stopped to thank me one more time for helping him with the auditions, and I told him it was a pleasure. All very formal. No last, lingering conversation on the corner. He said he would see me later, smiled awkwardly, and turned to go. Wondering what I had said to upset him, I also turned to go. But as I was standing on the corner waiting for the traffic to clear, struggling hard not to look at him getting on his Vespa, he called to me.

"Hey, Ms. Montclair!"

I turned. He was walking back toward me.

"I was thinking of going out to Ostia Antica on Saturday."

"What's that?"

"It's the port city of the old Empire. About an hour or so by train. Lots of ruins. There's a theatre there from the first century B.C. that I've always wanted to see. Would you care to join me?"

What an odd fish you were, Mr. Michael Cody. One minute all clamped down and chilly, the next Mr. Day Tripper. I have always wondered, what if I had said no to you then? I might have spared myself so much. But I did not say no. You were standing right in front of me, your hair still wonderfully windblown from the ride over, giving me the full value of that dimply boyish grin. I heard myself trying not to sound too eager as I said, "Sure. I'd love to."

He was full of exciting news when I met him Saturday morning at the Piramide Metro, where we were going to catch the train to Ostia. Adele had snagged him an audition for a part in Roberto's new film, an adaptation of a Muriel Spark novel set in Rome, *The Public Image.* The audition was scheduled to take place at Cinecittà the next afternoon.

"Do they show you the script beforehand?" I asked as the train crawled out of the station.

"Not a chance. Once you're in the room, they hand you a copy, say a few words about the character, and off you go. If they like me, they may ask me to come back and read with someone up for the role of Annabel Christopher, the female lead."

"Do you get nervous in auditions?"

"Only until I walk in the door. Then it's my moment to seize. What's the point of going out there tomorrow if I don't give them a show? If I fail, I fail. But at least I will fail having given everything I got."

I liked this confidence—a brio I had not seen at the café. It didn't strike me as bluff but as real experience talking. He had stood in the wings of a West End theatre waiting to go on, with butterflies like pterodactyls in his stomach; yet he had said to himself, "If I fail, I fail," and seized his moment with both hands. I yearned to be brave like that. Sure, I had been brave in front of college audiences and bar audiences here in Rome. But I had never gone before critics and seasoned, cynical theatregoers. I had never done anything professionally. But I had come to Rome to put in the work to become a professional writer. This was *my* moment, and I was going to seize it. I wasn't going to gag on it like some of the kids at the *Our Town* audition, so full of fear and self-consciousness.

"I've seen you writing," he said.

"When did you see me?"

"Once at the beginning of the year when I was at WIX for the dual faculty meeting. Afterward, you were sitting on the edge of the fountain going like mad in your notebook."

I smiled and looked down into the spongy brown froth at the bottom of my paper cappuccino cup.

"A girl with such commitment to her writing does not strike me as someone prepared to make a long-term commitment to the teaching profession."

"You figured that out, did you?"

"Do you mind if I ask what you were writing?"

"A short story."

"About up in Michigan?"

I pinged him right back, Hemingway for Hemingway. "Yes. The story was writing itself, and I was having a hard time keeping up with it."

He smiled back at me. I had surprised him, and he liked it.

"Maybe I could read it when you're done."

"Maybe." I smiled and turned to look out the window.

When we arrived at the historic section of Ostia, we played tourists for a while, walking through the ruined chambers of the ancient houses, examining the marvelously intact mosaics on the walls and floors. *"Tesserae in calcereous stone, marble, flint, and local rocks in a wide variety of colors."* Mr. Cody teased me for having brought a guidebook, but then he kept asking me to read from it, so I made fun of him in turn. Eventually, we started a game: If you were an ancient Ostian, which house would you like to live in? I chose one with a delightful floor mosaic of leaping dolphins, but Mr. Cody didn't think I'd like it. "The neighborhood is full of sailors and, what's more, the schools are bad." The house he wanted had a wall mosaic featuring a male and female figure. The placard told us that it depicted Odysseus on Calypso's island.

"Did you read the *Odyssey* in school?" he asked.

"I read some of it in college for a course on Joyce's *Ulysses*."

"We had to read it as freshmen in high school, and in my senior year AP Latin class we had a special unit where we looked at some of the Greek. Odysseus is supposed to be on his way home to his wife and son in Ithaca, but he gets shipwrecked on Calypso's island and remains there for seven years."

"And takes full advantage of Calypso's hospitality, if I remember rightly."

"Yes."

"Poor wife and son."

"She enchants him! There isn't anything he can do. Besides, for the Greeks, monogamy wasn't the big deal we've made it out to be. Even though she enchants him, I think he loves her in his way. And she certainly loves him. She wants to make him immortal so that he can stay with her forever, but he keeps telling her that he wants to go home."

"But he gets home, right?"

"Eventually the gods convince Calypso to release him from her spell."

"I hate being ignorant," I said. "My Catholic high school prided itself on having dumped the classics."

"You're Catholic?"

"Twelve years of Catholic school. Does that count?"

"Not by itself, no."

"I don't go to Mass anymore, if that's what you mean. Not willingly, anyway. I go on Wednesdays to the all-school Mass because I have to. I haven't really believed in anything since I was a kid. Are you Catholic?"

"No."

"Are you anything?"

"I don't think so, no."

"But you haven't decided?"

He laughed at this, or at himself, I wasn't sure. "I wasn't raised as anything. Unless you call Wagner a religion. My father was a great lover of opera. In the evenings, after a long day at school, he would shut himself in his office at home, pour himself a brandy, light a cigar, and listen to opera on his stereo. For him, opera was the summit of Western art and as close to religion as one could get in a godless world. I once heard him say that in his religion, Wagner's *Parsifal* was the Mass."

"Do you like opera?"

"I think of myself as a fallen away Wagnerian. When I joined a rock band at school, my father practically rent his garments. Shall we crack on?"

This Britishism reminds me that I haven't said anything about Mr. Cody's voice. All this talk of his growing up in London and going to RADA and his acting career might suggest that he had a British accent. He did not. Keep in mind that his father was an American, albeit an incorrigible Anglophile, as was his mother, though Mr. Cody's grandmother on his mother's side was British. All the same, his accent was not an American one, either. It is hard to put into words the difference. Later, when I began to devour British crime dramas on PBS and would hear a British actor speaking in an American accent, I would think of Mr. Cody's voice. His had the same, just perceptible note of inauthenticity. A flattening of the vowels that was just a little too forced or at other times insufficient. Having left the States before high school, he also didn't possess the armory of American slang and pop culture allusions that I did. He was more apt to use British slang, but here too his use of a word like *bloke* or *barmy* did not sound as natural on his lips as it did, say, on Adele's. Still, he thought of himself as British, despite his American citizenship; London is where he had come of age and forged his career. But if you listened closely, his voice betrayed his status as an exile.

The wine I had brought for our picnic lunch relaxed him, and inspired by the backdrop of the ancient theatre, he told me several funny stories from his student days at RADA—like the time he unthinkingly bent down to kiss Princess Di's hand in the receiving line after a RADA performance and was nearly taken down by three security guards; the dirty pictures that he and his friends used to hide in the books and newspapers used as props; the time in a television production when he had to light his "mother's" cigarette and set her wig on fire.

As the afternoon heat intensified, we also talked about me, but after his stories of thespian hijinks, I felt like a complete bore recounting my dysfunctional childhood in Virginia and my comparatively humdrum college years. But he showed a great interest in Five Hearths and asked me lots of questions about the house and grounds and history. I told him that my mother was a patron of the Middleburg Hunt, which caused him to chortle.

"So here I am living in England, while you're the one back in America hunting foxes."

"I never actually hunted a fox. I worked the refreshments tent. The only foxes I had to worry about were the tipsy old men trying to hit on me."

Later, we could not find the perfectly romantic trattoria, so we plumped for its ironic opposite: a hideous hotel restaurant with high-backed booths, garish chandeliers, and gaudy murals. The one right in front of us showcased a ghastly imitation of Botticelli's Venus. It felt like the restaurant of a third-tier Vegas casino. There was no one in the place but us, yet it took the *maitre d'* nearly fifteen minutes to find a waiter. When the waiter finally appeared—a small man with a sweaty moustache who looked at us as though we were, somehow, lowering the tone of the place—we ordered antipasti and wine followed by pasta. It was a hoot having the whole awful place to ourselves, and we became giddier and giddier as we worked our way through the bottle of wine.

When the waiter came to remove our plates, he asked if we were interested in a second course or at least dessert. Mr. Cody looked at his watch, then at me. We were both well aware that the last train for Rome departed in fifteen minutes.

"Would you like a tiramisu and coffee or—?"

"That sounds lovely," I said.

As soon as the waiter had taken our order and his attitude away, I extended my hand across the table, and Mr. Cody took it. I did not take my eyes off Venus. I was content just to sit there not looking at him but enjoying the brave new tactility of his hand clasping mine.

"You know," he said, "Adele has been trying to throw us together since that night at Mater Dei when you covered for her."

With my free hand, I placed a strand of hair behind my ear as I failed to suppress a happily embarrassed smile.

"Adele claims to have a special sense about these things. You and I, Ms. Montclair, just have to decide how much we're going to trust her."

Early the next morning, on the train back to Rome, we cuddled together listening to tapes on my Walkman. We didn't get much sleep in that grotesque hotel, but we didn't care. I let him wear the headphones, but he stretched them so that the little foam earpad nearest to me rested on my temple and we could both, kind of, hear the music. Springsteen, "4th of July, Asbury Park (Sandy);" Dylan, "Visions of Johanna;" Clannad, "In a Lifetime;" Van Morrison, "Rave On, John Donne;" Joni Mitchell, "Chelsea Morning." He was not very familiar with my mainly American tastes, nor was I with his British ones: The Smiths, Cocteau Twins, The Fall.

Later that morning, he dropped me at my apartment. He was going back to Mater Dei to shower and change before heading to Cinecittà for the audition. I asked him to call me with the news, whatever it turned out to be. Then I kissed him for luck, and he rode away. I watched him ride all the way out of sight, aglow with that intoxicating mixture of lust, curiosity, affection, and self-interest that most people call love.

Sunday dinner. Georgetown this time, thirty years later. Carly, unmasked, greeted me at the door. "You can take that off, if you'd like," she said, referring to my mask. "No fear of death in this house." As I complied, she told me that Adele was upstairs on a phone call and would be down momentarily. She escorted me through the foyer and past the living room of the townhouse, where several people sat chatting and drinking wine. I recognized only the obese undergrads from GW who had been at the symposium. I barely paused to nod hello at them because I was following Carly down the narrow hallway toward the kitchen at the back of the house.

The square kitchen was busy. Two female caterers in white shirts, black vests, and black neckties bustled about the stove and island laying out hors d'oeuvres and preparing the meal—the same caterers, I would learn, who every first Thursday of the month prepared the skeleton cake for the Death Symposium. Behind them in the breakfast nook were two more familiar faces: Julian, the hospice nurse, and Tina, the Asian marketing director from the Toy Theatre. They were talking and drinking wine with a tall, handsome man with dreadlocks and round tortoiseshell glasses.

Julian reacted to my arrival with delight. He placed a glass of wine in my hand; ensured I remembered Tina; and introduced me to their friend, Glenroy Fortune, an artist from Trinidad teaching as an adjunct at the Corcoran Gallery School of Art and Design. Instantly I was swept up into their company, listening to Julian as he told a hilarious story of the night at the Death Symposium when a poor elderly woman *actually died* in the middle of the discussion.

"When we broke for tea and cake, she remained upright in her chair, an expression of total, rigid confusion on her face. But Adele wasn't going to let this teachable moment pass! She ordered everyone to examine the poor woman, to make a study of death as an artist makes a study of his model."

While we laughed at Julian's story, I snuck peeks at the beautifully appointed kitchen with its stone countertops, double stove, and enormous fridge with separate wine cooler. The townhouse was on P Street in Georgetown. Rented, not owned. The owner was a friend of Dr. Ashton who was happy to rent it to Adele on easy terms. Which helped explain why DC became the Death Symposium's new mission field after New York.

"Kate, darling!" Adele said as she strode into the kitchen five minutes later. "Forgive my barbaric manners. Did Julian take care of you? Julian, did you put Kate through the initiation ritual?"

"We were waiting for you, Adele," said Julian.

Adele called to one of the caterers, "Do we have sufficient pig's blood, Andie? Are you keeping it fresh?"

"It's in the fridge," Andie called back.

There was a beat or two of uneasy silence, then a blast of Adele's laughter as she hugged poor bewildered me. "Oh, Kate! You must be thinking, 'What kind of sinister cult have I walked into?'"

The interior of the house was done up in Federal-era style. When we went in to dinner, I admired the pumpkin walls of the dining room and their mirrored sconces, as well as the long, plank-topped, farm-style table with its spindle-backed chairs. There were ten of us in all, including Adele but not including Carly, who disappeared as soon as she had handed me off to Julian. Six women and four men. Besides me, Adele, Tina, and Tess the GW undergrad, the women included Rhonda, a volunteer docent at the National Gallery, and Catherine, who did something involving economic policy at a think tank. Besides Julian, Glenroy, and Duncan (the other GW undergrad), the men included a distinguished white-haired gentleman in a blue suit and orange bow tie named Pierre, who had retired from the World Bank. Pierre became a favorite as soon as he held my chair out for me. His manners were as charmingly antique as the decorations of the room.

Adele sat in the middle of the table. "A little trick I learned from James Madison and the way he hosted his dinners at Montpelier. This way I can dip in and out of every conversation." But there was only one conversation— the conversation that Adele conducted with a deft hand. She made sure that Catherine, the other newbie, and I were assimilated before conducting a survey of what everyone was reading. Later there was a *soupçon* of political talk that created an opening for Adele to give a brief update about goings on in the international Death Symposium movement. In the muted glow of the candles in the pewter candlesticks and the punched-tin chandelier above us, I marveled at how such an eclectic group managed such good conversation in which no one was left adrift. They were a tribute to Adele's rare ability to establish friendships in every walk of life. I decided that I liked them all very much, and I was glad to be included in what Julian jokingly referred to as "The P Street Illuminati."

Dinner, after the peanut soup garnished with roasted peanuts and sippets, was a vegan ratatouille, vegetarian mushroom risotto with truffle oil, and an avocado caprese salad. Dessert was a gluten-free lemon cake in the shape of a coffin (!). Afterward, coffee and liqueurs were served in the living room. Julian and the GW undergrads were happy on the floor. Tina and Catherine scrunched up together on a gorgeous double scroll bench. Pierre took the elegant Windsor chair. And I made up a threesome on the sofa with Rhonda and Glenroy. When all were settled, Adele, from her period rocking chair, led us in discussion.

"At the end of our last synod we had just gotten into Nietzsche's idea of the eternal return."

"Which I did not even begin to understand," said Rhonda.

"Good," said Adele sharply. "I'm sure Rhonda is not alone. Who can help us?"

Julian, sitting yoga-style in the acolyte's position at Adele's feet, suppressed a self-satisfied smile and jumped in. "Imagine that you were to live your life over and over again in an endless loop, without anything changing from one repetition to the next."

Rhonda looked at him thoughtfully. "You mean reincarnation?"

"Don't think of it as a metaphysical theory as much as a thought experiment. It's an attempt to encourage us to get over the idea of—well, of regret."

"It's like this," said Adele, picking up the thread. "If you don't mind living the same life over and over again, that means that you're content with your life as you have lived it. It is what it is, for all its good and bad, and you are prepared to embrace it—eternally."

"But why not *want* to change it?" Glenroy cut in. His voice was deep, and he spoke with a half-British, half-sing-song Creole accent that I wished I could hear reading to me every night as I fell asleep. "I mean, if it's only a thought experiment, why not imagine changing it for the better? Why would I want to relive growing up dirt poor in Port of Spain? Or the day I didn't win the Future Generation Art Prize?"

"Excellent," said Adele, and with a quick movement of her eyes she deferred to Pierre, who sat with his chin on his chest as he frowned at the room over the top of his glasses. At Adele's prompting, his mouth opened as he gathered his thoughts and prepared to dilate upon the theme.

"Whatever the degree of literalness by which Nietzsche embraced the idea of eternal recurrence of the same—and scholars vehemently debate the point—it seems clear that Nietzsche was trying to underscore the necessity of embracing one's life to the full. Nietzsche's whole project comes down to the idea of *joy*, joy every day, joy in every moment, no matter what happens, it's all joy. Because there are no *Hinterwelten*. No 'other worlds' but this one. So let us live so as to will to *relive* every moment for all eternity. Even when things don't work out so well, like with not winning the prize or losing someone. The point is to seek joy even in the painful moments."

"The painful moments make possible the joy," added Adele. "To keep death constantly before your mind so that you do not forget to live—*that's* the philosophy of the Death Symposium."

This was the familiar cancer memoir trope, but on a much more impressive philosophical foundation. I understood better now why a dying memoirist should want to meditate upon it.

An hour or so later, after a second round of coffee and liqueurs signaled the end of the formal program, Adele and I slipped out the kitchen door onto the deck. We stepped down into the tiny square of yard, then across to the narrow alley. We walked in and out of pools of streetlight until the house was out of view.

"That darling Pierre!" I crooned. "Can't you just see him all those years at the World Bank? Like Wallace Stevens pushing papers at the insurance company all day while writing poetry in his head, Pierre was writing loans while thinking about Nietzsche. How did you find him?"

"His wife died not long ago. I helped them arrange her deathday."

"Carly mentioned that. What's a deathday?"

"A celebration of one's life. The bookend to one's birthday."

"With cake and ice cream and presents?"

"We tailor the celebration to the needs of the dying." After a moment, Adele inquired, "Have you thought about your final day, Kate?"

It was a shock to hear this phrase applied so bluntly to myself. *Your final day.* It still didn't seem real and no doubt never would.

"I'd like to die at home," I replied. "At Five Hearths. Looking out onto my Blue Ridge Mountains. I don't want to die in a hospital or even a hospice all strung out on morphine. I want to be awake and alert and at peace."

"You don't have to say goodbye in a hospital or hospice. The whole manner of your exit is entirely in your hands."

"I hope so," I said, not really understanding what she was saying.

Adele took my arm.

"When he was dying, the poet Rilke said to his friend Madame Wunderly-Volkart, 'Help me to my own death—I don't want the doctor's death—I want my freedom.'"

"Yes," I said. "That's what I want."

"Then know that I am here to help you."

"Then help me die at Five Hearths. Help me die without pain."

"I will."

"How?"

"There are ways."

"What do you mean?"

After a hesitation Adele replied, "Drugs."

"Morphine."

"No."

"Then what?"

"Drugs that will help you die when you think it best, consciously and peacefully, on your own terms."

"Wait. You mean—"

Adele cut me off sharply. "I don't like that word. It's not bad in and of itself. It's just that it's become tainted by bogus legal controversy. I prefer to think of it as celebrating one's deathday."

"So Pierre's wife—"

"Enjoyed the most beautiful of deathdays. If you could have seen how happy and peaceful she was."

"But I thought the Commonwealth of Virginia—"

"The Commonwealth of Virginia will see reason soon enough. An unjust law is no law at all, as I believe Aquinas said. Or was it Martin Luther King?

Anyway, all the best minds have said so. You have complete moral freedom to do as you please."

"And you supply—the 'goods?'"

"I can. It is one of my discreet services as a transition celebrant."

Adele smiled in understanding of my stunned surprise.

"We can talk about details later, darling, if you wish to. Right now we're simply expanding your menu of options."

Later, as we headed back to the house, I said through silent tears, "I'm not as strong as you think. I would probably panic. You would need to be brave for both of us."

"I will always be here for you, darling," Adele assured me as she put her arm around my shoulder. "Until the very end."

CHAPTER FOUR

The Tuesday after the dinner at Adele's. An especially hard day.

As I had other things to do in the District, I met Tabitha Davie in her office to resign my position at Brook Farm Academy. Actually, I didn't officially resign. Tabitha insisted upon making it an indefinite leave of absence, in the hope that I would beat my cancer and return to the classroom one day.

This was kind of her, though I doubt either of us held out much hope. Still, it was a nice way to finish with Tabitha. We'd always had an uneasy relationship. To her, as an old school feminist not as "woke" as she and my younger colleagues, I was part of the "reactionary" arm of the faculty. Absurd, really, to be characterized as reactionary because I fought hard for my elective, 19th Century American Women Writers. Of course I wanted my students to read contemporary women writers, especially ethnic women writers and those from under-represented populations. But how were they going to make sense out of them without reading them against the backdrop of Margaret Fuller and Emily Dickinson, Louisa May Alcott and Kate Chopin? And it's not like I needed to be pushed to include Native American women voices on my syllabus. Ah, well. Today in Tabitha's office, all faculty politics were put aside. We hugged and cried and laughed and cried some more. I told her that I was sorry for being an especially exasperating gadfly, and she didn't quite apologize for her lack of respect for my experience and judgment.

And then, it was over. A teaching career of more than thirty years laid to rest in one forty-five-minute conversation with someone I never really liked. I'd taught my last class. Graded my last paper. Had my last heart-to-heart with a distraught teenager. And—it's an ill wind that blows no good—said goodbye to faculty-parent conferences, the chaperoning of Sadie Hawkins dances, and cafeteria duty.

But that was only the day's first death. Next I had to head over to my apartment, my beloved Q Street pied-à-terre, and start packing up the place.

As my lease was set to expire at the end of September anyway, it was a good time to give it up, and I had emailed my landlord accordingly. I didn't plan on keeping much of anything in the apartment. All the furniture and kitchen items would be given to a halfway house for the homeless, and the books would be donated to Brook Farm. Mrs. Abrams (the school's librarian) would be so thrilled.

I worked at the apartment until about three o'clock, when I Ubered to the National Gallery to say hello, and perhaps goodbye, to my Vincent. Because during lockdown admission to the museum was by appointment only, that morning I had gone online and reserved a time. I was there with only a small band of loyal art lovers, many of whom also wanted to spend time with my Vincent. I hung around behind the main pack of onlookers to steal peeks at him while I pretended to flirt with the other paintings. Once or twice we exchanged glances of mutual understanding. *Let them look,* we said to one another; *they will never come between us.*

What moved you, Vincent, to paint this self-portrait in a single sitting? What inspired you, after a month of seclusion and silence, to come out of your room at the asylum at Saint-Rémy and take up your painting again? What did you need to say to me? Whatever it was, it was all there in your blue-green eyes. Was it apprehension? Or loneliness? Or a knowing commiseration? The answer was D: *All of the above.* In the end, I could not tear myself away from your eyes. O Vincent! How was I supposed to endure this?

Your eyes replied, *La tristesse durera toujours.* The sadness will last forever.

The day's third death occurred that evening. At nine o'clock, I met with Adele and Julian at Adele's townhouse, a meeting Adele and I had arranged before I left on Sunday night.

"Kate is dying," Adele announced to Julian. He had come into the townhouse about ten minutes after I did, but from the alley, like a secret agent. The three of us sat in the living room drinking limoncello, but this time I—not Pierre—sat in the Windsor chair.

"She doesn't want to put either herself or her loved ones through the torture of a slow, painful decline. She wants to make her farewells while she is still herself."

Julian only half-playfully genuflected before me and grasped me by the hands.

"You can do this, girl," he said. "You can stick it to the universe. The universe doesn't give two hoots about us, so why should we lie in bed waiting for it to tell us when our cue is? We'll die when we want to! You hear that, Universe! *We'll die whenever we want to!*"

Julian then flew around the living room shadow-boxing the Universe as Adele and I laughed.

"So," he continued, breathing heavily at the end of the round, "you'd like to organize your deathday."

"She's still thinking about it, Julian," Adele cautioned him.

"Of course."

"But no matter what, Kate wants to die at Five Hearths, her house out in the Virginia countryside."

"That will be no problem," Julian said, sitting down again. "No problem at all."

"It is Julian," Adele explained to me, "who will, if you choose, procure the elements you need."

"How much do they cost?"

"Don't worry about that now, Kate," Adele said. "There will be time for those details. And the Death Symposium will assist you in whatever way you may need."

"But what are the 'elements?'"

"Without getting too technical," Julian explained, "there is an initial cocktail taken about an hour before the culmination of the deathday ceremony. This is to prepare the intestines and to prevent nausea and vomiting. The second cocktail is the life-ending solution. Each cocktail is some two to four ounces. Not much to drink, especially if your strength and energy are pretty good, but they will taste bitter."

"And how long—"

"Coma ensues typically five to ten minutes after the second cocktail. You will experience no pain. It will be no different than falling asleep."

"And then—"

"Death will follow in its own good time," Adele intervened. "It is impossible to say when exactly. But it will be a quiet, beautiful time for your loved ones to be with you and cherish you."

I had assumed it would go down something like this, but still my mind went wobbly as I listened to Julian lay it out. "Assisted suicide," as it is called, is not an issue I had ever paid much attention to. Flickering through my mind were images from an old *60 Minutes* episode I had watched in school that featured a gaunt and gruesome Dr. Kevorkian with his crew cut, portable apparatus, and van. The legality, not to mention the ethics, of the thing had always struck me as preposterous. Of course we should be able to do whatever we want with our bodies. Why should anyone have the power to dictate to us when we die? But this was when it was a debate question, not anything to do with me.

"How do you get a hold of the stuff?" I asked Julian. "I suppose you have to steal it?"

"Do I have to answer that?"

"Is that what you did for Pierre's wife?"

"Kate, please," said Adele, "We cannot speak about the private decisions of other clients."

"But Julian is going to have to *steal* it?"

"The drug is for the dying," Julian replied. "And you *are* the dying."

"But I don't want you or Adele to get into trouble."

"Pish. Julian and I are happy to assume any risk that is required," said Adele. "But we would need to take care not to arouse suspicion. Dr. Ladd, I understand, is on record as saying that your tumor could take you more or less at any time. That helps us significantly. But if you decide to arrange your deathday, Kate, you need to be careful about who you invite to it. Don't invite anyone who is not of one mind with you."

Adele motioned for me to stand so that she could hold me as I cried.

"You wouldn't be alone, Kate," she whispered as she held me close. "It would be a beautiful day. A day of celebration. Can you see it?"

I couldn't see it. Not yet. But the thing was, even to deliberate the possibility of celebrating my deathday meant that I had to make my world one of secrets.

The day after I met with Adele and Julian, Lisa treated me to a "boozy happy hour" at a tiny table along the sidewalk outside Kramerbooks. For years, we had called such confabs our "boozy happy hour," but at this one, for me, there was nothing stronger than unsweetened iced tea. They don't tell you on the list of Glio symptoms that one of the first things to go, tragically, is the stomach for alcohol. Lisa, however, picked up the slack with a maple bourbon smash, with which she toasted my "three decades of *not-yet-finished* service to the virtually lost arts of reading and writing."

She also gave me a present. Two presents, actually. The first was an offer to help me clean out my classroom. The second made me weepy: a gift certificate for three days and two nights at the Fox Hollow Resort in Middleburg, including several booked appointments at its spa.

"Is the spa even open?" I asked.

"Restricted capacity, by reservation only. But I set you up, baby. I got you booked for a mani, pedi, hot stone deep tissue massage, and time in the aqua thermal suite."

Leave it to Lisa to know that what I really needed was a weekend in a thermal cocoon.

"Thank you, my friend." I stood up to give her a hug. "Thank you so much. I want you to come with me!"

"That would be fun," Lisa said after I sat down again. "But my presence would also restrict your ability to hook up with a tall handsome stranger from the pool."

"Lisa!"

"But maybe you could pass me off as your lady's maid. On hand to remove those little foam toe-dividers after your pedi. But then we'd have to get me my own room. Too expensive!"

I know she would have loved to go with me. But as she doubtless had already dipped deeply into her savings to finance my gift, her joining me was out of the question. Graciously, though not without pushing a point, she added, "I think a solitary retreat in a beautiful place, with a little pampering, will help you get your game on. Not that I'm against your meeting a tall handsome stranger by the pool."

She then asked me about my resignation—er, leave of absence.

"I don't know what I feel about it," I said. "Retirement is a little death, and like the big death, it doesn't give you a final summary chapter like in Austen or Dickens, where every loose end is tied up. You just fade to black and it's over."

After Lisa finished her cocktail, we ordered something to eat. Faint nausea was now a constant companion, and a small bowl of gazpacho was about all I thought I could handle, and I wasn't even sure about that. Lisa got a wagyu cheeseburger. By the time our food was served, Lisa must have figured that her remarkable restraint thus far had earned her a point-blank question.

"So. Tell me what's going on with your treatment? Have you started chemo and radiation? Did Dr. Ladd want to do them at the same time or sequentially?"

I could have lied, but I knew I couldn't make the lie hold up for very long. Especially when my hair didn't fall out. But I also knew that if I told the truth, I risked getting into an argument as well as having to evade Lisa's prying questions about what kind of strategy I *was* going to pursue. In the end, only one path seemed sustainable.

"I'm not doing chemo and radiation, Lisa. Not right now, anyway."

Lisa stared at me incredulously. I looked away and took a long sip of my tea while she continued to stare.

"Sweetie," she finally said, glistening tears in her frustrated eyes, "can you help me understand how you are proposing to treat your Stage IV brain cancer?"

"With disdain," I answered.

I thought it was a good line, but it only tried my dear friend's patience.

"Chemo and radiation can keep you alive, Kate. For *years*. Perhaps *indefinitely*. Does that not appeal to you? I'm not trying to be harsh here. I'm just trying to understand why my Kate is not fighting to save her life."

"There's more than one way to fight," I said.

"So, how are you fighting? Homeopathy? Antioxidants? Faith healing? What? Tell me."

"I'm researching alternative therapies, yes. I just ask you to respect my process. It's *my* brain tumor, not yours."

"What alternative therapies?"

"Can we talk about something else? Hey, did that dentist you went out with ever call you?"

"You can't tell me what you've been researching?"

"I haven't made any kind of decision yet, OK? I'm still researching. Sorry, Ms. Silverman, I didn't realize I was late with my homework."

I slumped back in my chair, exhausted and more intensely nauseous. Lisa gave me the shady eye. "Did you go to the Death Seminar?"

"Yes, Lisa. I went to the Death Symposium. And you know? It was interesting."

"Did that friend of yours—Adele?—did she talk you into not doing chemo and radiation?"

"Thank you, Lisa, for crediting me with a mind of my own."

"I just want to know. Did she or her group have anything to do with your decision?"

"Why are you grilling me like this?"

"I want to know why you're acting so—"

"So—"

"So *heedless.*"

"Good usage, there, girl. Does the thesaurus give that as a synonym for *stupid?*"

"I'm not calling you stupid. I just think you're not going about this in a way that's really going to help you. What happened at the Death Thing?"

"I don't really feel like talking about that right now. You'd only make fun of it."

"You got that right. I looked at their website. It's all about planning your funeral and deciding which one of your favorite childhood books you want in your casket with you. It's ridiculous. It's morbid. It's a waste of time and energy. *You have brain cancer, Kate, and you need to start getting it treated!*"

I paused and tried to assemble my warring thoughts before I delivered what came next.

"You know, Lisa. Even *you* have a line with me that you shouldn't cross. Maybe it would be best if I didn't accept your gift of the resort weekend."

"Kate. No. Please, Kate—"

"And maybe I should go now too."

"Kate. Please. I'm sorry. Kate, please sit down. I'm worried about you."

"Thanks for the happy hour," I said, throwing my purse strap around my shoulder.

"Kate," she whispered through pursed lips. Even with the social distance, we had attracted the curiosity of the people at other tables. "Please. Sit down. Just for a minute. *Please*."

I sat down, but only on the edge of my chair.

"I apologize for being a noodge. All right? I'm sorry. But I am really, really, *really worried* about you. I want to help you through this. Let me help you."

"Where do you think you'll be two years from now, Lisa? Most likely, I will be dead. That's the fact. No disputing it. In two years, I'll just be poor Kate, your old friend who 'lost her battle' with cancer."

"No! That's not—"

"I have seen how brutal chemo and radiation can be. I saw it with my mother. I don't want to go through all that just so I can soak up a couple extra months of cognitive impairment, speech loss, seizures, and blindness. I do not see the point. I. Am. Dying. The 'game,' as you and Dr. Brawny Ladd like so spiritedly to call it, is *over*."

During my hot stone deep tissue massage, I fell asleep, and when I awoke, it was the afterlife. I lay on the massage bed, face down in the facial cradle, dead. I had done it. I had passed over the threshold of consciousness. Easy as falling asleep.

The next hour of the afterlife, I spent in the aqua thermal suite. Only one other woman was present when I arrived, but then she was gone, vaporized, apparently, in a puff of aromatic steam. It was a good time to be at the resort: in the middle of September, all the kids back at school, still warm, a limited number of guests. I didn't want anyone else to suffer, but I couldn't help thanking you, COVID, for keeping so many people away.

After a Caribbean storm shower, I put on my robe and reclined in one of the three radiant-heated loungers. I sipped strawberry water and, to the ethereal pulsations of spa music, I watched soothing videos of waterfalls and trickling creeks.

I cried a lot more these days. I was crying again as I sweated in the sauna, and as I took my arctic mist shower, and as I inhaled the aromatic steam in the herbal cocoon. I cried until I had cried myself out. Then I took a plain shower and blow-dried my hair.

Back in my room, I put on my resort robe, as I was not going down to one of the restaurants for dinner. While I waited for room service, I scooped the little bottles of shampoo, conditioner, body lotion, and the unwrapped facial bar into the plastic laundry bag from the closet. I did this every day I was at the resort, not because I was ever likely to use them all but because they were superfluous and spoke of beauty and peace. This world does not often manage an overflow of grace, but when it does, one must seize it.

My room was on the ground floor of the hotel and had a large porch with a full patio set. I ate my dinner in a reclining chair and watched the evening sun go down. Dinner was steak and french-fried potato wedges with salad and bread. I took a selfie of me, or the lower half of me, with the tray on my lap, and texted it to Lisa:

> *Thank you so much for this fabulous gift. I am sitting here feeling so blessed that I have a friend like you in a time like this. Love, Kate*

> *P.S. Great resort but the pool was dismayingly devoid of tall handsome strangers.*

Lisa and I had cooled down and patched it up while still at Kramerbooks. I loved her so much. I knew I was making her crazy not doing chemo and radiation. But I also knew that I couldn't talk to her about what I was contemplating. Apart from Adele's request that I not tell anyone, I didn't think celebrating a deathday was something that Lisa could accommodate in her worldview. She was born to fight, even when all was lost. She wouldn't understand a decision to fall on one's sword.

Chloe, my therapist, might understand, and how I *longed* to talk with her. But if I told her everything, I would both break my promise to Adele and put Chloe in the awkward position of having knowledge that one of her clients was committing a crime. She would have to report me. I was scheduled to see Chloe the following week, but I would cancel that appointment. I couldn't go in and conceal things from her. I would break. After ten invaluable years of her support, I had come to the end with Chloe. I was beyond therapy now.

While I was looking at my phone, Benedict texted me. I still hadn't gotten together with him, and I had let his texts pile up in my effort to keep him at bay. Out of boredom, I replied to this one, telling him that I was "out of town" and would "be in touch" when I returned.

My desire to be festive was more robust than my appetite. I could hardly eat more than a few bites of the steak, potato, and bread, and the very sight of the salad repulsed me. Dessert was a chocolate cake which I, after sampling, wrapped back up and put in the mini fridge. In the middle of the night, when I couldn't sleep, I would be glad I had saved it.

When it was dark, I changed into jeans and a hoodie and ambled down to the tranquility garden, which stayed open until 9:00 p.m. A man and his wife in their late sixties, maybe, sat together holding hands on one of the cushioned wicker sofas by the fire pit. Happy days. They had already lived a decade more than I would, and they would probably live at least a decade beyond my time. I sat along the edge of the whirlpool and dipped my toes into the warm, churning water. When the couple vamoosed, I moved over to the fire pit. It was getting chilly. In my pocket, I'd brought a mini bottle of whisky—maybe my last drink if I could stomach it—which I did my best to do as I stared into the gas-powered flames.

In recent days, I had spent more hours online lurking in various cancer chat rooms. I knew this made me vulnerable to anyone spying on my surfing history (*Why was she talking with people about foregoing chemo and radiation? What other plan was she concocting?*), but I couldn't get enough of these conversations. Everyone was a perfect angel to everyone else: helpful, encouraging, generous with best wishes and prayers. It didn't hurt that no one was related or had to deal with any of the others face-to-face. But we all benefited by the enormous positive energy generated by the hive mind, and I considered some of these faceless, mostly anonymous people to be my friends. Here's to you, especially, LindaR, cancerNINJA, and GeeGee! From your grateful friend, ShelleyM.

The result of my research confirmed the following: chemo and radiation were pointless exercises that would likely destroy whatever quality of life I had left (as they did to poor GeeGee's husband). Sure, there were outliers, but they always had a spouse able to devote his or her entire life to their care. I didn't have that luxury, but even if I did have a devoted spouse, I'm not sure I would want to turn him into my twenty-four seven nurse. Steroids and painkillers would probably be enough, LindaR and cancerNINJA assured me, to help me manage my symptoms for a while. Which is why I had chosen November 2, my real birthday, as my deathday.

In Catholic school, I had learned that November 2 was All Souls' Day, but I hadn't retained anything more than the title. Recently, I had looked it up on Wikipedia. All Souls' Day was also known as the Commemoration of All the Faithful Departed as well as the Day of the Dead. All Saints' Day was the day before, November 1, anticipated by All Hallows' Eve. All Souls' Day was not for the saints in Heaven but for the souls in Purgatory, the ones who didn't quite make the A-team. That was me, certainly. I wouldn't even qualify as one of the *faithful* departed. Still, I liked the congruence of this bit of Catholic lore with the day I had chosen to take my life. Not because it meant anything to me in terms of religion but because I liked the poetry of it.

This date gave me about six weeks to set my lands in order, but it also wasn't so far away that I risked being incapacitated before I got there. That was as painless a death as was possible for me.

So, yes, I had decided to take my own life. If my health forced me to move up the date, then I would. But if my condition proved stable enough, then I had exactly forty-three days left of existence on this planet, not counting today or the deathday itself.

When did I make my decision? In the swimming pool that afternoon? In the herbal cocoon? I think I made it right there in the tranquility garden, staring into the gas flames of the fire pit.

I was not contemplating suicide. Adele was right: the tumor in my brain was killing me; I was simply choosing to confront the killer on my own terms. In the open field.

It helped to keep reminding myself: there was no real alternative. It was not like I was deciding between taking my life and going on living. There was no choice of that kind. I was going to die soon anyway; it was only a matter of how.

The act itself, the drinking of the cocktails, I thought I could manage, though it would be easier if someone were giving me a hot stone deep tissue massage as I shuffled off this mortal coil. What was hardest was the realization that my life was not going to add up to anything, that I was going to take to my grave an existence very much *manqué*. There was so much more I wanted to have done, so much more love that I had hoped to give and to be given.

How I wished I could do it all over again, even if I were only going to die again of cancer at the age of fifty-six. But those weren't the rules of the game. The *real* game: not Dr. Brawny Ladd's or Lisa's game. The real game was not designed for winning; it was not really designed at all. It was a maze of randomly shifting partitions that shunted you round and round in a circle while you thought—you hoped—you were making progress. Quite a trick.

While sitting there in the tranquility garden, I went back to Rome again. Quickly, Mr. Cody and I established a routine. Rarely did he ever come to my apartment. Once or twice I made us dinner there, but with roommates, it was never private enough. Adele, however, as she often went away on the weekends, encouraged us to treat her apartment as our own. She lived by herself, near the Vatican, in one of those typical Roman out-of-the-way apartment buildings situated at the end of an obscure alley with a plain door without any intercom buzzers outside. Yet when you turned the key and walked in, you found a metal-and-concrete stairway leading up to two floors of simple studios. The design of Adele's studio was functional, even dreary, and was perhaps not the least of the reasons why she was always on the move. Half of the main room was taken up by the queen-sized bed and the other half by her dining table and kitchenette. Down a little hallway was the bathroom, galley-shaped, with its signature Italian phone-booth shower stall and bidet. The place was not much to look at, and Adele did nothing with it, having neither time nor patience for even the simplest forms of interior decoration. Yet this was my and Mr. Cody's "Hidden Cave of Wonders."

I did my best to remain detached, but it was hard not to think about what today we would call our "status." "I don't know what he's thinking," I confided to Adele, "but I guess I'm simply taking each day as it comes."

"Hemingway described this kind of situation best," Adele advised me. "You live day to day as in a war. What is the point of wanting more than that?"

Mr. Cody got the part of the husband in the film adaptation of *The Public Image*. Over a celebratory dinner at a tiny trattoria near the Colosseum, we sang hallelujahs in praise of Adele, whose influence upon Roberto, Mr. Cody was convinced, had more to do with his getting the part than his audition. Filming would commence in the spring.

"And I'm back with my agent," he told me. "Helen was not a little miffed when I told her I was leaving the business for a while. I thought she'd never want to speak to me again. But she was a sweetheart when I rang her up the other day. She thinks the film will help fudge over the fact that I've been out of the game for two years."

I experienced slight judderings of panic as he continued to make references to a future in London, apparently without me.

"I'm going to ditch my position at Mater Dei if the head refuses to accommodate my shooting schedule. I'll wait tables until the shoot if I have to. But even if the head is grand about all that, I'm going to give him my notice as soon as I sign the contract, probably next week. My schoolmastering days, probably no one will be sorry to hear, least of all my students, are coming to a close. This film is my passport back to my real life."

As my inner organs dissolved into water, I began talking, in the most uninformed, schoolgirl terms, of moving to New York as soon as I began "publishing regularly." Then I burst into tears when he interrupted me by reaching for my hand and saying, "But I thought you might like to come to London with me."

Later that night, in our Hidden Cave of Wonders, we were up late talking, and I descried upon the floor a green scapular.

"Yippee!" I sang. "We got one!"

"What's that?" Mr. Cody said.

"Don't you know about the mystery of the green scapulars?"

"Is that an Agatha Christie?"

"It's the most exciting thing that's ever happened in these parts! Someone is sneaking into our abodes and planting green scapulars underneath our pillows. First it happened to Lucas and Shia Lu. Then to Astrid and Rory. Now us! They don't *steal* anything, nothing so much as a banana out of the fruit bowl. They simply tuck the scapular underneath the pillow and run. Lucas thinks everyone gets one who's having sex outside the marital bond."

"They leave it underneath the pillow?"

"Yes. Ours fell on the floor, though."

"Someone should call the police."

"What are we supposed to tell them? That there's a madman on the loose desperately concerned for our spiritual welfare?"

"It's breaking and entering."

"It's deliciously gothic! Do you think we're being watched right now? Oh, I'm going to keep ours forever and forever."

Early the next morning, I rolled over and discovered him standing by the window, peeking through the curtains.

"I hope I didn't wake you."

"What are you doing?"

He hesitated before answering. "Standing guard."

"Against what?"

"The fiends of the green scapular."

"Aw. You're being protective."

I went and stood beside him and rested my head on his shoulder. He smoothed my hair with one hand and pulled back the curtain with the other.

"You don't have to worry," I said.

"That's what they *want* you to think."

I lifted my head. "Are you really standing guard?"

"I don't like the thought of someone spying on us."

"I admit it's creepy."

"Breaking into people's apartments? That's not just creepy. That's a threat."

"A *threat*? You think they're going to try and hurt one of us?"

"I don't know."

He put his arm around me and pulled me close.

"I just don't like the thought that someone is watching us. That they know things about us. This is *our* world, Ms. Montclair, and I won't be trespassed upon."

"So what are we going to do, Mr. Cody? Run away?"

"That's right," he said. "We're going to run away. We're going to book tickets on a packet for the other side of the world where we'll go by Dr. and Mrs. Bram Carbuncle. I'll wear a fake beard and walk with a pronounced limp, and you'll dye your hair green, black out one tooth, and wear an eye-patch."

"I don't think I could kiss a man in a fake beard. Even if I were wearing an eye-patch."

"Well, you're going to have to get used to it, Mrs. Carbuncle. There's going to be plenty of sacrifice ahead."

You were right, Mr. Cody. There was plenty of sacrifice ahead.

For a long time there at the fire pit in the tranquility garden, I sat with him, imagining him in my arms as I stared into the flames. I couldn't help thinking of the way he looked when last I kissed him, when they were putting him in the ambulance. I remembered how as soon as we heard the siren in the distance, someone, maybe Adele, took little Miranda away. She called out for her daddy, not understanding why he wouldn't wake up.

I was still sitting with Mr. Cody and Miranda when a security guard came up to tell me that the tranquility garden was closed.

But before I left, I texted Carly, in code, that I wanted to schedule my deathday for the day of my birthday, November 2.

PART III

The Mad Flight

CHAPTER ONE

O n the Tuesday after my weekend at the resort, I had an appointment with Dr. Brawny Ladd. It was brief. I brought up my interest in alternative therapies for cancer: herbal remedies, homeopathic treatments, megadoses of vitamin C, and one or two other outside-the-box approaches. He rather curtly dismissed these "therapies," saying that there was no scientific evidence to support them and that, at any rate, they "weren't the object of his expertise." He probably wanted to ask if I was going to wear my tin-foil hat to the drugstore to get vitamin C, but he bit his lip and encouraged me one more time to undergo chemo and radiation.

"You're in your mid-fifties and in good physical shape," he said. "There's every reason to expect that your outcomes would be positive. There's also the cyberknife, remember."

Now it was my turn to be adamant. I thanked him for his time and efforts, but I had decided against conventional therapies. And with that, we parted.

I didn't expect him to understand my decision, but it was important to go see him anyway. As Adele and I had talked through beforehand, it would have been strange, and later it might have even raised a red flag, if I had disappeared from his list of gravely ill patients without any kind of explanation. He now had me pegged as an alternative therapy wacko, but that was all right. There was nothing illegal in drinking medicinal teas and vitamin C by the gallon. Not that I had any intention of pursuing such a regimen. My online research had revealed some anecdotal evidence of the effectiveness of these alternative therapies but no hard scientific support. I'd ordered some teas that promised some salutary palliative effects, but that was all I planned to do.

Later that day, after school, Lisa came over to help me clean the bathrooms and kitchen of my Q Street apartment. It was almost the end of September, and so I had only a week or so before my lease expired.

Before Lisa got down to cleaning and I got down to sorting and purging, we sat together with an afternoon cup of tea.

"This one is supposed to help with the headaches," I said as I raised my special herbal brew to her good health. The day before, I had told her that I was only going to see Dr. Brawny Ladd to talk about alternative therapies, that I had definitively made my decision not to undergo chemo and radiation or his cyberthingy. She did not express any desire to join in via Zoom. Now, watching me sip my tea, she looked inconsolable, like one of Socrates's friends watching the eccentric old philosopher drink the fatal hemlock.

"So, that's it?" Lisa asked sadly. "You're just going to drink tea and hope for the best?"

"Better than losing all this gorgeous hair to radiation, don't you think?"

"No, I don't. Your hair would grow back."

"Sure. Just in time for me to get a new 'do' at the funeral parlor."

"What does Adele think of your decision?"

I'm so proud of you, Kate, had been Adele's response. I told her of my decision by phone before I left the Fox Hollow Resort. In that conversation, she revised the suggestion she had made at Your Mama's Tandoor about my writing a general account of the Death Symposium. Now, she wanted me to write a memoir of the events leading up to my deathday.

"I want the whole word to know about you, Kate, and what you will have done," Adele enthused. "We'll call it *Apologia Pro Morte Sua*. The book will make you a hero and give a voice to so many now who are voiceless."

"Adele is fine with my decision," I replied to Lisa.

"But does she *agree* with what you're doing?"

"She respects my decision."

"Without taking a side?"

"She only said that she understands why someone in my situation would want to pursue the course I am pursuing."

"I don't get it," Lisa said, shaking her head. "I'm sorry, but I don't get it. Tell me, what's the philosophy of the Death Symposium when it comes to end-of-life issues?"

"It's not like that. The Death Symposium doesn't have a philosophy about anything. It only exists to provide people with a venue to talk about death."

"Adele has no views on these matters?"

"She facilitates the discussions. She doesn't give lectures."

"I see." Lisa quietly sipped her tea.

Why are we shy about encountering old friends, especially friends who knew us in our youth? Is it because it feels like extortion? Like they have pictures of us (in braces, with eighties blow-dried hair, with acne) and are threatening to sell them to the tabloids? Perhaps that's part of it. We've come a long way, baby, and we don't want to be identified with the gangly, dweeby youths we were then.

But when it came to Benedict, that was not quite everything. Seeing him again involved weightier baggage. The prospect gave me a paranoid fear of what he knew about me, as though at one time he had seen me turn coward and flee from battle.

Why did I finally cave and agree to meet him for a drink? It was hard to say. He rang me one afternoon while I was cleaning out Q Street, and I answered the call. As we caught up, I felt mean for having put him off so long. And as I didn't have a good excuse to put him off any longer, I accepted his invitation to get together.

I suggested we meet that afternoon. This was part of my plan to dispatch two difficult obligations in one fell swoop of a day. I had already agreed to meet Hailee Redfield and Rosamund Craig, two seniors from Brook Farm, at three o'clock. I had received any number of lovely notes and emails from students in the past couple of weeks, but these two insisted on taking me out for coffee at Cool Beans and a real farewell. I did everything I could to ease the pressure off them, but they struggled to be comfortable around a dying woman. I ended up giving them a little homily about never abandoning the search for solace and meaning in great literature. My farewell address. It seemed to touch them, but to me the words were ash in my mouth. As we hugged goodbye, poor Hailee melted down and Rosamund almost had to pick her up and carry her, bawling, out of the coffee shop.

After that, I fixed my face and Ubered down to the Hamilton to meet Benedict.

I let him order me a Manhattan, as I didn't want to answer any of his questions about why I wasn't drinking alcohol. I had no intention of telling him about my illness, but before I knew it, I was telling him all sorts of other stuff I hadn't planned to tell him about my not real marriage.

"What is a not real marriage?" he inquired politely. "I thought you were divorced."

"You don't know what a not real marriage is? It's totally a thing. After our so-called 'divorce,' Tim reconnected with an old friend from high school, a genuine Mass-every-Sunday-and-then-some Catholic widow. She persuaded Tim to take up again the faith of his childhood. Given what Tim told her of his and my attitude at the time of our nuptials, the widow convinced Tim to seek an annulment. That's Catholic for a piece of official paper that says your so-called marriage never happened. It may have looked like a marriage, it may have cost you emotionally like a marriage and taken years of your life that you will never get back like a marriage, but, when all the canonical dust clears, it was never really a marriage. 'But surely there have to be grounds!' Of course. The court of celibate priests found that we had never been open to children. If you're keeping score, that's a trespass against Canon 1101, section 2, *The willful exclusion of children*. On strictly legal grounds, it was no contest. Tim and I had signed a homemade prenup, one stipulation of which was that we would not have offspring. It was all Tim's idea. Something about changing diapers and dropping the kids at soccer practice in a minivan offended his sense of dignity as an *artiste*. I only went along with it because I was sure, once we were married, I would be able to change his mind. Alas.

"The widow, of course, had a dog in the hunt. As the resourceful mother of five children, she wanted Tim morally free so that she could marry him herself. So the irony is, Tim, who once reeled at the very thought of children and who all the time I lived with him thought about God about as much as he thought about the local economy of Whanganui, New Zealand, became absolutely and totally and canonically married with five kids. When last heard of, he was going to Mass every Sunday and running the spaghetti suppers at the parish with his brother Knights of Columbus."

"Where do he and the widow and the five kids live?"

"Down in Houston."

Benedict nodded, then said, "I'm sorry."

"I'm not," I replied.

Why was I babbling about Tim and my not real marriage? It couldn't be on account of the bourbon. I was only touching the Manhattan to my lips and pretending to drink. I made Benedict talk.

He had never married. "I've been in one or two lengthy relationships over the years, each of which began magically and each of which ended with us sick to death of one another and happy to get away." He told me more about his work, which was quite fascinating. He had left Mater Dei the same summer I left WIX and started a degree in architecture. Then he studied to become an historical renovator. After serving for several years as an apprentice, he opened his own shop.

"I love the work," he said. "It's satisfying to come upon something in a severe state of decomposition and to think through the problems of how to renovate it."

"Don't get excited," I shot back. "I think I'm beyond renovation." He laughed at the joke, and I said, "Tell me more about what sorts of buildings you work on."

"Lots of churches and castles. Renaissance era. Gothic and Romanesque."

"Like what's being done at Notre Dame in Paris."

"Actually, I've been asked to consult a bit on that reconstruction."

"Really?"

"I've become something of an expert on the use of laser scanning technology to reveal the structural secrets of old buildings. They've invited me in to do an assessment. A long way from teaching Italian and art history at Mater Dei."

"How did you get interested in historical renovation?"

He didn't seem to want to answer at first. Finally, he said, "My mother's villa—you probably don't remember—used to be a Dominican priory. The main house was built out of the remains of the original chapter house and dormitory."

"I remember it."

How many weekend parties did we have out there at the villa? Memory stacked them like emails, so that it seemed we were out there every weekend. But really there were probably only three or four parties. Sometimes the countess was there, sometimes not. She was a stock character out of a Golden Age Hollywood comedy: beautiful, pampered, witty. She breakfasted late every morning in bed before her maid helped her do her face and hair. At noon, she appeared downstairs in an elegant housecoat and slippers, with a cigarette burning like incense in an honest-to-Holly-Golightly cigarette holder. As for her ex-husband, the count, we never clapped eyes on him. Of dubious Italian nobility, he was, in the single photograph the countess kept of him, short and dapper with a goatee and the nose he gave Benedict. There were beaucoup bedrooms in the villa, but we didn't use them; we spent the nights sprawled all over the living room on couches or roughing it on the floor with a throw pillow. We were young with young backs. During their marriage, the count and countess collected modern art, and even after their divorce, the countess retained an impressive stockpile. There was a little Giacometti sculpture in a display case. A Miró on the wall. A Mondrian. Mr. Cody and I couldn't sleep one night, so we walked around the grounds until dawn talking about Joyce's *Ulysses*, a book I had made up my mind to finally finish that year. (I never made it past "Aeolus.") How intellectual I felt roaming about that house.

But I remembered, also, the villa on another dawn. No party this time. Someone escorted me into to a small bedroom tucked away in a corner upstairs. Brought me a cup of tea, then left and shut the door. There was a single painting on the wall at the end of the single bed. A Dalí. *A Study for the Madonna of Port Lligat*. I was in that bedroom a long time. It was very quiet. There was tumult downstairs, but it was whispered tumult. I must have been in shock because I did not remember thinking or feeling anything. It was as if my thoughts and emotions were in a perfect state of mindfulness. I sipped my tea, rapt by *The Madonna of Port Lligat*. Everything in the painting was splitting apart. The great blocks and arch of the Madonna's throne. The Madonna herself with a fissure breaking through her head. Her chest and womb opened like a window to the sea, revealing the Christ Child floating like a fetus in amniotic fluid, holding a tiny cross. All the gravity in the frame was giving way; the eternal was breaking through, absorbing into itself the Madonna and her Child. How I would have liked to be absorbed with them. And how I would have liked to find everything neatly put together again on the other side. But earlier that morning, I had held Mr. Cody in the crossing of my arms and, looking up into the rosy-fingered dawn, seen gravity holding the earth and sun in perfect tension, with absolutely nothing breaking through.

Benedict was still talking about how he got started on his career.

"Even though he was divorced from my mother and had given the place to her, my father hired a firm to complete the reconstruction project at the villa. The summer after I quit Mater Dei, I hung around the crew, watching them and asking a lot of questions. The process fascinated me. I guess I just like the combination of working with my hands, with beautiful architecture, and with history. I like the travel too, but it's a mixed blessing. You have to go where the work is. I keep apartments in Rome and in London, but I rarely spend a night in either one."

I asked him when he would head to Paris for the Notre Dame job.

"I have to stay on here for a while. Clear out Mother's apartment at Arcadia and settle her affairs, which are a complete mess."

"Adele said she was from DC."

"She grew up here and, I suppose, wanted to find her end in her beginning. At first she had an apartment on Connecticut Avenue, but about three years ago, she moved to Arcadia."

"How old was she when she pas—when she died?"

"Ah. You've been learning from Adele. Mother was eighty-seven."

"Were you able to be with her at the end?"

"Not at the very end, unfortunately. But we spent a lot of time together in her final three months. She was anxious during that time. I knew Adele had brought the Death Symposium to DC and thought Mother might find it helpful. She didn't have any of the equipment that might help her deal with death."

"Equipment?"

"Like religion. Or even a robust, scientifically informed stoicism."

"What do you make of the Death Symposium? Do you think it's all hooey?"

"To be honest, I'm not sure. It may be. Though about one thing, Adele seems to me to be right. We *are* repressed when it comes to death. We need to talk about it out loud. Are you religious?"

"Me? No. You?"

He swirled the question around his mind as he had swirled the first taste of the Manhattan around his palate. "I can sometimes work myself up to being a doubting nihilist."

"What does that mean?"

"Well. For example, Sunday mornings, when I want to sleep in, I'm definitely a nihilist. Wednesday afternoons, however, you might find me staring out a window, mulling over Cardinal Newman's argument for God's existence based upon human conscience." He stopped himself, smiled, and picked up his drink. "But I believe you've already heard enough from me on that subject."

"Don't worry, I can take it. Go on."

But he was intent on changing the subject. He asked me some questions about my teaching career, but I brought us back to the Death Symposium.

"Did the Death Symposium help your mother?"

"Not much, I don't think. Maybe a little. If she had found something like it when younger, it might have had more of an impact."

"What did she do with all that art, by the way?"

"You remember the art! She sold most it off to museums and private collectors."

He fidgeted with the laminated card advertising the daily drink specials. He was thinking hard about something. His lips began to make the shape of a word, like he had something he wanted to ask me. I pretended to sip my drink until he was able to get it out.

"Did you see that street woman at the Death Symposium earlier in the month?"

"Yes. I saw you give her money. Do you think that's a good idea? You're probably only supporting her drug habit."

Benedict cringed at this and sat back in his chair. After another lengthy pause, he said, "You never knew my mother as anything other than 'countess.'"

"No. Everyone called her 'countess.'"

"Her name was Irene. The street woman you saw at the Death Symposium used to work as an aide at Arcadia, a glorified gopher. I helped her get the job. She and Mother became attached. Mother helped her out in various ways."

"With money?"

"Sometimes. After mother died, she stopped coming to work and got fired. Now she works at a hotel, taking care of the—"

"Swimming pool."

"Among other things, yes. How did you know?"

"She told me. I tried to talk to her that night at the Death Symposium. So let me guess: you promised your mother that you would continue to help her."

"No."

"No?"

"I promised someone else. I promised *her* mother."

A wave of goose flesh spread down my arms and the back of my neck even as my chest constricted. I sensed a threat, a predator lurking. With barely enough air in my throat to voice the question, I asked, "Benedict, have I met this street woman before?"

He looked at me. "Yes, Kate. You have met her before."

I had met her before. And her mother. It was on a Saturday morning after the farmer's market in the Campo de' Fiori, and Adele and I were walking from the bus stop back to her apartment laden with our booty. I carried bags filled with artichokes and arugula lettuce, fava beans and fresh-cut flowers. After putting away her own stuff, Adele's plan was to tootle off to Perugia, where she would spend the rest of the weekend at the country house of one of her politically motivated friends. I, meanwhile, planned to stay at Adele's and make something involving artichokes for me and Mr. Cody.

But as we approached Adele's building, we discovered a car—a green Fiat Spider, cute as you please—parked at an odd angle in the alley. The driver's-side door was open, as though an international superspy had just hopped out of the driver's seat and raced inside. Our attention was then caught by a woman in sunglasses stalking back toward us from where she had been pacing down the alley.

"Kate," Adele said quietly, "I want you to go inside and wait for me."

Too late. The woman had already called out to Adele, and whether out of loyalty or curiosity, I wasn't going anywhere. The woman was tall and stylish—except for the absolutely bonkers, Halloween-worthy, platinum blonde glamor wig.

"Hello, Adele Schraeder." She smiled grimly. Her accent was British.

"Hello," said Adele. "How may I help you?"

The woman took off her sunglasses. "You can help me by staying away from my husband."

Adele was incapable of being nonplussed. "I'm quite sure I don't know what you're talking about. Would you like to come in for a cup of tea?"

"You can choke on your tea, you harlot."

"Oh my!" Adele laughed. "I think we will be going now."

Adele started to move toward the door of her building, but the woman moved with her, blocking her way.

"So where do you think you get off? You think you can just have any man you like, whether he's married or not?"

"This is a private alley," Adele said, still with impressive calm, "and you and your car need to leave, or I shall call the police."

"Listen to the adulteress lecturing me on the privacy of the home! What about *my* privacy?"

"I *will* call the police."

"I will call down legions of angels to fight for me."

Adele swept past her to the door but was slowed by the bags in her arms and the need to fumble with her keys. The woman followed as if to attack her. I dropped my bags and grabbed her from behind. I waylaid her for a moment until she thrust her car key, still in her hand, into my ribs. I recoiled in pain, and then she, taking advantage of my imbalance, pushed me to the ground. I bumped my head on the back tire frame of the Fiat, but I was all right. I got up, only to notice a strange bulk lying across the back seat of the car.

It was a child, a little girl about two or three years old, wrapped in a pink blanket, asleep.

I had lost my battle with the woman, but at least I had given Adele enough time to get inside the building. The woman impaled herself upon the door just as Adele locked it in time.

"Stay away from him!" she screeched. *"Do you hear me? Stay away from him or I swear I'll kill you!"*

Awkwardly, she kicked the door, then kicked it again even harder. She staggered back to the car, collapsed into the driver's seat without closing the door, and jammed the key into the ignition. The engine would not start. She tried it several more times, swearing more loudly each time the engine failed. After the fifth or sixth attempt, she started banging madly on the steering wheel with the hard palms of both hands as though it were a bongo drum. The little girl awoke after the third attempt to start the car, sat up, and wailed. I stood for some time stupefied by the scene before it occurred to me to do something.

"Let me help you," I said, but the woman refused to acknowledge me. Her glamor wig was askew, revealing the ends of her short, ragged brown hair. The little girl in the back wailed madly, as if her hot tears were scalding her rosy fat cheeks.

Once more, the woman tried to start the car, but it was no good.

"Do you have money for a taxi?" I asked.

The woman shook her head.

"Maybe I can help you get a jump or a tow, or you can at least use the phone at my apartment. You can't stay here."

I looked up to Adele's window, but she wasn't watching us. I wondered if she were standing and listening to us just behind the safety of the alley door. Wherever she was hiding, I didn't expect her to make a further appearance while this woman was around.

"Bring your daughter and come with me. My apartment isn't that far away."

The woman turned to me. The rage had suddenly vanished from her face. There was no expression on it, in fact. It was impossible to tell what she was thinking.

When she didn't respond to my offer of help, I started to gather my bags. "Come with me, and I'll try to help you. Otherwise, you can just sit there and wait for the police."

For whatever reason, the woman abandoned her wig when she decided it was best to come with me. She ripped it off and threw it onto the passenger seat of the Fiat. Then she picked up her little girl, still crying, and waited for further instruction, still no expression on her face.

We had a long, silent, awkward march to my apartment—about twenty minutes away—mother and daughter following me several paces behind. Eventually, the little girl's crying gave way to curiosity about where she was going and who I was, though she continued to soothe herself with a plush toy she had brought with her from the car.

Lauren and Consuela had gone out clubbing the night before with a group of their non-WIX friends, and they hadn't yet made it home by the time I left for the market. I dearly hoped they hadn't yet slouched back to home base, because if they got wind that a crazed woman had accused Adele of sleeping with her husband, it would be all over school before first bell on Monday. Fortunately, they were still out.

"Who would like some milk?" I said with affected brightness after setting my bags on the kitchen table.

Without replying to me, the woman turned to the little girl. "What do you say, miss? You want some milk?"

The little girl nodded shyly and hid behind her mother's leg. She held her plush toy, a frog, against her cheek with a tightly curled wrist.

I poured the milk in a small glass used for orange juice and, kneeling, handed it to the little girl, who tried to take it while still holding her frog.

"May I take Mr. Frog?" I asked. "I'll put him down for a nap here on the kitchen table while you drink your milk." She then gave me the toy and took the milk with both hands.

"My name is Kate." I smiled at her.

Gulping at the milk with slurps and smacks, the little girl looked suspiciously at me over the top of the glass.

"What is your name?" I asked.

She lowered the nearly empty glass and displayed her new milk moustache. "Mwanda," she said in her tiny British accent.

"Mwanda?"

"Miranda," clarified her mother. "You said I could use your phone?"

"Let me get it."

Each of us in the apartment had a phone jack in our bedroom, so our custom was to take the phone in behind the closed door whenever we wanted to talk to someone. I looked in Consuela's room first, though I found the phone in Lauren's. I carried it out and plugged it into a jack beside the couch in the living room and offered it to the woman. She wasn't that much older than I was—probably not yet thirty, I guessed. She was tall and beautiful, with enormous gray eyes framed by thick, well-groomed eyebrows. Her real hair was cut in a kind of messy pageboy look. On the walk to my apartment, I had decided that she was psycho, and I wasn't ready to give up on that assessment. However, if she were crazy, she hadn't lost her grip on a sense of style. She wore a full-length evergreen sweater with jeans, white tee, and black leather boots. She looked like she had just stepped out of a catalogue of fall styles for the mentally unhinged.

I was curious as to whom she was going to call, but I turned my attention back to Miranda. "Hello, Miranda. I'm Kate. Kate Kate Who's Now Your Mate."

The little girl smiled at me for the first time. She was like a toy figurine of her mother. The same enormous gray eyes and fair skin. She was dressed in a pair of elven-red pants with an elastic waistband and a white sweatshirt, dirty with stains made by her fingers and tears, featuring a cartoon frog that matched her plush toy.

"What is your frog's name?" I asked.

"Prince."

"Prince! He's a frog prince! Did a witch turn him into a frog? How are we going to rescue him? Do you and Prince want to sit up here at the table and have some more milk?"

She accepted my hand, and I led her to a chair. As I got the milk from the fridge, I continued to chatter. "I used to drink my milk at a table like that when I was your age. It was the color of mint ice cream, which I did not like but my mommy loved. Whenever I drank my milk at that table, I would look down at it over my cup and think mint ice cream was getting into my milk. Isn't that crazy? I begged my mommy, 'Mommy, please get rid of the mint ice cream table!'"

Miranda guffawed. "Minnie eye cream inna milk!"

"Do you and Prince want a cookie? You probably know them by their secret name, 'biscuits.' I have some super special chocolate biscuits I keep hidden from my roommates."

After I poured Miranda some more milk, I dug the cookies out from behind some pots in the cupboard. I hadn't yet heard her mother speaking on the phone, so I glanced over my shoulder into the living room, only to find the phone sitting on the couch, its receiver still in its cradle, and the woman standing in the middle of the room with her arms folded tightly against her chest and her lips tied shut like the strings of a leather purse. She glowered at the area carpet as though she might curse it.

I had an idea. On a shelf in my bedroom were two Mexican marionettes, a guitar-playing man, and a dancing woman in a colorful dress. They had sat in whatever bedroom I had occupied ever since I was a child. After bringing Miranda two cookies, I got the marionettes and brought them to her.

"Who would like to meet Señor y Señora Maravilloso!"

Miranda looked at the puppets with a wondrous gaze. Forgetting the cookies and milk, she took the marionettes from me and was quickly lost with them in play. I turned and addressed the woman. Recognizing her to be so obviously unwell, I addressed her with far more confidence than I ordinarily would have been able to summon.

"As I said, my name is Kate."

The woman looked up at me. "What do you know about Adele Schraeder and my husband?"

"Nothing."

"I don't believe you."

"Believe me or don't, that's your lookout. You won't even tell me your name. How should I know who your husband is?"

The woman wagged her head and seethed. "You're all alike. You live as if you're never going to die."

"You don't know anything about me."

"I know plenty about you, Kate Montclair."

My breath locked at the sound of my name. Now I was certain that I was standing in the presence of the mystery of the green scapulars. I was also fairly certain that I was in the presence of the woman who'd lit the storeroom on fire the night Mr. Cody, Dickie, Benedict, and I won the improv.

"I'm sorry," I said, "but you have the advantage over me. You know my name, but I don't know yours."

"You live like you're some goddess on Mount Olympus," she replied. "But one day you're going to have to answer for everything you've ever done. Everything and everything."

"How do you know my name?"

The woman returned a cool, disdainful smile. I looked back to see Miranda making the Mexican marionettes dance on the top of the kitchen table, oblivious to what was playing out in front of her. I turned back to the woman and said in a lowered voice, "Your little girl is the only reason you're still standing in my apartment. I'm trying to help you get your car started or towed or whatever it takes to get you out of here. Have you tried to call someone?"

"I thought I'd call my husband. Husbands are so useful on occasions such as these. Trouble is, I can't seem to find my husband."

"Is there anybody else you can call?"

"You mean, like a lawyer?"

Anger rising, I picked up the phone and dialed Lucas and Shia Lu's number. Even if he didn't have jumper cables, Lucas had enough Italian to call a tow truck. But no one picked up the phone, and each long, unanswered ring sounded like a taunt from the woman in the room with me.

After ten or twelve rings, I put the phone down again. I stood over it a moment, thinking about what to do, when the woman spoke to me in a voice that was haughty yet oddly serene.

"My name is Veronica Cody. Michael Cody is my husband."

Miranda's head jerked up at the sound of her father's name. "Daddy, Dadsy, Dads!"

I turned to Miranda and the puppets. She had started doing voices for the marionettes, and I heard Mr. Cody in her play, though she had gotten the puppets' strings horribly tangled and was feebly attempting to disentangle them with her tiny fingers.

"Maybe Daddy can help me," she said.

I went over and sat beside her at the table and began to work on the strings. My breath had become so rapid and shallow that patches of blackness flashed before my eyes.

"My friend isn't home," I said, not looking at Veronica Cody. "I don't know anyone else who has jumper cables."

"Perhaps if I waited at Adele Schraeder's, my husband would show up."

Blind with fear and fury, I picked at the strings of the marionettes. He had lied to me, and I had been a fool and hurt this poor woman and her child. But why did she think Adele was her husband's lover? Probably because she had seen him slip into Adele's building when it was really I who had been expecting him. But hadn't she seen *me* going into Adele's apartment? An impulsive—call it scrupulous—urge in me wanted to correct the mistake, to admit to her the truth. Because I wanted to fight for my man? No. Because I wanted *out* of the situation. Because his little girl's desperate desire for me to undo the impossible tangle of the marionette strings, his wife's brainsick efforts to force her husband back to her, and my own grasping obtuseness, which had been keeping the man they needed away from them, was too much brokenness to look at directly. It was a rupture, one that seemed to originate not from the shattered woman or from the little girl or even from me but from far beneath us all, from a fissure in the foundation of the world.

I could not unknot the marionette strings. And I could not cry out that I was Michael Cody's lover. The craven part of me was desperate to weather the crisis and escape without being discovered. Not because I was cold and conniving. But because I was wrapped in shame.

Veronica Cody took a seat cross-legged on the floor, her head cradled in both hands, a small child again. "There's one thing that's true, Kate Montclair," she said. "We have to pay for everything in this life. You can pretend you haven't anything to pay for, but that's a lie."

I handed the marionettes back to Miranda and went over to sit on the couch near Veronica Cody.

"How long have you been married to Michael Cody?" I had to catch myself from saying "Mr. Cody."

"Michael and I were married on the Feast of the Immaculate Heart of Mary, nineteen hundred and eighty-two. We were married here in Rome, but we lived in London. We rented a house on the Lincoln Road in East Finchley."

"But then you moved back here to Rome?"

"Yes. My mother, my brother, and my sister all live here. Michael and I thought that it would be good to be close to my family, so we moved in with my mother. But we were so happy on the Lincoln Road."

Gone was the defiant posture; now she just sat there broken, almost frozen, her expression again without affect, even catatonic.

"Can you tell me why you're putting scapulars under people's pillows?"

Her expression changed, and she said in an almost pleasant, confidential tone, "The green scapular has great power to convert even the most hardened souls. Even if a person is unwilling to wear it, it can still be effective. You just have to hide it somewhere close to them, and Our Lady does the rest. Isn't that wonderful?"

When did I realize that the street woman was Miranda Cody? Was it only when Benedict made it explicit over drinks? Or did I realize it beforehand, when Adele, at our dinner, deflected my interest in the woman and her green scapular? Or did I know it even when I encountered her at the Death Symposium, when she hid her green scapular from me? I cannot say that I knew the street woman was Miranda before Benedict told me; that would have been impossible. But I guess when I found out, I felt a certain inevitability, a kind of necessity which made it seem, in retrospect, that I had known the woman was Miranda all the time—almost that I had been expecting her to take her place on stage, with her mother and Adele and Benedict, here in the final act of my life.

"But she has the name NORMA tattooed on her arm," I said to Benedict.

"Yes. That was a nickname Cody gave her. Whenever she threw a fit as a little kid, Cody would call her Norma, for Norma Desmond, Gloria Swanson's character in *Sunset Boulevard*. Did you see her green scapular?"

"I did. How did Miranda get here to Washington?"

"She followed Adele from New York. She was living on the Lower East Side with her Aunt Bijou. Have you followed Bijou's career?"

"Oh, yes. You can't miss Bijou. But wait. Adele *knows* this street woman is Miranda Cody?"

"She knows all too well. Miranda won't leave her alone."

Then why did she lie to me? I wondered, rather angrily, but without expressing my feelings to Benedict. When I mentioned the street woman to her, Adele had acted like she didn't know who she was. I didn't like being lied to. But then Benedict explained why Adele had done it.

"I asked Adele if she had told you about Miranda. She said that it wasn't a good time, to leave it be. But I don't know. It seemed wrong not to tell you. I hope I made the right decision."

"You did," I said. "Thank you." So that was it. Adele had lied to spare my feelings because she didn't want me to get emotionally involved again, after all these years, with the Cody family. I understood her motivation, but I felt condescended to nonetheless, and not for the first time by Adele.

"Where is Veronica Cody? Is she still in Rome?"

"She's dead," Benedict said bluntly.

"No! When? Where?"

"Just over a year ago. Breast cancer. She had been living in a group home for schizophrenics run by some Catholic nuns up in Chappaqua, New York. That's where she died. I was with her in the final few weeks of her life. She asked me, then, to help keep an eye on Miranda. Miranda left Rome and came to live with Bijou in the States when she was in her early twenties. She was eager to get away from her mother and grandmother. But several years later, when she was twenty-seven or so, her own symptoms of schizophrenia began to appear. Her behavior became erratic. She started moving in with boyfriends who had no idea what she was going through. She was only inconsistently on her meds. She got into drugs. A few years ago, when Lucrezia Arden died, Veronica made the sensible decision to move to the States. She had an apartment in Manhattan close to Bijou's for a while. But when she heard her mother was coming, Miranda freaked out. She left Bijou's for good and has been on the street ever since."

I thought of the woman whom I had first seen wearing a ridiculous glamor wig, stalking down the alley toward Adele. I saw her banging on the wheel of her green Fiat Spider and sitting on the carpet of my Rome apartment, her head in her hands, her face incapable of expression. And I saw her on the morning of her husband's death, standing by the side of his body gazing madly up at the stars, unaware of what she had just done. She was such an odd, beautiful, damaged creature, who never, to my knowledge, learned of my role in the sad tale of her marriage. Surely enough, the world was broken, all the way down to its molten core, and I was broken with it. Still, I had made decisions that had caused irreparable harm to this woman and her child. *I* had been their catastrophe. All my adult life, I had borne the crushing weight of this guilt, and Veronica Cody's death did nothing to relieve me of it. In fact, it only intensified my sense of wrongdoing. Made it more emphatically unredeemable. For the only one who might possibly absolve me of what I had done was now no longer among the living.

"How did she end up with the nuns in Chappaqua?" I asked Benedict.

"Veronica was having trouble functioning by herself. She needed more hands-on support, and I helped her find the sisters. And she liked it there.

They really helped her get a handle on her schizophrenia. But then, just when she was doing so well, she received her cancer diagnosis."

What irony, that Veronica Cody and I, linked in life as rival lovers of Michael Cody, were marked for death by the same disease. The debt I owed to her had forced me, in a curious way, to live my life in her shadow, a shadow now working its insidious way through the tissue-folds of my brain.

"It's a horrific thing, cancer," Benedict concluded.

"It is, indeed," I said and then made my excuse to go.

CHAPTER TWO

As we waited outside the Hamilton for my Uber, I surprised myself by saying, "Is there no way we can find Miranda, Benedict? I want to help her, if I can."

"I'm not sure what you or anyone can do," he said. "And I don't know where she's staying. Likely on the street. But I know that on certain nights, at least, she's been camping out in my mother's apartment."

"Really?"

"The manager at Arcadia is allowing me a couple of weeks to clear out the apartment, and on one or two mornings when I've come in, I've found evidence that Miranda has been there: candy and gum wrappers, the odor from the joints she's smoked, a notebook. My mother must have given her a key."

"What's in the notebook?"

"Pages of incoherent, pretty much illegible handwriting. Some drawings too."

"Would you mind if I looked at it?"

"Not at all. If you'd like, you can come by Arcadia. How about Saturday? I'm going to be there sorting through Mother's stuff. Visitors are heavily restricted because of COVID, but if I tell the administration I need your help, I doubt they'll have a problem with it. They want their apartment back."

That Saturday morning, before I went to Arcadia, I met Adele at her townhouse, quite early, as she had a client arriving at 9:00 a.m. I had waited to file my complaint with her, as I didn't want to do it on the phone, and on Friday I hadn't been feeling well and had remained in my Q Street bed most of the day.

"I wish that you had told me who she was," I said to her.

"You'll have to forgive me, darling. But the last thing you need to be worrying about is Miranda Cody."

"I'll decide what I worry about."

"The error was mine," she admitted. "*Mea maxima culpa.* Just know that it was done out of concern for you."

Was she thinking, as I was, of another time when she had withheld vital information from me, from the same misguided motive? I didn't really want to go there with her after all these years, but part of me was eager to challenge her astounding lack of sensitivity. Instead, I changed the subject. I asked her to tell me how Miranda had found her.

"She tracked me down on the internet while we were still in New York," Adele confessed. "Started coming to the Death Symposium. Believe me, Kate, I tried to help her. She's as schizoid as her poor mother was but even more erratic in her behavior, and that's saying something. She drove poor Bijou to tears. Bijou had to keep pulling Miranda out of the beds of seedy men.

"But when she came to me, I took her in hand. Found out from Bijou who her doctor was, had Carly drive us to her appointments, made sure she got back on program. And it worked for a while, but only for a while."

"Then she followed you down here to DC?"

"Much against my wishes, let me tell you. The poor thing practically stalks me. It's everything I can do to keep Carly from throwing Miranda into the boot of her car and hauling her down to the police."

"Why does she follow you?"

"I suppose because I'm a connection to her father."

"She told you that?"

"No. Of course not. That's just my pet theory. She never really knew her father, so she has the luxury of divinizing him in her fractured mind. You are so brave and good, my Kate. Tell me how you are feeling physically."

"Tired. Headachy sometimes. But not bad."

"And how about emotionally?"

"Can't say I feel much emotion. I'm distracted and fidgety. I sit in rooms for hours and just stare at the walls."

"Because you're still in shock."

"I suppose."

"Which is why I don't want you to get involved with Miranda. I'm sorry, but it's just transferred anxiety. I can tell you from experience that it won't come to any good. Bijou is her guardian, and I keep her informed about Miranda as best I can. Beyond that, there really isn't anything anyone can do."

"Benedict said Miranda spends the night sometimes in his mother's empty apartment. He finds candy wrappers and such when he comes in to pack up the place. Found a notebook of hers too. I'm going over tomorrow to look at it."

"Whatever for?"

"I don't know. Maybe it will tell me where I can find her."

"Kate. I'm begging you to stay out of Miranda's life. It will only lead to frustration. I promise to be more proactive again in trying to help her. I'll put Carly on watch. I'll notify Bijou. But, Kate, please don't get involved with this yourself. Think. Do you want to spend this special time taking up a project that will only bring you sorrow?"

As I entered Arcadia's lobby, I felt like I had walked into an exhibition at Disney World's Epcot. *Retirement Living of Tomorrow—Today!* Thick navy blue carpets and white columns, faux colonial furniture and flatscreen TVs flashing the day's menus and COVID-truncated recreational agenda; walls adorned with stylish black-and-white photographs of laughing geriatrics playing around DC; a coffee station, juice station, and healthy snack station—all up to COVID standard; a bank of public-use Macbooks; a sitting area with touchpads and digital reading devices set out invitingly upon the coffee table; disposable masks and sanitizer dispensers every five feet. The homepage of the Arcadia website featured a quartet of slim, silver-haired Arcadians standing around a baby grand, glasses of Chardonnay lifted in a toast. I spied the baby grand in a corner of the lobby, playing itself, and I almost expected to see audio-animatronic versions of the silver-haired quartet enter and start singing along with it. Except for the concierge, no one was in the lobby, save for one elderly gentleman sitting alone in a wheelchair in the corner, his head in his hand, a horror-struck expression on his face. *Et in Arcadia ego.* Of course, the long-term nursing care facilities were kept discreetly offstage. No one was to see where the silver-haired quartet went when they were forced to put down their glasses of Chardonnay and confront their final agony in a hospital bed.

The concierge had me on a list of visitors with permission to enter the building. But I was given strict instructions to keep my mask on, to sanitize my hands, and not to fraternize with any of the residents.

"Hello," Benedict said, squinty-eyed, as he opened the door of his mother's apartment. I wondered if I had woken him up, but no. "I was out on the balcony having a covert smoke. In this penitentiary, there is no sin greater than smoking. Except maybe using the phrase 'old folks,' which I did once and got reprimanded for it by one of the aides."

He had left his cigarette out on the balcony, so as I entered and took in the surroundings, he stepped outside in his slippers to put it out. It was a spacious apartment. From the foyer, a left down a narrow corridor led into the shared living, dining, and kitchen space. There were some packing boxes, more or less filled, on the floor. All of Benedict's mother's furniture, wall hangings, chintz curtains, and chinoiserie had remained untouched since the day of her death. From the living area, I could see into the kitchen, where dirty dishes—some encrusted with the remains of what I hoped were Benedict's meals—were piled on the counter. Though I did not see any bookcases, a good number of books lay spread around on the sofa, armchairs, and coffee and dining room tables. Many of them were open or straddled the arm of a chair-cum-bookmark, as if Benedict spent his day moving about the apartment dipping into a series of readings. On the dining room table, next to piles of business mail, was an open notebook filled with scrawl.

"That's not it," Benedict said as he re-entered the apartment and locked the sliding glass door. In one hand, he carried a little homemade foil ashtray, which he placed with two or three others on the counter of the pass-through. "That one's mine. Miranda's is over here." He pointed to a closed notebook on the coffee table.

"Your mother certainly opted for the premium floorplan," I said, perhaps not too tactfully. Maybe I was feeling a little nervous, still not sure of my bearings when it came to Benedict.

"Mother always wanted the biggest and best, whether she needed it or not."

"Can you believe we qualify to live in this place?" I laughed.

"Do we? I cannot imagine it."

"Fifty-five is the minimum. I saw it on the website."

"I've never understood the impulse to place oneself voluntarily in a persistent vegetative state," he said. "I don't think that's how a human being should die."

"And how should a human being die?" I tried not to make my question sound too pointed.

"I've only known one person who seemed to do it right."

"And who was that?"

He looked at me with a wan smile, and I guessed that he meant Veronica Cody. Then he asked if I would like a cup of coffee. I really didn't want coffee—I hadn't had an appetite for a couple of days—but it seemed rude not to pursue some social preliminaries before I sat down with the notebook. As he went into the kitchen to make a couple of pour-overs, I drifted over to inspect the pictures on the living area wall, the remnant of the countess's once spectacular collection.

"What are you going to do with all this gorgeous art?" I asked Benedict after he had finished grinding the coffee beans.

"I just had them all appraised by someone from the National Gallery. I'm hoping they'll take them off my hands—and quickly."

"You don't want them yourself?"

"No. I prefer to travel light."

"Light, but rich as fudge."

"I won't keep the money."

"No? What will you do with it?"

"Maybe I'll give it to Adele. Maybe I'll give it to the Notre Dame restoration project."

"You're a good egg, Benedict. Sorry, have you heard that one before?"

As I turned toward the kitchen, I noticed another painting hanging on the wall near the hallway leading to the bedrooms. Thirty years dissolved like a dream upon waking, and I was both in this apartment and in the little corner bedroom in the countess's villa. I stepped over to see her, my Madonna of Port Lligat. I was transfixed. She was exactly as she had been before. Her cracked head remained bowed as she contemplated her child floating in the open sky of her womb. Her throne still rose gently upward even as it broke apart. *Do you remember me, my Lady?* But she was as silent now as she was then.

"Do you worry about security?" I called to Benedict.

"You mean the paintings? I suppose I should. But until the National Gallery calls, Arcadia's security will have to do."

"Have you alerted security about Miranda?"

"No. I *want* Miranda to get in. It's the only way I know she's safe. Besides, I think last time she might have left a clue as to her whereabouts. At least, I hope it's a clue. Why don't you take a look at Miranda's notebook?"

He brought me my pour-over and invited me to sit down with it on the sofa in the living area. I scanned the titles of the books lying about on the coffee table. Dante's *Inferno* in what looked like the original Italian. *Romanesque Churches of Umbria. Crime and Punishment.* John Henry Newman, *An Essay in Aid of a Grammar of Assent.* Bookish Benedict still.

"Mind if I put on some music?" he asked.

"Go for it."

He put on the latest Dylan album. I smiled and said aloud, "The more things change..." He smiled back and settled in with Dante on the opposite sofa. I took a sip of coffee, set it on a coaster, and picked up the notebook I had come to see.

It was a cheap, dollar-store purchase, its black cover falling away from its spiral binding. It had a deep horizontal crease across the middle, indicating that it had been folded over like a sandwich and probably stuffed into a back pocket. It was a workaday notebook; a spy's notebook; a notebook intended for observations on the run.

I opened it and discovered that reading it in the ordinary sense was not possible. Written in blue, black, and red ink, it was simply strings of random phrases, many of them illegible or badly misspelled, broken up only occasionally by three or four-word flashes like *I am the prophet* or *she made a promise.* None of it was punctuated, but it was illustrated. Miranda, true to her genes, was an extraordinary artist. Sketches, cartoons, and doodles adorned the margins of every page, making it look like a demented *Book of Kells.* And unlike the text, the drawings brimmed with intelligibility. There were several small portraits of Adele; various interior views of Cool Beans Coffee and exterior views of Adele's townhouse; sketches of birds and District landmarks; portraits of what looked to be vagrants, Miranda's fellow denizens of the streets.

While Dylan murmured and growled the stream-of-consciousness litany of "Murder Most Foul," I turned the pages of Miranda's notebook and came upon a drawing that took up an entire page, brilliantly executed with nothing more than a dime store black ink pen. The drawing was of a woman in bed, her head sunk into her pillow out of exhaustion. The woman stared straight up at the artist, as if Miranda had done the drawing standing at the woman's bedside. The eyes were tired, with dark rings underneath them, and they clawed at me with an Oedipus sorrow that could not bear the knowledge of what it had seen. I knew those large, gray eyes. The starlight had gone out of them, and they were set in a face much older and thinner, with all the voluptuous fat over the cheekbones eaten away. But I knew those eyes. And I knew that expression too. I had seen it once before, the day when we were caught in the marionette strings with her little girl and the broken car.

"She was very sick then," Benedict said. I didn't know how long he'd been standing behind me, looking over my shoulder at me looking at the drawing. "It was the first time I had brought Miranda to the sisters to see her mother. Miranda didn't want to speak to her, but she did want to draw her."

"Did you stay in touch with Veronica all through the years?"

"Pretty well, yes. I would visit her at Lucrezia's house whenever I was in Rome. But Lucrezia never much cared for me, and my visits were never welcome. She didn't like the fact that I was an apostate."

"What is that?"

"Someone who renounces the faith."

"Sounds dramatic."

"It fits the facts. I can't argue with that."

Benedict took his seat again on the sofa opposite mine, then picked up the thread of his story.

"One evening as I was leaving her house after visiting Veronica, Lucrezia said to me, 'Why are you an apostate, Benedict? Why have you separated yourself from the sacraments? I know your upbringing has been an irregular one, but that is no excuse. Don't you understand that Baptism gives you an indelible mark? An *indelible mark*. You are a child of God, and don't think for a moment he's going to let you go without a fight.' She made their house a fortress, a fortress against the modern world, and once she had got Veronica back, she was determined not to lose her again. Peter the monk with the leading man looks was her pride and joy—but she couldn't see him but a few times a year. Bijou was a lost cause, having gone into the film biz and married a man outside the Church. All she had left was Veronica and Miranda, and the three of them lived together for years in that house like cloistered nuns.

Lucrezia wouldn't even get Veronica the help she needed. She had this insane distrust of the psychiatric field."

"But Veronica was better, you said, after Lucrezia died and she came to the States?"

"Not right away. Bijou got her the proper help, but poor Veronica had been conditioned to distrust doctors and medicine. She would pretend to take her pills but then flush them down the toilet. And off her meds, she was a mess. But yes, after years of struggle, she turned the corner with the help of the sisters in Chappaqua."

"That's where Miranda drew this picture?"

"Yes. That was about a month before Veronica died."

I wasn't sure if I wanted to ask the next question on my mind, but my curiosity would not be denied. "Did she suffer much?"

"She suffered enough. The sisters took good care of her, but her last few months were hard."

At these words, the drawing of Veronica Cody swam and blurred before my eyes.

"I'm sorry, Kate," Benedict said. "That was insensitive, forgive me."

"No worries."

We sat in silence for a few moments. I wasn't able to stop myself from crying, but at least I was able to do it quietly, and Benedict had the good sense to let me cry without offering sympathy.

"You know what you were saying at the Death Symposium," I said with a loud sniff after I had pulled myself halfway together, "about how sometimes you feel like you're being judged?"

"Yes."

"I was too proud to admit it at the time, but sometimes I feel that way too. Judged…or maybe not even worthy to be judged. Just simply forgotten. I've had a wonderful life in so many ways. Great friends, terrific students, fantastic colleagues. Yet none of it has done anything more than momentarily numb the loneliness. The sense of being *abandoned*." I paused, unsure whether I wanted to share my next thought. "Ever since that awful night, it seems I've been wandering this earth alone. Did I do something wrong? Am I being punished for it? Or is it that I'm stupidly expecting the cosmos to be well-suited to my happiness?"

He didn't answer for a good while. He had something to say to me. Like at the bar the other night when he fingered the specials card and seemed to be searching for the words.

"Kate," he said at last, "I was the one who told her."

I looked at him, thinking that I might know what he was talking about but not absolutely sure.

"Veronica came to the villa that night because I told her Cody and Miranda were there. She'd spent that afternoon lurking outside Adele's apartment, waiting—hoping—for them to show up. When they didn't, she came looking for them at Mater Dei. When she found me there late that night, she was hysterical. She begged me to tell her where Cody was 'hiding' himself and 'her baby.' So, I told her that they were at the villa. Then I volunteered to drive her out there. I didn't do it out of spite. I did it because I had fallen in love with her. I know it sounds crazy, but I thought I could prove myself to her by helping her come upon Cody—"

"Benedict—"

"Please, Kate. Let me say this. I didn't tell her—"

"Benedict. No. Please. Not now." I stood up. I was breathing heavily, appalled by his revelation but also angry with myself for broaching the subject of that night in Rome. Miranda's notebook was still in my hand. "May I keep this? I want to study it some more."

He stood up too. "Of course. But Kate—"

"Not now, Benedict. Please. I have to go."

As I walked toward the door, I thanked him for having me over, but I could not look at him. It was only when I was in the hallway, when I turned to nod my thanks again, that I saw his helpless, broken expression.

Once outside the building, I started walking blindly, wholly absorbed in what Benedict had just told me. *I didn't do it out of spite. I did it because I had fallen in love with her.* I rode along on the back of this revelation as it careened backward and forward through the events of my life like a misguided missile. *Why did he have to tell me that? Why couldn't he have kept it to himself? Would my punishment never end?*

At some point in my tortuous rumination, I found myself sitting on a bench in a neighborhood park. Absentmindedly, I reopened Miranda's notebook and flipped through the pages. I had almost flipped to the end when another drawing caught my eye, one I hadn't noticed before. Two women in blue ink, one with her arm around the other, speaking consoling words into the other's ear. It was me and Adele in the alley behind her townhouse. Any doubt was removed by the fact that Miranda had drawn us in the very clothes we were wearing that night, along with the streetlight and the garbage bins that lined Adele's alley. Then I noticed the jumble of words wrapped around the drawing, out of which a sentence of oddly coherent syntax thrust forward and into me like a knife:

Kate Montclair is going to celebrate her deathday.

CHAPTER THREE

I went for a long walk too, that day in Rome, after I had managed to rid myself of Mr. Cody's wife and child. I was never able to contact Lucas or anyone who could help them with the car, and Veronica Cody refused my money for a taxi, but eventually she got a hold of her brother Peter, who came round and picked them up. Once they were gone, I stormed out onto the streets, needing to move, needing to expend all the hurt and bewilderment, fury and self-loathing that were raging inside of me. More than once on that walk, I cried so violently that I had to stop and support myself in the doorway of an apartment building or behind a news kiosk until I regained a measure of control over myself. The head waiter of a *hosteria*, standing outside the door of his establishment trying to drum up business, asked me in Italian if I needed help. The poor man. My response to his kindness was to burst into tears again and run away.

It was a gorgeous autumn day in Rome, and the city looked serene and redolent of ancient beauty and wisdom, but its charms no longer had power over me. I wanted to raze every last stone of it and then salt the ground.

I have been involved with a married man who has been keeping his marriage a secret from me. This damning statement was on continual loop inside my head. And, believe me, I didn't want it to stop. I wanted all the humiliation of it, like an acid, to penetrate and destroy every shred of romantic naiveté within me.

As for Adele, I could not believe what sort of idiot—what sort of needy, witless *child*—she took me for. Was it possible that she had been duped as badly as I had been? Possible, but not likely. "Mr. Cody needs rescuing," she wanted me to believe. She knew his marital situation. She used me to divide Michael Cody from his crazy wife when she didn't want to do the dirty job herself.

By eight thirty that night, having been out for nearly six hours, I was exhausted. I couldn't walk any longer. I needed my bed. I needed sleep. I had held on to some cash, so I was able to take a taxi back to the apartment. I imagined Mr. Cody waiting for me on the walk outside, but the street was empty as my taxi rolled up to the curb. But when I entered the cubicle of the building's foyer, hardly bigger than an elevator, there he was, sitting on the dark floor, his head sunk between his knees.

His head jerked up, and our eyes met. My first instinct was to turn and run back into the street, but I was out of juice for that. Instead, I blew right past him up the stairs.

"Kate!"

My plan was to get into the apartment, lock the door, and burrow away in my room. But the sound of his voice calling me hit me like a provocation. How dare he call me back as if I owed him something? Halfway up the first staircase, I stopped and unleashed my fury upon him.

"We are *done*, Cody." I'd never just said "Cody" before, and the strange word further unbalanced us both.

"Kate—"

"You *lied* to me. You lied to me *about a wife and child*. There's no coming back from that." I was shaking wildly, and my voice was someone else's.

"Please, Kate. Let me explain. You don't know everything."

"Not 'everything?' What *else* is there beyond a *wife* and a *child* and a *lie?*"

He was crying now, and I was repulsed by the sight of him.

"Kate!"

"Leave me alone!" I screamed and ran up the stairs and escaped into the apartment.

One down. Why not get them both out of the way? When I entered the apartment, everything was exactly as I had left it several hours earlier: a sign that Lauren and Consuela were on quite a party. How thankful I was for that. I grabbed the telephone from the couch, plugged it in in my bedroom, and closed the door—just as Mr. Cody began knocking on the apartment door outside. I dialed Adele's number before I had more time to think.

"It's a simple question," I said to her. "Did you or did you not know that he was married?"

"Of course I knew. Why is that important?"

Her cocksure complacency versus my quavering, near-hysteria. I wanted to punch her in the face.

"When did he tell you he was married?"

"I don't know."

"When he was trying to get *you* into bed?"

"Oh, stop it, Kate!"

"When was it? Before you encouraged me to get involved with him, I suppose?"

"Yes."

"And you didn't think that was information I might have a certain right to? Did you know about the little girl?"

"Yes. If you're going to blame anyone, Kate, I'm glad you're blaming me. It was my idea, not his. *I* convinced Michael not to tell you about his past."

"*What?*"

"Admit it, Kate. If you had known about his wife and daughter, you would never have gotten involved with him."

"Exactly right!"

"Which is why I begged him not to tell you. Not until later. Kate, you saw her today. The woman is schizophrenic. She's not in her right mind. He's done everything he can possibly do for her, Kate. *Everything*. He can't do any more. She's been terrorizing him, making his life a living hell. You have no earthly conception. He hasn't dared tell her about his role in the Spark film or his plans to return to London because he's scared what she might do to him or even Miranda if she were to learn he's trying to start his life again."

"What does any of this have to do with his *lying* to *me*?"

"When Veronica became too much for him in London, he brought her to Rome. Her mother was here, and Michael needed help with both her and Miranda. But the mother is a religious fanatic who doesn't believe in modern medicine. She will not get Veronica under proper care. It's been an absolute nightmare for him, Kate."

I was silent for several long beats. There was no sound of Mr. Cody knocking on the apartment door.

"Kate, *talk to him*."

"I'm not going to talk to him. I'm never going to talk to him again."

"Just give him a chance to explain. He wasn't using you. He wasn't just out for a good time. There's a lot more to this story than you realize. If you don't find what he says convincing, then tell him it's over. But I think you will be persuaded by what he has to say. I wouldn't have encouraged you to see him if I didn't think he was emotionally available. He loves you, Kate."

These words ambushed me, and I began to cry. "Why couldn't you both just have told me the *truth*? Am I a child?"

"I thought you wouldn't even look at him if you knew he was married. I thought that would scare you away. I wanted you to find out who he is apart from his past."

"Well, that's just not possible, is it? His past is a seriously ill woman and their child."

"Michael has no intention of shirking his responsibilities. He's going to do everything he can to take care of them both. But he also needs to take care of himself. You can't imagine what his life has been like, Kate. He's been playing nursemaid to Veronica while trying to maintain some measure of stability for Miranda. Meanwhile, he's sacrificed his career and is supporting his family as a schoolteacher, a position far below the level of his talents. He doesn't deserve to be shackled to a mental invalid for the next sixty years. Veronica Cody belongs in an institution. She will never recover from her malady. They will never enjoy a normal married life again."

"How did you come into possession of all this top-secret information?"

"He and I have been friends, Kate, almost since his arrival in Rome. As you know."

"Just friends?"

"Just friends."

"Because I'm tired of the lies, Adele."

"*Just friends*, Kate. A man will feel all sorts of silly emotions when he first gets to know a woman, but we've sorted all that, and anyway his feelings were superficial. He's in love with *you*, Kate. I know that. And I think you love him, too. The salient point to consider is whether you would have discovered your love for one another if he had introduced himself as the husband of a schizophrenic and father of a three-year-old girl?"

"I don't think either of you gave me much credit. I don't think either of you *respected* me."

"I think you're right, Kate. And I'm sorry about that."

At this I slammed down the phone, slammed it down again and again into its cradle like I was beating someone's skull in with an iron.

I did not walk for six hours the afternoon I left Benedict at Arcadia and discovered, from her notebook, that Miranda knew about my deathday. That kind of energy would never be mine again. When I had tired myself out after maybe thirty minutes, I called an Uber and, for the second time that day, journeyed to Adele's townhouse. It was about four o'clock in the afternoon when I arrived. The brilliant, blinding flame of the receding sun cast her cobblestoned street in bronze. There was a marked chillness in the air, and a light wind that only just disturbed the leaves that had begun to gather in bunches along the curbs and the front stoops of the houses. I felt that plangent melody that is the leitmotif of autumn, and I fell sadly with it, like the leaves helplessly falling, toward my last end.

Once we were behind the closed door of her office on the second floor of her townhouse, I showed Adele what I had found in Miranda's notebook.

"How could she possibly have heard us?" Adele said as she peered through her glasses at Miranda's handiwork. "We were whispering."

"She was hiding behind one of the garbage bins? I don't know," I replied. "The point is, she was there in the alley. She knows. How likely is it she'll talk?"

"Not likely."

"Really? Why not?"

"I don't think her mind works that way. You're imagining that she would want to stop what she sees as a terrible crime. That's imputing a lot of rationality to a most irrational person. I think she'll be happy simply knowing that she's found out a secret. Anyway, you shouldn't be alarmed. All you have to do is destroy it. Easily done."

"The whole notebook?"

"Why not? She's probably forgotten she even lost it. Besides, she shouldn't have been snooping. She has no right to evidence from a private conversation."

"But what if Benedict saw it? Does he know what a deathday is?"

"I don't know. And so what if he did? Even if he takes what Miranda wrote seriously, he'll respect you enough not to intrude upon your business."

I worried for a moment. Then Adele said, "Kate, if she were going to call the police, she would have done so by now. And just imagine what would happen if she did call the police. They'd know in a couple of ticks that she was mad as a hatter."

"Did you know that it was Benedict who brought Veronica Cody to the villa that night?"

"What?"

"He admitted it to me this afternoon. He told her everything, then drove her out there himself. Did you know that?"

"He never told me, but I guessed it long ago. He was in love with Veronica. Until the very end, apparently. He spent the last weeks of her life with her, in that nunnery in New York. Don't let Benedict trouble you, dear. And watch out he doesn't fall in love with you."

"Benedict? Oh, please."

"Have you told him about your diagnosis?"

"No."

"Do you plan to?"

"No. Look, I haven't seen him in decades, and it's not like we were that close in the years when we were supposed to be close."

"All the same, watch out. Benny has an ugly, misshapen, crookbacked conscience. He's been flagellating himself for years for betraying you. He knows his intentions were hardly disinterested. I can easily see him trying to make up for it by concocting a compensatory romance with you."

Adele saw how tired I was and insisted that I stay not only for dinner but for the night. Several hours later, before going to sleep in the guest bedroom, I opened Miranda's notebook again and stared at the drawing of me and Adele in the alley. The same hand that made it, I had taken in mine so many years before as I led her to the kitchen table in my Rome apartment. The day I found out that her father was married. How badly I wanted to take her hand again and rescue her from her half-life on the streets, to get her the care she needed. I also wanted to talk to her about my relationship with her father, if it was possible for her to understand. I'm not sure what I wanted to say to her about it. Did I want to apologize? Maybe that was just my own crookbacked conscience talking. But I did want to let her know how terribly sorry I was for what happened and to explain that her father and I had plans for her to be with us.

I didn't believe in fate or the ways of God, but maybe this was what I was supposed to do with the time I had left: find Miranda and help her. Maybe this was all the meaning I could expect from my life. The chance to repair this one small part of the catastrophe.

But how, Miranda, was I going to find you, and before I had to catch my bus?

It took me two weeks after my discovery of Mr. Cody's marriage to decide that I wanted to see him again. What changed my mind?

Three things.

The first was my friend Madeleine from Washington and Lee. She lived in Geneva and worked for the Swiss section of Amnesty International. Desperate to get out of town, I called in sick on a Friday and took the train to Milan, where she and I had agreed to meet and rough it in a hostel for the weekend. After I poured my heart out to her over a bottle of cheap wine and some pasta, she said something that surprised me.

"Imagine someone who is an airline pilot, or a train engineer, and suddenly they go blind. Would you expect that person to continue flying an airplane or operating a train? Of course not. Well, this woman has gone worse than blind. She's lost her identity. Given that, why would you expect her to continue being a wife and mother? She's no longer capable of it. In the same way, how can you expect Michael to continue being her husband? Absolutely, he should continue to help her and support her in every way he can. But the person he married no longer exists." I told her that my friend Adele had said something similar. Then Madeleine added, "It doesn't sound like he was using you. It just sounds like he panicked and did something massively stupid. But think about this: What made him panic were his feelings for *you*."

The second thing was Adele. Not only the fact that her argument concerning Veronica Cody's incapability of sustaining a marriage was confirmed by Madeleine, but what she said in the letter I found on my bed the Sunday night I returned from Milan:

The only life is a life lived on your terms and nobody else's. One day you're going to die. When that day comes, you will want to look back on your life and say, "I lived my choices. Not the life that other people chose for me or expected of me. But my life. Mine. Kate Montclair's life."

Adele's hypothetical had a special resonance for me when I was twenty-two. In college I had taken a Death & Dying elective that began with an unusual exercise. We were to write our own obituary, and in doing so imagine the elements of what would make up a happy and fulfilling life. I loved that exercise; I found it so energizing to put together a list of everything I wanted to do with my life: become America's female Mark Twain, and a film director, and a mother of four prodigiously gifted, Glass family-like children. Putting my dreams on paper made them all seem so much more possible. Adele was encouraging me to repeat that exercise and ask myself whether I would want to add Mr. Cody to my list, even given his massively stupid lie. Did I want to imagine a life in which I had not given our relationship a real chance?

And the third thing that changed my mind about seeing Mr. Cody? Oh, yes. Last, but certainly not least, and certainly the one I least wanted to admit to myself: I missed him like crazy.

So we met on neutral ground. The Caffè Ogygia.

"I want to know the story of you and her," I said as soon we had sat down with our coffees. "Just do it. Tell me."

So, he told me. Though I think, in describing her talent and achievements, and the grace and beauty that went along with them, he held back somewhat, not wanting to inflame my scorn both for him and for her any more than was necessary.

"We were in the same year at RADA. Veronica was a special talent. Everybody sensed that she was the one who was going to make it big. We started dating seriously in the spring of our first year. In our second year, she agreed to move in with me. That was a big step. Her family still referred to it as 'living in sin,' so Veronica wanted to keep it secret. But our secret eventually got back to Lucrezia. Long story, but it was Bijou who inadvertently spilled the beans. Lucrezia flew to London in a blaze of maternal wrath. There was a big showdown. But Veronica didn't budge—not completely, anyway. Afterward, she told me that she would continue living with me but only if she were convinced that we were moving in the direction of marriage. And by *marriage* she didn't mean a pit stop before a justice of the peace. She meant all the smells and bells of a Catholic wedding.

"I was serious about her, believe me, but marriage wasn't on my radar screen at all. Veronica got upset when I hesitated. We even sort of broke up for a few days. But then she realized she was pregnant, and I was faced with a much more momentous decision. We planned a small wedding in London and not the large one she had always imagined in her family's parish church in Rome. Even so, Veronica asked me—begged me, really—to become a Catholic before we married. So, I took instruction with a priest she knew in London.

"We were married the summer after we graduated from RADA, and that August Miranda was born. We were happy that first year, but even during our happiest days, Veronica was starting to have trouble coping with day-to-day reality. She'd gotten a part in a television show but dropped out because she was depressed. Soon she stopped working entirely. Stopped paying the usual attention to Miranda. It became hard even to get her out of bed. For a long time, I thought it was post-partum depression, and maybe it was, to a point. Then I would catch her talking to the voices in her head. And then began the grandiose delusions. She started to think she was a handmaid of the Virgin Mary. She would say the Virgin Mary needed her for a special mission. Which, as you now know, involved the hiding of green scapulars.

"After one particularly nasty argument, I convinced her to see a psychiatrist, who diagnosed her with schizophrenia and put her on meds. Thus began the long war of getting her to take her meds regularly. She would stand right in front of me and pretend to take them, then spit them out as soon as my back was turned. She refused to believe she was ill. But I should say, this wasn't just stubbornness on Veronica's part. Refusing to believe one is ill is actually part of the illness. She blamed the meds for whatever problems she was experiencing, so from her point of view, not taking the meds was the path to recovery. This led to some crazy paranoia. She thought that I was in league with her doctor to keep her from fulfilling her duty to the Virgin Mary. She thought the meds made it impossible for Mary to speak to her. But even when she was in a somewhat better place, she still wouldn't take the meds because the side effects were so awful. They made her feel jittery all the time, made her feel antisocial, made her lose an appetite for sex.

"We struggled on in this way without much help. By this time, my parents had divorced and were on opposite sides of the Atlantic, busy trying to restart their lives. Lucrezia, for her part, was a positive nemesis. No matter how much evidence was put in front of her, she refused to accept that Veronica was ill.

"Meanwhile, in the thick of all these troubles, we were trying to launch our careers. There was one stretch when Veronica stayed on her meds, and we experienced a happy period of normalcy. She managed to land the role of Juliet in a West End production of *Romeo and Juliet*, and I got the part of Edmund in *Long Day's Journey into Night*. But Veronica had an ugly relapse in the middle of her run—stopped taking her meds—and the producers had no choice but to replace her. After this, her grandiose delusions really started to get out of hand. Lucrezia kept insisting that I bring Veronica 'home,' that if she were on hand to help with the baby and Veronica were given time to rest in familiar surroundings, everything would be all right.

"What else could I do? I couldn't take care of a schizophrenic wife and an infant daughter while still trying to make a living as an actor. So after the run of *Long Day's Journey*, we gave up our rental on Lincoln Road, put our careers on hold, and moved to Rome.

"But things only got worse. Lucrezia and I fought constantly about how to care for Veronica as well as for Miranda. Lucrezia was livid that I had stopped going to Mass, as if that was the cause of all our problems. Veronica grew more and more distrustful of me. She was hardly ever on the right meds, and there were some really frightening episodes. One morning we were awakened by a phone call. The Swiss Guards at the Vatican had stopped her from trespassing. She had told them she had a secret message from the Virgin Mary. Someone was going to try again to assassinate the pope.

"I did some research on various treatment options, and I started to make the case to Lucrezia that Veronica would do better in a group home for schizophrenics where she would receive round-the-clock attention. Lucrezia erupted when I suggested it. 'How can you separate a mother from her baby?' she kept saying. Which made no sense because Veronica had already stopped functioning as a mother. She never so much as fed Miranda or gave her a bath, much less played with her. But Lucrezia was adamant, and when I tried to persuade Veronica, her reaction was all grandiose paranoia. She accused me of being an agent of the Antichrist.

"Now, I had Veronica's health care power of attorney; I had the legal power to do for Veronica whatever I thought best. But I had no money, no health insurance. I hadn't worked at all since we moved to Rome; we had been living entirely off Lucrezia. My hands were tied, so Lucrezia won the day, and Veronica remained at home.

"One evening, I felt so desperate, I went to Veronica and tried my best to make her understand that our lives would be better if we went back to London. She pretended to agree with me, but later that night, she attacked me with a kitchen knife. The next morning, I called in a social worker to help me force Lucrezia into getting Veronica better help, but Lucrezia played her like a fiddle.

"Luckily, just about that time, I found and was offered the job at Mater Dei. The head also offered me a position as a rector's assistant, which meant extra money but would also require me to live on campus. I jumped at the offer and moved out of Lucrezia's house. My plan at first was to make enough money so that I could afford rent on an apartment where Miranda and I could live together until I could convince Veronica to come with us back to London. Our returning to London—away from Lucrezia and back to the place where we had enjoyed a semblance of happiness—was an imperative in my mind. But that was a fool's dream. Even if I could get Miranda away from Veronica, even if I could afford a place for us in Rome, how was I going to take care of my little girl while teaching all day? I was getting pretty depressed myself and would have gotten worse if Adele hadn't been there for me. Once, when I went to the house to see Miranda, Veronica said to me, 'I wish I had never met you.' That's when I knew it was all over between us. And about a month after that, I met you."

I didn't respond to this. I didn't know what I thought about any of it. I just waited for him to go on.

"Kate, I think I have enough momentum now to take Miranda with me back to London. Money from the film will take care of us for a while, and if my agent's predictions prove true, then I'll be able to get other work.

"Kate, I want you to come with us. I want us to be together in London. I have a second chance on my career, and I want you to share it with me.

And London is a much better place for you to pursue a writing career than Rome. You'll be surrounded by all kinds of magazines and other outlets. And if you're interested in performance, well, London is the best place to be outside of New York. It'll be easier to find a teaching job there too, if that's what you want."

"You've got my life all mapped out for me, don't you?"

"Kate, I'd be humbled and honored and eternally grateful if you would forgive my asinine behavior. I made a horrible decision out of fear, and I hurt you, and I'm sorry. I will never fail to be honest with you again."

I leaned forward and whisper-smacked him through gritted teeth.

"You didn't tell me you were *married.* With a *kid.* You told *Adele,* but you didn't tell *me.* Adele was wrong to persuade you to keep it a secret, but you were wrong to go along with it."

I'd hit him hard enough that his eyes welled up with tears. "You're right," he said, his voice cracking. "What can I say? I was an idiot, and I'm sorry."

"What hurts the worst, though, is that you underestimated me. You *assumed* I wouldn't be able to handle it."

"I should have known never to underestimate you, Kate Montclair. But I did, and I'm sorry. Adele encouraged me, at the beginning, not to say anything. She said that it would scare you away. But the longer we went on, and the more my feelings for you deepened, the more I feared losing you if I told you the truth. I was a victim of my own lie. But I knew we were coming to a crossroads where I would have to say something. I wasn't going to go to London without telling you the truth and begging you to come with me. I was still figuring out how to talk to you about it when Veronica showed up at Adele's with Miranda."

"Yeah, that pesky wife and child. They tend to show up, don't they?"

"I don't have a wife, Kate."

This was what I wanted to hear. By this point, after reflecting on what Madeleine and Adele had said, I had become inclined to believe—and desperately wanted to believe—that he no longer had a wife. But I wanted to hear him make the case for it.

"In what sense is it," he said, "that I have a wife or that Miranda has a mother? I have a *patient,* one who wishes she had never met me. I will do the honorable thing and take care of her as well as I can for the rest of my life. I will make sure she has the highest quality of life she can possibly have. But meanwhile, what am I supposed to do? Go on as a schoolteacher for the next fifty years? I have to live my life, Kate, or I'm going to die. And I want to live that life with you."

"You're planning on getting a divorce?"

"I guess. Yeah."

"Well, I'll let you figure that out."

I got up from the table. While walking down to the café, I had given myself a stern warning to keep the meeting short, to listen but to show no sign of thaw in the iceberg. It was time for me to go.

"What can I do to win back your trust?" he pleaded as I buttoned my coat.

"Maybe nothing." I hoisted my backpack onto my shoulder. "Sometimes, you prove yourself so untrustworthy that there's no going back."

That was my parting line as I swept out of the café. Though I can't say I believed it anymore.

A few days later, I was just closing my classroom door at WIX, on my way home, when I saw Veronica Cody coming down the corridor with a glamorous stride, like it was a runway in a fashion show. She wore a smart, gray plaid, knee-length skirt, high at the waist, matched with a black turtleneck and sunglasses pushed stylishly back onto her head as a hairband. No wig this time. Her hair and makeup were perfect. It seemed she had dressed to intimidate and had done a swell job of it.

I finished locking my classroom door and steeled myself for the confrontation. Surely her presence here meant she had discovered that I, not Adele, had been her husband's lover. An unstoppable urge came over me to admit to her the truth, to beg her forgiveness, and to assure her that I, also, had been duped by Michael Cody. It was everything I had been dreading, and it might mean losing him forever, but in that instant, all I wanted was to spew it out of my mouth.

When she stopped ten feet away from me, I said, "Hello, Mrs. Cody."

Upon hearing her married name, she giggled. Then she came forward to enlist me as a conspirator:

"At Fátima, Our Lady asked us to make sacrifices for poor sinners. Will you join me in making a sacrifice so that my husband and Adele Schraeder will break off their affair? It is putting their souls in jeopardy. Prayer and fasting are the only effective weapons."

"Is your husband here?" It was four o'clock, and he was likely downstairs at an *Our Town* rehearsal. But she didn't reply to my question.

"Perhaps we could say a rosary together? Out on the grounds, perhaps? It's a lovely afternoon."

"Veronica, may I say something to you? I want to tell you something about your husband and Adele Schraeder."

For a moment, the manic affect drained from her face. But then, just as suddenly, it returned. She snatched my arm and whispered hotly into my ear. "*Adele Schraeder is an agent of the devil!* But do not be afraid. I have put everything in the hands of Our Lady. Our Lady will crush the serpent under her heel!"

Still in the grip of her arm, I said, "It's not what you think."

She froze for an instant, giggled, then released her grip and ran away down the empty corridor. She was a good runner, even in her chic flats, and I watched her sprint merrily away until she turned the corner and was out of sight.

The next day was Saturday, and after going alone early to the farmer's market in the Campo de' Fiori, I took the bus to Adele's apartment. I had brought her some flowers, a bottle of olive oil, and some bread as tokens of peace, hoping to further heal the breach in our friendship. When she answered the buzzer, her voice sounded flat and unnerved.

"It's me, Adele. Are you busy? May I come up?"

She buzzed me in without a word.

When I reached the top of the stairs and turned into the poky hallway, she was standing outside her apartment door with Mr. Cody. She was pale and puffy-eyed, and her unwashed hair was tied behind her head. Mr. Cody was in his leather riding jacket and cradled his Vespa helmet. He must have just arrived.

"I stayed at Roberto's last night," Adele said, "and when I came home early this morning, I found this." She gestured toward the opened door of her apartment.

I looked in and saw that the main living space had been torn apart. Furniture was upturned. Drawers emptied. Books and papers and silverware thrown about. Most disturbing were the gashes made through the mattress and pillows of the fold-out bed—gashes made with a large kitchen knife left stuck into the wall behind the sofa.

I stepped into the apartment and gaped at the damage. "Who did this?" I asked, but even as I uttered the words, I found the answer. Hanging from another kitchen knife plunged into the near wall was a green scapular.

"I called Michael and asked him to come over," Adele said as she and Mr. Cody followed me into the apartment. "I don't quite know what to do. I suppose I should call the police." I had never seen her so rattled.

Alarmed by the state of the apartment, as well as highly conscious of Mr. Cody's presence, I set my market bags on the counter of the kitchenette and continued to survey the damage. This could have been my apartment, if Veronica Cody had known the truth, if she had listened to what I tried to tell her the day before. And if I had been present when she had broken in, it might have been me at the end of her knife.

"Adele," I said, "we have to get you out of harm's way." I turned to Mr. Cody. "Is there no way we can convince your wife that you are not having an affair with Adele?"

Mr. Cody sighed. "I've told her many times. I don't know what else I can say. She's not in her right mind. And now I'm really afraid for Miranda."

"You think she'd hurt Miranda?"

"Veronica has come after *me* with a knife before, but I've never seen her do anything like this. Miranda or anyone else around her could be in danger."

He gaped at the knife stuck into the wall, no doubt imagining the horror his wife might do to their child. I had to struggle against a maternal urge to comfort him.

"You kids need to take Miranda and leave Rome," Adele said.

I didn't acknowledge this comment. It was bold as brass, but I was also feeling too many things at once. Still angry at Mr. Cody, though wanting to be with him, while worried about Adele, worried about Miranda, worried about myself if Veronica Cody found out about my relationship with her husband.

"I'm so sorry about this, Adele," was all I could manage to say in the moment. "You're welcome to stay at my place for as long as you need to. I'm sure we can think of some way of explaining it to Lauren and Consuela."

"Thanks, but I'll ask Roberto first if I can bunk in one of his apartments," Adele said. "If only I can get there without being followed. The real problem is Miranda."

"I would take Miranda out of Lucrezia's house this very morning," Mr. Cody said, "but they'd tell the police that I kidnapped my own child."

"Let them!" Adele snapped back. "Let them! Then *you* can tell the police about Veronica's savagery here. This apartment is more than enough proof that the woman needs to be in a padded cell under lock and key. I'm sorry, Michael, but that's how I feel. In fact, I'm going to take pictures of all this. Should anyone challenge you, it'll be hard evidence that the woman is not competent to care for her child. Get Miranda to safety. You're going to London anyway. Go now."

"I have no money to go now."

"We'll pass the plate among our friends," Adele insisted. "Pool our resources. We'll get you and Miranda on a plane, and you can figure the rest out later in London."

"Maybe Helen, my agent, can help me," Mr. Cody murmured.

"She'll be delighted to help you," Adele said. "She can ask Roberto for a little advance on your film money."

"But another thing is, I don't have anywhere to take Miranda right now. There's no place for her to sleep at Mater Dei even if the head would allow her to stay with me. Which he probably wouldn't."

Adele considered this, then said, "OK, then don't take Miranda until you're ready to go. But get ready to go *now*."

During this exchange, I had been standing to the side, not knowing what role, if any, I might play in the evolving scheme. Was I watching Mr. Cody prepare to depart my life forever? Or was this my moment to seize? It was all coming at me so quickly, and all while I was unable to speak with him alone—if I wanted to speak with him alone—which I wasn't quite sure about.

Apparently, he was thinking along the same lines.

"Kate," Mr. Cody said, "could I have a word?"

Adele picked up her cue well before I picked up mine. "I'll leave you two to talk," she said. "But let me call the police first. Then I'll go out and get us some pizza or sandwiches or something. I'm drinking before five o'clock today, folks, trust me!"

When we were alone, standing there in the middle of Adele's devastated apartment, Mr. Cody said, "I think Adele is right, Kate. I need to leave Rome with Miranda as soon as possible. And I want you to go with us. I made a mistake in not telling you right from the start about Veronica and Miranda. But my mistake had nothing to do with my feelings for you. Quite the opposite, in fact. I love you, Kate Montclair, and I want you with me, and I *need* you with me because I cannot take care of Miranda all by myself."

I put my hand over my mouth to stop myself from crying, and with my other arm gripped myself around my torso to stop myself from shaking. Neither measure did a jot of good.

He took a step toward me, but he restrained himself from taking more. "It's all happening fast, Kate, I know. I'm sorry."

For several minutes, we just stood there. Me silently weeping and shaking. He unsure how to proceed.

"I love you, Kate Montclair," he said again. "Do you love me?"

"I loved you when I thought it was just us."

"It *is* just us, Kate, along with Miranda, if you'll have her."

"If I'll have her? Sure! I'll just make a snap decision about whether, at the tender age of twenty-two, I want to be, for all practical purposes, a *mother*. While at the same time I decide whether I want to get back with the man who humiliated me; and whether I want to run away with him to a city in which I know not a blessed soul; and whether I think it's right for the man to abandon his mentally incapacitated wife and his baby daughter; and whether I want to leave my job without notice and without a reference. Just give me a minute, Mr. Cody. I'll be right with you!"

"Come with us, Kate Montclair," he said in a quiet, deliberate tone. "It's crazy, I know. But come. It will be just us again, I promise." He took a step closer. "I love you, Kate."

And then he was holding me while I sobbed onto his shoulder my anger and confusion and fear.

And yes, too, my relief.

CHAPTER FOUR

On the first Thursday of October, I once again attended the Death Symposium, now daringly maskless myself. My second and already my last meeting. All through the first half of the evening's discussion, I had half an eye on the stairs, hoping to see Miranda creeping up them. But she never came. Benedict was not there either. I hadn't spoken to him, really, since that Saturday at Arcadia. He had texted me another apology, and I had replied, again, "No worries," but neither of us made any further effort to communicate. Was I angry with him? For being in love with Veronica Cody and wanting, by his twisted logic, to prove himself to her? For undermining my future with Mr. Cody? No, I was not angry with him. Those events were too far in the past to admit that kind of feeling. More than anything else, I felt sorry for him. No less than myself, he had allowed love—or feelings that surely seemed to be love—to lead him, most unwittingly, down a path toward a tragic end. We were paired, Benedict and I, by our youthful indiscretion and lifelong regret. No, I was not angry with him.

During the break, I was pouring myself a cup of tea at the refreshments table when he appeared at my side.

"Benedict! I'm glad you've come."

His attempt at a smile fizzled. He could not look at me as he wrung his hands. I took him by the shoulder and led him over to a quiet corner of the mezzanine. Then I looked him squarely in the eye.

"Listen to me, Benedict. I forgive you. We were both young and stupid and got ourselves caught up in events beyond our control. But that was a long time ago. It may be impossible, but we have to do our best not to brood on it anymore. OK? You with me?"

Without a word, he kissed me on the cheek, and I decided that I liked this grownup Benedict and wished I hadn't been so cool to him at the beginning.

"I've learned something you might find interesting," he said.

"Oh?"

"There's a geezer at Arcadia named Roy. I ran into him today when I was hauling a load of stuff out of Mother's apartment. An aide was pushing him along the hallway in a wheelchair. He's a friendly bloke and we got to talking, and as soon as he found out who I was, he described himself as my mother's last boyfriend. The reason I hadn't met him before is that he had been at his daughter's home in Florida since before Mother died, recovering from a hip replacement. He had to get to clay works or haiku class, but he invited me to come up to his apartment sometime for a drink.

"'Don't worry about the COVID laws,' he said. 'There's an exception for those of us on the way out.' Poor guy. Right after his hip replacement, he found out that he has Stage IV lung cancer.

"I told him that I would certainly come by for a visit. But before we parted, it occurred to me to ask him if he knew Miranda. His reaction to hearing her name was not what you would call subtle. Like he had cartoon eyebrows flying off his forehead. He admitted having seen her, but the more questions I asked, the more uncomfortable he became. But his parting word was to encourage me to visit him."

"So—"

"So I thought I'd visit him tomorrow. Bring him a bottle of Jameson's to loosen him up. See if he's got any more to tell us about Miranda. Want to join me? We'll get you into Arcadia on the same pretense of helping me clean out Mother's apartment. When I tell Roy you're with me, I'm sure he'll be delighted to see you."

I did want to join him. To see if this Roy could help us find Miranda, but also because, admittedly, I was enjoying Benedict's company. We knocked on Roy's door at Arcadia at precisely five o'clock the next afternoon. A pretty Latina aide let us in. Before leaving, she advised us to keep our masks on during the visit and to maintain social distancing.

The air of the apartment was close, with a faint whiff of urine. We found Roy in a wheelchair in his tiny, gloomy living area, hooked up to an oxygen machine. Before Benedict could introduce me, Roy asked if I was his girlfriend. "Just a friend," Benedict replied. "Kate is here to help me clean out my mother's apartment."

Roy was a good-looking, though frail, eighty-seven. You could tell that once he had been the tall, rugged, military type. He was dressed in a red and black flannel shirt (with a crusty splotch of what looked like scrambled egg on the breast pocket), navy blue sweatpants, and compression socks with slippers. His raven-dark hair still held out impressively against the grey, though around each furry ear he wore a hearing aid the size of a transistor radio.

I took a seat on the couch while Benedict poured the drinks. "Irish whiskey!" Roy beamed when Benedict presented his gift. "I would love some, though strictly for medicinal purposes." He laughed at his own joke in wheezy cackles that rattled his wheelchair. We toasted Irene and then chitchatted a while. We heard more from Roy than was necessary about an unfortunate incident the previous day involving an enema.

At last, Benedict segued into the subject of how Roy met Irene. "I wanted to ask you something, Roy," Benedict said loudly, having adjusted his volume to Roy's near deafness. "You knew my mother well, I take it."

"Yessir. I did. But I was always a gentleman."

I nearly laughed aloud at this, but I caught myself.

"Yessir," Roy continued as he held his glass in a shaky, twisted hand, "your mother was a great lady, God rest her soul. You know, she and I were quite an item. Our first date was an Arcadia excursion out to the Leesburg Corner Premium Outlets. We also went to the zoo here in DC a lot. It pleased your mother that I walk out with her there. If the Lord hadn't come for her, I might have been asking your permission to marry her!"

"Is that so?" said Benedict. "And you were telling me that you knew her friend Miranda."

"Who?"

"Miranda. Mother's friend."

Roy shifted in his wheelchair, and there was a lull in which the only sound was the soft mechanical thrum from his oxygen machine.

"How did she become friends with my mother?" Benedict inquired.

"I dunno," Roy said. "I think they used to see one another in the chapel. I never accompanied your mother to the chapel because it's nondenominational and I'm Methodist. But your mother always said God was nondenominational, and so we agreed to disagree."

"I never knew my mother to go to the chapel."

"Yessir. There are no atheists in foxholes. Your mother was a very sick woman and felt like she could use some divine succor."

"I see. So she and Miranda used to meet in the chapel."

"Yessir. Your mother befriended her. I didn't like it."

"No? What didn't you like?"

Roy scowled and rubbed his hands, which were the color of raw steak.

"Didn't like what, Roy?" Benedict asked again.

Before he replied, Roy inhaled some oxygen through his nasal tube like a drug. "I dunno. I guess I didn't like the fact that she was always hanging around."

"Where? In the chapel? In mother's apartment?"

"In the apartment, especially. Before I went to Florida, she seemed always to be there. Sometimes your mother let her stay the night, which wasn't exactly house rules."

"She let her stay in the apartment? Did she ever give her a key?"

"Yes on both counts. But don't tell anybody here I said that, especially about the key. I don't want no trouble."

"Don't worry, Roy. I just want to know about Miranda's relationship with my mother. Is there anything else you can tell us about her?"

"I don't think she had a regular place to live. Your mother once told me she liked to sneak into churches to spend the night. She was a weird one."

"Miranda suffers from some pretty serious psychological issues. That's why we're interested in her. We'd like to get her some help. Was my mother aware of Miranda's mental illness?"

"Your mother thought she was a schizo. Miranda made her a little scared sometimes."

"She did? Then why did she let her stay? Why did she give her a key to her apartment?"

"Your mother was a soft touch. How else do you think I got her to go out with me?" He gave me a wink and tried to change the subject, saying how popular Irene was with the men of Arcadia, how it was an honor for him that she should single him out, but Benedict wouldn't let him go.

"You think mother was afraid of Miranda? Tell me about that."

"Maybe more uncomfortable than afraid," Roy said.

"So what did Miranda do or say that made my mother uncomfortable?"

"She was just kinda nuts, ya know? She'd say and do crazy things—"

"Like—?"

"Eh?"

"Like what kind of crazy things did she say and do?"

"Well, like one time she said she was talkin' with the Virgin Mary. Now, I'm not Catholic, and I mean no disrespect, but that's kinda nuts, don't you think? And she used to give herself cuts all over her arms. That kinda freaked your mother out. But, I must say, at other times she was completely normal. She and your mother liked to watch TV together, *Jeopardy* and that *Downton Abbey*."

"Have you seen Miranda since you've been back from Florida?" Benedict asked.

"No. I hear she got fired."

"And you wouldn't happen to know if my mother had a phone number for her or any other contact information?"

"Sorry, I don't."

"Well," Benedict concluded, "it sounds like my rather eccentric mother had one of her rather eccentric friendships with this rather eccentric woman. Mother liked to take in strays. She once loaned her car to her hairdresser for a week so that he could use it to look for a new job."

"Your mother was a wonderful woman," Roy agreed. "Wasn't an inmate in this place who didn't love her. I miss her every day. Every day."

In the midst of this testimonial, Roy got a little weepy, and Benedict gave me a look that said it was time to go.

"Thanks for talking with us, Roy," Benedict said.

We got up to go. But we hadn't left the living area before Roy asked us to wait. His head was shaking; his watery eyes were bright with fear.

"There's one other item. I don't know if it means anything, but I think maybe you have a right to hear it, being her son. I still have it on the answering machine. You see, your mother left me a message the night she died. I don't want to alarm you, but you should take a listen to it, if you want to."

We all went over to the telephone on the dining room table, with me pushing Roy's wheelchair. The dining room table, apparently never used for eating, was covered with newspapers, junk mail, medical documents, pill containers, and a landline. The answering machine next to it showed a red digital number one.

"I didn't hear it until I got back last week," Roy said. "I guess she thought she was calling my cell because she knew I was in Florida."

I felt apprehensive for Benedict, who was about to hear his dead mother's voice. But he did not look concerned as he pressed the playback button.

The first thing we heard was an automated female voice saying "*Sunday, 6:32 p.m.*" This was followed by several seconds of ambient noise before Irene's voice broke in, anxious, disoriented:

> *Roy? Are you there? Can you pick up, Roy?...I don't want her here....Tell her not to come, I don't want her to come....I don't want to die...She's coming to kill me, Roy...She's coming to kill me!...Please, Roy...please...Lord have mercy, I don't want to die....*

There was then a second or two of ambient noise before a loud crashing sound and the line went dead.

Roy blinked away tears. I was pretty shaken myself: the brassy voice in my audial memory of the countess did not match the small, terrified voice I had just heard. Benedict wanted to listen to the voicemail again. After the second playback, he asked Roy, "Did you tell anyone else about this?"

"I played it for Selena, the aide."

"What did she say?"

"She said, 'Poor Ms. Irene. Bless her heart,' and told me not to worry about it."

"*Do* you worry about it?"

"Listen to her! She says she don't want Miranda there. She was afraid that woman was going to kill her."

"Why would she think that?"

"Because Miranda is a schizo lunatic. Capable of anything."

Roy was getting more upset, and now it was my turn to tell Benedict with a look that we had pushed Roy too far and had better leave him be.

"I'm sorry you had to hear that, Roy," Benedict said. "I'm not sure what was going on when my mother recorded it. But don't erase it, OK? It's important that you don't erase it. In fact, if you don't mind, I'd be happy to take the answering machine with me."

"I wish you would," Roy said. "I can't stand the thought of spending one more night alone with her voice in there."

Back in Irene's apartment, we regrouped.

"Are you OK?" I asked Benedict, though I was the more visibly upset of the two of us.

"I'm fine. Need another drink?"

"No, thanks." I was relieved he hadn't noticed that I had barely touched the Irish whiskey down at Roy's.

"How about some food, then? There's an Italian place down the street that I've been trying to support through the pandemic. Really good food."

"Sounds great." I wasn't hungry either, but clearly he was, and I didn't want him not to order something because of me.

As he rummaged through the papers on the pass-through looking for the carryout menu, he asked what I thought of the possibility of Miranda having killed his mother.

He didn't seem to mind discussing the topic, so I didn't see any reason to pussyfoot around. "I think it's a possibility, yes. Do you think we should call the police?"

"I do."

He found the carryout menu for Ciao Amici! and handed it to me. I was still trying to decide whether I could best choke back a forkful of eggplant parmesan or the spaghetti Bolognese, when he said, "I always thought—in the back of my mind, you know—that Mother slipped away a little too precipitously at the end."

"What do you mean?"

"I've been around the dying, and I have a sense of—what would you call it?—the *rate of decline*."

"You're talking about Veronica Cody."

With his sad eyes, he affirmed my hunch.

"I had been with mother that morning. She was weak, sure. But I didn't think she was in the final throes. I wouldn't have left her if I had thought that."

"Where did you go, anyway?"

"I popped up to New York on the train to meet with a potential client. I stayed the night and was back late the next morning."

"At that stage, was your mother in bed the whole time?"

"Yeah. She needed help to get to the bathroom, but she could still use the facility without assistance. She wasn't on full hospice alert. The hospice nurse came in to check on her that morning, gave her a dose of morphine for her pain, but when I asked the nurse, privately, where we were in the process, she said the end would most likely occur anywhere from several days to two weeks."

"But it's not a science, Benedict."

"No. I'm just saying that when they called me and said that she had died, my first reaction was, 'There's no way. How could she decline that fast?' They said the time of death was sometime in the early evening. I left her about noon."

"It's possible Miranda was involved. Though I'm not sure how she would have done it."

"Easily with an overdose of morphine," Benedict said. "Yet there were no doses of morphine that hadn't been accounted for. The hospice nurses keep records of all that."

"Do you think your mother could have been having an adverse reaction to the morphine or any of her other meds?"

"Possibly."

"Or maybe Miranda simply frightened your mother in some way. Threatened her, even. But maybe didn't actually kill her."

"And what would be her motive anyway? Couldn't be money. There's lots of valuable things in this apartment, not least the paintings, that she might have taken but didn't. And there's no evidence that she has access to mother's bank accounts. Maybe from a misguided sense of compassion?"

"Maybe. But let's recall, Miranda is mentally ill. She wouldn't have needed a rational motive."

For a while longer, we turned over the grim hypothesis in our minds. Then Benedict asked for the menu so he could decide on an entrée and place our carryout order. I walked down to Irene's bedroom. Except for the mattress, bedframe, and furniture that belonged to Arcadia, Benedict had cleared out the room. I leaned in the doorway, and onto that spare backdrop inserted an image of the dying countess in that bed and Miranda somehow murdering her. Surely someone—the hospice nurse, the folks from the funeral home— would have noticed signs of a struggle, like marks on her neck from strangling. The more I thought about it, the more I was convinced that Miranda had said something to frighten Irene—frighten her enough to call Roy—but that was all. I felt badly for Benedict that on top of the death of his mother, he had to hear that voicemail and consider the prospect that she was murdered. I was thinking of how to express my sympathy when I heard something behind me.

The muffled sound of someone crying.

I whipped around, heartbeat thumping. The sound was coming from the guest room across the hallway. Benedict was on the phone with the restaurant giving our order. I took a deep breath, then tiptoed silently back to the dining area.

After finishing the call, Benedict turned to me. I held my finger to my lips.

I mouthed the words, "Miranda is here," while motioning in the direction of the hallway. When Benedict looked at me with surprise, I added, barely in a whisper, "I think she's hiding in the guest room closet."

We tiptoed to the guest room. In the doorway, I peered over his shoulder and saw no one in the room itself. I was right; she was in the closet. But there was no sound of crying now. Benedict turned and mouthed the words, "Wait here."

His first step into the bedroom made the floorboards under the carpet creak. That, and the fact that we had stopped talking, was surely enough to alert Miranda that we were aware of her presence. Benedict must have thought so too because after the creak, he gave up tiptoeing and walked over and yanked open the closet's accordion folding door.

Miranda sprang up from where she had been crouched on the floor and pushed Benedict back. In her hand she held the recording device I had seen her with that first night at the Death Symposium.

"Miranda!" Benedict shouted as she scurried past him. "It's all right!"

She came straight for me as I stood in the doorway. I pleaded with her, "Stop, Miranda! Please!"

I didn't tackle her—she was younger and far stronger than I—but I grabbed her arm as she tried to rush by me. I pulled, but she ripped her arm away. In doing so, however, she dropped the recording device on the floor.

"Let me through!" shouted Benedict.

I went flat against the door as he raced past me. I heard the click of the door unlocking, then Miranda yanking open the front door of the apartment. She was fast. Benedict was no slouch, but I didn't know if he was fast enough to catch her.

After I closed the front door, it occurred to me go out to the balcony, to see if I could see the chase from there. I looked down at the landscaped entrance to Arcadia for five minutes or more, but neither Miranda nor Benedict ever appeared. I went back inside. There was no calling or texting Benedict; his phone was on the dining room table. I went to the doorway of the guest room and picked up the recording device off the carpet. I pressed play and heard Miranda's chilling monotone:

> *You want to know my motive, dearest chucks? I am the angel of mercy. I am the angel of death. I am the handmaid in service to the prophet...*

CHAPTER FIVE

Benedict returned to the apartment after failing to catch Miranda, and we called the police and offered them our suspicions. Two officers came directly to Arcadia, but given the lack of hard evidence of murder, there wasn't much they could do. The cassette on the voice recorder didn't hold anything more than various random segments from the Death Symposium and assorted strange yet inconclusive ramblings from Miranda. Later, after the cops had left and we sat down to our Italian carryout, Benedict mentioned that we had better bring Bijou into the loop.

"Why don't you let me call her?" I asked. He'd been through enough today already. He agreed and gave me Bijou's cell number. I texted her, and we set up our video chat for the next afternoon, a Saturday, when I would be back at Five Hearths.

After we finished eating, Benedict offered to drive me to Lisa's, where I would spend the night. I was beginning to feel tired, headachy, and vaguely nauseous, and I was glad not to have to wait for an Uber. Before we left Arcadia, Benedict left his Airbnb address at the front desk in case Miranda, for some obscure reason of her own, came looking for him.

It was about seven thirty when we pulled up to the curb outside Lisa's building. As I got out of the car, Lisa, coming down the street laden with shopping bags, hailed me. I hadn't expected this; I thought surely by that hour of the evening that she would be upstairs. There was nothing for it but to introduce her to Benedict. This was not a bad thing, of course, but given that I hadn't told Benedict about my illness, I was anxious about what Lisa might let slip. My hope was to make a quick introduction and send Benedict on his way.

But Lisa said to him, "Why don't you come up for a drink?"

Great.

I wasn't feeling at all well by this point, and now I had to get through another round of drinks for which I had no stomach.

Ten minutes later, the three of us were sitting in Lisa's living room, and I was doing some slow breathing exercises to calm my rocky stomach. But it was no use. As Lisa asked Benedict all about his and my past in Rome, I excused myself to the bathroom and hurried away.

I only just made it, and no doubt the delightful sounds of my retching and dry-heaving, insufficiently muted by the bathroom fan, raised an alert in the living room. When I came back out, they were both standing up, waiting for me, with looks of terrified sympathy on their faces. Benedict's especially distraught expression indicated that my secret was out.

Lisa made a deft excuse about needing to make a phone call and shimmered away to her bedroom. Benedict and I sat down again.

"Do you need anything?" he asked.

"Only a miracle cure."

"Another cup of tea?"

"No, thanks."

"Why didn't you tell me, Kate?"

"Oh, I wanted it to be a surprise. Surprise!"

Benedict ran a hand over his face.

"I thought sometimes you looked tired," he said, "but I didn't want to say anything. If I had known, I wouldn't have had you come to Arcadia today."

"Then I'm glad you didn't know. I wanted to be at Arcadia today. I want to find Miranda."

"You're not doing chemo? Radiation?"

"No, I'm not."

I thought about telling him more. I will confess that. But in the end, I was not too sorely tempted to unveil my one remaining secret.

"I can't believe it," he said. "This can't be happening."

"I'm sorry, Benedict, to be checking out while you're still grieving your mother."

"Forget about me. It's *you* my heart is breaking for."

His sincerity got to me, and once again I was crying. He came over, sat beside me on Lisa's couch, and held me until my waterworks ran dry.

"Lisa is going to spend the weekend with me at Five Hearths." I reached for a tissue on Lisa's coffee table. "Why don't you join us? Or do you have to keep working on your mother's stuff at Arcadia?"

"I suppose I can take a break."

"How much more do you have left to do?"

"Not too much."

"Does that mean you'll be leaving soon?"

"I—I'm in no particular rush." He smiled sheepishly. "If you don't mind, I kind of like hanging around."

"I don't mind. Come hang around at Five Hearths this weekend. There are horses to ride if you're interested. But if you want to just hole up and read, drink wine, or nap, that's fine too."

"Thanks," he smiled. "I'd like that a lot."

"But no going around all mourny-faced, OK? That's the rule at St. Kate's Monastery for Lost Souls. You think you can obey the rule?"

"I can't promise anything," he said, "but I'll try."

When Bijou Arden appeared on my cell phone screen on Saturday afternoon, she looked like she was ready to be photographed at home for a *New York Magazine* profile. As we gushed our hellos, I half expected a hair stylist or makeup artist to flit into the frame for a final touchup. She had on jeans and a modish zip-up jacket with a scarf. Her hair was dyed chestnut brown, shoulder length with bangs, as she'd been wearing it for her Netflix series, which made her look younger than her forty-nine years. The Botox-smooth forehead and utter lack of glabellar lines between the waxed brows also helped. She sat upright, shoulders slightly back, framed elegantly in perfect light against the open concept of her Manhattan loft.

She didn't return my compliment on how gorgeous she looked. When I first appeared on her screen, I caught the reflex of astonishment in her eyes followed by the polite recovery. It had been an especially hard day for me physically. I hadn't slept well and had woken up with a headache, dizziness, nausea. Overwhelming lassitude. Spent half an hour using petroleum products to cover my gaunt—let us not say cadaverous—features. End result: like a beginner embalmer's failed homework assignment.

I looked hard into her face. Bijou Arden favored her mother. Her angular features were more Italianate than the softer Anglo-Roman mix of her sister. But she had her sister's preternaturally translucent complexion, and whenever she stopped talking and listened, her sister's face peeked out as though from behind a scrim.

"Golly jeepers! Is that really my Ms. Montclair!"

She repeated this refrain several times at the beginning of our conversation. She kept calling me Ms. Montclair until I had to tell her to cut it out and call me Kate.

"Can I do that?" she said. "You won't give me a lunch detention?"

"You used to call me Kate when you were eighteen, pert miss, and not even behind my back either. I don't see why you can't do it now."

She laughed heartily at this. "I must've been a royal nightmare!"

"You were, let us say, 'spirited.'"

She asked me where I was calling from, and I said from my home in Fauquier County, Virginia, just over an hour (with no traffic) west of DC. I had put my cell phone stand on a stack of books in the sunroom, and I leaned aside to give her a sense of the place.

"You haven't updated your social media lately," she said, very much as a rebuke. "Are you on our WIX Facebook page? Did you see the post about Jenny Dyer? Remember Jenny? She just died of colon cancer. Can you believe it? Jenny Dyer! One of the immortals!"

After I negotiated her inquiries about my life, she brought me up to speed on hers. Most of what she told me I knew from her own social media accounts, the celebrity news, or what Benedict had lately said. Her Netflix series, *The Middle Agent*—an espionage drama in which a middle-aged suburban housewife is enlisted by the CIA to spy on the family next door (Chinese operatives)—was a big hit in its third season. Bijou, with a more-than-passable American accent, played the star's hard-as-nails CIA handler. It was a good role for her. The previous year, she had been nominated for an Emmy for best supporting actress in a drama series. Now, the show was madly trying to work through logistics as it geared up production for its first COVID-era shoot.

Though we had been connected for years via social media, this was the first time I had spoken to her since she graduated from WIX in the spring of 1987. During my second and last year at WIX, she'd been in drama school at the London Academy of Music & Dramatic Art, after which she went on to quite a stellar film career. My friends are impressed when I tell them that I taught the future star of *Brush Against a Stranger* and *Lady Chatterley's Lover*. "But when a woman hits forty, the scripts dry up," Bijou explained to me. "At least film scripts. In television the scripts are more plentiful and usually better quality." Accordingly, in recent years she had transitioned to the small screen. On the personal front, she'd been married twice—"the triumph of hope over experience"—but had no children. In the tabloids, she had been romantically linked with the younger actor who played the star's husband on *The Middle Agent*, but I made no inquiries into that.

"So you've been in touch with Benny," she said.

"He's staying here for the weekend, in fact, along with my friend Lisa. I sent them off to a local winery for a couple hours."

"Hey, girl," Bijou said, "save Benny for yourself. Don't let your friend get her claws in him. You know, Kate, you could do far worse than Mr. Aquila. I'm serious! His face is *ravaged*, unfortunately, but it's still got a certain rugged manliness, don't you think?

I tried to laugh at this girly banter, but my thoughts were running along different lines. I detailed for her all that had happened the day before at Arcadia. By the time I was done she was practically bent over, hands covering her mouth as she stared aghast at the screen.

"I don't know what I'm supposed to do about that girl." She moaned and tilted for a moment out of frame, then returned with a tissue. "She refuses to get help. I can't keep her prisoner. What am I supposed to do?"

"I want to help you find her, Bijou," I said.

"You know, I wasn't exactly trained to be a psychiatric nurse. But for years now I've had to look after *two* women with schizophrenia—first Veronica and now Miranda. Neither of whom, by the way, was ever a model patient. I've read a few books, but I've never really known what I was doing. *And* I've had a few other things going on as well. When my mother died and Veronica came to live with me, I was still trying to salvage my marriage to Bill and struggling to keep a career afloat. I'd go out to LA to audition for something, and when I'd return, Bill would say, 'Your sister's off again.' By some miracle, I finally got Veronica to recognize that she needed real professional support. Thank God Benny found the sisters in Chappaqua! That's where Miranda needs to be. They'd *transform* her just like they did Veronica. I know it. But if I ever so much as *mention* the sisters to Miranda, she becomes absolutely *violent*. Anything connected to her mother just sets her *off*. My therapist tells me, 'You have to let it go. You've done your best. You've given them both your blood, sweat, and tears, but you can't control their actions.' She's right. But at the same time, am I supposed to *forget* that my schizophrenic niece is living on the streets of Washington, DC, high on opioids and sleeping with one stoner after another?"

While she blew her nose, I told her again how sorry I was and assured her that I was going to do everything in my power to get Miranda off the streets and into that halfway house in Chappaqua or some place that could help her.

"She won't listen to you," Bijou snapped. "She doesn't think anything's wrong with her. That's the problem. She won't do anything her mother did, however sane. She blames Veronica for everything that's happened to her. She's read some of Veronica's notebooks from that period of her life. She knows how she hounded Michael and Adele. Veronica kept a *vivid* account of it. She knows all about what happened at the countess's villa that night. In Miranda's schizoid mind, Veronica *caused* poor Michael's death, and *Adele* is the real mother-with-all-the-marbles she never had."

I gathered from all this that Bijou still did not know that it was I, not Adele, who had been having an affair with her sister's husband.

"That's why Miranda started stalking Adele," she went on. "I haven't a clue how she found her. But one day, I glanced at her 'dumb' phone—she doesn't use digital because she thinks the pope or the president or the Gates Foundation is listening in—and I saw a text from *Adele Schraeder's assistant*. I said to Miranda, 'Is this Adele Schraeder from WIX? How did you find her? Why didn't you tell me?' But Miranda just shrugged. It's the schizophrenia. Makes her so secretive about *everything*. But behind my back, she had reconnected with Adele and started haunting this Death Squad or whatever it is. You've heard about it? At first I thought: Is this a *cult*? Is Adele going to invite Miranda to her island utopia and make her drink the Kool-Aid?

"So I rang Adele. We hadn't spoken in years. She tried to get me to come to one of her coffee shop death klatches, but I said, 'No, thank you! I think I'll give it a miss.' Can you believe it? People sitting around drinking tea, eating cake, and talking about the day they're going to peg out? I suppose it's all very enlightened. My therapist said I might try it, but I'm depressed enough without having to sit around imagining what I'll look like in an open casket at my wake. I've got a mirror that tells me that every morning!

"Anyway, Adele confirmed that she had seen Miranda a couple of times at her coffee shop meetings but that they had hardly exchanged ten words. Miranda had been acting strangely, and Adele guessed that she was suffering from serious mental health issues. In the end, Adele offered to let me know if she ever saw Miranda again, but not long after that, she became embroiled in some lawsuit, and next thing I knew she had pulled out of New York and gone down to DC. I haven't spoken to her since."

"A lawsuit?"

"Yeah! Can't remember where I heard about it or any of the particulars. Anyway, Miranda disappeared again, and I realized she had followed Adele to DC. That's when Benny got involved. The countess was dying at the time, and as he was with her in DC, he volunteered to try to find Miranda. I told him, 'If you want to find Miranda, keep an eye on Adele Schraeder.' Sure enough, Benny found her shadowing Adele at the Death Squad. Benny tried to talk sense to her, but Miranda wouldn't listen to him, either. She'll take his money, but she won't listen to him. And now I'm afraid she's got some sick fantasy going on in her mind about being Adele's evil minion. What did you say she said on the recording? *I'm the angel of death in service to the prophet?* Poor Benny! How horrible that he had to hear his terrified mother crying out for help in a voicemail! He didn't deserve that. He's such a *sweet* man. Always so devoted to Veronica and me and Miranda. He was in love with Veronica, you know. Since he was a teenager. He actually *proposed* to her on her death-bed! I can't decide whether that's romantic or just plain creepy."

There was an awkward pause in which neither of us was sure what to say next. There was one thing, however, I very much wanted to say. And, as this was quite possibly the last time I would ever speak to an Arden or a Cody, I girded my loins and said it.

"I'm dying, Bijou. I have a brain tumor. Glioblastoma Multiforme Stage IV. I don't have long to live. Just some weeks. I know you want to ask me questions, but please just listen to me first. I need to say this. I never got a chance to say this to your sister, so I'm going to say it to you. It was I, not Adele, who was Michael Cody's lover. Your sister was mistaken, that's all. *It was me.* And I'm sorry, Bijou. I'm sorry about what happened that night. I'm sorry that Michael and I didn't make a different choice. I'm sorry I betrayed your sister. I'm sorry I hurt your mother. I'm sorry I sent Miranda on this destructive path."

When I stopped, I was breathing heavily.

Bijou's reaction was not at all what I expected. No gasping, wild-eyed surprise. No peppering me with unbelieving questions. She simply looked down, as if to gather her thoughts, then leaned in toward her phone's camera.

"Kate, I know about your past with Michael."

"What? How? Did Benedict tell you?"

"No, Benedict didn't tell me."

"Then how?"

She didn't answer my question.

"Don't be too hard on yourself, Kate. You can't take responsibility for everything. *You and Michael were simply trying to live your lives.* Michael tried his best, but he couldn't help Veronica. Mother wouldn't let him. And who knows? He might have been more use to her once they were apart. Maybe that would have helped her see reality better. I don't know. But you can't blame yourself, Kate. It's as bad as Miranda blaming Veronica for Michael's death. No one is to blame."

"It's how I feel," I said. "But again, I want you to know that, in whatever time I have left, I'm going to do everything I can to find Miranda and get her the help she needs. That much of the mess I made I'm going to try to put right."

Bijou smiled her thanks and said, "Kate, I want to send you something. I'll put it in the mail. You'll get it in a few days. I think it's something that will help you better understand."

I didn't know what she was talking about, and she didn't seem to want to tell me, but I gave her my mailing address.

"Isn't it strange," she said after she wrote it down, "how life's gone in a big circle? It's like we've been wandering in the woods for years, each on his own path—you, me, Benedict, Miranda. We thought we were making progress. We thought we were finding our way out of the woods. But now we're all back together where we began, and we have to start all over again."

That weekend with Lisa and Benedict at Five Hearths was the most pleasant I had enjoyed in some while. The early October weather was perfect: a cloudless, deep blue sky; a temperature in the low seventies during the day without any hint of humidity, yet cool enough for a hoodie or sweater in the evenings. Lisa and Benedict got on well together. They had a fine time at the winery, and late in the afternoon, I put them on Lucy and Ethel, and they rode around Evie and Everett's place as well as around Five Hearths. On Saturday night, I invited Evie and Everett to join us for dinner, and Benedict grilled steaks. For some inexplicable reason, I had an enormous appetite for that steak and devoured the entire thing. After Evie and Everett left, Lisa, Benedict, and I stayed up late streaming a double feature, *Knives Out* and *Little Women*. On Sunday, we made brunch around noon, which was followed by books and naps. It was a weekend that made one want to live to see more, though I had to keep reminding myself that the relative good health that enabled me to enjoy it would soon diminish. If only there were a heaven, a heaven just like this weekend, then I would be more than happy to catch a bus even before November 2.

I was in the shower on Sunday morning when I had an idea about how to get in contact with Miranda—an idea I hoped to execute that evening at my second Sunday dinner with the P Street Illuminati. I was so excited by the idea that as soon as I got dressed, I shared it with Benedict. I found him alone in the kitchen making up a batch of waffle mix. He liked the idea and thought I should go for it.

I leaned against the kitchen counter and watched him pour batter into my waffle maker. It felt increasingly awkward not telling him about my deathday. I had never brought up the subject of the drawing Miranda had made of me and Adele. Perhaps he had not seen it in Miranda's notebook, and what Miranda had written around it: *Kate Montclair is going to celebrate her deathday.* Or perhaps he had seen, but hadn't understood?

He closed the lid of the waffle maker and smiled at me. I managed to smile back, though I felt a stab of regret that we would not be able to get to know one another better. Would it be easier to go if I let him in on my secret? But how could I tell him—on this most perfect of Sunday mornings—that in a few weeks I was going to take my own life?

Lisa left Five Hearths around four o'clock that Sunday afternoon, and at about four thirty, Benedict drove me into Georgetown. Adele wanted me at her house well before dinner so that we could have some time to talk, just we two. When I arrived, Carly showed me upstairs to Adele's bedroom. I found Adele there in a white satin kimono with a print of peacock feathers and her short, icy white hair tucked into a matching cotton turban. Her face was un-made, and the cross-hatching of lines beneath her eyes and the skin around them was as brittle and cracked as an ancient papyrus. I had entered the star's dressing room an hour before the performance, though even this dressed-down version of Adele couldn't help, with a guest backstage, performing just a little.

I took a chair in the little sitting area next to the fire. Adele had a nice blaze going, and scented candles burned on the mantle and on her makeup table. She offered me a glass of wine or a cup of tea, but I declined. "How about some nosh?" she asked, but I wasn't hungry. "Of course you're not," she said. "Lie down if you like, Kate. Don't stand on ceremony around me."

We talked about several things before I brought up the subject of my FaceTime call with Bijou.

"How is dear Bijou? I hear she's got a hit show on the telly."

After I said one or two general things about our conversation, I asked Adele about something Bijou said that had been worrying me. "She men-tioned there was some lawsuit you had to deal with in New York?"

"That was an unfortunate episode," Adele said. "But there was no lawsuit."

"No?"

"There was the *threat* of a lawsuit. The sister of one of my clients wasn't happy that my client had planned a deathday ceremony, and when she found out about it, she went bonkers."

"How did the sister find out?"

"My *client* told her, wrongly assuming that her sister would understand. That's why you have to be careful about who you invite to your deathday, Kate."

"Understood," I said. "But the sister threatened a lawsuit?"

"She didn't have a shred of evidence."

"But she threatened a lawsuit."

"Please don't worry, Kate."

"But what grounds did the woman *think* she had?"

"She had her sister telling her that she was planning to take her death into her own hands. That's it. She had her sister's expression of a *wish*, a desire. Nothing that could be linked to a deed, much less to me in particular. In brief, she had rubbish. No, you have nothing to worry about. But, if you do invite family members and friends to the ceremony, make sure you give their names to Carly."

"I wasn't aware Carly was in on my deathday."

"Carly is my right hand. I trust her with everything. But I shouldn't have assumed you knew that. Forgive me, Kate. She won't be present at the celebration itself. Have no worries."

"That's fine." I was already sick of talking about my deathday. "What I really came to talk about is Miranda."

I told Adele about Benedict and I coming upon Miranda at Arcadia and her running away. I concluded by saying, "I need to find Miranda, Adele."

"And if that's what you want, Kate, I'm going to help you find her. But you can't run around playing detective. You need to enjoy these days in peace, seeing and talking with the people you want most to be with."

"Miranda is the person I want most to be with. She's the only one I can do anything for at this point in my life."

"Are you thinking of telling her the truth about you and her father?"

"I don't know. I'm not sure it would be a good idea."

"I'm quite sure it wouldn't be. You wouldn't get the response you're hoping for. She's not capable of that. There would be no closure."

"Perhaps not. But I want to help her."

"I understand. And I admire you for that. But let me take over the job. After all, it's me she wants to stalk. Maybe I can lure her out into the open."

I was just about to tell Adele the idea I got in the shower when the doorbell rang and she had to play hostess. I followed her down the stairs, but instead of joining the party, I slipped out the back door. I headed to where a streetlight threw a bright disk upon the alley and found my mark right in the center of it. Then, from my pocket, I took out the voice recorder.

"I brought this for you, Miranda," I called into the darkness. "Sorry I made you drop it the other day. I'd like to give it back to you."

I said this three times over several minutes. On the fourth attempt, she took the bait. Out of the darkness behind me, I heard her voice.

"Just leave it on the ground."

She had been behind me the whole time, hiding in the shadows by the deck.

"I don't think so." I turned toward the house but did not move from my spotlight. "You're not getting rid of me as easily as that. I'll give you back your voice recorder if you come visit me one afternoon. How's that for a deal? Hey, did you know that I knew your dad? We were teachers together in Rome all those years ago. I have a picture of him I'd love to show you. Come out to my house in Fauquier County one afternoon. Benedict would be glad to bring you. We could have lunch. And my neighbors have two horses they let me ride. Their names are Lucy and Ethel. Have you ever ridden a horse? Ethel's a sweetheart. She'll take you for a nice gentle ride."

When she didn't reply, I slowly began to walk back toward the house. Before I got to the deck, I had found her. She was crouched by an azalea bush just outside the penumbra of porch light. I made sure to look in the opposite direction as I mounted the stairs of the deck. But when I opened the screen door, I turned right toward her. "It's a great deal, Miranda. Lunch and a horse ride for your voice recorder."

Then I put the recorder back in my pocket and went inside.

At dinner, I sat next to Julian, who brought me up to speed on the reading for that evening's discussion, Don DeLillo's novel *Zero K*, which I had started with enthusiasm but wasn't able to finish due to mortality issues. The novel dealt with themes of transhumanism and cryogenic preservation, which dominated the after-dinner discussion around Adele's living room fire.

"But at what point do we *stop* trying to preserve ourselves," Adele kept pressing, "and blow the final whistle on our existence?"

After the discussion, Adele assigned Carly to drive me back to Five Hearths. Since I had last seen Carly, she had acquired a new tattoo: a small Jolly Roger on the side of her neck. The dreadful thing grinned at me through the shadows the whole drive out to Fauquier County. Our fitful conversation was mostly banal, except for the declaration she made almost as soon as I got into her car.

"I just want to say that Adele didn't leave New York because of any lawsuit. Or *threatened* lawsuit, I should say. That's utter twaddle. Bijou Arden is, I'm sorry, a posh git who doesn't know what she's talking about. Adele don't need to run from nobody."

The Jolly Roger on Carly's neck grinned in agreement.

CHAPTER SIX

It had been a cool autumn, and for the second weekend of October the leaves were in splendid array in their russet, burnt orange, and amber colors. That Saturday morning, Evie took me in her car down Skyline Drive. I hadn't been in the Shenandoah all season, and it was the perfect day for it. Bright sun in a deep-blue watercolor sky. Zeppelins of cumulus casting their shadows on the mountains. I imagined that in her prolonged silences Evie was playing the last time game, wondering whether I would ever again round this curve and see the storybook valley open up below me or feel myself taken up in the arms of the mountain and swaddled in this canopy of trees. But for myself, I could not manage to formulate the long thoughts or summon the wistful pangs that such a journey should inspire. Thomas Stearns, you were right: Humankind cannot bear very much reality. It was too much for my fading energy. All I could do was lean my head back on the headrest and in a semi-catatonic state and let the terrible beauty of this earth overwhelm me.

As we drove higher and deeper into the mountains, I considered telling Evie about my deathday. *"Three weeks from now, Evie, I'm going to take my life."* It would be lovely for her and Everett to be with me on that morning. But in the end, I thought better of it. Maybe it was a generation gap, but something told me that Evie wouldn't understand and that I would only leave her more saddened and confused. I did want to say something to her, however. She was driving with her left hand only, her right hand resting on top of the flip-open storage bin between our seats, and before I began, I took this hand and squeezed it.

"I'm so sorry you lost Cricket, Evie."

The pain had been right there all these years, awaiting its moment at the top of her throat, but as it sprung forward, she choked it back. "What can you do? None of us gets out of here alive."

"She was a beautiful girl."

"Yes, she was."

"How did you and Everett handle it?"

"We didn't handle it. We just tried not to dwell on it. We got up every morning and muddled through."

So that's how you did it. By doing your best not to think about it. How much saner Adele's approach seemed to me: square up with arms akimbo and look death in the eye. Not, though, as an antagonist. "It's absurd to think of death as something that you fight or try to overcome," Adele liked to say. "It's as absurd as trying to overcome yourself. Like Oedipus, you must learn the awful but cleansing wisdom that you *are* the plague."

Earlier that week, I had decided to leave Five Hearths as a gift to the Death Symposium Foundation and hired Everett as my lawyer for the transfer of the property. Adele had told me that she'd always wanted a piece of property to serve as a retreat center. My first idea was to surprise her with it in my will, but then I decided that I wanted to enjoy her reception of the gift. I invited her out to Five Hearths for that Saturday afternoon. Evie and I returned from our drive about one thirty—slowed by leaf-peeper traffic on Shenandoah Drive—but I had time for a nap before Adele arrived an hour later.

"Simply gorgeous!" was her reaction to the property.

We were standing at the top of my favorite hill, looking back at the house and the line of the Blue Ridge Mountains in the distance. I thought it odd, on a day of such stunning fall weather, that Carly did not even get out of the car to stretch and get a breath of fresh air. I could see her still sitting behind the wheel, head bowed, entranced by her phone.

I told Adele that I wanted to give Five Hearths to the Death Symposium. She couldn't believe I meant it at first. We hugged and cried, and afterward I listened as she dreamed her dreams of what the retreat center might one day be.

"And we will call it the Kate Montclair Retreat Center," she exclaimed. "No, your name on it is essential. That is the condition on which I accept the gift. Everyone must know of your generosity to the Death Symposium. And they will learn of your bravery when they read your memoir. We will have a little bookshop in the retreat center, where your memoir will be prominently displayed."

"Careful there," I joked. "Remember, it's the memoir of a crime."

"Well, until the law changes, we'll pass it around among our friends in a plain brown wrapper. It will join Joyce's *Ulysses* among the most famous banned books of all time!"

Adele and I were walking back down the hill when I saw Lisa's familiar metallic blue Subaru Forester rolling up the drive.

I had not been expecting her. She had come to surprise me with a pot of chicken soup. After introducing her to Adele, I led them both into the kitchen so that Lisa could put the soup on the stove.

"Isn't this a beautiful place?" Lisa asked Adele as the three of us stood awkwardly in the kitchen.

"Absolutely lovely," said Adele. "I still cannot believe that our big-hearted friend here just gifted it to the Death Symposium."

"*What?*"

Lisa's gasp contained a note, or perhaps a few bars, of deep revulsion. I was shocked that Adele had blurted this out. It wasn't like her.

I attempted to put a buffer of reasonable explanation around Adele's blunt revelation, but it did no good with Lisa. She beat a hasty retreat.

"Are you thinking of inviting her to your deathday?" Adele asked when Lisa was gone.

"No," I said regretfully.

"That's good. I'm sure she's a brilliant gal, but I wouldn't trust her for a minute with your secret. Oh, Kate! What a marvelous thing you've done! Who says there's no such thing as life after death? Your spirit will live on in the very stones of your retreat center!"

All through the following week, my strength declined. Headaches and nausea increased in intensity. I spent much of my time in bed, and when I wasn't asleep, I was drinking herbal tea, pounding Advil and vitamin C, and writing this memoir.

Whether out of passive aggression or just being busy with school, Lisa didn't call me that week. Benedict drove out almost every day, but despite my offers of a guest room, he would only visit for an hour or so before leaving.

The next Saturday morning I felt somewhat more myself, so I accepted Evie's offer to drive me to the grocery store. It was another gorgeous autumn day. When we returned to Five Hearths, Benedict's rental car, a white Toyota Camry, was parked by the house. As I got out of Evie's car, I could hear Everett having a "therapy session" (shooting at targets behind his house). A moment later, I was surprised when my front door opened—I had left the house locked—and Benedict appeared, holding a cup of coffee.

"Everett let us in," he smiled. "He and Miranda are next door shooting up the joint."

They had found Everett in the house when they arrived (I'd given him and Evie a set of keys long ago). Everett had walked over with some papers for me to sign regarding the transfer of the property. He was just setting them on my kitchen table with a note when he heard the crunch of car wheels on my pebbled drive. The three of them, or at least Everett and Benedict, chatted as they waited for Evie and me to return from the store. Benedict introduced himself to Everett as an old teaching friend of mine from Rome and Miranda as the daughter of one of our mutual friends. When they had run out of chat and we still weren't back, Everett encouraged them to make themselves at home. He mentioned wanting to get some practice shooting his new rifle, and when Miranda heard this, according to Benedict, she touched Everett on the shoulder in shamelessly kittenish fashion and begged him to allow her to join him.

Everett was delighted to have the company of an attractive, albeit unbathed, woman, and off they went.

Evie drove me and Benedict to her house. We walked around back to where Everett and Miranda were shooting at a bull's-eye Everett had set up on his portable target stand. He'd fitted Miranda with a pair of safety glasses and earmuffs and was giving her tips on how to position her arms. On the walk from the car, Benedict and I had a few seconds alone.

"What happened?" I asked. "Did she call you? Wait. She doesn't use cell phones."

"No. Last night I was at my Airbnb when she just knocked on the door and announced that I was to bring her this morning to your beautiful house. I gave her my bed for the night while I slept on the couch."

"It's been two weeks since I invited her. I thought she would never come."

Miranda was so fixated upon hitting the target with Everett's rifle that she barely registered Evie's presence when I introduced them. I caught Evie taking in Miranda's grimy oddness and trying to guess what was wrong with her. By contrast, she warmed immediately to Benedict's understated charm, though I was sure she thought that he had come to say his final goodbye.

Despite Everett's coaching, Miranda was having trouble hitting the target with the rifle, which gave me an idea.

"I think Miranda would do better with my little pink pistol. Benedict, would you mind running over to the house and getting it out of my nightstand drawer? And yes, it's loaded. Be careful."

Miranda looked at me, impressed that I owned a firearm. She was even happier when she discovered that the pistol was much easier to handle and when she started hitting the target with regularity. She laughed at her newfound accuracy. An unnerving, childish laugh. With every blast of the target, she cackled and danced about, and we all had to jump in to caution her from waving the pistol around in the air.

The therapy session succeeded in setting the tone for the day. After we said goodbye to Evie and Everett, I put Miranda on Ethel, climbed up on Lucy, and led Miranda on a gentle ride around Five Hearths. She kept asking me to make Ethel go faster, but the most I allowed was an easy trot to the top of my favorite hill. Not that Miranda was into views. She wanted speed. So, for the sake of a final trust exercise, I relented. I led her back down to the bottom of the hill, where I took Ethel's reins. Then I kept Lucy right beside Ethel as we galloped hard across the flat meadow. The whole way, Miranda's mouth was open in a frozen gasp of ecstasy.

Afterward I was desperate for my nap. While I slept for nearly two hours, Benedict made a fire in the family room and read while Miranda binged *The Great British Baking Show*. I had more steaks in the freezer, and later Benedict braved the chilly evening and grilled them for us. I microwaved some potatoes and made a salad. I hadn't exchanged ten sentences with Miranda since she arrived. It was like being around someone who didn't speak English. To keep the burden off conversation, the three of us ate on tray tables by the fire with the television on so that Miranda could see more of her show. She ate ravenously, sawing at the meat and shoving oversized hunks of it into her mouth.

I was determined to get her into the shower, so after dinner, I took her upstairs and showed her to the guest room with the private bath. On the bed I had already laid out towels, soaps, shampoos, and a pair of men's flannel pajamas that I had bought for cold weather.

"I want you to spend the night," I told her. "It's supposed to be another beautiful day tomorrow. Maybe we can go for another ride."

I went into the bath and turned on the shower. Before closing the bedroom door, I said, "I'll be back later to make sure you have everything you need."

Before my nap, I had texted Carly and asked her to tell Adele that Miranda was with me at Five Hearths. When I checked my phone while Miranda was in the shower, I saw that Carly had relayed a message from Adele asking if I'd like her to come out. I replied that Benedict was here and that I would be back in touch in the morning.

After I heard Miranda turn off the shower, I waited another ten minutes before knocking on her bedroom door. To a point, I was pleasantly surprised by what I found. She was sitting cross-legged on the bed in the flannel pajamas, her skin brown and blotchy but at least shiny clean, her wet hair combed not prettily but neatly straight back off her forehead. But she was just sitting there staring with no affect at the bedspread and playing with the green scapular she had replaced around her neck.

I had brought my fireproof box of treasures with me. I sat down with it on the edge of the bed and opened the lid. "My first-class relics," I said. The item I wanted was at the top of the box. "Take a look at this." I gave it to Miranda.

It was a framed photograph, in color and in a cheap frame, from the combined WIX-Mater Dei field day held in the Villa Borghese Gardens, October, 1986. Both faculties were in the picture. Mr. Cody and Dickie Grobbelaar, our soccer captains for the day, were each on one knee in front. Together they held a shlocky plastic bust of Dante discovered by someone at a tourist stand in Florence, which for some reason served as the trophy for the winner of the annual faculty versus students soccer game. I had always loved the boyish grins on Mr. Cody's and Dickie's sweaty faces. They'd just "kicked the collective, impudent backside" (Dickie's words) of the Student XI, and they were immensely proud of themselves. Dickie's competitiveness in the game didn't surprise me. He played as if the comparative youth of the students had been a personal insult, relentlessly charging forward with the ball and then contemptuously carrying it back to the center spot after each of his several goals. Mr. Cody's competitiveness, however, did surprise me. At twenty-six, he must have seemed positively middle-aged to many of those kids, and maybe he felt it, too. But as soon as the opening whistle blew, he'd cast all teacherly decorum aside and played with an abandon I found darling. I hadn't known beans about soccer, and I'd begged not to be put in because I hadn't wanted to embarrass myself in front of Mr. Cody. But I'd played for a few minutes in each half. In the picture, I stood on the left edge of the back row, red-faced, skinny as a bean pole, and holding up a Churchillian V for victory.

Miranda held the picture with both hands and peered into it so closely that her nose almost touched the glass, as though she wanted to fall into the picture through time.

"I have a green scapular too," I said. "Where did you get yours?"

"My mother hid it in my father's rooms at Mater Dei," Miranda replied, "because Adele Schraeder and my father were having an affair."

"So how did you come by it?"

"After my mother killed my father, she snuck back into my father's rooms and reclaimed it. She kept it in one of her notebooks for the rest of her life. That's where I took it from."

"Did your mother also put a green scapular in Adele Schraeder's apartment?"

Miranda nodded. "But in her notebook she said that when she went back she wasn't able to find it."

I lifted my old class planner out of the box and took from it my and Mr. Cody's green scapular. "*This* is the scapular your mother put in Adele's apartment."

Miranda looked at me for the first time since I had met her.

"We found it. Your father and I. You see, your father wasn't having an affair with Adele Schraeder. He was having an affair with me."

She put down the picture and began to tug on a strand of wet hair behind her ear.

"Your father and I were going to move to London, Miranda. With you. That was our plan. Your mother got it wrong. Your father and Adele were good friends, and she would always see them together."

For several moments, I let her tug silently on the strand of wet hair.

I dug into the box for another item. A love letter he wrote to me in the last days, his playful way of trying to convince me that I was going to be wonderful with his little girl.

Even though the letter was written to me, I considered leaving the room while she read it. But it wasn't that long, and I didn't want to do anything that would jeopardize the moment. I remained seated on the bed, my eyes cast down.

> *Besides being beautiful, bright, and the proud owner of a frog named Prince and an imaginary horse named Rollo, you should also know that Princess Miranda does not like sauce on her pasta; prefers Palestrina at naptime and Chopin's nocturnes at night; refuses, often quite peremptorily, to listen to any bedtime story "not done with all the voices;" and insists upon wearing her tiara in the bath...*

Unlike the photograph, she held the letter slightly away from her, as though afraid to get too close to his neat, cursive hand. As she read it, she showed no sign of emotion; her expression remained utterly impassive. Oh, Mr. Cody! We did not foresee this day on the day you gave me that letter, the day when I actually began to believe that I could be her mother.

"Where do you live, Miranda?"

No reply.

"Where do you live?"

"I live with Manny."

"Who is Manny?"

"Manny Manny Bo-Banny a Fee Fi Fo-Fanny Banana-Fanna Fo-Fanny. MA-NEE!"

"Who is Manny, Miranda?"

"He takes care of the pool at the hotel. He likes to watch Plague Baseball on his laptop and bet on every at-bat. *DiamondBet, the easiest way to bet MLB online!*"

"Are you in a relationship with Manny?"

No reply.

"I don't suppose you're seeing a doctor?"

No reply.

"Are you on medication?"

Still no reply.

"When you were a child, Miranda, I wanted to be there for you, but that chance was taken away. I hope you will let me be there for you now. With proper care and medication, you can live a much happier life. I know that's what your father would want for you."

She responded in a flat, uncurious voice, "In sixteen days, Kate Montclair, you're going to celebrate your deathday."

"Yes. I saw from the notebook you left at Arcadia that you overheard Adele and me talking about that. But I still have time to help you. Will you let me, Miranda?"

"The angel of death is coming for you."

"I'm going to be all right. But it will be much easier knowing that you will be getting the care you need." I wanted to touch her knee, give her some sign of affection, but I was unsure how she would react.

"Are you afraid to die?" she asked, her voice still flat and uncurious.

"Very much. But I'm more afraid of dying needlessly in great pain."

"Irene Aquila was afraid to die."

I waited to see if she would offer more before I said, "Were you there when she died, Miranda?"

She began to tug even more forcefully at the strand of wet hair, as though she were going to pull it out of her head. Unthinkingly, I reached up to make her stop, and she slapped my hand away. Hard.

She resumed tugging at the strand of hair, not the least concerned that she'd hurt me. I stood up. "I'd like you to keep the picture and the letter. Why don't you get some sleep? In the morning, we'll have a nice breakfast and go for a ride."

I picked up my box of treasures and started to leave. But then I remembered. Shifting the box of treasures in my arm, I took the voice recorder out of my hip pocket and tossed it lightly on the bed in front of her.

"After all," I said, smiling at Miranda, "a deal's a deal."

When I left Miranda, I went downstairs and found Benedict still reading in front of the fire. He had picked off my shelf Muriel Spark's biography of Mary Shelley. As he drank another glass of the Rappahannock Cellars Cab Franc that I had opened for dinner, we talked about my conversation with Miranda.

"She became anxious when I asked if she was there when your mother died. What'll we do if she admits to something? Call the police again?"

"I suppose," Benedict said. "But what she really needs is a doctor and medicine."

After we sat for a while looking at the fire, I concluded, "But it was a good day, all in all. I'm grateful for it."

Benedict smiled a sad, heartrending smile, and I excused myself and left him with Mary Shelley.

I brought to bed my old class planner bulging with its contents. I re-opened the blue cover and began turning the pages, each page marking a week, the plans for each class indicated in my ridiculously loopy handwriting:

Jane Eyre Unit, Day 1. Background on Romanticism, Contrast w/ Austen, Reading Aloud Chapter 1 w/ Discussion of Setting and Character. Homework: Read & Annotate Chapters 2–4.

The planner bulged with other treasures from those years: programs from dramatic performances, essay assignments, thank-you notes from girls and parents. Once, in college, I'd read about archaeologists discovering several versions of the ancient city of Troy, one buried underneath the other like the layers of a lasagna. My life was like that. Although my childhood and adolescence contained one or two broken pottery shards of interest, it was my years in Rome and at Wildwood that made up the deepest stratum of anything resembling the person I was today. That young woman I remembered—the sensitive *ingénue*, the romantic artist, the star-crossed lover—had been taken up into the poetry of my mind and shaped and burnished into a heroine. Yet, as with Troy, that mythic heroine had a basis in fact. In some related form, she had really walked this earth. She was not wholly imaginary.

I ran the tips of my fingers over those pages. My original lesson plans were written in pencil, but written later, in red felt pen, was a much more personal diary, lightly encrypted, of my days with Mr. Cody. I turned the page to that pivotal Friday night in November 1986 when we set our course definitively for the lands beyond the sun.

The plan was this. We were both going to resign our teaching positions on the upcoming Monday and, with our abundant savings (about 500 pounds after the exchange), not to mention our two shiny new credit cards, fly with Miranda to London early on Tuesday morning. The countess's villa was to be our staging area. Adele and I were to meet Mr. Cody and Miranda there, and we would all spend the night. Then, long before sunrise, Adele would drive us to the airport.

Once we were in London, while Mr. Cody awaited the shoot for *The Public Image* to commence in the spring, he would look for other acting work. Meanwhile, I would scour the city for my own job. Somehow our schedules would have to work so that one of us could always be home with Miranda.

Pretty lousy plan, admittedly. But how perfect it seemed at the time.

The night we finalized the plan, he brought me home on his Vespa. All the way from WIX, as we slalomed through the Friday night Roman traffic, the gelid November air like cut glass on our faces, I felt as though I were being rocked on a fast and powerful boat moving farther and farther out into the unknown. We talked for a long while outside my apartment building. He sat on his Vespa, his chin resting on my shoulder blade, and I sat kind of side saddle on his right leg, holding the arm that wrapped round my waist.

"I love you, Kate Montclair," he whispered into my ear. "I love you, and I don't want to live without you."

"You won't have to live without me, Mr. Cody. I love you too, and I'm never going to let you go."

I fell asleep at Five Hearths in the arms of Mr. Cody, and my light was still on when I was awakened, an hour or so later, by the presence of someone in the room with me.

It was Miranda. She was standing next to me by the bed, fully dressed, the voice recorder in her hand. "Listen," she said, her voice nearly a whisper.

"Wait. What time is it?"

"Benedict is asleep now. Listen."

She took the cassette out of the recorder and replaced it with another one she slid out of the pants pocket of her pajamas. "You haven't heard this one." It took her a moment to find the place on the cassette she wanted. But when she did, she pressed the play button, and a loud grating sound burst forth. In the background a woman was wailing and screaming. I recognized the voice from the recording on Roy's phone. It was the countess. It was Irene.

"NO!...NO!...GO AWAY, PLEASE. STOP! STOP!"

Then I heard another woman.

"Hold her still, Miranda!"

It was Adele's voice.

"Calm yourself, Irene," Adele shouted over Irene's screams. "Everything is going to be all right!"

Irene: *"I DON'T WANT TO DIE! I DON'T WANT TO DIE!"*

Further sounds of scuffling ensued. Adele shouted at Miranda and again tried to calm Irene. I shouted at Miranda to turn it off.

The screams echoed all around me in the stunned silence.

"Oh, Miranda, what did you and Adele do?"

The faintest twitch of interest appeared on her face as she registered my horror. Then, dropping the recorder, she bolted from the room.

Next it was I who was wailing and screaming, beside myself with confusion, terror, and worry as I shook poor Benedict awake.

"She's gone, Benedict! Help me find her, please. I'm going to die, Benedict, on November 2, and you've got to help me find her now!"

CHAPTER SEVEN

After Benedict left, I was awake the rest of the night, sick with worry about Miranda, sick to the point of nausea with a cancer migraine. Sometime after dawn, I fell asleep and was still asleep at midday when Adele arrived bearing pho.

"How we doing, love?"

I could not manage any kind of answer.

She looked at me as if she knew I had just rounded the final turn, but she covered up with smiles and solicitude. She helped me freshen up a bit, put clean sheets on the bed, and gave me my pain meds. While she went downstairs to heat up the soup, I had to decide what I was going to say. I was still thinking when she came back into my bedroom and asked me what I had an appetite for.

"Not much. Let me start with just a little of the bone broth."

Ten minutes later, she returned with a bowl half-filled with pho broth. She set me up with a folded tray table on my lap, then arranged a tray table and chair for herself at the end of my bed. I watched her tear the basil and sprinkle it into her bowl then squeeze her lime wedge into the soup with incantatory swirls of her hand.

"One cannot eat pho with delicacy," she declared. "Send the servants away." Then she lowered her chin to her bowl and gobbled up the strands of rice noodles clamped in her chopsticks.

I tried a sip of the bone broth, but it was too savory for me. I was feeling much better than I had in the night, but I didn't have the appetite for anything this extravagant. As I put the bowl down, Adele watched me.

"Let me get you something else," she said. "Maybe some tea?"

"Nothing right now."

"What's on your mind, Kate?"

"How does it usually, you know, go at the end?"

"You've asked me this before."

"Yes."

"You'd be surprised. You'd think there would be anguish, tears. But it's quite the opposite. The fortitude and composure I've witnessed, well—it's mighty edifying."

I ventured further onto the ice. "Has anyone ever changed their mind?"

She reached out and began to rub my foot wrapped in the sheet and the comforter. "No, my darling. At that ultimate point, the mood of celebration generates a tremendous grace. Everything is serene. There is only gratitude and love. Tell me what's the matter, Kate. You're feeling some anxiety about your deathday?"

I was still trying to figure out my next move when we heard Benedict enter the house though the kitchen. When Adele had gone to heat the soup, I had checked my phone and saw that he had texted me a few minutes before eight o'clock that morning.

Still looking.

Had he found her since then and brought her back?

"That's Benedict," I said.

"I'm glad." Adele once more lowered her chin to her bowl.

I listened intently to the noises from downstairs, and my heart sank when I could only make out one set of footsteps. Benedict used the powder room off the foyer, then joined us upstairs.

"Hello, Benny, old chap," Adele said. "Good to see you."

He nodded at Adele, then turned to me. His dejected look disappointed the anxious expectation in my eyes.

"Where have you been, Benny?" Adele inquired. "You look like you spent the night in your car."

"I did." He swept the oily, drooping strands of hair off his forehead.

"What's going on, guys?" Adele inquired again.

Benedict looked at me to gauge how much I had told her about Miranda's cassette.

"Miranda's gone missing," I said.

"Miranda? The girl's always missing."

I started to explain but didn't get very far before the effort exhausted me. Benedict, still standing on the other end of the room, picked up the thread but told only so much: how he had brought Miranda to see me but that she had run away in the night.

"I'm sorry," Adele said as she turned to me. The expression in her eyes couldn't help adding, "Can't say I didn't warn you."

"Did you find Manny?" I asked Benedict.

"Not yet, but I'm still looking. Adele, how did my mother die?"

He asked this question calmly, wearily, but there was no doubt it was an accusation.

"I think you know how your mother died, Benny."

"I think I do too. You killed her, shoving secobarbital down her throat even as she was pleading with you to let her live."

"Ah. So you've been talking to Miranda. Perhaps not the most trusted source of information: a schizophrenic who suffers from hallucinations."

"There's evidence that my mother changed her mind. A voicemail she left for her boyfriend, Roy. She doesn't mention your name, but it's clear from the message that she was afraid of your coming."

"Your mother had a moment of indecision, Benny, to be sure. Bad luck I was on my way home from England. If I had been able to be with her earlier, I would have been able to give her something to calm herself. But my flight was delayed, and I only returned to DC that evening."

"She revoked her consent, Adele."

"Benny, you can't listen to Miranda."

"I'm not listening to Miranda. *I'm listening to my mother.* I can hear her screaming at you to stop on the recording."

"What recording?"

"The recording Miranda made of the whole business."

As if on a jutting slab of sidewalk, Adele's regal self-possession stumbled with a flicker across her eyes. But just as quickly, she righted herself again. She wiggled her torso to full upright position and placed her shoulders back. "How did Miranda make a recording?"

"A device in her pocket."

"Blimey, what an age we live in! Would it be possible for me to hear this recording?"

"Adele," I interrupted, "Benedict doesn't need to hear it again."

"I'm fine," Benedict said. "Do you have it, Kate?"

I had been keeping the device in my bedside table drawer. I took it out and played the recording—which *I*, at least, didn't need to hear again. But I did hear it again, glad, at least, that Benedict was there and that I didn't have to confront Adele with it alone. As the recording played, I watched Adele, head cocked to one side as she listened, hands clapped between her knees while she stared placidly into her cooling soup. When the recording finished, she sighed and addressed Benedict.

"I'm sorry you had to hear that, Benny. It wasn't fair of Miranda to play that for you. It wasn't fair of her to make the recording in the first place. But I want you to know, Benny, that your mother enjoyed a lovely, peaceful death. The death *she* wanted. What you hear on that recording is only a minute out of the entire deathday celebration—a *minute*, I might add, not anywhere near the celebration's climax. Irene had a *moment*, and I'm sorry you had to learn of it in this horrid fashion. But please, hear me on this: Irene got through the moment and regained her peace."

"When did she arrange her deathday with you?" Benedict asked.

"Not long after she received her diagnosis. She asked me not to tell you, so I was professionally bound to respect her wishes."

"Did she say why she didn't want to tell me?"

"She thought you might not agree with her decision. Was she right, Benny?"

"I don't know what I would have agreed to if I had been brought into the discussion. But from that recording, it certainly sounds as though she revoked her consent."

"She gave me a consent that by her own express desire was irrevocable."

"Do you have that written down?"

"Of course not! We don't have the freedom at present to carry on normally with the business of dying. We are forced to operate in the shadows."

"But what does that mean, anyway? To give consent that's irrevocable? I don't think freedom of choice works that way."

"But the anxiety of *dying* works that way, Benny. If the sufferer does not make an absolute commitment, then the moments *in extremis,* which should be moments of joy and celebration, turn into an intolerable game of chicken. *Irene wanted to die.* She looked me in the eye more than once and told me so, fully composed of mind, absolutely determined. She didn't want to die in a hospital bed, and I am proud that I was there to help her avoid it."

The three of us fell into a brooding silence. Adele finally turned to me and broke it. "So, you've brought Benny into the picture?"

"Yes," I said.

"And what are your views, Benny, on keeping Kate's deathday confidential?"

"I'm happy to honor Kate's wishes."

"Good."

"But I need to find Miranda before I do anything," I said. "Even if that means delaying."

"Kate—"

"No! This is nonnegotiable. I need to find her, and I need to get her help. *If it's the last thing I do!*"

With the outburst of this brilliant cliché still ringing around the room, Adele came and sat on the side of the bed close to me. "I promise to take care of Miranda," she said. "As well as anyone can. Don't put yourself through the torture of delaying your decision, Kate. One delay can easily lead to another and, before you know it, you'll be in a place where you do not want to be. Why did Miranda run away?"

"She was upset because I reacted badly to that recording. She thought I was accusing her. I didn't mean to. I was just so shocked."

"Can you think of any place you haven't looked, Benny?"

"I haven't tracked down this fellow Manny whom she seems to be living with. It's the only lead I have left."

"Then follow it," Adele said. "But, Kate, you have to realize that girl can disappear for *weeks* on end."

"I *have* to help her," I repeated.

"Not everything broken can be fixed. That's nothing to feel guilty about. It's simply the way the world is." I watched as Adele surveyed the class planner on my nightstand. "Rejoice in the memories of your youth, Kate. Be confident that, if you could, you and Michael would live it all over again. Exactly the same way. Without regret. Miranda's problems, like her mother's problems, are a piece of fate out of your control. Accepting that is wisdom and peace."

It was not quite four in the morning. By the light of the flashlight on my phone and to the tune of Benedict's snoring, I had been up for an hour already, writing. It was difficult to write. My energy flagged easily; I had a constant, ever-sharpening ache behind my forehead; every five minutes, I had to close my eyes and steady my breath before soldiering on. I didn't know whether I would be able to continue writing much longer.

Adele had left about three o'clock the previous afternoon, and afterward I fell into a deep sleep. When I awoke a solid twelve hours later, I felt refreshed, all head pain subsided. Likely only the eye of the hurricane, but I was determined to make the most of it while it lasted. I used the bathroom quietly, careful not to wake Benedict, who had grabbed a blanket out of the linen closet in the hall and made a bed for himself on the chaise lounge. But either because of the tapping I was making on my laptop or because of his subconscious awareness of my being awake, he stirred.

"Is there anything I can get you?" he asked me.

"No, thank you." I continued to write. I still didn't have an appetite, but I was thankful for whoever had placed the full Bethany Beach water jug on my nightstand. "Sorry I woke you."

"It's OK. I think I got eight hours. I was exhausted too."

"You don't have to stay in here. You have your pick of guest rooms."

"Adele warned me that if I abandoned this post I would be shot."

Several minutes passed. I was aware of him awake and thinking and probably wanting to talk, but I continued to write as fast as I could go. For these, I thought, could well be the last words I would ever write, and, though no one would probably ever read them, it was important to get them down. After I had finished and read it over, I lay back upon my pillow.

The room remained quite dark. At this time of year, the dull light of sunrise would not appear through the closed slats of the window shade until after seven o'clock. But my eyes were quite used to the dark, and I could see the silhouette of Benedict's wild, dirty hair as he sat upright in the chaise lounge, bare feet peeking out from under the blanket spread over his legs. He was in a thoughtful mood, and, as I was tired, I closed my eyes and let him talk.

"I had an experience of God that morning," he said. "But not in the way you'd think. After everything was over, I went into the *cortile* and sat underneath the pear tree and smoked. No flash of light. No getting knocked off my horse. Quite the opposite, in fact. I didn't have an experience of God's presence but of his absence. As though, with Elvis, he had left the building. Let the place fall to ruins. I don't mean that I realized he didn't exist. It was more that now I had proof he *did* exist, but that he was angry with me. That I had been exiled from his presence. Kind of like how you described yourself, that day at Arcadia when you came to see Miranda's notebook."

Benedict continued, "All this agonizing, you might say, is nothing more than Catholic guilt. Maybe so. But if it is the superego-father castigating the ego-son, then I want to know why my psyche would turn on itself in *that* particular way. What evolutionary purpose is there—I recognize it is a paradox to speak of evolution's purposes—in punishing myself for trespassing against a table of commandments that is only a mirage? How does this help me achieve security? What does it have to do with propagating the species? I am an exile to myself. That's a curious drama for my psyche to be playing out, is it not? Why do I keep rehearsing in my mind the role of the prodigal son hankering after the husks meant for the pigs, a prodigal son whose father would only be too glad if he never came back?"

As I listened to Benedict, I realized that I too knew this God. I didn't believe in him, but for one moment long ago on that harrowing morning, as I held Mr. Cody's dead body in my arms and looked up at the morning star, I had believed *enough* to think that he was angry with me. That I had wronged him in some way.

"Do you want a baby?" Tim surprised me with the question on a lazy Sunday morning. Oh yes, I wanted one, but I didn't tell him so—not only because I knew he didn't want one but because I didn't think I deserved one. I couldn't bear the thought of holding my baby all scrubbed and tubbed and ready for bed and seeing the tentacles of that other cancer, my guilt, winding around its dimpled arms. That other cancer strangled my dream of a baby, and it strangled my marriage, just as it strangled my desire to write and to love—really love—my students.

What was it really? A little black dot on my lily-white soul? When the sisters made us go to confession, we would contrive ways to skip out. Excuse ourselves to the bathroom and hide in the stalls. Then later, we would sneak into the pew with the kids saying their three Hail Marys so that sister would think we'd gone. *Bless me, Father, for I have sinned, though I have no idea what that means. I last went to confession when I was twelve or thirteen, when my mother made me go before Easter, when she drove me to a parish I had never been to before because she didn't want to talk to a priest or be seen by anyone she knew.* What was I supposed to say to that sniffly man behind the screen? What had I done and to whom? Was I supposed to tell him that my father had run away with some young chippie whom I often imagined killing in dozens of unspeakable ways? Was I supposed to tell him that my mother was usually buzzed when I came home from school and that when I hated her I didn't understand that she was punishing herself for a crime that didn't even exist, the crippling, misunderstood pain of her own mother visited upon her?

Bless me, Father, but I was just a kid with lots of daddy issues and mommy pain, and I never knew what it felt like for a man to tell me he loved me and didn't want to live without me.

I truly thought that I was doing something good, and maybe I was. I don't know. My therapist told me to forgive myself and forgive them too, and I had done it, yes, on my favorite hill out there. I had looked into that heartless sky and said the words aloud, longing to be cleansed.

Did I break the universe, Lord? Is that why you're angry with me? Is that why you've gone away? Speak to me. Why won't you speak to me? Speak.

A few moments later, I had drifted off into a light sleep when Benedict asked, "If Miranda showed up here in the morning, and she allowed you to help her, would you still—"

"Go through with it?"

"Yeah."

"You mean, would I go through with it, as opposed to living a happy, healthy life until I'm ninety-five?"

"But do you ever think—"

"What?"

"That maybe the decision isn't yours to make?"

"Then whose decision would it be, Benedict?"

A few moments later, I said, "You told Adele that you are happy to honor my wishes about my deathday. You didn't say that the other night when I first told you about it." Perhaps it wasn't fair of me to hold Benedict's reaction up to scrutiny. I had been so upset about the recording on Miranda's cassette and Miranda's subsequent running away, and I was feeling so afraid of not finding Miranda before my deathday that I vomited my secret all over Benedict. His stunned response was simply an "OK, I understand," before he turned his attention to searching for Miranda. But I wanted more from him.

"Will you be with me on the day?"

After a moment's reflection, he said, "Thank you for asking me. I am humbled that you would want me to be present with you in that moment. But, if you don't mind, I'd like to think about it."

"Of course."

I was disappointed by his reply. Hurt by it, actually. But I deflected attention from myself by asking him another question. "Do you believe what Adele said about your mother's deathday?"

"I don't know. It's hard to imagine my mother regaining her peace of mind after the episode on that recording. But I don't know."

"You think Adele killed her?"

"She would never call it that. She would say she was simply taking things in hand. Like not telling you at first about Miranda."

"She wanted to protect me," I said.

"Protect you from what?"

"From continuing to go through life haunted by guilt. She thought my discovering Miranda would dredge up my past with Miranda's father."

"But is that why she didn't tell us that Miranda was staying at her house?"

"What?"

"Miranda stayed at Adele's the night she ran away."

"Wait. How do you know that?"

"Yesterday morning, early, I saw Miranda coming out of Adele's house in Georgetown. It was one of my stops as I went round looking for her. I called to her, said you weren't angry with her, that you were only surprised. That you wanted to see her."

"What did she say?"

"She didn't say anything. She just looked at me for a moment with that blank expression on her face, hopped into some stranger's car, and left."

"Why didn't you tell me this yesterday?"

When he didn't answer, I answered for him. "Because you wanted to see if Adele would admit she had seen her."

The past stretching into the future; the future stretching into the past. Never now, never in the center of the chiasm. The antagonists of my life are memory and hope.

I have beheld, all these years, myself being held, wrapped in Mr. Cody's arms. I have craved, cravenly, a future filled with that same feeling.

I have lived, on the one hand, like an old man—like my grandfather—as he tore through the rusted filing cabinets of his mind, searching for the memory he wanted. His mouth would gibber momentarily, desperately, as he groped for it, and, when he found it, his eyes would brighten as he lunged for it. Then he was off again. And as he talked, a solitary tear would edge over the corner of one eye and slide sideways down the slope of his jagged nose. His stories were told not so much from joy as from fear. Fear of losing just one of those scattered leaves of memory. And me? Events that took place in my life more than thirty years ago, over the space of less than three months, had defined all my attitudes and aspirations, all my fecklessness and failures since then. Here, in my dying days, my thoughts were of Mr. Cody and holding his dead body as I gazed into the last of the night sky before that awful dawn, with the stars spilled across the dark expanse as from a child's jar of glitter, with the pale moon floating away like a lost balloon. So empty and desolate that endless, pointless space.

But I have lived, on the other hand, like a child. Expecting everything to turn out all right in the end. A child playing before her father, knowing the love with which she is looked at. How strange it is that we do not, cannot, give up hope. We still long for fullness, even when we've learned it is not possible. Even now, here, in my dying days, my longing is like that of a little girl who lays her head on her deceased father's tummy, fully expecting him, after a snuggle, to get up as always, tickle her and begin to roughhouse, as the fullness comes rushing in.

But I am finally ready to live like an adult. I am ready to accept that nothing that is past can be preserved from catastrophe; nothing that is to come can answer to our longings. There is only now and how one decides to negotiate the tragedy.

This morning, Adele came to see me. She had hardly stepped into my bedroom when I torpedoed her with the question: Why hadn't she told us that Miranda came to her house on the night she fled Five Hearths?

Adele was taken aback by my question. "I didn't know Miranda came to P Street, darling! And I'm quite sure Carly didn't know either or she would have told me. We were both asleep, all through that night. Did Benedict actually *see* her exiting the front door? Miranda must have broken into the house—she's clever that way—to steal food. Or more likely liquor. I'll have to talk to Carly about getting an alarm system. Anyway, darling, you have to believe that I am on your team. I am committed to helping find Miranda and getting her the help she needs, however long it takes."

After that discussion, Adele helped me down to the front porch. I sat in one of the rocking chairs with a blanket around my knees. It was a cold, cloudy day, and I was feeling weak. Nonetheless, I wanted to sit on my front porch and look out on Five Hearths under the low ceiling of iron-gray cloud that was sliding over my life like the lid of a sarcophagus. Adele and I sat on the porch for about an hour, and she helped me finalize the liturgy for my deathday celebration.

The reader will wonder: Why did I trust this woman? Had Adele really killed Irene Aquila? I doubted that. Had she been involved in some other shenanigans in New York? It seemed to me that she had only been confronted with a disgruntled family member. While I might not have approved of every decision Adele had made along the way, I did appreciate that she had always, in her own inimitable fashion, been there for me, helping me not to seek myself anywhere but inside myself.

So, no, dear reader, I did not trust her, if by that you mean expecting her not to meddle; expecting her not to conspire; expecting her not to think that she always knew best. But I did trust her, in this most critical moment of my life, to help me negotiate the tragedy on my own. And my own decision was not to concede anything to the senseless proceedings of the universe. On the morning of November 2, I was going to end my life.

What of my promise to help Miranda? Four days had passed since she had disappeared again. Benedict had continued to scour her customary haunts, to no avail. I knew I could trust him to keep looking for her after my death, and Adele had just pledged, once again, to do the same. If I changed my deathday plan, I would only become weaker as time went on and, thus, more useless to her cause. Enlisting the aid of Benedict and Adele was the best I could do, at this point in my life, to help Miranda. But I despaired that even their aid would be enough.

CHAPTER EIGHT

I awoke early on the Thursday of the third week of the October, feeling, if not "myself," at least as though the alien being using my body as its host had chosen to sleep in. While my energy was decent, I got down to some writing, but around nine o'clock I was interrupted by a visit from Lisa and Benedict. They had come—unexpectedly—together. Lisa made me us a fresh pot of my herbal tea, then sat down beside me on the edge of the bed. Benedict took the end of the chaise lounge.

"I want to talk to you about something, Kate," Lisa began ominously. "I asked Benedict to be here too because we're both your good friends who love you very much."

Lisa then told me that she had been doing some research into Adele and the Death Symposium.

"I went to the Facebook page of the New York City Death Symposium," she said. "Started going through their posts, scrolled back more than a year. I came upon one post that was a picture of Adele with an invitation to come to one of their coffee shop meetings. There were tons of LIKES and positive comments. I started randomly clicking on the names of the people who liked the posts just to get a sense of who these people were. I came to the page of this one young gal, Emily—she's a fitness and health guru in Manhattan–and she had a post pinned to the top of her page. It was a picture of her kid sister, Alexis, and underneath it Emily described how Alexis died in early 2019. Then she added, rather cryptically, that her sister 'unfortunately was a regular participant in meetings of the NYC Death Symposium. Those with inquiring minds, please message me.'

"So I messaged her. I just said, 'I'm sorry for your loss. I'd like to get more information on Adele Schraeder and the Death Symposium.' She messaged me back within five minutes, and we set up a Zoom call.

"Kate, you won't believe what Emily told me. Alexis had arranged with

Adele this thing called a deathday, this suicide ritual where at the end you take some pills or whatever that end your life. Well, Emily found out about her sister's plan beforehand—Alexis herself told her—and she was able to put the kibosh on it. It's actually *illegal* what Adele and Alexis were doing. Emily lawyered up and went after Adele and the Death Symposium—"

"But she didn't have enough evidence," I said.

"That's right. How do you know?"

"Adele told me."

"But wait. Does that mean Adele *admits* to this deathday thing?"

I did my best to explain that the Death Symposium has no philosophy of its own about end-of-life issues or anything else. It provides a forum for—

"Emily originally posted a comment on the NYC Death Symposium page, to the effect that Adele practices assisted suicide," Lisa interrupted me. "But Adele, or whoever moderates her Facebook page, hid the post. That's why Emily pinned her sister's picture to her own page and made her comment cryptic so that Facebook wouldn't take her post down."

"I'm not sure what any of this has to do with me," I said.

"Kate," Lisa said, taking my hand in hers, "tell me that you and Adele are not planning your deathday."

The combination of Lisa looking at me with such dreadful anticipation and Benedict, behind her, looking away abashedly, shattered what was left of the defenses to my secret. Choking on the words, I said to Lisa, "I would like you to be there with me."

"Oh, Kate!"

Lisa grabbed me off the pillow, enveloped me in her arms, and rocked me back and forth as we wept together.

"Don't do this, Kate!"

"It is either *this* or extreme pain," I sobbed. "There is no third option! I don't care if it's illegal or immoral or whatever. I just want the pain to be over."

Benedict excused himself for a good half hour, and when he returned, Lisa and I had achieved a different mood. Lisa was in my bathroom washing her face, while I was opening up the bedroom windows to let in the crisp October air. She and I were laughing uproariously about something—if memory serves, about whether it was too gruesome to use my shoe collection as an auction item at the next Brook Farm fundraiser. Benedict was, understandably, a little confused.

Turning from the window, flush with excitement and perhaps a touch of hysteria, I said, "Benedict, Lisa wants to be there with me on the day."

"Who am I to tell this girl what to do?" Lisa, coming in from the bathroom, explained to Benedict. "If this is what she wants, then I'm going to be there for her."

"Will you be there too?" I asked Benedict. "Please? I trust both of you with my life—and my death. I want both my good friends with me at the end."

Just over a week to go now. Am in a good deal of pain. No news of Miranda. No energy to write.

Non te quaesiveris extra.

From my bed, I stare at my picture in the framed poster above my desk across the room. My twenty-year-old self hiking on my Morning Mountain. Bright eyes and bright teeth. All topped up with estrogen and idealism. *This is my moment, and I am going to seize it.*

Six days to go now. Still no news of Miranda. And Benedict still has not told me whether he will be there on my deathday.

My deathday in two days.
More intense pain in my head.
Is this the promised end? Or image of that horror?
Either way, I shall soon fall and cease.

Editor's note. *Kate's last entry in her memoir was not written on her laptop but in her own hand in a small notebook she kept by the side of her bed. On the day before her deathday, she wrote several lines in this notebook, most of which are illegible. The last line, however, can clearly be made out:*

Miranda, where are you? God forgive me.

PART IV

SHIPWRECK

KATE'S STORY COMPLETED POSTHUMOUSLY
BY HER EDITOR

Fauquier County Intelligencer

Katherine "Kate" Montclair

November 2, 1964–November 2, 2020 (age 56)

Beloved teacher and writer Kate Montclair died at 8:23 a.m. Monday, November 2, 2020, at her ancestral home, Five Hearths, 4457 Exodus Road, Hume, Virginia.

Since 1997 Kate taught English literature at Brook Farm Academy, a private secondary school located in Washington, DC. Her students will fondly remember her as the demanding but devoted (and wickedly funny) "Ms. Montclair," lover of the Oxford comma, the droll riposte, the designer handbag, and all things Austen. Her students will also not soon forget the signed "Apprentice's Affidavit" they had to turn in with each essay and the phrase they hoped to find written at the bottom of the last page when it was graded: "Acceptable, with alterations."

Katherine "Kate" Montclair was born on November 2, 1964, in the same home in which she passed away, the only daughter of Stephen Montclair and Germaine (Harris) Montclair. At Washington and Lee University, she helped found the comedy troupe Funny Ha-Ha or Funny Strange that still flourishes on that campus. Upon graduation, she taught for two years at Wildwood International Catholic School in Rome, Italy. After returning to the States in the summer of 1988, she spent the next several years in New York City forging a career as a comedy writer. In the fall of 1992, she returned to teaching, taking up first a position at The March School, Middleburg, Virginia, and later at St. George's School, Houston, Texas, where she remained until she returned the Washington, DC, area in 1997 to take up the position at Brook Farm Academy, where she taught for the remainder of her career. But Kate always kept up her writing. She was most proud of her humorous, Austen-inspired essay on the lives of single female schoolteachers, "Poor Gentlewomen in Love," that was published in the April 8, 1994, edition of The New Yorker.

A lover of the busy streets and bookstores of the District no less than her cherished Fauquier County, Kate also will be remembered for her dedication to her friends and students, her passion for Virginia wine, horses, a good novel, a good bath, and, not least, good dark chocolate.

Kate's final work, a memoir, is being edited for publication.

Burial will take place privately.

Expressions of sympathy may be offered to the Sisters of the Compassionate Heart of Jesus, 427 Stratford Avenue, Chappaqua, New York, 10514. Online condolences may be expressed at eltonfuneralhome.com.

CHAPTER ONE

I understand your frustration at not being able to hear anymore from Kate directly. I understand and share it. But I hope you will forgive me if I take up Kate's story in my own voice. The story of her final illness is not yet complete, and I feel bound by what she asked me to do on the eve of her death to complete it. Besides, as I've said, this is my story too, mine and Miranda's and the Codys and, of course, Adele's. So, here after the ending, allow me to tell you about the beginning.

Again, it was a cold November morning, that first day of the month. I awoke early, and flailing about for something useful to do, walked down the drive to get Kate's mail. After I brought it back, I made her a pot of tea and carried it up to her on a tray with the stack of mail.

"There's a package for you from Bijou," I told her. "What would she be sending you?"

"No idea," Kate said. "Just put it on the desk. Got no juice for mail at the moment. I'll open it later."

I poured her a cup of tea, then sat beside her on the bed. This was when she asked me to edit her memoir. I refused her, and then told her I loved her, as I have written. When she had finished telling me where I could find her manuscript in case I changed my mind, I launched into my plea. "Don't do it, Kate."

"Please, Benedict—"

"Don't do it. I'll stay with you through the pain. You won't be alone. Let me and Lisa help you. Let us help you bear the burden. We *want* to help you bear it."

"There's no point, Benedict. I will be in utter misery. As a matter of fact, I'm not feeling too spiffing right now. There is no helping me bear it. I've made my goodbyes in my own fashion. Now let me go."

"I can't."

"You have to."

She held my hand as we cried. She pulled me toward her, and I leaned over awkwardly so that she could kiss my hand. I thought, *Less than twenty-four hours from now, this hand, these lips, will no longer be warm. She will no longer be here. And I can't stop it. The unendurable is coming, and I can't stop it.*

I released my hand. "Then I can't stay."

"Benedict."

"I can't, Kate. I can't just sit here and watch."

"I want you here."

"But I can't do it. I told you I don't think—

"I'm sorry you had to hear that recording, Benedict. But Adele said your mother recovered her balance. Wasn't that better than weeks or months more of suffering?"

"What I know is, I can't watch you take your life."

"I'm not asking you to 'watch' me. I'm asking you to be with me."

"I'm sorry, but I can't."

"You think what I'm doing is wrong."

"I'm not your judge. I can't imagine what you're going through. If I could change places with you, take your suffering on my shoulders, I would do it."

"But you can't. No one can."

We sat for a long while without speaking or looking at one another. I might have relieved the tension by agreeing to stay, but I could not do it. I tried to imagine, if I were to stay, where I would sit. Here on the side of the bed? While Adele, sitting on the other side of the bed, handed Kate the last lethal cocktail? No, I could not do it. What inside me resisted the thought of staying, I had no idea. It certainly wasn't logic. I *was* glad my mother was spared further suffering, yet I found the manner of her death appalling. I didn't want Kate to suffer one minute longer, but I could not just sit here and watch the woman I loved—yes, loved—drink her own death.

Now, holding a green scapular up to the light from the windows, Kate said, "Do you think it could possibly be like what they used to tell us, when we were in school?"

"I don't know. But I must say, I prefer the poetry of it."

Kate was worn out and already half asleep. Like the close air of the room, our disagreement still hung about us, but it would have to wait. I tucked her in, kissed her on the forehead, and went downstairs. I felt like I was going to be sick. I hadn't eaten all day, but couldn't bear the thought of food. I thought about drinking myself blind. Tempting, but no. That's not what I wanted. I wandered the house aimlessly in a woozy cold sweat. Out the windows, I could see the leaf-blown day passing, but it felt as though the world had stopped. It was waiting upon me. Waiting for me to do something.

Which was—

To go upstairs, quietly pack up the morphine and other meds, and put it all in my backpack. Then, throwing my backpack over one shoulder, to pick up Kate and carry her down to my car. I would take her somewhere safe. An Airbnb, whatever. I would nurse her there; call Lisa to help me; we would be there for her...

What was to stop me? A hospice nurse was scheduled to come that afternoon. But until then we were alone.

Could I do it? Would Kate fight me? She would protest, kick and scream maybe, but she wouldn't be able to stop me. Later, she would even thank me.

No more thinking. *Go!*

I bounded up the stairs, two at a time. The fact that Kate was sleeping would make it easier. When I stopped at her bedroom door, the pulse in my throat knocked in my ear. In five minutes or less, we would be in the car. Slowly, I turned the knob of her bedroom door and opened it.

She was out of bed and at the window, her hands on the sill, bent over in almost a perfect right angle of exhausted determination.

"Kate?"

"I wanted to see my Morning Mountain."

I rushed over and took her in my arms, as though pulling her back from a precipice. To the pressure of my hands her skeleton was as fragile as a bird's.

"Don't do this, Kate."

"Oh, Benedict!"

"I love you, Kate. Come with me now. I'm taking you away from here. Right now. We're going someplace safe."

"Benedict!"

I kissed her on the cheek, felt the cold hollowed flesh on my lips. "Let me take you away from here, Kate."

"No, Benedict."

"I don't want you to die."

"And I don't want to die. But there's no point, don't you see? It wouldn't be better. It would only be longer."

"But Lisa and I would be with you!"

"But I wouldn't be with *you*. I'd be lost in all the pain. Go, Benedict. If you can't stay, then go."

"I cannot leave you alone."

"Call hospice. They'll send someone. But I can't do this anymore."

"Kate!"

"Let me remember this moment, please. Just this. You telling me you love me. I love you too, Benedict. Now go, please. Please. *Go!*"

Where did I go?

Not back to my Airbnb. I could not bear the thought of driving back into DC and just sitting, waiting, looking at the clock and helplessly imagining the horror that was happening at Five Hearths.

So I drove. First on the winding, two-lane country roads of Fauquier County. Then onto I-66 heading west. I made sure not to go over the speed limit. The last thing I needed was to be pulled over.

The police. It occurred to me that I could still call the police. Inform them that a crime was about to be committed. I imagined with some satisfaction Five Hearths being raided just as Adele was concocting the final, lethal cocktail. She and Carly being taken away in handcuffs. The same thing happening simultaneously to their accomplice in DC, whose name Kate would never divulge.

But why would the police believe me? They would want some proof first, proof I didn't have. Miranda's recording of mother's death was back at Five Hearths. But even if they heard it, the police would hardly know what to make of it. And even if they did suspect that Adele killed Irene, they probably would be inclined to look the other way, not interested in pursuing an arrest for a crime they weren't convinced was a crime in the first place.

And would I be able to bear the look of disbelief and resentment Kate would give me when she realized what I had done?

I drove on. Into the Blue Ridge Mountains Kate had loved all her life. I wanted to think of her regretting sending me away. I wanted to think of her changing her mind about her deathday. I imagined her willing me back to her like Mr. Rochester using his metaphysical tractor-beam to bring back Jane Eyre. But what was I supposed to do? Turn the car around and have another scene with her? How much anticlimax could either of us endure? She didn't want me there anymore protesting her decision. The only thing to do was to pretend that she was already gone.

I drove on.

When I got to I-81, I headed southwest. It was eleven thirty in the morning. At a liquor store in Woodstock, I loaded up on provisions. One plan emerging in my mind was to drive a mazy route all the way across the country to California. I had done this once before, one summer during the years I was working on my MA in historical conservation at University College London. At the time, I was chain-reading Kerouac, and, as I had by that time only been to New York for long weekends, I had the itch to see the rest of America by car. With no Neal Cassady to accompany me, I made the trip alone. Money was not an object, as my recent twenty-sixth birthday had triggered the release of my trust fund. I spent some three weeks on the road, finally ending up in San Francisco and a luxury suite at the St. Francis Hotel. I had a grand time. Every day, I found some interesting piece of architecture and sketched *en plein air*: the Haas-Lilienthal House, the Palace Hotel, the Palace of Fine Arts Theatre, the Victorian houses along Postcard Row. When I wasn't sketching, I was walking. Miles and miles over the hills of the city, one time over Golden Gate Bridge and the entire eleven miles up to Muir Woods. The defining episode of that visit was an all-night, Dickensian saunter through the city, climaxing at dawn in Golden Gate Park. As the sun came up behind me, I walked all the way out to the beach. Fifty yards down I saw a thin, grey-bearded pensioner in a swimming cap stroll toward the water and continue strolling until he was up to his waist in the frigid water. I watched with awe as he then casually torpedoed into his breaststroke. I wasn't about to be outdone by this old geezer. I stripped down to my underwear and, shaking with cold and anticipation, I closed my eyes and prepared myself for a little death. With a barbaric yawp, I sprinted forward and crashed into the breakers. When the freezing water reached my thighs, I let myself go and plunged in.

Let this be the end of it. No more. No one is to blame for falling in love. After all, isn't that why Cody himself was there?

I surfaced with a victory cry, and when I looked back toward the beach and the golden metamorphosis of the city in the rising sun, I could believe, if only for a moment, that I was born to a new life.

Somewhere between Harrisonburg and Staunton, Virginia, it struck me, as it no doubt has struck you, that a reprise of such a sojourn was doomed to failure. But then another idea flashed across my mind. One strategic phone call later, I was set. I turned around and drove back in the direction from which I had come, drove through the gloomy mizzle with a sense of grimly poetic satisfaction.

It was just after two o'clock in the afternoon when I arrived at the Fox Hollow Resort in Middleburg. The place was deathly quiet for more than one reason. It was a Sunday; it was off-season; and Virginia was still in COVID semi-lockdown. The enormous lobby, the length of the main building of the hotel, was empty save for a listless elderly couple sitting on a sofa looking at their phones and, at the far end, several workmen busy erecting a floor-to-ceiling Christmas tree. The alarmingly chipper desk clerk was gracious enough not to appear shocked by my lack of mask and luggage and handed me my key. I went to my suite on the ground floor and ordered a room-service lunch with a beer. I was saving my Woodstock provisions for later.

After lunch, I didn't know what to do with myself. I could not possibly sleep or read or sketch. When Kate spent her three days here in mid-September, her so-called Last Wellness Before Dying Tour (alternatively, the Decadence for the Decaying Tour), she indulged in hot stone massages, age management facials, and thermal cocoons. I had never had a massage in my life, much less an age management facial, and it seemed ridiculous to start now. Not that I had the reservations I needed anyway. I did think, however, I might manage a walk out on the grounds, so I tramped outside in the strengthening rain. The point was to keep moving, to keep my mind distracted from what was going to take place at Five Hearths in the morning.

When I returned to my room, wet and shivering but with new clothes and a puffy winter jacket purchased from one of the shops off the lobby, I took a long hot shower, changed into my new duds (after blow-drying the wet underwear), and gaped at mindless TV. Around six o'clock, I ordered a room-service dinner. I would need this solid base for the drinking I planned to do that night. The only question was where. The rain had let up, but the evening promised to be damp and cold. I could stay inside and drink, but this was not a night for getting drunk in one's room in front of *Men in Black II*. Grander gestures were called for.

With my provisions hidden inside my new puffy winter jacket, I left my room about eight thirty. During my afternoon's roaming, I had spied a kind of luxury corral with a sign out front that said TRANQUILITY GARDEN. Basically, a private pool and hot tub (covered with tarpaulins) for those who did not choose to mix with the great unwashed at the central pool and lazy river. The low fence of the corral would have been the work of a moment for someone not already taking swigs at the whisky. But I still made it over reasonably unscathed and with provisions intact.

I remembered Kate telling me that she had sat on one of the cushioned wicker sofas by the fire pit. But I chose a chaise lounge deep in the shadows of an overhanging tree, well away from any of the accent lights, better to escape the notice of scrupulous security guards. I opened the bottle of Jameson's and raised a silent toast to my dearly departing friend. About nine hours to go. What was she doing? Sleeping? In pain? Still up and alert as I had seen her last? Was I a coward for not staying with her? If I called the house and demanded to speak to her, I might still hear her voice. It would be cruel to do it, but it amazed me to think that she was, for a little while longer, still with me on this planet, conscious, breathing, touchable—

It didn't matter. I had left my mobile in the room.

The whiskey did its work warming me up, and with that and my new jacket, with its hood, I felt I could stay outside for some time, at least until the real biting cold set in.

The cloud-crammed evening sky showed no stars. On her midnight walks around this property, Kate would have looked into that very sky and wrestled with the question: To be, or not to be.

You think what I'm doing is wrong.

Did I? What would that even mean? That I believed the Everlasting had set his canon 'gainst self-slaughter? Canon. Commandment. Binding tenets. I had lived my life outside their jurisdiction. One Sunday morning in the upper bunk at school, I had rolled over, slept another hour, too bored by the thought of Mass to be bothered. Thus, easily and dully, I launched my revolution with the snooze button. Then, after one mindless act of rebellion, the sluice gate opened and others followed. Yet I did not cease from worship. What did Chesterton say? When a man stops believing in God, he doesn't believe in nothing; he believes in anything. In my adolescent years, I believed in the oblivion of drugs and alcohol, and, as you see, it remained for me a minor deity. But most of all I believed in Beauty. On a trip to Berlin as a boy, at the Neues Museum, I was given a premonition of my vocation. I was brought to see the bust of Nefertiti, and I remembered the catch in my breath as I stood before it marveling at the towering neck, the smooth *café au lait* skin, the high cheekbones and full lips, the complacency of the teardrop eyes outlined in black, the regal elegance of her tall headgear. I remembered my heart breaking with an intoxicating sadness as I gaped at her. From that moment I was, like one of the Egyptian queen's retainers, enslaved to that sadness. I gave it service everywhere: when at Cambridge I first delighted in the Italian of Dante; when in Rome I first looked up into the oculus of the Pantheon and wondered how the weight of the dome was distributed; and when in San Francisco I wandered the streets on that white Dickensian night. And I gave it service on the day when I first saw Veronica Arden, soon to be Veronica Cody. Michael had brought me to see her play Cleopatra in a student production at RADA, and when she came on stage, it was as though, except for Veronica's fairer skin, the bust of Nefertiti had come to life. The same sadness was in her eyes too. I had seen it long before I ever learned she was ill. Sometimes, I would stare furtively at her and, before she turned and caught me, I would see in those gray eyes a desperate look that seemed to say, "Will this exile never end, or must I wander in this desert forever?"

We were all Catholic once. Me, Michael, Veronica, Kate. Even Adele, one morning in her infancy, was carried into a Roman church and with the water and the oil marked forever as a child of God. But we had all of us abandoned that religion. Why? Not that any of us worked out the reasons beforehand. But why? For me, I guess I had come to believe, or to assume, that all of that had been demolished by science, rendered mythical, silly, even dangerous. The heavens had been emptied. As delightful as it sounded in poetry, love did not move the sun and the other stars. It was only gravity.

Yet our freedom left us sad and lonely, burdened by the weight of what we had given up. We became adult human creatures careening through life like toddlers knocking things down, with no one to come along and clean up the mess. For my part, I could not stay away from you, Beauty, though I knew you could never satisfy me. You were even worse than drugs and alcohol because you tricked me with the promise of so much more.

Follow me. I can give you all the joy you're looking for.

And I followed you, just like the sluts I would sometimes pick up on the streets of Rome and Paris and London, only to wake up not with the promised joy but with the same yawning maw of sadness.

Did I include Adele in this assessment? Had she also spent her life sad and lonely? I believe she had. I was not fooled by her bluster, the Nietzschean bird she flipped at the universe. That was only the mask she wore to protect herself against the brutal unconcern of being. I could not prove it. But what else was all the constant moving about, the various enthusiasms that ebbed and flowed, her inability to see or hear anything beyond her own fanatic concerns? I would not say that she and the Death Symposium had got it all wrong. But the skulls and other lurid accoutrements struck me, finally, as so many campy props. *Do not suppress the thought of your mortality.* Adele was right about that much. But in the end, what can genteel discussion over tea and cake do to unbind the shackles of the dead?

At some point I fell asleep, and my snoring alerted one of the hotel's security guards. He helped me up and gently asked me to take my party back to my room.

The walk back through the nipping air stirred my consciousness, and I needed once more to anesthetize it. I crawled into bed with a nightcap. It was almost one o'clock in the morning. Five hours to go.

I slept again, or passed out, until eight thirty that morning, November 2. Mouth like a fur boot and unnerved by my strange surroundings, I crashed about the room looking for my mobile. I found it in the pocket of my trousers, which I had left deflated, half standing up, by the side of the bed, right where I had stepped out of them. The phone was out of juice, so I plugged it in and waited in agony until it had enough battery to turn on. Who was I expecting to call? And yet, I had missed a call. In a most indecorous position, on all fours in my underwear, I squinted at the caller IDs in my recent calls list. At 8:17 the previous evening, a call from Kate's phone. *Did she not go through with it?* Heart in my mouth, I punched the button to return Kate's call. I was greeted by an electronic voice. The person at that number was unavailable. Voicemail had not been activated.

CHAPTER TWO

Twelve days earlier, with Adele's help, Kate had finalized the liturgy for her deathday celebration. Lisa would be the only guest present in the room besides Adele. Carly would wait downstairs during the entire ceremony.

At five o'clock that morning, Kate would begin with the *lustratio*, a long bath in scented candlelight while enwombed in the transporting strains of a *schola cantorum*.

After the bath, Kate would lie upon the bed while Adele gave her a massage using hot stones and scented oils.

Next, after she was peacefully tucked in, Kate would enjoy her Desert Island Playlist, her favorite songs played in ascending order, beginning with the silly "I Wanna Dance with Somebody" and culminating with Van Morrison's "Someone Like You."

Then the Liturgy of the Word: a collection of Kate's most beloved poems, novel episodes, and prose pieces read aloud by Lisa or played from audiobooks, culminating with Dylan Thomas reading his own, "Do Not Go Gentle into That Good Night."

Finally, at precisely six o'clock that morning, Kate would consume the initial draft intended to prevent nausea and vomiting. An hour later, she would drink the secobarbital. After that, if she were able, she would wash the bitter taste of the secobarbital away with a mug of hot tea and honey, accompanied perhaps by a square of dark chocolate.

While the medicine did its work, Adele would read aloud the Litany of Gratitude, the list of the names and things, events, and experiences that throughout Kate's life had "brought her into being."

When the celebration was complete and Kate had made her farewell, Adele and Lisa would each give Kate a kiss. Then, with a rolled washcloth, Adele would settle Kate's jaw before rigor mortis set in. Following that, Adele would leave a message at the funeral home. Lisa would depart. There would be little evidence to dispose of, only to stoke the fire in Kate's bedroom and burn the paper bag which had contained the secobarbital. Then Adele would go downstairs, rinse out Kate's drinking glasses and tea mug, and add them to the load that she had started in the dishwasher. In another ten minutes, she and Carly would have packed up the candles and hot stones and rinsed out the bathtub.

There would be nothing else to do. Adele would take a brief nap while she waited for the gentlemen from the funeral home, who when they arrived would not even think of questioning the cause of death.

The morning did not go as planned.

"Benny!" Adele greeted me later that afternoon at the door of her townhouse.

"*Is Kate alive?*" I shouted at her. I knew no more now than when I had left the resort. When I had called Lisa for news, she was in the ER of all places, having been rearended early that morning on her way to Five Hearths by some high school kid in a Ford F-150. She had suffered a concussion, but she was far more distraught by the fact that she had missed Kate's deathday. I promised I would come see her later that day. After we hung up, I called Carly, but she didn't answer her phone. I stopped by Five Hearths, but the house was quiet and locked. Somehow, I thought it still possible that Kate was alive.

"No, Benny," Adele corrected me, "Kate celebrated her deathday this morning."

I nearly collapsed right there on the doorstep. Adele helped support me as she ushered me inside.

"Come in and have a drink, Benny. In fact, I'll join you. I'm knackered. I've been hours with the police and the coroner. I also had to have a devastating telephone call with Carly's mother. Where in heaven's name have you been?"

"Where's Carly?" I asked as I sank into a chair in the parlor. "I'm going to be blunt, Adele. I want to hear the story of the day without Carly hovering about."

"Carly's dead, Benny."

"What? *Dead?* How?"

Adele poured us each a large martini, and after she served me mine and sat down, she told me the story.

"Carly and I arrived at Five Hearths about four this morning. When we got there, we found Kate in a bad way—"

Kate's head pain had increased significantly in the night, beyond anyone's expectations. She was unable even to respond to Adele's questions. The plan was not to give Kate any morphine before the liturgy, so that she would be as clearheaded as possible in those final hours, but as soon as Adele saw Kate's condition, she knew the liturgy had to be scrapped. Adele gave Kate a dose of morphine, and in a few minutes, Kate had settled into a heavy doze. Adele and Carly then discussed whether to administer the life-ending medications right away rather than let Kate's torment continue for another hour or more. Given that there was to be no liturgy, and the fact that it was necessary for Kate to drink between two and four ounces of anti-nausea medicine an hour before the final, lethal cocktail, it seemed a good idea to get the process moving.

It took some effort, but Kate was able to get down the anti-nausea medicine. Afterward, there was nothing to do for the next hour but keep Kate as comfortable as possible. But half an hour later, Kate's head pain spiked again. Adele judged that the anti-nausea medicine had had sufficient time to work, so she went into the bathroom and prepared the final cocktail.

She had just come back into the bedroom with it when she heard the rustling of the shower curtain in the bathroom. When Adele screamed, Carly ran up the stairs and into Kate's bedroom. She found Miranda and Adele in the middle of the bedroom, with Miranda training Kate's pink pistol directly at Adele's heart. The rest happened in seconds. Carly dropped her phone, pounced upon Miranda, and in one fluid move had thrown her to the floor. Carly tried to grab the pistol from Miranda, but Miranda bit her arm. As Carly recoiled in pain, Miranda scrambled free. They were both on their knees. Again, Carly sprang to tackle Miranda, but this time Miranda fired into Carly's chest. For a moment or two, Miranda looked at her victim with mild curiosity before she dropped the pistol and fled the house.

Later that night while lying awake in bed, numbed by alcohol, I turned over in my exhausted mind another catastrophe, another death, one oddly connected to Miranda's murder of Carly Brownhill. That terrible morning thirty years ago in Rome fell upon us like a curse. Fell upon us as though we were the members of a great house in a Greek tragedy, signed by the gods with a dreadful and unavoidable doom. Since that morning, we had wandered the earth as exiles, marked as unclean, bearing the curse in our bodies and incapable of repairing the damage we had done.

Just two nights earlier, on Halloween, as we sat up late talking, Kate and I, for the first time together, had recalled the tragedy of that morning. Decades before, by letter, I had asked for her account of Michael Cody's death, and she had refused to answer. But on this Halloween, when I asked again, she was ready to talk. She was in a lot of pain, but she knew this was her last chance to talk about an event that had been so significant to her life. What she told me filled in certain gaps. I knew some things firsthand, and others from Adele's and Veronica's accounts. But given that I had left the scene before the climactic event, that Adele did not witness it either, and that Veronica's memory was impressionistic at best, there were still things I never knew until Kate revealed them.

It began with Veronica finding me at Mater Dei. She was beside herself with fear and worry. Her mother had told her that earlier that day, when Veronica was at church, Michael had come and taken Miranda, and Veronica suspected that they were hiding out at Mater Dei.

"What is he going to do with her?" she kept shouting at me.

I knew, of course, and considered telling her outright. But then the idea came to me: not to tell her but to show her. This thought was my hubris: that if I could help Veronica *see* that her husband was in love with another woman—enough to plan an escape with her to London—then Veronica would feel herself in my debt and thereafter depend on me for her comfort and support.

Next thing I knew, I was in my mother's lovely yellow Citroën driving Veronica to my parents' villa. I had only told her that Michael and Miranda were there. Veronica expected to find Adele with them, but I did not correct her. I did make her promise, however, not to tell anyone how she got to the villa.

Once we arrived there, I went back to Mater Dei, as I had classes that morning. Meanwhile, Veronica entered the house, there to be—as she put it later—an instrument of chaos.

There was no one in the living room, but she could hear voices upstairs. Miranda's voice. Michael's voice. Adele's voice. On the chimney piece was a little bell. She took it and began to ring it as loudly as she could, calling out, "Compline! Everybody's late for Compline!"

Michael, Adele, and Miranda rushed to the staircase, but as soon as Michael saw Veronica, he ordered Miranda to return to her room. My mother and Kate came in from the kitchen. Veronica kept ringing the bell, laughing at everyone's looks of astonishment.

Michael charged at her and took the bell out of her hand. Then began the scene proper. Veronica attempted to get upstairs to Miranda, but Michael and Adele held her back. Veronica worked hard to get free of them: clawed, scratched, bit. Adele barked at my mother to call the police.

Veronica bit Michael hard on the shoulder, and he pushed her away in pain. He didn't push her hard, but she tumbled to the floor. Michael and Adele stood over her. Kate raced upstairs to see to the terrified Miranda. My mother was on the phone to the police. Suddenly, Veronica got up and ran out of the house.

She ran a long way down the winding driveway of the villa. It made no sense why she was running, and eventually this fact dawned upon her. She turned and ran back toward the house. When she got there, she saw Miranda come out of the villa holding Kate's hand, with Michael right behind them, but Veronica still did not realize Kate's role in these events. Miranda and Kate got into a car parked in front of the house—my mother's Maserati. Kate buckled Miranda into the back seat, then got into the passenger seat. Michael got into the driver's seat and turned on the engine. But then he got out of the car again, having remembered something. He dashed back inside. Veronica seized her chance. She sprang forward and jumped into the driver's seat of the Maserati.

As she sped away, she looked into the rearview mirror. She saw Adele running out of the villa. The sight of her standing there looking so helpless set her laughing. She had to keep slowing down to take the tight curves of the winding driveway, but when she hit the main road, she really opened it up. One hundred and twenty kilometers per hour? One hundred and thirty? She didn't know. She was just trying to make the car go as fast as it would go.

Kate begged her to slow down, to stop, to go back. "For Miranda's sake. You don't want to do anything to hurt your precious girl," she said.

Through the rearview mirror, Veronica looked into Miranda's nervous eyes.

"Fine," she said and crushed the brakes. "Let's go back. For precious Miranda's sake."

She flew back down the highway. She nearly missed the entrance to the villa, but she swung into it just in time. When she came out of the fishtail, she roared ahead up the drive. She never saw Michael. Desperately, he was running down the winding driveway, as if he could stop her. She never saw him. She was just going up the straightaway toward the first turn when she was jolted by the collision.

When she got out of the car, she was displeased that Michael just lay there by the side of the road and would not get into the car so they could go home.

But then, from Kate's bawling explanation, she grasped that he had been killed. She attempted to raise him from the dead but found she could not. She was awfully put out. "I have faith the size of a mustard seed," she told Kate. "I have faith that can move mountains. I am handmaid to the Mother of God; no one has ever had more faith than I."

Yet he would not rise.

Later, a policeman tried to get her story from her. Quite calmly, she instructed him that objectively speaking her act was vehicular manslaughter, whatever her subjective responsibility might be.

After they took Michael's body away, she became confused again. She turned to Kate, who now was standing in the driveway with Adele, holding a sobbing Miranda.

"Where's Michael?" Veronica snapped at Adele. When Adele didn't answer, Veronica asked her again, this time more sharply. "Where's Michael?"

"They've taken him to the morgue," Adele replied.

"What a silly place to take him," Veronica said. "He needs to be here with me. A husband's place is beside his wife. When will he ever learn? Miranda, go wake up your father."

That was all thirty years ago. But now, our doom had been visited upon us again. Kate had taken her life without benefit of ceremony; a woman had been murdered; and Miranda, the fugitive killer, had disappeared once more. What was I to do? Keep up a fruitless search for Miranda, as I had promised Kate? Keep wandering the earth as an exile? Was there nothing that could save us from this unbearable curse?

EPILOGUE

MORNING MOUNTAIN

Veronica Cody, age fifty-seven, died at 7:24 a.m. on a warm and bright Friday morning in July, the First Friday of the month. As most of the sisters were at Mass at the local parish and the hospice nurse wasn't due until after lunch, Veronica was accompanied in her final moments by Sr. Rose Sharon, who had volunteered to stay behind from Mass and help Veronica keep watch for Our Lord. Sr. Rose Sharon had been reading in the chair in Veronica's room for some time before she realized Veronica had found her heaven. Her "descent," as Sr. Rose Sharon put it, or "ascent," as Sr. Agnes Virginia corrected her, could not have been gentler. There had been nothing labored in her breathing, no discomfort or unrest of any kind. The day before, she had received Viaticum from the parochial vicar at the parish, and a week before that had received the Sacrament of Reconciliation. She died holding a green scapular in her hand. "It was a good death," Mother Dulcis Maria declared. "The sort of death we should all pray for while remaining abandoned to whatever death Our Lord should choose to send us." The body was interred next to that of her husband in Westchester Hills Cemetery, Hastings-on-Hudson, the two plots having been purchased by her mother at the time of Michael Cody's death.

The few personal belongings that Veronica kept in her room were boxed up and mailed to her sister, Bijou. Included among these items were several notebooks, cheap spiral items of the kind mothers load up on during back-to-school sales. These notebooks comprised the journal Veronica had kept in the last year of her life. Bijou opened the first of these notebooks with interest, an interest that quickly faded when she realized that the entries were mostly concerned with her sister's struggles as a resident in her halfway house for schizophrenics. Bijou skipped the second notebook entirely, the one with the reclaimed green scapular pressed in its pages, and in looking through the third skipped right to the culminating entries written just days before her sister's death. Bijou was absorbed in what she found. She kept this notebook for herself, letting the others fall into the hands of Miranda. She considered showing Veronica's final entries to me, but as they cast me in perhaps not the most flattering light, she decided in the end to keep them to herself.

However, as she told Kate she would, Bijou sent Kate this third and last of Veronica's notebooks, but given the complications of her shooting schedule and the abysmal state of mail service during COVID, the notebook did not arrive until the first day of November, when Kate asked me to put the package, with the rest of her mail, on her bedroom desk. It is scarcely surprising, given how badly she was feeling and the events that soon followed, that Kate didn't open Bijou's package right away or that I never thought of this package again until, ten months later, it was brought back to my attention.

"With respect, they've been a total pain in my posterior," Everett said as we stood together, those ten months later, in front of the new addition to the house. "First of all, there's the current HOA rule that says no property can be occupied by anything other than a private domestic unit. No for-profit or nonprofit businesses or organizations allowed. So, what do they want me, as their lawyer, to argue for them? That they're *not* occupying the house as a nonprofit organization; that they're essentially a *family*; that for everyone here this is their primary *residential* address. Can you believe it? And on top of *that*, there's a deed restriction on Five Hearths going back almost 100 years. No one thought to have a look at the title before breaking ground on construction. The deed stipulates that there are to be no additions made to the property 'in deference to its historical significance.'"

The addition was a square, cabin-like structure with multiple large picture windows and a flat solar roof. It had a modern aesthetic that somehow didn't clash with the rest of the house.

Everett had just been coming down the porch steps when I drove up to the house. After I parked my rental car, we said hello, and he asked if I wanted to come around back and see "what they're doing to the place."

"Are you going to continue to represent them?" I asked.

"Oh, sure. What else am I going to do? It's what Miss Katie wanted. Quite literally her dying request. Can you believe Miranda shot that woman?"

"I'm afraid I can."

"Yeah. I guess I can too. She gives Evie the jitters, but I like her. I'm glad they're letting her do her probation here. She's not going to get better rotting in jail. Where are you staying?"

"I booked a room at the Marriott Ranch B&B."

"Miranda says you'll be here for dinner. Why don't you come by later for a drink?"

"I'd like that. Say, Everett—"

He didn't realize how little information Miranda had given me over the phone. When I pressed her in that phone call, she only teased me and said I would have to flap my wings and fly over from Scotland to find out.

"When did Kate make this decision?"

"The afternoon before she died. Miranda ran over and got me."

"Miranda? She was *here* the day before Kate died?"

"Sure."

"When did she arrive? She wasn't here when I left that morning."

"I don't know. I didn't ask. I got to the house right around four that afternoon. I followed Miranda up to Miss Katie's bedroom, and Miss Katie dictated to me the change to her will. I wrote it on her laptop and printed it out in her office downstairs. Poor kid barely had the strength to sign it, but she did. Miranda and the hospice nurse served as witnesses. All perfectly legal in the Commonwealth of Virginia."

"But why?"

"I asked Miss Katie that, and she only said it's what she wanted. I didn't feel it was my place to inquire any further."

"I understand."

"C'mon," he said, "let's see if we can find the lady commander of the place. She must be one of God's favorites to get an addition like that built so fast, what with all these supply-chain issues going on because of COVID."

In the past year, Five Hearths had changed dramatically, and I don't mean the addition on the back. It had changed in the way it presented itself to me. Now it was no longer Kate's home in the Virginia countryside. It was the place I had fled in fear. The place where she had died. A sacred space desacralized, transformed into something that I could not understand.

Everett rang the bell, and the door was opened by a tall, lanky young woman with a COVID mask covering the big smile in her jutting jaw. She was so tall that her habit hardly made it to her ankles. We greeted one another at the approved social distance, then she loped away to get the "lady commander." A moment later, a second woman appeared, also in full religious habit and mask. She was a short, not particularly thin woman, with a cheerful but not over-sweetened expression in the blue eyes behind her glasses. Gray hairs were visible in the few strands of brown peeking out along the sides of her veil. Like the younger sister, she wore no makeup.

Everett made his goodbyes and headed home for "forty winks."

"We really love the house," my hostess said as she led me on a tour of the downstairs. She began in the formal living room to the left of the foyer, a room with which I had no associations. "We moved in at the tail end of July, after we had the basement remodeled. Put in two bedrooms down there, added to the four upstairs. We have capacity for twelve in all, three sisters and eight guests. Only three guests at present, counting your friend. The place belonged to a single woman who died of cancer last year. She never had any direct contact with us. But she had a friend who was a guest in our house in New York."

Apparently, Miranda had told this woman nothing of significance about my connection to Kate, to this house, to Miranda herself. I was not in a mood to set her straight. I was glad to be anonymous, free to take it all in without the static of the backstory.

"Let me show you the chapel," she said. We walked across the foyer into the main living room, where I had sat and read, drank, and kept vigil in those final days leading up to Kate's death. The furniture and other items in the house, down to the books in the bookshelves, were almost entirely Kate's, which lent the atmosphere of my tour another dimension of eeriness. I almost expected Kate to call for me from upstairs, asking me to fill up her water jug or simply to come up and sit with her.

But when we got to the chapel, there was no imagining that the house belonged to anyone but these sisters. The structure subsumed what had once been Kate's sunroom, and extended further than the sunroom had into the yard. It was small but sufficient, seating maybe twenty-five. With its three picture windows framing the alluring line of mountains, it gave me a feeling of vertigo as I looked out at the familiar vista through this exotically different prism. The sisters wanted that vista enough to eschew stained glass. I could not blame them.

Mother Dulcis Maria genuflected before the altar and tabernacle. I stood behind her, the awkward pagan. There was no holy water in the font by the door—another casualty of COVID. I admired the three-dimensional, car-pentered characters in the Stations of the Cross that lined three of the four walls.

It was no perfunctory genuflection. Mother Dulcis Maria remained on both knees for a full minute. Even from behind her, I could tell she was look-ing intently at the tabernacle, a squat marble box with golden doors built into the wall behind the altar. A large candle in a tall red holder flickered beside it, signaling to the woman that she was in the presence of her king.

Between my knees and this woman's there was an infinite distance. How many times over how many years had I stood before such tabernacles, in churches old and new around the world, and never humbled myself in the way this woman was doing?

When she rose, she stepped before me down the aisle and told me the story of how they got the altar stone and who the architect was and who designed the stations. I was sure I confused her. I did not genuflect, but then here I was talking about church architecture and furnishings like an old hand. Again, I was in no mood to straighten her out. These were merely preliminar-ies before the main event, and I was anxious to get them over.

Something caught my eye. I turned, and there was Veronica standing just inside the door. Not Veronica, but her very image. She had lost a fair amount of weight in the past year, but she looked as healthy as I had ever seen her. Her skin was clearer, and her eyes were brighter. Her hair was now much longer too, though she wore it pulled back off her wide forehead and bundled carelessly on top of her head. Gone was her street uniform, replaced by a pair of dungarees over a long-sleeved black tee that hid the sleeve of tats. A new pair of Converse All-Stars, fire-engine red, served as a larky complement. She was beautiful; her natural beauty was more evident to my eye in this tomboy outfit than it would be otherwise, and I wondered about the man who might one day fall in love with her.

We walked out together onto the porch, just we two. Mother Dulcis Maria had gone back to her duties. It was a ripe September afternoon. The first nip of cold was in the air. I was bleary-eyed with jet lag, but the fresh air and Miranda's presence revived me.

"Good to see you, Miranda," I said. "Everything all right?"

"I've been back on my meds for two weeks," she said. "Sr. Rose Sharon and I are going riding now. I always go out on Ethel."

"Ethel was Kate's favorite. It's a lovely day for a ride. You've been hanging out with Evie and Everett?"

"Everett is making *jihad* with the HOA over all these changes to Five Hearths. Evie says don't listen to him complain because he loves nothing better than sticking it to the HOA. Evie is chairing this year's Hound Show. First one since the Big Lockdown. Everett's sleep apnea device is driving Evie crazy. You've been in Scotland?"

"Most recently. Before that, Paris. Spain."

"In 1984, you took the train to Scotland with my father to see the Edinburgh Fringe."

"Yes. How do you know about that?"

"They told you I shot Carly Brownhill?"

"They did."

"She's dead now." Then she quoted, "Yet not, in hope, beyond the reach of Our Lord's mercy."

"How do you like your life here?"

"What's not to like? Three square meals per diem. God's own scenery. I ride pretty much every day in the afternoon. They don't let me shoot with Everett, though. Not a good optic, Sr. Rose Sharon says. I want you to read something."

She'd been carrying a simple red spiral notebook and handed it to me.

"You can read this while we're out riding. Start where I put the sticky note. Go read it up on Kate's favorite hill. You'll be able to watch us from up there."

As it happened, I did not go up on the hill. After Miranda and Sr. Rose Sharon—the tall, lanky sister who greeted me—went off to Evie and Everett's barn, I sat my weary bones down on one of the rocking chairs on the porch—Kate's rocking chairs. As soon as I put on my glasses and opened the notebook to the page with the sticky note, I recognized the artistic neatness of the hand, the homemade script with the elvish flourishes on the tails of letters and at the ends of words. This was not one of Miranda's own notebooks. Nor was it one of Kate's. This notebook had been kept by Veronica Cody.

> *I am awakened by the sounds of Lindsay wailing in her urine.*
>
> *I lie in bed listening to her. Fuming. Waiting for Sr. Agnes Virginia, who is on night duty, to come and deal with it. This is the third straight night Lindsay's done it in the sheets. How long are they going to let this situation go on? It's intolerable. I need to sleep. I'm on chemotherapy, for the love of muck. I couldn't even go down for the baking lesson on Tuesday, which I was really looking forward to, because I couldn't keep my eyes open.*
>
> *I told them not to put that nutter in here with me. I don't do well with roommates, even when they're not peeing the bed like a toddler. I'm an introvert. I need my space. (Which is why, along with my accent, my housemates call me "the queen.")*
>
> *"When I decided to come, you promised me a single room," I reminded Mother Dulcis Maria yesterday.*
>
> *"Not promised, dear. I said we would accommodate you as far as we were able. But now we have Lindsay to take care of. We need a place for her."*
>
> *Penny-pinching old bat. This isn't about taking care of Lindsay. This is about getting her rent. You don't have enough money to run this place. It's a shambles. It's not even up to code. There are supposed to be fire sprinklers in every upstairs room as well as the landing, but there's nothing anywhere. If there were a fire blocking the stairwell, I'd have to leap from the window*

and hope I could grab onto a branch of the oak tree before I broke my neck!

Sr. Frances says that Lindsay is anxious about her new surroundings and regressing in her habits, just as a child would. Peeing the bed. An uptick in her hallucinations. Lindsay thinks she's from an alien planet and that we're all government agents working to keep her here so that we can do experiments on her. Sr. F. says Lindsay got the idea into her head from some American film I haven't seen. My only hope is that she's not, in fact, hallucinating and that the mothership finds her and takes her away as soon as possible.

When it is clear that Sr. Agnes Virginia isn't coming, I get out of bed and go over to Lindsay.

"Get up and let me change the bed."

She doesn't move, so I say, with the irrational irritation one can only have toward the irrational, "You have nothing to be afraid of. No one here is out to get you. You're having a hallucination. You're in a halfway house for schizophrenics. My name is Veronica. I'm you're roommate. We sat next to one another at dinner last night, remember? I said how awful the pudding was and you said, 'That's not pudding. It's brownies.' You told me you're from Long Island. That you used to teach religion at a parish school. Remember?"

She then starts to spout some nonsense that of course I would know these things because we have her under such tight surveillance, etc.

She resumes crying. The room reeks of the warm, earthy, intestinal stench of urine and the plastic-perfumey smell of store-bought nappies. I'm living in an infant's bedroom.

In the linen closet in the hall there are fresh sheets and pillowcases. I leave the bedroom door open while I go out to get them, hoping that Lindsay's sobbing will awaken Sr. Agnes Virginia. Even though we're way up on the third floor, Sr. A.V. didn't have any trouble the past two nights waking up with Lindsay's wailing. But I guess she's as exhausted as I am.

When I come back to the room, I throw the fresh linen on my bed and bark at Lindsay to come with me into the bathroom. She's frightened of me and does what she's told. In the bathroom, I tell her to throw her nightie into the laundry hamper and to put the soiled nappy in the trash. I rinse her down in the tub with the shower fixture, and while she towels herself dry, I go back into the room to get a fresh nappy out of the box by her bed, along with another nightie out of her suitcase. She only packed one nightie, so I grab Daddy's old Brentford football jersey out of my drawer. I give it to Lindsay, then start making her bed. The jersey comes down almost to her knees, and she stands shivering in it while she watches me make the bed. Once I'm done, I tell her to go to the bathroom one more time before getting into bed, but she doesn't move. She just stares at me as I get into my own bed.

"You lied to that sister," she says.

"What?"

"Why did you lie to that sister?"

"What are you talking about?"

"Tonight she asked if you wanted to come to the mindfulness talk at the parish, and you said you were sick. But you weren't sick. You were up here reading and writing in your notebook."

"And this is your business?"

"I just don't understand why you lie. We don't lie."

"Who's 'we?'"

"The beings on my planet."

I give her the withering and say, "Go to the bathroom, Lindsay, then get to bed."

Benny likes to bring me books. Today it was Trollope's Palliser novels (the entire set!), which I will need half my time in Purgatory to finish, a book of Advent sermons by Cardinal Newman, and a volume of Wodehouse's Jeeves stories. He's noticed that I often speak in Wodehouse. "Ankle over there, would you,

Benny, and fetch me my sweater?" "Five o'clock. Who's ready for
a tissue restorer?" "The way sister always knocks over the pictures
on my shelf when she dusts it really gives me the pip." I think
it's because I've been thinking a lot about Daddy lately and my
childhood generally. Wodehouse was Daddy's favorite, and his
talk was always replete with Woosterisms.

Benny tells me that Adele Schraeder has resurfaced, on the
Lower East Side of all places, running some kind of book club
focused on death. He says Miranda found her. Now, how did
Miranda get into contact with Adele Schraeder? Benny hasn't
the foggiest.

I haven't seen Miranda in seven weeks, not since that Sunday afternoon Bijou brought her and she was so full of venom.
I wish I could scrub from my memory the image of her hunched
in that chair, hugging herself and rocking. (I always seem to
bring out her tendency to repetitive motion.) She had nothing
to say to me. Couldn't bring herself even to look at me. She'd put
on weight and wasn't taking care of herself. She refuses to let
Bijou touch her hair.

The day after that visit, she bolted from Bijou's, upset by
seeing me I can only suppose. She needs a scapegoat for her life,
and what better candidate than her batty mother?

I have no idea where she is now. Living on the streets? Living
with some man? Under the sway of Adele Schraeder? Almost
certainly not getting the help she needs. And there's nothing I
can do to help her.

And time is running out.

Benny comes to visit me on a Saturday morning. Not his
usual self. Seems agitated. I try to draw him into a conversation
on St. Thérèse of Lisieux, but he doesn't have the patience for it.
He asks me if I had ever thought of acting again.

"You were the most talented young actress anyone had ever

seen," he says. "*Fiercely intelligent. Daring. Beautiful. You're still beautiful.*"

"*That's rot. And my voice was always kind of reedy, don't you think? And my nose in profile? Ghastly.*"

"*You had a marvelous voice, and a nose that would make Cleopatra reach for the asp.*"

Then he comes back, bang again next morning. Is waiting for me when I come in from Mass, like Mr. Darcy come again to Huntsford. He declares his love for me. A torch he has carried since we were kids. Poor man is shaking as he summons the words. He wants me to come live with him in the East Village. He even makes the absurdly extravagant offer to take instruction as a Catholic so we can be married in the Church.

"*But, Benny, I'm not even sure* I *believe in it.*"

"*Don't you?*"

"*I don't know. How can I believe a divinity is in charge of the disaster of my life? I'm ending my days as a recovering schizophrenic trapped in a room with another schizophrenic who wets the bed while she waits for her alien friends to come get her in their spaceship. There are Beckett plays not as absurd as that. I think you should just go ahead and take instruction for yourself, Benny.*"

"*What do you mean?*"

"*You want to, don't you?*"

"*I've never said that.*"

"*It's been the story of your life, Benny. The Hound of Heaven chasing you through the years.*"

He doesn't really expect me to return his affection, and, anyway, I don't. Can't. "*I'm not that young slip of a thing you met in London, Benny. Time's arrow moves in only one direction.*"

I find it hard to imagine what it would feel like to be absorbed in a man's life again, emotionally, psychologically, sexually. That part of my apparatus has, apparently, been removed.

It's not that I don't have feelings. I feel everything deeply, though not in the way people expect. As Benny was making his *pitch, I was profoundly moved, not by the fact that I was the object of a good man's love but by the sadness in his eyes. Sadness because he wasn't getting what he wanted, but more than that. While he had seen the mystery flicker for a moment among my ruins, it had disappeared again, and he didn't know where to find it.*

Benny here this afternoon for his customary visit. His new proposal is that we live together as "brother and sister." As he makes his case, I realize that there is going to be no perfect time to tell him my news.

"I can't, Benny. I'm dying, you see."

"What?"

So I explain the whole thing. The swelling in my armpit. The tests and diagnosis: Stage IV breast cancer, metastasized all over the county. Nothing to be done.

Benny just looks at me, devastated. His face hangs from his skull like an old coat upon a hook.

"How long?" he asks.

"A few months at most."

He buries his face in his hands.

I then have to crack the whip and move him quickly through the denial phase. He wants me to get a second opinion; he offers to pay for me to see a specialist at Sloan Kettering; he speaks of new clinical trials and homeopathic treatments.

"How about a trip to Lourdes?" I suggest.

"If you think it'll work."

I smile at his unaffected sincerity, and I apologize when it makes him peevish.

"It's no good, Benny. I'm dying. I don't want to spend my last days fighting a battle that's already lost."

"I really will take you to Lourdes if you think it'll work."

"Thank you. But if Our Lady has a miracle for me, she knows where to find me."

"But isn't there something special about the water?"

"Supposedly. But I don't feel called to go, if you know what I mean."

"Veronica. Please. If you're not going to fight it anymore, then at least let me take you out of this place. I'll rent a nice flat or even a house for us. We'll bring in hospice."

I cannot deny that the idea appeals to me. "Could there be a view of the mountains?"

"Pick your mountain range."

I surprise myself by how excited the prospect makes me. "How fast could you make it happen?"

"Give me a location and I'll have a place in forty-eight hours."

"And we'd just drive away?"

"You're not a prisoner here. You entered on your own free will, and you can leave anytime you want."

"Indeed I can," I say, pretty chuffed. "Indeed I can."

About three in the morning, I am on my knees in the bathroom being sick. When I haul myself, clammy and shaking, back to bed, Lindsay addresses me through the darkness.

"Where's your husband?"

"Who says I have a husband?"

"I saw a piece of mail for you on the table downstairs. It was addressed to Mrs. Veronica Cody."

A Mass card from Peter. He's the last person on earth who still sends handwritten notes and letters, and he always addresses mine to Mrs. Veronica Cody.

"You shouldn't be snooping."

"Couldn't help it. Where is your husband?"

"He's dead."

"How?"

"Car accident."

"When?"

"Long time ago."

"Do you have children?"

"A daughter."

"Where is she?"

"She lives with my sister."

"You're lying again. Why do you keep doing that?"

"Who says I'm lying?"

"You do. You wrote in your notebook that your daughter ran away."

"Daft maggot! You're reading my journal? I thought your alien kind weren't into sin?"

"It wasn't sin. I had to make sure you weren't taking notes on me to send to the government. It was an act of just self-defense."

"I see there are ethicists on your planet. Stay out of my notebook, missy, or in the middle of the night while you're sleeping, I'll cut off all your hair."

"Go missy yourself, missy," Lindsay snarls. *"Conscience is the herald of the king."*

After this tussle with Lindsay, I cannot get to sleep. I find myself thinking, again, of the morning of the accident...

After they take Michael away, someone leads me into a small guest room. I am left there for a long time, sitting on the side of the bed. When I remember that I have a green scapular in my pocket, I take it out and hide it under the mattress.

Eventually someone brings me a cup of coffee and a yesterday's cornetto. I devour them both. When I am in a phase, I can go two or three days without eating.

I hear crying from somewhere deep inside the house. I get up and wander about, looking for Miranda. There is no one around. Just the sound of crying from behind a closed door somewhere.

I drift into the kitchen hoping to find another stale cornetto. That's when I see them on the counter. Three plane tickets.

Rome to London. Departing 8:05 that morning, arriving at 10:37 a.m. The top one is smeared with blood, but I can make out Michael's name. I lift it up and find the second ticket is for Miranda. Then I lift up the third ticket and read the name.

"So, you've known all these years?" Benny gapes at me when I tell him this, more than thirty years later, here at the halfway house. "Does Kate know that you know?"

"I don't believe so. I never told anyone."

"No one? Not Bijou or Miranda?"

"No one."

He sits for a moment, stunned.

"You suspected Adele," he says.

"I did. And it might have been Adele, before Kate Montclair. Michael was confused at the time and very lonely. Have you ever seen Kate Montclair since those days?"

"No. For a few years afterward I wrote to her, but she stopped writing back. I heard from someone—can't remember who—that she's divorced and lives in Washington, DC. Still teaching."

After a pause, I say, "I used to pray that the grace of the green scapular I had hid under Adele's pillow would ultimately have its effect. And I prayed that somehow Miranda would be the means by which God's grace would work. Not until I saw their plane tickets did I realize that my prayers were meant not for Adele but for Kate Montclair.

"My anger and resentment toward her are gone. Now I feel only pity. She was hardly more than a girl at the time. Of course she thought she was in love! How romantic it must have seemed to plan a new life in London with a handsome older man—an actor!—and his bright, beautiful child. From her point of view, she couldn't allow the man she loved to waste his life with a mentally disturbed wife he no longer loved."

Benny looks forlorn.

"Stop blaming yourself, Benny, for taking me to the villa that night. You were trying to save my marriage."

"No," he says, "I was not."

I take his hand and kiss it.

"You know I can't go live with you, Benny. Not even as brother and sister."

"I know," he says.

"You understand, I need to end my life here."

"I don't understand," he says. "But yes, I know that you have to end your life here."

Tonight we've just finished grace when Sr. Agnes Virginia asks me how I'm feeling. Being not in the mood for the question, I give her a rather dismissive response. While the frost descends upon the table, Sr. A.V. prongs a fried potato wedge and, with the spud just beneath her double chin, says in that cheery, reductive, jejune, deadening tone that only a religious sister keenly distracted by a well-oiled starchy carb can manage, "A wonderful opportunity to pick an intention and offer it up."

I shan't write what I say in reply.

But after I say it, I get up and sweep rather dramatically out of the dining room.

Offer it up. What the sisters at school used to say when you banged your knee on the playground.

Offer it up. What Granny used to say when refereeing one of my adolescent spats with mum.

What does it even mean?

I go to the chapel because, though I want to go back and jam the whole bowl of potatoes down Sr. Agnes Virginia's pious pie-hole, I feel badly speaking like that to a sister. She's given up everything to take care of the likes of me—sex, career, her own home, her independence. She's the one who might be changing out my own soiled sheets in my final hours.

Mother Dulcis Maria finds me after dinner. I can talk to her. She never stops being a human animal. She never condescends.

"What made you angry," she says, "is that she only gave you the map."

"What does that mean?"

"She only gave you the map of the journey you are on. Your via dolorosa *of Stage IV breast cancer, on top of a history of schizophrenic illness, on top of the painful story of your marriage. You are in the thick of it. You're picking your way through difficult terrain. Sr. Agnes Virginia reminded you of the map in your pocket. The map that says, 'Offer it up to Our Lord. Join your sufferings to His. That is what the suffering is for. Atonement. Reparation. Healing.' But the map is not the territory. The map doesn't tell you what to do when your roommate wakes up in the middle of the night sitting in a puddle of her urine. It doesn't say how you're supposed to get through the day when you know your days are nearly over. You understand what you must do, not by looking at the map but by going on the journey. There's no substitute for it. And that's why you got a little testy (shall we say) with Sr. Agnes Virginia. She's not on the journey with you. She doesn't need to figure out what you need to figure out. No matter how much we're here to help you—and we're here to help you all the way until God calls you—in the end you'll have to figure this out for yourself."*

A silent tremor then rises out of Mother Dulcis Maria's sensible shoes. It rattles and shakes her entire body as she shuts her eyes and buries her face in my shoulder in a vain attempt to stifle the laughter.

"Oh, honey! We were breaking up in there after you left, Sr. Agnes Virginia most of all. I don't think we're ever going to get that image out of our heads!"

A couple of hours later, I'm reading Trollope but feeling Lindsay's eyes scrambling over me like an insect. Finally, she tells me that she wants to show me something. She gets up on one elbow and grabs a small purse off her bedside table. She pulls the zipper and takes out a picture that looks like it was printed off the internet. She holds it up to show me.

"You're going to have to bring it over here," I tell her.

She comes over and stands beside my bed.

"Sit down," I say.

She looks at me dumbly.

"Sit down, Lindsay," I bark at her. "I'm not part of any government conspiracy."

"I know," she says, as if she's no longer speaking schizoid.

"Then sit down."

She sits on the side of my bed.

"Aren't you going to show me your picture?"

She holds it out to show me.

"What's this?" I ask.

"The Madonna and St. Giovannino."

It's Mary in the manger kneeling over the baby Jesus.

"Check that out," she says, pointing.

In the corner of the picture is a green object shaped like a rugby football, rays of glory or of fire emanating from it as it flies off into the heavens.

"What's that?" I ask.

"What's it look like?"

"A spaceship."

Lindsay nods.

"What is it really?"

"It's really a spaceship."

I'll be blowed if it doesn't look like a spaceship, though I say, "You've been watching too much History Mysteries *with* Sr. Agnes Virginia."

"*The painter must've heard a legend,*" Lindsay says, "*about a spaceship appearing on the night Jesus was born. That's my spaceship.*"

"*You came here in a spaceship on the night Jesus was born?*"

"*We came to see the newborn King.*"

"*You're an intergalactic magus?*"

"*A what?*"

"*Forget it,*" I say and nod at my book. "*If you don't mind, I'd like to find out whether Lady Glencora is going to marry Plantagenet Palliser.*"

"*I was left behind the night Jesus was born.*"

"*Why?*"

She stares at me with her wondering child's mouth hanging open.

"*I didn't know you had cancer,*" she says.

"*Breast cancer. Stage IV. One of the sisters told you?*"

"*The young pretty one.*"

"*Sr. Rose Sharon.*"

"*I was left behind for you. Your cancer is the sign.*"

"*The sign of what?*"

"*The sign that you're one of the ones I'm supposed to rescue.*"

"*You can't rescue me, Lindsay.*"

"*I'm going to take you to my planet.*"

"*What planet?*"

"*There's no name for it in this language. But it's lovely. We don't suffer like you do. Your cancer is the sign I'm supposed to rescue you.*"

"*Fine. So how do we get to your planet?*"

"*When the ship comes, it will take us through the black hole.*"

"*I see.*"

"*But it's not like any black hole. It's not empty space.*"

"*No?*"

"*It's a black hole made of blood and flesh. It's like being inside one of those tiny cameras that surgeons use to look inside the body. But then you come out the other side and you're free."*

The map is not the territory. I am in a night black as pitch. There is no way back, and I cannot see the way forward.

My God, my God, why have you abandoned me?

A rough brushstroke of violet light appears along the eastern horizon. I see the morning star. Kate Montclair's arms clasp Michael around the neck as he lies with his crooked head on her lap. Little Miranda cuddles beside them with her head on Michael's tummy.

How I let you down, Michael. Forgive me. And if God will hear your prayer, pray for me. Because I am alone in a city that is not my own, in a house that is not my own, in a room that is not my own, getting ready to depart from a world that is not my own. What a strange, alien life I have led. What a senseless, pointless, unbearable, heart-rending life. But I will go inside it now, through the black hole caked with black, desiccated blood and drenched in the stew of his sweat. I will feel my way through the nerves and blood vessels of the wound, through the cartilage and muscle all the way down to the bone.

Though I cannot see my way, I trust, Lord, that you see the way. Beyond all my feelings, I trust. Beyond all my brokenness, I trust.

My muffled gasps and sniffles awaken Lindsay. I feel pressure on the bed behind me, and when I turn I find her sitting there. I look at her, expecting her to say that she's wet the bed again, but instead she leans down and kisses me on the forehead. She then settles the extra pillow against the headboard and makes herself comfortable beside me, and I rest my head on her shoulder until I fall asleep.

This suffering, this death, I offer up:

For Benny. That he may know the consolations of your mercy.

For Lindsay and all my housemates here. That they may know healing.

For the sisters. That they may receive your reward for the sacrifice of their lives.

For Bijou. That she will allow herself to be surprised by you.

For Peter. That his prayers may rise like incense to your altars.

For our parents and the sweet repose of their souls.

For my darling Miranda. That wherever she is tonight, you will shelter her from harm and lead her to the help she needs.

For my Michael and for myself. That in your mercy you will forgive our betrayals of one another and that our vocation, even now, when all seems lost, will bear the fruit that it was meant to bear.

For Adele Schraeder. That all her many gifts may be turned to your glory.

For Kate Montclair. That she may know every grace and peace and joy and that, somehow, she may know that I forgive her and that I offer up for her my illness and my regret and my aloneness. They are all the gifts I have left.

An hour later, Miranda and Sr. Rose Sharon returned from their ride. After Sr. Rose Sharon went inside, Miranda came over and looked down at me in my rocking chair.

"Maybe you dodged a bullet," she said. "If she had said yes, you'd be my father."

"I'd be satisfied to be your friend. You want to talk about where you've been the last year?"

"Everywhere and nowhere. It doesn't matter now."

"No, it doesn't. But I'm glad you're here safe and that your meds are what you need. Can you tell me what made you come back here last November?"

"I came back the day before Kate died. To beg her not to do it."

"You came back here on November 1?"

"Yeah."

"Where did you go after you ran away, after you played Kate the recording of my mother's deathday? You went to Adele's, right? Remember I saw you coming out of Adele's townhouse that morning?"

"I wasn't there long. I went there to beg her not to go through with Kate's deathday. I didn't want Kate to suffer, but I didn't want it to be like what happened with Irene."

"What did Adele say?"

"Told me I didn't understand what a deathday was. Tried to change my mind about what had happened to Irene. Carly *really* tried to put the squeeze on me. But it was a stalemate. I was just leaving when you saw me."

"Adele lied to Kate about your going to Adele's that night," I said. "She told Kate that you must've broken into the house and that she and Carly slept through the whole thing."

"She didn't want Kate to know that they were trying to shut me up. I knew what Adele did to Irene."

"So," I said, "after you left Adele's, you went back to the streets, and on November 1, you came back here to Five Hearths to try to talk Kate out of her deathday."

Miranda nodded. "Why didn't you go up the hill?"

"I'm tired. I started my day in London."

"We can go up there now. There's something I want to show you."

"All right. If you insist. I suppose it would be good to stretch my legs. Am I staying for dinner?"

"It's brisket night with mac 'n cheese. You'd have to be crazier than I am to miss it. Hey, and I invited Lisa too. She should be here soon."

"That's great. I was going to text her."

Miranda and I began the walk up the hill.

"Where did you get your mother's notebook?" I asked. "Have you always had it?"

"My Aunt Bijou had it, and she sent it to Kate. I read it to her the day before she died. And when I got back here this summer, I dug it out of a box of Kate's stuff that the sisters had stored in the basement. Got it before they mailed Kate's stuff back to my Aunt Bijou."

Realization struck me. The package I'd put on Kate's bedroom desk contained Veronica's last notebook.

"When did you get here on that first day of November?" I asked. "I left the house about eleven."

"I don't remember. No one was here but the hospice nurse. Kate was in bed. She was in a lot of pain, but she wouldn't let the nurse give her morphine. She had a lot she wanted me to do. She told me how to get into her laptop with her memoir on it that she kept in a lockbox in her closet, along with a zip drive with another copy. Kate wanted me to print out the memoir in her office, tape the zip drive to the top page, then put it all in the bottom drawer of her office desk so that you could find it there. Then she asked about my Aunt Bijou's package. Wanted me to open it. When I told her it was my mother's journal, she asked me to read it to her."

"Did you read the whole thing?"

"The same part I asked you to read. When I finished, she told me that she wanted to take a nap. But I don't think she slept. An hour or so later, she called for me."

"What did she want?"

"She told me that she had changed her mind. That she didn't want to die."

"She didn't want to go through with her deathday?"

"No."

"Why not? Did she give a reason?"

"No. She just said she had changed her mind. Then she told me to go get Everett."

"Do you know if she called Adele? Or rather, Carly?"

"She said she would talk to Adele when she came. She wanted to tell her in person. Adele was supposed to come at four the next morning."

"So when you got Everett, he came right away?"

"Drove straight over in his late-in-life crisis. Typed up the change to Kate's will and printed it out. Then Kate signed it, with me and the hospice nurse as witnesses."

"What time was it when all this happened?"

"I don't know. It was the middle of the evening, I guess, when we finished."

"Is that when Kate asked you to call me?"

"Yeah. She gave me her phone and said, 'Call Benedict.' But when you didn't pick up, Kate said not to worry and that we'd try you again in the morning. She didn't want to leave a message."

So Kate wanted to tell me that she had changed her mind. But then what about Adele? Adele had said nothing about Kate changing her mind. I asked Miranda what happened next.

"The hospice nurse ended her shift at midnight. She got Kate to take some morphine right before she left. Kate was in a lot of pain. She also gave Kate a sleeping pill. I don't think Kate realized what it was, and I didn't say anything because it's not like I could say, 'Hey, don't give her a sleeping pill because she's got to call off her deathday in a few hours.' But the morphine didn't seem to do much for Kate and neither did the sleeping pill. She was moaning and thrashing. She got sick into the towel she kept by the bed. The nurse said I could give her another half dose of morphine if she needed it in two hours, so about two in the morning I gave her another dose. But nothing was working. I didn't know what to do. And before I knew it, Adele and Carly were downstairs."

"And you hid in the bathroom."

"I lay down in the tub. Adele even came in once, but I held my breath."

"Was Kate able to tell Adele that she had changed her mind?"

"I could hear her trying. But she was totally out of it. She couldn't really form words. She was full of too many chemicals and in too much pain."

"So Adele killed her."

"Pretty much. When I heard Adele trying to force Kate to drink the death brew, I came out to stop her. I fought with Carly and shot her with Kate's gun. Then I ran off. As soon as I was gone, Adele finished off Kate. I told the cops everything, eventually. Told them what I heard while hiding in Kate's bathtub. They talked to Adele too, but in the end they didn't think they had enough to pin anything on her."

"Where is Adele?" I asked her.

"Who knows? Sydney. Dubai. A suburb of Philadelphia. She bolted soon after the cops paid her a visit."

"I would love to play for the police the recording you made of my mother's death."

"I don't know where that recorder is," Miranda said. "Last I saw, it was in Kate's bedroom. I bet Adele took it and destroyed the tape. Just like she took the strongbox with Kate's laptop in it."

"Adele took the laptop?"

"She must've. I haven't found the strongbox in Kate's stuff."

I then told Miranda about the voicemail that my mother left for Roy.

"You think that voicemail would be enough to send Adele up the river?" Miranda asked.

"I'm not sure. I'm no lawyer. I hope so."

But as a matter of fact, though I did not say it aloud, I knew Adele would get away. Cody was dead. Veronica was dead. Kate was dead. My mother was dead. Yet Adele—she operated in the shadowy regions beyond the law. She was a force of nature. Try to get her in London and she'll escape to New York. Try to get her in New York and she'll escape to Washington, DC. Put the cops on her and she'll still slip the noose, only to appear again in Sydney or Dubai or a suburb of Philadelphia, eager to stir some pots.

Surely she had attended Dionysus in the age of gods and heroes. With her fennel wand in hand, had she not run through the Attic woods with the other frenzied Bacchae, ravenous and orgiastic? Had she not served as a medium at Endor and come out of the desert at Nag Hammadi, a mother-goddess and spirit-guide, offering the secret knowledge of the hidden texts? Had she not drunk tea in London with Madame Blavatsky and ushered in the Age of Aquarius in Haight-Ashbury? Had she not been watching from the covert when lightning fell from the sky?

Words cannot express what a privilege it has been for me to be included in the intimacy of Kate's thoughts and feelings during the months of her final illness. Before reading her memoir, I was well aware that Kate was quite a special person, but after reading and editing these pages, after viewing her trial from the inside, I am profoundly aware of having witnessed someone with true greatness of soul. She was a most remarkable woman—humble, generous, perceptive, boundlessly good-humored. I am so grateful for the chance we had to reunite in the final months of her life.

I have endeavored to edit Kate's memoir with a light touch. What the reader finds here is what Kate wrote, but here and there I have removed entries and passages that seemed repetitive or that concerned topics well outside the narrative of her death. The subtitles are Kate's, made in the spirit of her mythological method—save for that of this epilogue, which I added myself. I have also added, of course, the final entries from Veronica Cody's journal.

One other writing not officially part of the memoir I also include. Miranda explained its importance to me on our walk to the top of the hill. That last evening of Kate's life, after the change to her will had been prepared and signed and Everett had left, Kate gave Miranda a last set of instructions.

"Go down to the desk in my office downstairs," she said. "In the top right-hand drawer you'll find a stack of forms. Bring me one."

Miranda went down, got the form, and brought it back to Kate. It was the form found at the head of this memoir, an unsigned copy of the "Apprentice's Affidavit" Kate's students had to sign when handing in the first drafts of their essays.

"Get me a pen from the desk," Kate said.

It was a struggle once more to prop Kate up to sign her name, but Miranda did it.

"That needs to go at the top of the manuscript you put downstairs," Kate said after crashing back against her pillow. "And I need to write a final entry. The surprising plot twist. But I can't do it now. I'll do it tomorrow."

Kay lay there panting. Miranda went downstairs and placed Kate's signed "Apprentice's Affidavit" with the manuscript of her memoir.

Now," Kate said when Miranda returned, "will you get the green scapular that's in my planner there?"

Miranda found the green scapular and handed it to Kate. She watched as Kate examined it, then kissed it.

"You're going to talk to Adele?" Miranda asked.

"Don't you worry. I'm going to be here for you tomorrow, and the next day, and however many days it takes. Now open up those blinds." She gestured toward the window. "I want to see my Morning Mountain when the sun comes up."

Through the small hours of the morning, Kate clutched the green scapular as her pain grew worse. The scapular was later found in the bedclothes when Lisa came with some of Kate's former students to pack up Kate's things. No doubt clueless as to what it was, one of them tossed it into a moving box that was eventually placed by the sisters in the basement, which is where Miranda found it again when she returned to Five Hearths.

At the top of the hill, in the cool of the evening, I stopped and looked up at Kate's Morning Mountain. The trees on the back of it were thick as sheep's wool. Farther out to the west, the Blue Ridge Mountains, ply over ply, with their clean-shaven faces of deep azure, glowed in the twilight.

What would I have done if, that night at the resort, I had picked up the call from Miranda? If I had known Kate had changed her mind? I would have raced back, of course. I would have been able to stop Adele. I would have had more time with Kate Montclair.

"Here is what I wanted you to see," Miranda called from behind me. "This is why you were supposed to read the journal up here."

I turned around and discovered Miranda standing beside the giant oak tree that dominated the top of the hill. She pointed to a simple headstone that I hadn't noticed. I walked over and took it in. We stood there for a long time just looking at the stone, alone with our respective thoughts, saying nothing.

Finally, Miranda took one of the green scapulars from around her neck and offered it to me. I hadn't noticed that she'd been wearing two. "This one was the one Kate was holding when she died."

"I can't take it, Miranda."

"Yes, you can. Take it."

I took the scapular from her and then, surprising even myself, I kissed it. Tears pleaded with me to let go, and I let them go.

I asked Miranda who chose the inscription for the headstone, and she replied that it was Lisa. Lisa chose better than she knew. As we continued to stand there, silently gazing upon Kate's headstone, I clutched the green scapular Kate had clutched as she followed Veronica in making her very good death. For the first time in many years, I prayed, or tried to pray, which the spiritual masters tell me is the same thing. As I did, I glanced at the tiny garment in my hand through which so much that was unexpected had been revealed. Scoffed at by us in our youth, this piece of holy cloth had delivered its promise despite our faithlessness. We were not the protagonists we thought we were. We thought we were creating our own story, when in fact we had been bound by the strands of this scapular and led to a place where we did not wish to go. But behind the veil of the scapular beat a mother's heart, itself pierced, going before us always, knowing the real logic of our desires, keeping vigil through the barren years when we worshipped our half-gods and tin-pot idols. This was the heart that guarded me when I sought beauty among its mortal ruins. This was the heart that led Veronica by an Ariadne's thread out of the labyrinth of her mind toward that small room in Chappaqua where she fought her final battle and won. And this was the heart that had broken for Kate Montclair and supported her as she wandered through the aftermath of the catastrophe, until finally she was ready for the catastrophe that alone could make her, in the words of the inscription on her headstone:

ACCEPTABLE, WITH ALTERATIONS

COME BEHIND THE SCENES BY JOINING
DANIEL McINERNY'S THE COMIC MUSE

danielmcinerny.substack.com

And receive the FREE short story,
"PURSUIT AMONG THE RUINS,"
(which follows the young Benedict in the aftermath
of the events depicted in the novel),

as well as other exclusive stories and content
from the world of *The Good Death of Kate Montclair.*

Follow Daniel McInerny on Instagram
@danielmcinerny_thecomicmuse

And on Twitter
@comicmuse

Learn more about his work at
danielmcinerny.studio

YOU MAY ALSO ENJOY

Shooting at Heaven's Gate
by Kay Park Hinckley

In the wake of death and destruction, the town that used to be called Heaven's Gate will find no easy answers, but there may still be hope for redemption. Shooting at Heaven's Gate is a Theology of the Cross novel in which genuine goodness, bona fide evil, and suffering truly live side by side.

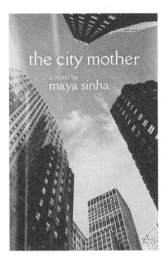

The City Mother
by Maya Sinha

As her marriage falters and friends disappear, Cara seeks guidance from books, films, therapy, even the saints, when she's not scrubbing the diaper pail. Meanwhile, someone is crying out for help that only she can give. Cara must confront big questions about reality and illusion, health and illness, good and evil—and just how far she is willing to go to protect those she loves.

See all of Chrism Press's titles at
www.ChrismPress.com

Made in the USA
Las Vegas, NV
10 August 2023

75914503R00173